RUSH WEEK

RUSH WEEK

ALARIC JAXARTES

PAGETURNERS PUBLISHING COMPANY
Jacksonville, Florida

Pageturners Publishing Company
Greg Sampson, Publisher
P.O. Box 6, Jacksonville, Florida 32234-0006

Debuted in perfect binding: October 2004
Printed in the United States of America

Publisher's Cataloging-in-Publication
(Provided by Quality Books, Inc.)

Jaxartes, Alaric.
Rush week / Alaric Jaxartes.
p. cm.
ISBN 0-9755102-0-7

1. Greek letter societies--Fiction. 2. College stories. 3. Love stories. I. Title.

PS3610.A88R87 2004 813'.6
QBI04-800039

Library of Congress Control Number: 2004096421

DESIGN: ALBERTINE BOOK DESIGN, SANTA MONICA, CA | ALBERTINEBOOKDESIGN.COM
COVER DESIGN COVERED UNDER ABOVE COPYRIGHT. ALL RIGHTS RESERVED.
COVER IMAGES: GETTY IMAGES

Dedicated to all those
who have ever been told,
"Not At This Time."

CONTENTS

| CONTENTS |

CONTENTS

PREFACE

IN OFFERING THE STORY of Montgomery Lee to the general reading public, the author finds it necessary to offer two notices that the reader must heed. First, although the story relates the experience of a college freshman who pledges a fraternity, nothing in the story depicts the process used by actual college campus fraternities in recruiting, testing and accepting new members. The events of *Rush Week* were inspired by a different process altogether, and were shaped by the developing plot along the general outline originated by the author.

Second, the story is loosely semi-autobiographical. Plot devices and events did not necessarily occur but are symbolic of key episodes that the author underwent. Furthermore, dramatic license has been taken to present an interesting tale, so that the sequence of events may be altered, several events may be condensed into one, or a scene may be played up. Or maybe not.

THIS IS A WORK OF FICTION.

Everything is made up, including names, persons, groups, fraternities, colleges and so forth, except that parallels between the story and the process used by a mainline denomination in admitting ordained ministers to their ranks are intentional although subjective in nature.

THIS IS A WORK OF FICTION.

Enjoy!

Alaric Jaxartes
July 9, 2004

Prologue

THE CALL

MONTGOMERY STARED THROUGH HIS TELESCOPE at the night sky.

"Did you see it?" he whispered to his companion, a dark-haired girl of sixteen.

"See what?" she replied in a slightly annoyed voice.

"Comet Traveler," Montgomery whispered excitedly. "Just past Jupiter—I'll show you." He pointed to a bright spot in the sky. "Focus on Jupiter, the bright dot in the scope. Then, look up at 330 degrees, eleven o'clock if Jupiter was a watch face. No more than a couple of ticks off the planet."

Judy pretended to be interested. She liked Montgomery; she had dated him since the tenth grade and had known him since they were toddlers in pre-school care. Even then, her earliest memory was Montgomery lying on his back watching the stars in the sky. He was fascinated by stars, and by age five had learned the names of the constellations the way most kids learned dinosaurs.

Judy's interest in the stars never progressed beyond the newspaper horoscope. But Montgomery was cute with his boyish features, naturally blond hair, scruffy goatee and neat sideburns, intense green eyes and slender physique. Judy knew she was the envy of her clique of girls. Montgomery was shy and faithful; he went to church every Sunday and led Bible study in his youth group. He was very smart, and

Judy knew her C's and B's would slide to D's without Montgomery so she put her heart into his hand and feigned interest in his pursuits. Montgomery had a fascinating presence that made him popular among his peers; Judy had decided that compensated for his nerd-like absorption with the stars.

Judy looked into the eyepiece. She made what she hoped would be noises of wonder.

Montgomery sat down on the toolbox attached to his pick-up truck's bed. He looked at Judy and smiled. The points of her figure punctuated the loose t-shirt and shorts she was wearing. Small and petite, she had a natural, innocent beauty that animated her dark skin, brunette hair and brown eyes. Montgomery adored her.

"Do you believe in space aliens?" asked Judy.

"What supermarket rag sheet have you been reading?" laughed Montgomery.

"American Gossip. Have space aliens been sighted? Have they talked to anyone? Do you think they're out there?"

"No, no, maybe. Perhaps there are worlds in other solar systems where intelligent beings exist who have mastered the technology needed to travel through space. But the distances are too great for any such beings to arrive at the Earth. Even at the speed of light, the travel would take thousands of years—far too long for any expedition to be worthwhile. After all, these are supposedly intelligent beings."

"Do you think they're communicating? They could be calling us over the radio but we can't understand their language."

"The radio waves would degenerate long before our antennae could receive them."

"You don't hear a call from out there—somewhere far away in the universe?"

Montgomery grinned. "Trick question, Judy. Yes, I hear a call, but not from aliens. The universe itself calls to me: Come look at me, Study me, Regard me, Find out how I work, Discover my secrets—strange worlds, new stars, echoes of the Big Bang.

"I want to explore the great unknown regions of space in every way I can. Next month, I begin my last year of high school. After that, I'm going to Florida Sawgrass University in Bacon. They've already accepted me. All the Lees have always gone to Sawgrass in Bacon, joining Sigma Omicron Beta as the fraternity of scientists, engineers and artists. This is my calling; it's what I'm going to do."

Judy sat next to Montgomery. "How do you know this is your call? How do you know that you're meant to study astronomy?"

Montgomery said dreamily, "When I look at the stars, I hear the voice of God telling me I was made to discover their secrets. Not the astrology nonsense you love to read, but the physical laws that govern matter and motion. I understand physics intuitively; God has written the knowledge into my brain cells. I have a talent for scientific work and accurate observation. I'm fascinated by astronomy and derive great satisfaction from its study. God has asked me to pursue the stars, through Sawgrass and Sigma Omicron Beta. I do not know His entire purpose, but I do know the path on which He's leading me."

"Anything out there tonight?" boomed a hearty voice.

"Barney!" cried Montgomery with delight.

In the dark, they could see the approaching figure of Montgomery's older cousin, Kyle Barnsworth, who had graduated the previous month from Sawgrass University and the presidency of the Sigma Omicron Beta fraternity.

Barney arrived at the truck and jumped into the bed. He leaned over the telescope.

"Two ticks off Jupiter 330 degrees," said Montgomery. "Comet Traveler."

Barney squinted at the eyepiece. "Yes, I think I see it—very faintly. Only you could find it. Some day soon we'll ooh and aah over Comet Montgomery."

Montgomery blushed. Judy squealed, "That would be fantastic!"

Barney pulled a five gallon Igloo water cooler to the telescope and sat down.

"I'm leaving tomorrow for Dallas," Barney said. "I want to talk to you about Sigma Omicron Beta."

"What about it?" asked Montgomery.

"The fraternity is in disorder. The Sawgrass chapter is holding on, but nationally, the SigBees have been losing members for a long time. Chapters are closing. We need a turnaround, and that will take talent—talent like you, Montgomery."

"I plan to join."

"Good. Even the Sawgrass chapter is having difficulty—we've had a hard time finding quality men to induct. Too many compromises have been made, I'm afraid. Join your first semester. Get into leadership. You're top notch material. You'll attract the best university men—like the days when our Daddies were there. It's your calling, Montgomery, all the Lees have been SigBees, and it is your responsibility to wear the mantle at Sawgrass."

"Done deal, Barney. I'm already accepted at Sawgrass with a science major in astronomy. I want to join Sigma Omicron Beta. The rest will come as God wills. Remember, I have a year left in high school."

Barney stood up. "Glad to hear it. You were made for leadership, Montgomery. Everyone sees it. Write your name into the Wall of Legends as a SigBee. You're destined to be remembered for a very long time."

Barney jumped to the ground, then turned. "Make me proud, Montgomery. I'll come by when I come back for Thanksgiving."

"Good luck with your new job," called Montgomery after his cousin's departing back.

Montgomery knocked on the door marked "Guidance". A moment later, and Montgomery was staring at a short, rotund man wearing wire glasses and a dazed look. The man blinked several times. Rumors periodically swept the school about the guidance counselor. Some students claimed he was a narc; others, that he used his office to deal and consume narcotics. Others thought he conducted surveillance through hidden cameras and microphones; some held that he was a great thinker. Each story tried to account for the fact that wherever his body was, his mind seemed to be someplace else. Montgomery thought he was mildly retarded and was hired to fill a mentally disabled quota.

"Oh, Montgomery," the man exhaled. "Come in."

"You sent for me, sir?"

"Sit down, yes, sit down," the counselor replied as though he was only then making up his mind to talk with the young man.

Montgomery sat.

"You're applying to college." The counselor scanned an open folder on his desk. Montgomery noted that the folder was labelled "Junior Drop-out Risks" and held pictures of the last school dance, a cafeteria menu from October, a traffic ticket, and yellow sticky notepapers with Internet and web addresses scrawled in blue ink and pencil.

"Yes sir," Montgomery replied.

"I've known you since a baby," the counselor continued. Montgomery wondered if he meant since the counselor was a baby, or since Montgomery was a baby.

"You have an air of destiny around you," the counselor said. Montgomery began to squirm in the chair. The conversation was too weird.

The counselor slapped the folder shut. "Have you ever thought of going Greek?"

"Sir?"

"Greek. Have you ever thought of being Greek?"

Montgomery rapidly skimmed through every slang phrase he knew, and to what each referred. He had no clue as to what being Greek meant.

"Montgomery, it's natural at this time in your life to be undecided about so many things. Where to go to college, what major to select."

"Sir, I have already been accepted to Florida Sawgrass University, and I plan to study astronomy."

The counselor blinked rapidly as if this was new information he did not know.

"Of course, Montgomery, of course. I knew that. But I was sitting in my office last week, looking over my notes of the post-graduation plans of the seniors ..." He waved his hand over the folder he had closed. "... and the thought came crashing in on me that I should talk to you about joining a fraternity when you enter college."

Montgomery opened his eyes wide. "Sir?"

"You have the gifts and graces to be a campus leader," the counselor said earnestly. "The Greek system on campus, that is, the fraternities, will offer you the best opportunity to use your gifts. It's a calling, Montgomery, a calling to the best and brightest to offer themselves for service for the welfare of society, in this case, the school. You have the call. Have you not heard it? Felt it?"

"Sir, all the Lees have joined Sigma Omicron Beta at Florida Sawgrass. I plan to follow in their footsteps."

"Great! Glad to hear it!" the counselor enthused. "I heartily recommend it!"

Montgomery stood. "Is this interview over, sir?"

The counselor blinked several times as if he had suddenly thought that he needed to change the oil in his automobile. "Yes, yes, you may go."

Montgomery left quickly, and wondered what had made his guidance counselor decide that he had been called to join a fraternity when he went to college.

That evening, Montgomery slid to his knees before his bed as he prepared for sleep.

"Jesus, I love you and I want to please you," he prayed. "I gave you my life when I was seven. I love the stars and feel you have blessed my fascination with the night sky so that I could make its study my life's work. I have kept myself from the temptations of drinking and drugs, and have kept my virginity even though Judy would let me have sex with her if I made a move. I want to serve you. I thank you for my family, and its traditions, and thought I would join Sigma Omicron Beta at college next year. But if you have other plans, let me know. I'll be obedient to your call. My guidance counselor's speech was weird. But if you were speaking through him, please let me know. Let someone I know and trust come to me, and indicate that you're calling me to that purpose, or tell me openly what other plan you wish me to follow. Amen."

| PROLOGUE |

As he lay back on his bed and closed his eyes, Montgomery thought back to the night he had first looked up and seen the stars. Even then, as a small child, he had understood that God had created the heavens. He had been fascinated, and wanted to know how the sky worked. He was headed to the stars; it was his destiny. He was a Lee, and the destiny of every Lee was Sawgrass University, and Sigma Omicron Beta. But now he was wondering, "Is this really my call?"

The following week, Montgomery's cell phone rang. "Montgomery Lee?" sang out a tenor voice. "Wilson Dole, president of Sigma Omicron Beta, SigBees for short, Beta Sigma chapter."

"Pleasure to greet you," answered Montgomery. "What may I do for you?"

"The pleasure is mine; glad to make your acquaintance. I'm calling you to issue a special invitation to pledge Sigma Omicron Beta when you arrive on campus in the fall. Unusual though it may be for me to make an invitation to pledge, you're someone special and we'd be honored to receive you into our membership. Your cousin Barney told me that he had already talked to you."

"Last summer," Montgomery confirmed.

"Right. Look, Montgomery, I'll be candid with you. Pledging is not the easiest of experiences. Especially with our current pledge committee who like to give everyone a very hard time. Especially those who don't insinuate themselves into their special group.

"Please consider pledging. It will not be a pleasant experience. Many of the members will want you to bow down to them and kiss their rings. My own experience was pretty hellacious. But I made it and so can you. Please think about it, okay?"

Montgomery agreed to think about it. He mashed the off button on his phone. *Tell me openly ... If that wasn't an answer to my prayer, I don't know what is. I'm going to be a SigBee!*

Chapter One

Freshman Orientation

BEIGE AND PINK WALLS with teal doors and windows gleamed in the August sunshine as Montgomery guided his truck through the streets of Florida Sawgrass University. With him was his best friend and freshman roommate, Travis Lewis. Travis was a dark-haired, dark-eyed, bronzed and muscular young man who had spent his afternoons and summers working cattle on his grandfather's farm and his weekends and predawn mornings surfing the waves if the offshore winds drove in big swells. Travis was an outgoing, engaging boy; he plunged directly into whatever activity presented itself. He liked fast cars, girls and the outdoors; he was not the studious type. He passed high school with Montgomery's help, and he figured he could do the same through college. Travis had no religious faith; he did not object to it but his goal was to party through life.

"There—there it is," exclaimed Travis. "Somerset Johns Dormitory."

Montgomery spied a parking spot near the door. He perfectly parallel-parked his truck and turned off the engine. The two boys simultaneously released their seat belts and jumped out of the truck.

Travis let a big whoop. "We've made the big time now!" He exchanged a high-five hand slap with Montgomery. The two boys headed toward the door and went inside.

Inside the lobby, a big table had been set up. "Welcome Freshman Class" read a banner hanging from the ceiling. Montgomery pulled a letter from his pocket, opened it and handed it to one of the women sitting behind the table.

"Welcome to Florida Sawgrass University," she smiled. "My name is Sarah Moore. I am the head of the Somerset Johns Residence Hall. Cindy Wang is one of our floor advisors—on the women's side, I might add." Sarah laughed. "Although she can take on any guy and come out on top (Travis grinned; Montgomery gave him an elbow in the side), so I don't advise trying her."

Sarah looked at Montgomery's letter. "Montgomery Lee," she read aloud. "So your friend is Travis Lewis."

"Yes ma'am."

"You're assigned to Quad F, room 3, on the third floor. There is an elevator inside to help you take your things to your room. But I must tell you that the elevator is always locked except on moving days. You must use the stairs normally. While you're living here, your address is made up from your floor, quad and room. Your campus address is 3F3 Somerset Johns, Bacon, Florida 33555. There are twelve quads to each side—twenty-four quads total per floor. A through L are the male quads that are on the west side of the building; N through Y are the female quads, which are on the east side of the building. Your student I.D. will gain you access to the building; always carry it with you. Since you will not receive your I.D. until this afternoon, the dormitory doors are open until 7:00 p.m. After that, you will need your I.D. to enter the building. There are luggage carts by the elevators; do not try to remember anything—it's all written down on these papers. Further orientation will take place in the lounge behind us tomorrow morning at nine a.m. Sign here for your keys."

Montgomery and Travis each took the stylus from the two card readers that Sarah was indicating. They signed their names across the window and were fascinated to see that their signatures were electronically reproduced.

"Hope you can type," Cindy said. "The campus has gone completely paperless. Some day we will no longer have keys but card readers on every door."

Sarah finished the briefing. "Starting with lunch, you will eat your meals in the Jeff Davis Dining Hall which is next to the dorm. Until Tuesday evening, your meals are free as part of your freshman orientation. Starting Tuesday at supper, you may eat according to the meal plan you selected which you may adjust at any time by going on-line to the Bursar's Office. Then you can eat at any campus food facility. Until then, only Jeff Davis is serving."

Montgomery and Travis thanked the women for the information and their keys. Then they ran to the elevator to look at their room. The two women looked at one another and laughed, "Freshmen."

Montgomery and Travis exited the elevator on the third floor and ran across the bridge that connected the women's and the men's sides. Breathlessly, Travis inserted his key and opened the door.

"Wow," he exclaimed. The two boys looked at their new living quarters, enthralled by the sight. Straight ahead was a half moon desk with a telephone. To the left, couches made a viewing pit for the 20-inch color television that was perched on a corner shelf. A small refrigerator and microwave oven stood beyond the couches; a table and chairs filled the remaining space.

The boys walked directly back and entered the bathroom. There were two showers and two toilet stalls. Two sinks flanked a ladder of towel bars that extended from the floor to the ceiling. On either side of the door were vanity cabinets where the boys and their quad mates could store their soap, shampoo, and other personal items. The boys exulted over the provisions; best of all, they had maid service.

Next they unlocked the door to their room. Two desks sat side-by-side on the far wall. Flanking the side walls were two beds. The rest of the room was given over to walk-in closets, which had two bars for hanging clothes, and drawers on one side for folding clothes. Montgomery grinned at Travis, "I'm in Heaven."

The boys headed back for the elevator, snagging a luggage cart along the way. Retracing their steps to the lobby, they went around the two women at the table, and outside to Montgomery's truck. They unloaded their trunks that held their clothing, plus boxes of reference books, CD's and video games, video game machine, Travis' surfboard, Montgomery's telescope, computers and various other items that the boys had tossed onto the truck at the last minute.

An hour later, they had set up their room and were playing a video game when they heard the outer door open. Two boys were struggling to push an overloaded cart past the couch. Entering the common area, Travis introduced himself and Montgomery.

"Hi," said the shorter boy, who was stocky and sported a shaved head with spikes on the top, which he had dyed blond but was allowing his dark roots to show. "Darrell Cattlip. My friends call me Cat. My roommate, Joseph Boxer." The boys shook hands. Cat continued, "We live in Miami, and we both played football. We were the only two from our high school coming to Sawgrass so we decided to room together. Our assignment is room 2."

Cat walked to the refrigerator and opened the door. "Looks like we need to make a beer run."

Travis laughed, "You read my mind."

Montgomery helped Joe wheel the heavy cart into room 2, Cat following. "First thing, Joe, we take the drawers out of my closet and install them in yours. Then we can set up the weights."

Joe grunted his approval. He opened his toolbox, and assembled his drill with a screwdriver bit. He hooked up an extension cord, and the drill whined as it removed the screws and bolts that held the dresser to the wall. In the other closet, the sound of hammering was heard.

Montgomery and Travis were about to return to their video game when another boy came in. "Is this Quad F?"

Montgomery nodded his head.

"Whew," the new boy blew out a sigh of relief. "I have been so lost ..."

"Travis Lewis," said Montgomery as he pointed to his roommate, "and Montgomery Lee. We moved in earlier this morning."

"Michael Raike," the boy replied. "Pleased to meet y'all. Everyone calls me Mick."

"Room two is under construction," said Montgomery. "We're going to have a weight room."

"And game room," added Travis. "If the video game has been made, by us it has been played. Plus we have a stereo that went AWOL from a flea market."

"Better than me," said Mick. "All I brought were my clothes and computer."

"Do you know your roommate?" asked Montgomery.

"No, he's some out-of-stater from Michigan. Probably thought he'd stay warm in the winter. I talked to him on the phone a few times. His name is Art Sullivan. He was flying down to Orlando, and then switching to a prop plane. He won't arrive until this evening."

Mick opened the door to room four. He slung his backpack and satchel onto one of the beds. "That's it; I'm home."

Travis looked at him strangely. "Don't you want to unpack?"

Mick grinned. "I'll take it out as I need it. With any luck, by the time I'm out of clean underwear and socks, I'll have a girl to do my laundry for me. Beware, boys, and watch your girls. My one talent is conning females to do my will."

Travis grinned back. "I'll be watching to pick up a few pointers."

Mick laughed. "What about the General?"

Travis lifted his eyebrows.

"General Lee." Mick was one of those guys who gave nicknames to everyone he met. He had the charm and hubris to pull it off so that people welcomed the changed moniker; in fact, people felt insulted if he did not rename them.

Travis caught the reference. "Oh, Montgomery. His head is always in the stars; he's no competition for you or me. If a girl goes for him, guys like you and I have no chance."

Mick changed the subject, not wanting to give away his mental note to meet the challenge when Montgomery found a girl to date. "Who's our construction crew?"

Montgomery answered, "Short and stocky is Darrell Cattlip who goes by Cat. His roomie is Joe Boxer. Really, it is," he insisted as Mick was laughing.

"I'll call him Shorts," Mick said.

"What do folks call you if they don't use Mick?" queried Travis.

"Drunk!" roared Mick.

"I've been here two hours and already I have two drinking buddies," said Travis. "Montgomery, excuse me, the General, does not imbibe. None of the Lees do. I've told him for three years that drinking is good for his heart—it lowers cholesterol—but he won't listen. 'All the Lees abstain,' he says. I'm so glad the Lewis's have no family history or tradition. Nothing to uphold and get in the way of fun."

Montgomery laughed. "You need me sober so I can keep you out of trouble. How many times have I rescued you from the tangled situations you get yourself into?"

Travis laughed too. "I lost count a long time ago."

Mick smiled. It was clear that these two roommates had very different temperaments, yet they enjoyed each other's company and friendship. They had an easy-going way that readily accepted newcomers into their social circles. He had been concerned, coming to a university where he knew no one, but now he was relieved.

From the center of campus, a carillon chimed the noon hour and began playing the university anthem. The sounds of construction stopped. Joe and Cat came out of their room and were introduced to Mick. The boys descended the stairs and headed for lunch.

Afterwards, the group split up to find their different advisors and to register for classes. Montgomery headed for the science building. Upon entering the building, he checked the lobby registry to find the office for Dr. Peterman, his academic advisor for his astronomy major. Dr. Peterman's office was room 205.

Montgomery moved to the stairs and took them two at a time. At the top of the flight, he paused, and then he turned right. His guess was correct. Three doors down, the name Peterman was etched in frosted glass with the numerals 205 underneath. The door was closed. Montgomery knocked, then opened the door.

Books, charts and telescopes were stacked haphazardly around the office. A desk faced a solitary window; a telescope was mounted on the desk. To one side, a computer stand held a desktop model, which displayed a moving model of the solar system as a screen saver.

Overstuffed chairs were arranged in front of the desk. The office was empty.

Montgomery went over to the telescope and examined it. He was disappointed to note that it was an economy model with insufficient magnification and less than average clarity for the lens. He looked through the eyepiece, not expecting to see anything in the daytime, and he was correct.

Montgomery cast his gaze upon a star chart. These were more interesting. One of them was tracking asteroids, which grazed the Earth's orbit around the sun. Another documented all the known space junk orbiting the Earth that was larger than a marble. Another held details of comets and their trajectories.

"Mr. Lee," observed a calm, deep bass with a Southern accent thick as wads of cotton.

Montgomery spun around, blushing, "Dr. Peterman."

"I've been expecting you," said Dr. Peterman. "Welcome to Florida Sawgrass University. I don't receive many freshman declared majors; in fact, you're the only one. What do you think of my telescope?"

Montgomery continued blushing and stammered, "It suffices for a casual scope, but its magnification and clarity are lacking for charting observations." Montgomery wondered what he should add because he had insulted an university professor.

"Excellent, Mr. Lee. You are at the university level now; never be afraid to speak your mind. Academic freedom means that you form and express your opinions without fear of reprisal as long as you can defend them. As you have well noted, this telescope is lacking in features for the professional astronomer. I keep it in my office more for show than anything else. People expect an astronomy professor to have a telescope in his office. No sense in wasting money on a good model to place it where it is useless for observing the skies."

Montgomery relaxed. The professor sat down in a chair and indicated that Montgomery should do the same. Dr. Peterman reached to a bookshelf, and pulled a folder from one of its shelves. Then he gave Montgomery a current catalog and a registration form.

"First-time registration is routine," he noted. "Freshman English is a requirement; you're already placed in a 9 a.m. class for Tuesday, Wednesday and Friday. Even as a science major, you must receive a grounding in the humanities. Two semesters of Western Civ should work well; start with Ancient Greece and Rome. We offer that Monday and Thursday from 1 p.m. to 2:30 p.m. For a soft science, you could take sociology, psychology or anthropology. With your fascination for the stars, you most likely would enjoy anthropology. That runs from 9 a.m. to 10:30 a.m. Monday/Thursday. That's nine hours so far.

"For hard science, go with chemistry. 11 a.m. Tuesday and Wednesday; take the Tuesday lab from 3 to 5 p.m. Finish off with mathematics. 2 p.m. Tuesday, Wednesday and Friday: Calculus/advanced mathematics. Have you got all that down?"

Montgomery had marked the form as fast as he could. "Yes sir."

"Good. Let me sign it, and you may drop it at the registrar's office as soon as we're done."

Dr. Peterman sat back, and smiled. "Mr. Lee, you're embarking upon the adventure of a lifetime. The most important thing for your first semester is to establish good study habits. You're on your own—no one will hound you to complete and turn in your assignments. No truant officer will search for you if you skip class. But if you are slack in your academic pursuits, you will fail. So make study your first priority.

"You'll have extensive reading for all your classes. Stay on top of it. Get ahead of the assignments in the first three weeks; then the rest of the semester will be easy for you to handle. Don't be anxious to join organizations; they can take all of your available study time. Be especially careful of the fraternities—it's best not to rush until your second year."

"But sir, all the Lees have belonged to Sigma Omicron Beta. I was going to pledge immediately."

Dr. Peterman's smile faded. "Don't select a fraternity based upon family tradition. Fraternities change, especially S.O.B. It's not what it was in your father's day. My advice is to rethink your decision. At least, visit several fraternal houses to see which one is best for you. But, above all else, keep your academics first."

"Yes sir." *But I have a calling to become a SigBee, and I'm going to be true to my calling.*

Dr. Peterman scrutinized the young man in front of him, hoping that Montgomery would not waste his years at the university as Montgomery showed promise of developing a first-rate mind. Dr. Peterman then shifted the topic to astronomy, and soon the two were engaged in an energizing conversation that occupied the remaining length of an hour.

Travis had made his way across campus to the library. There he found his advisor surrounded by a couple dozen students. As an undeclared major, he had been foisted upon a graduate student who had been hired to keep track of a large number of undeclared freshmen. As Travis joined the group, the grad student was telling the new students "... you'll be assigned a faculty advisor when you declare your major." Travis was unconcerned; for the most part, academics did not interest him. College was a place that offered better opportunities to party and kept him from getting a job.

Travis, therefore, embraced a volunteer, experimental program called "freshman seminar." Under this program, he would receive instruction in writing, research, history, music, literature, philosophy, art, politics/government, law and anatomy/biology. The program was for five days a week, 9 a.m. to 12 p.m., and 2 pm to 5 pm every Wednesday and Thursday. Upon successful completion, he would receive 18 hours of academic credit non-graded. That part appealed to Travis—no grades. The program would enroll 48 students; each would be assigned to a study group of six students who would work on projects together and help keep one another on track. The university's interest was to see if collegiate academics worked better under this format than the traditional lectures to hundreds of students, and T.A. groups of thirty.

While Montgomery and Travis were registering for classes, the occupants for room one arrived at the quad. Mick introduced them as

Red and Caveman. It was easy to see why one boy had received the nickname Red. He had a flaming head of wiry, thick red hair. Blue-eyed and freckled, he introduced himself as Daniel Punt.

The other boy extended his hand, and introduced himself as Kyle Grinsby. Montgomery supposed his new name came from his dark hair, which grew in abundance all over his body and his longer arms. Montgomery was surprised to hear himself introduced as Monkey. He wasn't sure he liked the moniker, but it was better than General.

The boys whiled away the afternoon by watching a movie on a DVD player. At 5:30, the boys left the room and clomped down the stairs. Montgomery, Travis and Mick climbed into the cab of Montgomery's truck; the other four jumped into the back. Travis opened the rear window.

The freshman picnic was being held on the edge of the Everglades that the school property abutted. The Natural Sciences building and lab was located here as well as the Administration Building. A commanding view of the unique ecosystem that made up the Everglades attained to those who were on the acre-sized pavilion which attached to the back of the Administration Building.

Upon arrival, each student drew a token from a barrel. The token directed its holder to one of the food stations with separate tables. The freshman class was approximately 6,000. The tokens were a means to help them meet one another outside the normal avenues of residence halls and classes. Montgomery drew a swallowtail butterfly, and headed toward the butterfly banner. Travis drew a bullfrog, and made his way to the back.

As he looked ahead, Travis saw a group of three girls headed for the line. He adjusted his pace so that he arrived half a step ahead, and then he stepped back. "Please, go ahead."

A honey-shade blonde spoke, "You were here first."

Travis smiled, and she smiled back. "Ladies first, or have manners gone out of style?"

"Honey, manners are never out of style," drawled the honey-blonde. "Park Longstreet. My friends are Rose Hill and Elizabeth Stuart."

"Charmed," said Travis. "Where do you hail from?"

"Alabama," replied Rose. "We went to school together, and decided we'd all come to Florida for college."

Elizabeth giggled. "We decided on this school because we liked the mascot."

Travis raised his eyebrows. "The snook?"

Elizabeth nodded. "Best fighting game fish in Florida, but we liked the sound of the word—snook. Who would not want to be a fighting snook?"

"Maybe the Gators, Seminoles, Rattlers, Bulls, Hurricanes, Owls and other assorted animals and weather events that represent Florida colleges."

Park gave Travis the once-over. "You haven't told us your name. What bad manners for such a fine southern boy."

Travis grinned. "Travis Lewis, hailing from Sparksburg, a small-town in Central Florida. Born and bred, I'm a native Floridian for several generations back. There aren't too many of us around."

Park winked, "We come from Montgomery. Native Alabamans, or should I say native Alabamen?"

"Y'all are native Alabawomans, southern belles and three peaches in the basket. By the way, my roommate's name is Montgomery—Montgomery Lee."

Elizabeth laughed. By this time, the quartet had moved through the line and piled hot dogs, potato chips, baked beans, coleslaw and fresh veggies onto their trays. They sat down at a nearby table. Travis volunteered to go for drinks. He went to the open station, picked up four cups of ice and four cans of Diet Coke.

As he returned to the table, Elizabeth said, "You'll have to introduce us to your roommate. We have a Longstreet, a Hill, and a Stuart. Lee would be a fine addition to our group!" She laughed at her own joke.

Travis asked in mock seriousness, "Are y'all still fighting the War of Northern Aggression against the Southern States?"

Park answered, "We're Daughters of the Confederacy. In our hearts, we'll always fight the Lost Cause until it's lost no more. As a native-born son of the South, don't y'all want to whip the Yankees?"

Travis flexed his arm muscles behind his head. Out of the corners of his eyes, he could see the girls admiring his biceps. He was glad he had worn a sleeveless shirt to the picnic. "All I care about is whipping the waves when the surf's up."

Park was impressed. "You surf? Great, could you show me sometime? I'd love to learn."

"It would be an honor." Travis checked her out without looking directly at her. *Yes sir, I'm going to enjoy college.*

At his table, Montgomery had sat down with two other boys. They introduced themselves as Joel and Nathaniel.

"Get the classes you wanted?" Joel asked Montgomery.

"Not much choice," Montgomery said. "It seemed like the university already had me assigned to classes before I registered."

"I would like to major in marine biology," said Joel. "But it's a crowded major. So I got sloughed into Freshman English, U.S. History, Principles of Logic, Basic Biology, and Basic Spanish. I figured I had it in high school so it should be an easy credit."

"My major is physical education," said Nathaniel, "so I signed up for Basic Humanities, Biology and Physics. I have to get my sciences done my first year so I can begin to take the courses on the mechanics of sports."

"Either of y'all going to pledge a fraternity?" asked Montgomery.

"To help my major, I'm working as an assistant trainer for the football team," said Nathaniel. "I want to visit the houses during rush week just for fun. But I have no spare time between the team practices and studies. I'll be a GDI."

"The Greek scene is not as important as it used to be," added Joel. "Still, the social contacts with the sororities are valuable; much less work to meet chicks."

"I plan to pledge Sigma Omicron Beta," said Montgomery. "My family has always joined. I'll follow in their footsteps—it's a calling. The Florida Lees are Sigma Omicron Beta. My father, uncles and cousin were in the house."

Joel gave Montgomery a funny look. "You want to be an S.O.B.?"

"I was warned that the character of the members had deteriorated.

But I'll be at the front of a fresh generation to restore the honor of the house."

Joel was still regarding Montgomery with an odd expression. "Hercules to the stable. You're aware that they abandoned the Greek honor system? They tolerate all sorts of behavior and philosophies—anything goes as long as the tap is running and the women are coming. It's even rumored that they deal drugs out of the house."

"No wonder they're in decline. Well, the brothers dealing drugs will be easy to fix: narc them and expel them. They won't have much to do with the fraternity from prison. As for the rest, why abandon something good to the bad guys? I want to take it back, and those who won't abide by the Greek code can get out."

Joel now looked amazed. "You almost convince me to pledge."

After dinner, Food Service cleared away its serving stations while a d.j. set up his equipment. The young people broke into small groups, walking around, talking, some staying with their new friends and others rejoining the friends with whom they came to dinner. Montgomery located Travis; the girls stayed. The young people danced until the sun began to set; then the d.j. wrapped the session with a final number. Afterward, Montgomery and Travis walked the girls to a campus bus. Travis found an opportunity to get Park's phone number. The boys found Montgomery's truck and arrived back at their dormitory around 9 p.m. Inside, they noted the announcement that their next orientation session would begin at 9 a.m. in the dormitory lounge. Stopping at the vending machines, they bought several cokes. Then they went upstairs to see what their quadmates were doing.

The next morning, about three hundred young men and women assembled in the lounge for the second day of orientation. Sarah Moore began by introducing herself and her staff of floor advisors, one advisor per floor. The third floor men's advisor was Rick Early, a junior from Lakeland. He was tall and lanky with a thick mustache.

"We'll leave in groups of thirty," Sarah announced, "for the campus tour. Before we do, I must review the dorm rules. One, carry your i.d. at all times. You need it to get into the building, to eat, to purchase books, snacks and other items on campus, to use the library, and to use the gym. You'll need it several times a day; no cash is used on campus except for vending machines.

"Two, every bedroom desk has an connection to the campus computer through which you may access the Internet. The service is free and essential, but know that your visiting habits could be monitored. The computer service department swears that they do not keep tabs on who is doing what. Be aware that it is possible—so stay away from porno and hate group sites.

"Three, D.E.A. and local police actively enforce the drug laws. If you're caught with illegal drugs in your room, you will be arrested and expelled. Four, alcohol bureau undercover cops keep watch on the places where beer, liquor and wine are sold. The drinking age is 21. Underage students who have alcohol in their rooms will be evicted. We don't inspect your rooms, but if we have to come to your quad for some reason, and see alcohol, someone living in the quad had better be old enough to legally possess it—enough said.

"Five, parking will be enforced beginning Tuesday. If you have a vehicle, get a sticker from the Bursar's office. By the way, freshmen have to park so far away you need the bus to get back to the dorm. If you don't have a sticker, your vehicle will be ticketed and towed.

"Six, you may rearrange your furniture however you like. But you aren't allowed to disassemble or detach any furniture—although I've been known to go temporarily blind when lumber and tools go past my door, or temporarily deaf in the halls. However, whatever you do to fix your quad the way you want it must be undone at the time you leave. You will be billed for any damages, and the university makes very expensive repairs.

"Seven, the nearest campus bus stop is out the front door at the curb. Buses run every 10 minutes from 7:30 a.m. to 7:30 p.m., then every 20 minutes until midnight. No charge, but you must show your student i.d. if the driver asks for it.

"This is your home for the next nine months. Let's keep it clean and orderly." Sarah fielded several questions about mail delivery, visitation, fire drills and quiet hours. When the students understood the dormitory's routine, Sarah efficiently sorted them into tour groups and sent them out five minutes apart. Montgomery and Travis, along with their other quadmates, were in the last group to depart.

Outside, Rick Early halted his group at the curb. "The bus stops here." Only a few freshmen had any idea that he was making a quip off President Harry Truman's famous saying. "It's half a mile through Ambrose Bay, which is actually a swamp, to reach the main campus. The mosquitoes are big, and they bite. Because we love all the little critters and respect the environment, the university does no spraying. So when you leave this area, you have a few options: wear long sleeves and pants, use bug repellent, run, swat or ride the bus. Most of us ride the bus. But you are on the walking tour. So today we swat."

As the group walked along the street through the bay, Rick talked about the University's history and major strengths. When they neared the main campus, he pointed to a pentagon-shaped building. "We call that the Bureau—short for bureaucracy. You'll spend much time in that maze paying bills, depositing money into your student account, withdrawing money to go to town—it functions like a bank, registering for classes and the like. Really, it's not too bad. Since everything went online, you can do most of your school business over the Internet. Every once in a while, though, you have to go in person—like all you who need parking stickers."

Moving onto the main campus, Rick took his group under an archway into the center of several buildings connected by covered walkways. "We call this the Ring. These buildings are connected to form a large circle. I won't bother telling you which building is which; you'll never remember. Consult your campus map when you receive your class schedule.

"Beyond the ring is the library." The group entered through the revolving door. "The main library's in this central building. The checkout desk is to your right. Study carousels are distributed throughout. You can access the catalog as well as library records over the Internet from your room. The library is almost irrelevant except as a place to study. You can research your papers on the Internet."

Rick took the group outside; pausing, he pointed out the concert hall. "The administrative building is across the street. It has no relevance for you. Four buildings at this end of the campus house our colleges of Engineering, Business and Economics, Teaching and Nursing. The easy way to remember is that the Ring is straight academics; this end is where the professions are taught. Across the street from the Nursing building is the campus bookstore. Connected to it is the Student Center. You're not likely to use the Student Center much because we have excellent recreational facilities in our residence complex. The Student Center is mainly for commuters. This is the beginning of the Bacon business district. You'll have time to check that out as the semester progresses. There are a couple of drugstores, clothing places, bookstores, and several Wal-Mart wannabees for those odds and ends you may need."

As the group walked on, Rick pointed ahead to the laboratory annex and classroom buildings. He then took the group through two blocks of faculty housing. "If any of you guys are thinking of pledging a fraternity, here is where the houses are located."

"Is it a good idea to join?" someone asked.

"I'll be honest with you. All the fraternities have lost strength. They're not that important anymore. They have little influence and virtually no power on campus. They're trying very hard to recruit new members, but their old habits are too difficult for them to break. I tried to join the S.O.B.'s my first year—that is, Sigma Omicron Beta—but their hazing was too brutal for my taste. I gave it up. That's the problem with these old-line frats: they work hard to sell you on how great they are, but once you commit, they treat you like dirt. They do anything they can to humiliate you—the sicker, the more they like it. You can tell I'm still bitter about my experience with the Sick-Bees. If you want to join a fraternity, check it out carefully. Their rush, that's what they call their recruiting, begins next week."

Montgomery looked at Travis, but did not say a word. He did not need to; his worried look told Travis he was becoming concerned.

The tour ended with the athletic facilities and a look at the stadium complex. The boys rode the bus back for lunch, and then back to the main campus for the afternoon's agenda. They came into one of the classroom buildings, and located the room for the L's. A proctor handed them a pencil, booklet, and several different kinds of sheets of paper.

Montgomery and Travis sat down in the seats indicated. Montgomery looked at the booklet. It read Professional Organization of Psychologists Research Center Multi-Phasic Inventory. The front cover read POP Research, which afterward Montgomery said stood for the Panel Of Pinheads. Travis, however, after viewing his results, decided that they should be PAP: Professional Association of Psychologists because they had done a smear job on him. Cat said they merely left an O out of the name because it was all poop.

Montgomery carefully listed his name and student i.d. number on all the papers. He opened the booklet, and began reading the questions. The questions were multiple choice, whose answers the students would record on an answer grid for machine scoring and analysis. Montgomery noted that many questions were about his background: age, sex, years of education completed, height, weight, religion, etc.

More interesting were the questions about his personal habits: use of alcohol, sexual activity, use of drugs, hours of sleep, grooming, cleanliness, work, and health. It asked about homosexuality or latent attraction to the same sex (*like anybody would answer yes,* thought Montgomery), perversity, or other fetishes; then it asked emotional questions about periods of sadness and insanity. It asked if he heard any voices. It asked if he had additional personalities. It asked about family history of mental illness.

Interests and hobbies were another topic of the questionnaire. Montgomery found it curious that the questions were not organized into topical sections but were haphazardly mixed up throughout. Then he noticed that several questions were repeating word for word. He wondered what would happen if he changed his answers, but decided to play it safe.

Finally, Montgomery finished answering the 500 questions of the booklet. Then he moved to the next sheet of paper. It was full of fill-in-the-blank statements. Montgomery looked them over. He had no idea what to write. "My father is ____________; My mother is ____________; My hero is _____________." He conferred with Travis.

"We have to write something," Travis said. "Make it up."

Montgomery stared at his paper. Feeling like he was about to fail a final exam, after five minutes of attempting to think of answers, Montgomery began to list background information: My father is a Lee of Florida; My mother is married; My hero is Carl Sagan. Travis fared no better: My father is a man; My mother is a woman; My hero is a sandwich.

Then there was a sheet of word associations: a series of words would be listed, and then the next word in the series had to be written down. By this time, Montgomery was tired of psychological testing and wrote "telescope" beside every series. Travis looked on Montgomery's sheet, and decided to do the same thing except that he wrote "sex." *What if they conclude that everything makes me think of sex? That's not so bad. Better than Montgomery—they'd better know he's into astronomy big time, or the Freudians will crucify him for his answer of an instrument for looking that one expands to use and contracts when done.*

Montgomery raised his hand, and asked the proctor why the proctor was jotting notes upon a clipboard. The proctor responded that he had to submit a report on the manner in which the students filled out the papers, and any questions they asked or comments they made. Montgomery felt Travis' hand on his back with the middle finger extended. He grinned, "My sentiments exactly."

They were now getting near the bottom of the stack. The boys whipped through the Meyers-Briggs Personality Inventory, and then considered the final questionnaire, a multiple-choice survey of incoming college freshmen. By now, neither cared how accurate their answers were. They filled out the answer sheet as fast as they could, turned all their papers in, and split.

Friday morning opened with thunderstorms. Heavy rain lashed the buildings as dark grey clouds scudded across the front of a tropical wave. Travis and Montgomery had taken advantage of their proximity to the bookstore the day before to purchase their textbooks, so they both slept in. When they got up, they decided to handle all their remaining business over their Internet connections. They raced one another to see who could purchase a meal plan faster, print off class schedules, read e-mail, check the status of their student accounts, activate their library accounts, and try to hack the system. Montgomery applied for his parking permit, saw that his account was automatically debited for the fee, and that he could obtain it in the afternoon. Montgomery then found a way to shortcut the student i.d. process. He set up his mini-cam, and took pictures of Travis and himself. Adding their names, addresses and student i.d. numbers to the picture files, Montgomery sent them to the security office for processing. Fifteen minutes later, an e-mail arrived that their i.d.'s could be picked up at the Bursar's office.

After lunch, the students dashed for the bus and headed for the fieldhouse for the Campus Cavalcade. Clubs, intramural sports, fraternities, sororities and activities of all sorts had set up booths so that the incoming freshmen could investigate the parts of campus life that interested them.

Montgomery's first stop was the Astronomy Club. He signed up immediately as an interested freshman. He had a good conversation with a sophomore and a junior. He was excited about joining the club and was not surprised to learn that he already knew many of the members through the Internet.

Travis was not interested in any clubs unless there was a party club. "They ought to have one for beer-tasting," he groused good-naturedly. He did, however, stop at a surfing booth. To his delight, he found people who had a network that provided instantaneous alerts when the waves were strong and transportation pools to head to the best beach. No one in Florida is ever more than two hours from a shore. Travis added himself to the network.

The boys talked to many of the groups, and slowly made their way around to the fraternities. Montgomery led the way to the Sigma Omicron Beta booth. A small, slender boy wearing a yellow, deep purple and black polo shirt was standing in front of the booth, making eye contact and shaking hands. Montgomery stepped forward and said, "Montgomery Lee. My friend is Travis Lewis."

A delighted look came over the boy's face. "Montgomery! Wilson told me to keep a lookout for you. Glad you stopped by."

Montgomery was relieved by the pleasant and happy reception. *Perhaps it won't be so bad after all.*

The boy scribbled both the names down on his clipboard. Montgomery asked if many boys had expressed an interest in the fraternity.

"Not yet, not yet," the boy enthused. "But it's early. The list doesn't really grow until the end of Rush Week when the prospective pledges have to make a decision. But you—you're a shoo-in. Nothing to it—a few weeks of pledging, some harmless fun, you come live in the house for a few weeks and we vote you in. Wilson said only the best and the brightest this year. We want the cream of the crop."

He turned to Travis. "And any friend of Montgomery's will make it as well. I've already signed you up; you can't say no. Be sure to come to our smoker on Monday. It starts at seven. We'll have a few beers, show you the house, introduce you to some brothers, and talk about the advantages the Greek system offers on campus. See you then!"

The boy immediately began talking to other boys in the crowd. Montgomery heaved a sigh of relief and began to move away. Travis came alongside. "That was easy," Travis said. "I wonder why Rick told us that scare story?"

"I heard they had some problems, but it looks like the fraternity is on top of things. Maybe all the mysterious difficulties and rough members mentioned by my cousin and others were to convince me that I had to pledge right away. Sometimes my family thinks all I care about is stars."

Travis grinned. "Montgomery, you do scare us at times. But how bad can a fraternity be when they're going to be so hospitable? Did you catch his name?"

"No, but he has to be the head of the pledge committee. Why would they send anyone else?"

Chapter Two

Rush Week

LOUD VOICES SPARRED in the front room of Sigma Omicron Beta.

"We want good pledges this year—quality material: more character, less vice."

"Intolerant *******! There's more to fraternal life than high grades and study hours."

"Watch your mouth! Have you forgotten the honor code? We're the laughingstock of campus because our house is notorious for allowing any sort of cheating and rowdiness."

"That depends upon how you interpret the code. It allows for a wide diversity of views on what it means and how it applies. You moralists want it only your way. Besides, the code is only a guide, not authoritative."

"Of course it's authoritative. Why bother having a code if it doesn't apply?"

"It's a historic relic; a tradition, but it's not binding."

"Make sure we weed out the ones who don't believe in our ideals."

"Like the past few years, we're going to solicit a wide range of pledges. A diversity of backgrounds and interests makes a healthier fraternity."

"You mean you're looking for party boys who will drag down our grade average, blacken our already bad reputation, and act in drunken, lewd ways: pledges like you."

"Face it, Wilson, you've lost control of the house. We're going to run it the way we want; we're going to get pledges who will fit in with how we run things. We only let you be President to look good to the Dean. You have no say in how we're going to choose pledges or how we're going to test them."

"I still have power. I can shut you down—"

"That's rich. Who's going to listen to you? The house charter gives you certain powers, but no one will obey unless we give the say-so."

"Unless who gives the say-so?"

"Me, Jack, Rip, Brendon, and Pete. Don't believe me? Then try something."

"This isn't over—not by a long shot."

"Calm down, Wilson. We don't want to scare anyone away until they agree to pledge. Then we nail them."

Harsh laughter accompanied this final statement. Wilson stormed upstairs to prepare for the night's smoker, which would begin in thirty minutes. Downstairs, the five-member pledge committee supervised the efforts of the other brothers to put everything in place.

At 7 p.m., the lights blazed around the exterior of the house, throwing the Cracker style architecture into high relief. Several stereos in different parts of the house began playing the latest C.D.'s from the most popular bands. Several of the SigBees gathered in the front room while others went into the front yard. Still more were in some of the other common areas, some waited upstairs in the bedrooms, and some were out back in the service area.

Young men from the university began to drift in. A subtle screening process began. Promising groups were ushered up the front steps into the front room, and handed off to one of the brothers for conversation and evaluation. Duds were taken aside, carded, informed that they were underage at a function serving alcohol, and shown out through a side gate in the fence. Those showing up only for free beer were sent to the back patio where they could be served, and receive a special pitch to pledge.

Inside the front room, brothers were leading groups of two and three to side alcoves to talk about the fraternity. Upon obtaining a name and campus address, the brother would take his group into the back for a beer, and lead them on a tour of the house. Few of the rushing visitors knew that the casual conversation was laced with qualifying questions: how much partying have you done since you came, what classes have you registered for, do you study much, have you ever tried marijuana, what church do you attend, and others that were so subtly introduced that the topics seemed to have arisen spontaneously. However, the host brother was monitoring the answers and extra recruiting efforts were made for the boys indicating that they were light on academics, loved to get rowdy and take risks, and oriented toward an active life of socializing under the assistance of intoxicating substances.

Boys who were more reserved and academically oriented were not discouraged, but if they wanted to pledge the house, they had to put out the effort to get themselves asked back for Thursday afternoon's barbecue.

Montgomery and Travis arrived around 8:30 p.m. They were taken into the front room, where they looked around for the member who had signed them up at the Cavalcade. He was nowhere to be seen, but Jack came over and introduced himself.

"Jack Canter, pledge committee. Welcome to the house. Best frat on campus—all the girls say so." Jack winked.

Travis grinned. "You speak my language. Travis Lewis, and Montgomery Lee."

"Are you the Lee we've been expecting?" Jack asked.

Montgomery blushed. "Probably so. My daddy, uncles and cousins have all been Sigma Omicron Betas."

Jack appraised Montgomery carefully. "The Lees have been an important part of Sigma Omicron Beta from its beginnings. Following in the footsteps, then."

Montgomery nodded. "It's like I'm called to join—destiny, fate or whatever."

Travis laughed. "You'll love Montgomery. He has this big family heritage that sits on him like a straitjacket. All the Lees have done this, the Lees have never done that. But he's a real friend—he's pulled me out of many a mess; you can always count on Montgomery Lee. I rode his coattails through high school, and figured what the hey—I can do the same through college."

Montgomery smiled. "I got the grades, and Travis got the girls: an even trade-off."

Jack laughed. "We need both talents in Sigma Omicron Beta. You guys want a beer?"

Travis replied, "Love one. But (here he joined with Montgomery) the Lees do not drink alcohol." To Jack he said, "See what I mean? You'll get used to it."

Jack was wondering how to split them up when he caught a warning glance from Cody. He led the way through the dining room into the kitchen. "Here's a brew, Travis. Coke for your pal."

He led the way up a back stairway to the bedrooms. "Our rooms sleep two to four. Every year we have the opportunity to change rooms on a seniority basis. Usually we pick our roommates and then the room. We don't have many house rules—live and let live. We are one big happy family. We do like to party and get rowdy on occasion."

Travis interjected, "Only on occasion?"

Jack smiled broadly. He liked Travis. "As much as you want—every day's an occasion to get messed up. Of course, if we did that, we would get fat from all the calories."

Travis thought Jack sounded like a fun guy to know. Montgomery thought he sounded like a jerk. Jack finished the tour of the house. "Are you two signed up?"

Travis answered, "We did that Friday."

"Great! Then we'll see you back here on Thursday."

After Montgomery and Travis left the house, Jack conferred with Cody. "The Travis kid is a possible, but we need to dump the Lee kid—all grades, no fun."

"Careful. We have to let him pledge—his family has too much clout in this place for us to refuse him. Then we'll see—sometimes these stiffs loosen up with a little encouragement. He might be one of us waiting to cut loose."

"I hope so. The last thing we need in the house is moralizers."

"You said it, brother. We need a couple of brains to get us through our courses. But they have to be tolerant of our lifestyle." He snickered.

"And our occupation."

"And our occupation."

Tuesday morning Montgomery woke up with a charge. He hurried into the showers, excited about his first day of classes: English at 9, Chemistry at 11, and Math at 2. He carefully shaved and trimmed his sideburns, dried his hair and applied a little gel for body, scratched the few, wispy hairs that passed for a goatee beard, and splashed some aftershave about his face. He hopped under the jet of water pouring from the showerhead, then toweled off. He went back to the room to dress.

Travis was still in bed asleep. He had stayed up late after they had visited some of the other frat houses. Each one had offered him a beer, which he accepted, so he had been quite inebriated when he went to bed. He remained in a heavy sleep as Montgomery left the room to go to breakfast with some of the other boys.

It was 8:30 a.m. when Montgomery returned to the room to pick up his notebook and pen. "Hey! Sleepyhead! Get up!" he cried as he kicked Travis' bed. Travis mumbled something and rolled over. "Travis! Buddy! Thirty minutes to class!"

Travis opened his eyes. His mind felt dull, and his spirit lazy. He took in his surroundings, and slowly remembered that he was at college. His mouth was dry. "Morning, Montgomery," he mumbled. "What time is it?"

"Eight-thirty," Montgomery said. "Get a move on—you'll be late."

Travis sat up, swung his legs to the floor, and stumbled into his closet. "You go ahead," he said. "Meet you for lunch at Jeff Davis." He watched Montgomery leave the room and returned to bed. *Another ten minutes,* he thought. *Then I can dress in five, catch the bus and be in class the moment the clock strikes nine.* Travis fell asleep.

Montgomery rode the bus to the main campus and entered The Ring. He took a moment to get his bearings, then walked around the central green to the English building. His classroom was on the second floor. He ran up the stairs two at a time. Reaching the top, he turned left and proceeded to the second door on the left.

The classroom was filled with chairs that had writing surfaces attached. Montgomery winced—every chair was built for a right-handed person. The exterior wall was lined with windows. The Ring was the original campus built in the 1920's so all the buildings had oversized windows designed to catch the prevailing breezes. Since central air conditioning had been retrofitted into the buildings, the windows were superfluous, but Montgomery thought they made the room much more pleasant than the jailhouse architecture of his high school: all metal doors, cinder block walls with narrow horizontal windows 12" x 30" six feet high. The back, front and interior walls were covered with black slate chalkboards. A desk and straight-back chair were in the front of the room on a platform eight inches off the floor.

A few persons had already sat down. Halfway back, Montgomery saw Park Longstreet smile at him and wave him over. Montgomery smiled back and took a seat next to her. "Hi."

"Good morning," Park said in her slow, melodic way of speaking. "How's the astronomer today?"

Montgomery was surprised that she would remember. "Head in the clouds, as always. I'm glad there's somebody in this class that I know."

"Me, too. You reckon it will be hard?"

"Shouldn't be, unless your high school didn't prepare you for writing papers. All college-bound kids at my school had to take writing classes."

"We didn't have special classes, but my teachers were always pulling the excuse that we had to write papers because we would have to know how in college."

Montgomery grinned. "I heard that a lot myself."

"How's Travis? I haven't heard from him since Wednesday night."

Montgomery was surprised. "That's not like him. Last I saw him, he was getting dressed for class. He overdid it when we visited the frats last night; I think he's a little hung over."

Park laughed. "Why do I always go for the good-looking ones who love to party hearty? Don't tell him I said that."

Montgomery smiled. "I won't."

"But drop a hint to call me—would you do that?"

Travis has a new girl. "Sure thing."

More students had come in and taken seats. At nine, hallway bells rang as a man in his older twenties came in and sat at the desk. "Good morning, I am your teacher for Freshman English. I'm a graduate student working on my thesis for my master's degree in American Literature—19th century. In particular, the writings of Samuel Clemens, also known as Mark Twain. My name is Kyle Appleton—please call me Kyle. The syllabus will be prepared and distributed on Friday. This is the English Department's sneaky way to make sure you come to class on Friday."

The students laughed. Kyle continued, "For this class, you will be responsible for completing grammatical exercises and turning them in every Monday and Wednesday. The syllabus will have your assignments. There will be eight writing assignments plus one term paper. Four of your writing assignments will be assigned a week in advance; four will be written in class with no advance preparation."

The Teaching Assistant noted the eager glances on the students' faces. "Today is the first assignment. Take out a sheet of paper, and write a one-page essay on your favorite candy bar. Be sure to write your name on your paper; every year somebody takes a zero because they do not identify their work."

The students' unanimous groan mixed with the sound of paper being pulled from notebooks and the scratching of pens. Silence reigned as the students gathered their thoughts, and tried to organize them into a coherent essay. Some struggled to fill up their paper; others were writing much smaller than normal to fit in all their words. Thirty minutes later, the first student finished and handed in his paper. The others looked up, annoyed that someone was already done and also at the involuntary reminder that they only had fifteen minutes left.

Montgomery and Park finished at the same time and left the classroom together. "Travis is taking that experimental program in one of the classroom buildings. Want to walk over and find him on his break? I'm free until eleven."

"I'd love to," said Park. The two left the English building and walked to the building marked Classroom Annex A. Park remarked, "I can't believe they haven't found somebody to name it after."

"They're waiting for a large donation."

Inside the building, they found Travis in the hall. "Your break start already?" asked Montgomery.

"No, I overslept," Travis replied somewhat unsteadily. He was dressed in a wrinkled t-shirt with baggy shorts and flip-flops. "I ran all the way. I can't get into the room until the class takes its break. Hello, Park," he added. "What brings you this way?"

"Your roommate and I are in the same English class. We walked over to see you. Long time, no hear."

Travis looked at her slyly. "Here now."

The hallway bell rang. "There—bye," retorted Park. She was leaving for her ten o'clock biology class.

"By where?"

"Over there."

Montgomery grimaced. "I hate to say it, but for romantic banter, this is awful."

Park laughed, and ran down the hall.

Travis shrugged his shoulders, but watched her receding form until she disappeared around a corner. "What gives?"

"She's peeved because you haven't called her. Don't tell her I told you, but she likes you."

Travis smiled. "It's going to be a great weekend."

"First get through your classes."

"Yes, Mom."

An e-mail message was waiting for Montgomery when he checked his on-line campus mailbox after he returned to his dorm for lunch. "Montgomery: Our district manager is visiting the house today. Could you come over this afternoon to meet him? Wilson/Sigma OB"

Montgomery whipped off a quick reply, "Wilson, I have a 2 o'clock and a 3 hour lab 3 - 6. I can come before 2 or after 6."

Montgomery checked his e-mail again after eating. "Come as soon as you can. Wilson." Montgomery confirmed he would leave in ten minutes for the fraternity. He grabbed his notebook, and headed for the bus stop.

Travis was in a bad mood because of the stinging lecture he received from his professor for being late to class. He also had a pile of homework to complete and turn in the following morning. "This was supposed to be the easy option," he grumbled.

The steam of a hot August Florida afternoon rose into the sky in visible waves. Despite his precautions, Montgomery found himself sweating as he waited for the bus. He saw it coming down the street and pull over. The driver got out and opened the front hood. Steam lifted a large cloud over the driver's head.

Montgomery checked his watch, and began walking to the campus. He half-ran, half-slapped his way across the bay and cut across the main campus by the library. By the time he arrived at the fraternity house, his mood had soured, his skin was red from slaps and mosquito bites, and he was covered with sweat, his t-shirt and shorts soaked.

He walked up the front steps and knocked on the door.

Rip Tilden opened the door and snarled, "What do you want."

"I'm supposed to see the district manager."

Rip was about to tell him to beat it when the door was pulled all the way open by Cody Spung. "Come in," Cody said. "He's really busy, but he likes to meet our most promising pledges." Cody gave a warning poke to Rip that Montgomery could not see.

"Cody Spung. You are—"

"Montgomery Lee. I was here last night."

"So you were. Were you as impressed with Sigma Omicron Beta as we were impressed with you?"

That line went out before the Apollo moon landing. "All my family have been SigBees. It's a family tradition."

"We believe in family traditions. That's what makes Sigma Omicron Beta strong and great."

Such patronizing! Does he think I'm falling for it?

Cody knocked on a side door, ushering Montgomery inside upon hearing, "Come in." A twenty year-old junior extended his hand, "Wilson Dole, president of the Bacon chapter of Sigma Omicron Beta. This is Mr. Allegra, our district manager. His territory covers the states of South Carolina, Georgia, Florida and Alabama."

Cody introduced Montgomery and left him with the two men. "You're Montgomery Lee," said Mr. Allegra. "Kyle has told me much about you. He said you were prime Sigma Omicron Beta material: good head, solid character."

"Thank you, sir."

"I like to meet the new pledges. It helps me to know who they are."

Montgomery, feeling shy, was silent.

"Do you have any questions about the fraternity that I can answer?" asked Mr. Allegra.

Montgomery thought a moment, then he began to ask, "How does the process—"

"Oh, Wilson can help you with that. I'm glad you could stop by." Mr. Allegra stood, indicating that the interview was over.

The meeting's over? But it never began. Why did this man make a special point of asking me to go out of my way when he had no reason for seeing me? What was so urgent that I had to be here this afternoon? All he did was shake my hand. He never mentioned my name; he won't remember it by the time I shut the door.

As Montgomery put his hand on the doorknob, Mr. Allegra said to Wilson, "Madison here is a good candidate. We need more like him—remember, it's the personal touch that makes the difference." Montgomery shut the door in disgust.

In the hall, Rip Tilden was leaning against the wall. "How did it go?"

"It never went. He shook my hand and showed me the door."

"It never does with these executive types. Too highbrow to get to know us common people."

Montgomery felt sweat drops dripping from his armpits. "I have to get to class." He hurried to the front door. Outside, he paused for a moment and took a deep breath. *What am I getting myself into?* Then he bolted for the Mathematics Building.

Math class and chem lab passed quickly. Because it was the first lab of the semester, the experiments were simple and Montgomery was through by 5:15 p.m. He made the happy discovery that Cat and Red were also in his chemistry lab; not only would he have someone with whom to eat dinner and someone with whom to study, but the trio also joined together as lab partners.

They went straight to the dining hall. At 5:30 p.m., the dinner hour was in full swing. They took trays and entered the line. The main dish was baked chicken breast with peas and potatoes. Montgomery took a full serving. He added a salad and cake to complete his meal. A few chairs emptied by a window. The three boys took those places.

"Montgomery, how goes the rush?" Cat asked.

"Very strange. They called me last spring to ask me specifically to pledge this fall. At the Cavalcade, the frat rep knew I was coming. The president of the chapter wants me badly. But when Travis and I visited last night, they acted indifferent. In fact, they seemed more interested in Travis than me, even though Travis was only there because of me. This morning, I get an e-mail asking me to come by and meet the district manager. Real important it seemed. But when I go over, the man shakes my hand, gets my name wrong and shows me the door. I got a creepy feeling in the hall like I wasn't wanted. Now why would someone make a special effort to ask me to come only to tell me that I was not wanted? It's weird."

"You can never figure those frat boys out," said Red. "I'll never pledge—I don't want to become one of them, nothing personal, Monkey."

"No insult taken. That's exactly what I thought when I reached the porch and could breathe the fresh air. What am I getting myself into?"

"It's simple," said Cat. "Some are recruiters and the others are hazers. The recruiters tell you that you're special, fate has brought you to their door, you have all these wonderful qualities about you, you're prime material. It's one long line of bull. Once you commit, your life becomes hell. The hazers take over. They tell you that you're dirt, scum like you is a dime a dozen, and you're lucky they're taking pity on you by allowing you the great privilege of serving their every twisted, disgusting desire. What you feel is the hazers' impatience to get started when the recruiters are still doing their thing."

"I've never understood the point of hazing," said Red. "In the military, the boot camp sergeant is viciously mean toward the recruits. After he's broken them down, he rebuilds them into good soldiers. The end result is tight cohesion among the unit. But fraternities, and my Dad told me it goes on in most professions, too—even ministers get hazed by their colleagues when they take their first churches—there's no point. It does not produce loyalty; quite the opposite—the recruits hate the guts of the older guys who hazed them. Not exactly a fraternal feeling, is it?"

"The only means they have to handle their rage," added Cat, "is to become what they hate. Most frat boys take their revenge by savagely hazing the recruits that come after them. A most unhealthy atmosphere for the development of one's mind."

"I feel like I'm supposed to do this—like there's a purpose for pledging that I don't know. I might go again tomorrow night. See if I can observe what's really going on behind all the glad-handing and polished speeches. Y'all interested if I do?"

Cat and Red shook their heads. Cat said, "There aren't many places to get beer in this town, and it has the advantage of being free. But I won't swim in a shark-infested pool for a free beer. No thanks."

Montgomery said, "I'll go alone if I have too."

Red asked, "Wouldn't Travis go with you?"

"Nah, y'all won't see much of Travis for about two weeks. He's got a new girl interested in him—met her at the picnic the first night. He played her slow—didn't call her but waited until he ran into her on campus. That happened this morning. She's hooked; he won't do another thing until he's landed her in the boat."

In his room, after eating, Montgomery read his e-mail: *Gone to see Park. Don't wait up, T. // First meeting of the Astronomy Club will be on Monday, the 26th at 9 p.m. in the Student Center.* Montgomery clicked on his scheduler, and entered the meeting on his calendar. *Montgomery, sorry the meeting with Allegra was so brief. Come tomorrow at 3:15 and we will enroll you as a pledge. Cody Spung, pledge committee chairman.*

The next day, Montgomery went straight to the fraternity after his class. Pushing open the door, he called out, "Hello. Anyone here?"

Rip Tilden was sitting in the front room reading a magazine. "Oh, it's you," he said without any enthusiasm. "Up the stairs, first door on the left."

Montgomery stepped into the house and closed the door. He went up the stairs in a deliberate fashion, the palms of his hands tingling. He knocked on the door and received no answer. Montgomery slowly opened the door and looked into the room. *No one's here. I hope I'm not being set up for a prank.* In the room were couches, stuffed chairs and end tables. A television was at one end of the room—a 35" screen that was hooked to a mini-satellite dish.

Montgomery sat down on one of the couches, dropping his notebook beside him. He studied the décor: *off-white paint, badly stained walls and carpet, worn furniture. I wonder what scarred the walls and broke through the wallboard at those patched places. No pictures, either—I wonder what that means, if anything.*

Thirty minutes later he was still waiting. *Maybe I have the wrong room—I'll go see.* Montgomery went down the hall, but found no one. He went back down the stairs. Rip was still in the front room. "What," he snapped.

"No one's here. I had an e-mail to come for a meeting to enroll as a pledge."

"Right. Up the stairs, first door on the left."

"I've been sitting in that room for thirty minutes. No one's come."

"If you're going to pledge Sigma Omicron Beta, the first thing you need to know is never, ever, ever question an order. Go up and wait, Pledge; someone will come when he's ready, and not before."

Returning to the room, Montgomery discovered that his notebook was missing. He was now angry. *Let them play their little game; I'll wait them out.* Another thirty minutes went by. Montgomery got up and began pacing. "Five more minutes," he grumbled. "Five more minutes, and I'll search the house for my notebook and leave."

Ten minutes later, Montgomery was still pacing. *I should go. But then they win—I don't want to let them do that.* He sat down again. *If only I had brought my cell phone. I'd call Barney and get this situation straightened out.*

At 4:30 p.m., Cody Spung nonchalantly walked in. "Good to see you, Montague," he said cheerfully.

"Montgomery, Montgomery Lee."

"Yes, right, well Mozzarella, we have the results of your psychological profile and, as the Pledge Chairman, it's my responsibility to review it with you."

Montgomery's jaw dropped open. "What profile?"

"The one the psychology department prepared from the tests you took during orientation."

"Those are confidential," objected Montgomery. "You have no right to those results."

"If you are going to pledge Sigma Omicron Beta, Misdemeanor, the second thing you need to know is that you have no secrets from us and there is nothing we can't find out. We know everything about you, right down to the first time you soiled the sheets while dreaming."

This entire procedure, from the moment I entered the house, was planned. Cody and Rip have been communicating; they're being deliberately rude and obnoxious—why? They're trying to gain a psychological hold on me; at the same time, they're trying to gall me into leaving.

"My name is Montgomery," he said firmly.

"Whatever, Mockingbird." Cody opened the folder he had brought. "Let's see, well, well. You scored well in academic inclination—bit of a bookworm, I'd say." His eyes probed Montgomery. "We do look for well-rounded individuals. There's more to life than books."

After thirty seconds of silence, Cody continued, "Shy and inexperienced with females—you've had intercourse, haven't you? Mohair, it's the man of the world that makes the best fraternal brother. Teetotaler, no drug usage, what's wrong with you? Don't you know how to have fun?"

Speechless, Montgomery agonized over a response. *Everything I thought was a plus this guy is turning into a minus. Why would it be bad to wait for sex until I'm ready—in a committed relationship? I've always believed that drinking and drugging are moral failures in a person's character. My morals are a part of my Christian commitment, giving me the happiest possible life at eighteen years of age. What's going on?*

"It says here you once stood up for what you thought was right even when an entire high school class opposed you. Are you one of those moral crusaders? We don't need that kind in Sigma Omicron Beta."

"But they were going to shaft an immigrant student to make her take the blame for stealing something she didn't steal. She was innocent, but she would have been kicked out of school. I had to defend her."

"Mm-hmm," ejected Cody loudly. "Subject tends to intolerance of others different from himself, and is unwilling to try anything new." Again, his eyes probed Montgomery. "You're peeved, aren't you, that you had to wait. You couldn't tolerate my schedule or be respectful of my needs."

This guy is a jerk with a capital J. He was disrespectful to me to ask me to come for a 3:15 appointment when he was unavailable until 4:30 p.m.

"Subject tried to anticipate analysis by giving cagey responses to the open-ended questions—detailing basic facts that revealed nothing about himself. His obvious attempt to manipulate the questionnaire shows that he is distrustful of others, and one who keeps his motives hidden. His choice of a university professor for a hero shows he can be a sycophant when he believes it to be in his favor.

"You ******* toady.

"Finally, Subject reveals that his sexual energy is self-focused as everything makes him think of an object that is an obvious phallic symbol. That the object is worked by extending and contracting its length means the Subject is fixated on self-gratification which the researcher suspects is several times a day." Cody laughed rudely.

The room was swimming around Montgomery's head. *How could they say these things about me, especially when they're wrong?*

Cody jumped to his feet. He opened the door and yelled down the hallway, "Hey, Rip! Wait till you hear this! Sexual energy is self-focused as everything makes him think of a phallus that works by extending and contracting its length. Subject is fixated on pleasuring himself several times a day!"

Loud, vulgar laughter blasted from many rooms in the house. Montgomery slid low in the couch. Cody delivered his coup de grace, "Masturbation, you are a challenge worthy of this house. You are officially a pledge, you might make a good brother if we can beat it out of you."

Laughing, Cody held out Montgomery's notebook. Humiliated, Montgomery grabbed it and fled.

His quadmates were startled when Montgomery came flying through the common room into his room, locking the door behind him. He slammed his notebook to the floor, then he shredded his pillow into tiny pieces of foam. *I should packing my things and go home. Who else in the university was going to see this scathing report? My advisor? Psych classes? They'll say, "Now here we have a really sick puppy." No one knew what to put down. Anybody could interpret the answers any way they want. How can someone presume to sit in judgment on me when they never met me?*

Outside, his quadmates knocked on the door. "Montgomery, something wrong?" When they heard no answer, Cat said, "Somebody get Rick."

A few minutes later, Rick Early entered the quad. He knocked on the door. "Montgomery, it's Rick. Let me in, okay?" A few moments later, the lock turned. Rick went into the room, closed the door and sat on Travis' bed. "What's wrong?"

Montgomery started to say, "I can handle it," but instead the story spilled out in a rush: deliberately being made to wait, violation of confidentiality by the university, and the humiliating way the pledge chairman had broadcast the findings for the entire house to hear.

Rick cursed, "Whoa. They did a number on you—that's for sure. Are you sure they had the real papers?"

"Yeah. They knew I put Carl Sagan down as my hero; from what they said about the sexual stuff they had to be referring to my telescope. I don't know how I can face anybody after this."

"You were violated. What that frat house did was wrong. Nobody should have to undergo what they did to you. I can help you file charges if you want. Getting those psychological papers alone will get them kicked out of school and the frat closed."

When Montgomery said nothing, Rick added, "You're not thinking about going through with pledging, are you? After what they did to you?"

"But that's the point. I'm supposed to be pledging so I can help run those guys out of the fraternity. If I give up now, they win." *Plus, God called me to this mission.*

"That's something that you'll have to decide for yourself. But it's not as bad as it sounds. The rotten guys—if it weren't this, it would have been something else. The good guys, if there are any good guys, will be so embarrassed by this incident that they'll leave you alone during your hazing period. I'd like to go after those rip-roarers for stealing university records that contain restricted information but I won't do anything without your permission. One thing I can tell you—they may have had copies of your test papers, but they did not have official university interpretations of your responses. The university doesn't evaluate the papers until a specific need comes up. All they do is computerize the records. So none of this is going to get around campus. Those of us who know you know that you're normal. Those nimnockers must have hacked the system. There are lots of folks on campus, professors even, who have asked the university for years not to computerize the information for this very reason. If you decide to pursue a case, you could make a permanent change in university recordkeeping that would make you a major campus hero. Think about it, will you?"

Montgomery stood up as relief purged him of shame, anxiety and tension. Rick stood, and Montgomery hugged him. "Thank you, Rick." A few moments later, Rick and Montgomery moved into the central room. His quadmates gathered round. "Everything okay, Monkey?"

Montgomery smiled, "Yeah, it's okay now." He hesitated, then shared the story with his friends. They were shocked but Joe said it best, "I can't believe how well you're handling it."

Red added, "They must do everyone that way. I have an older cousin who was trying to enter a monastery. Y'all would think the last people on Earth who would be having psychological evaluations done would be a church, right? They have God; why do they need Freud to tell them about their people? But they did. He too was savaged by an extremely critical report. He was going to quit, but then the other monks told him, "That's the way Razor Lips does everybody." They called the psychologist who did the evaluations Razor Lips. When my cousin heard that, he relaxed. Instead of being shamed and humiliated, he was one of the guys. He belonged."

"They haven't done Travis that way—yet. They must think he's the same as them. They're wrong about that. But it's not right—there's no need for a fraternity to perform psychological evaluations of its pledges."

The phone rang. Travis was on the line. "Montgomery, grab some cash and get yourself over to Alyssa Hawkins, room 312. We're going out for pizza." Elizabeth Stuart grabbed the phone, "Bring your telescope, please." Montgomery froze, then realized: *There's no way she could know. It's going to take some time to fully get over this experience.* "I'll be there in ten minutes," he said, and hung up the phone.

Thursday heralded change for the freshman: their twice-a-week classes would be in session. Inside the lecture hall for Western Civilization, Elizabeth was waiting to surprise Montgomery. *I hope he doesn't realize that I changed classes this morning just to be with him. It's a bit silly, really. And if I seem too forward, he'll shy away. But those green eyes of his—so full of passion, curiosity, intelligence—so expressive of the stars he loves. Montgomery Lee: extraordinary, handsome, he knows who he is and where he's going. I wouldn't mind going with him.*

Montgomery entered the room, walking toward the front for a seat. Elizabeth followed a minute later.

"Is this seat taken?" Elizabeth asked.

"Not to my knowledge," Montgomery answered as he shifted his notebook to his desktop.

"Montgomery?"

"Elizabeth! How—I thought ..."

"I changed classes this morning. This class made a better fit with my overall schedule. I didn't realize you were taking it."

"Humanities requirement."

The bell rang. Three Teaching Assistants began passing out the course syllabus. Up front, the professor began taking attendance from the class roster. Montgomery paged through his syllabus. *Lecture, reading and three tests: simple. The deep pools of her intelligent brown eyes ... doggone, there's another text needed ... she's shaped like an hourglass—very sexy in those denim shorts, white blouse and gold choker around her neck. Like a pool at the bottom of a waterfall. Travis can have Park; she's a splashing fountain. I'd rather dive into Elizabeth.*

Montgomery's face was turning red. He started, and tuned into the professor who was beginning his lecture. To cover his unease, Montgomery uncapped his pen and began taking copious notes.

Elizabeth intuited the awkward moment. *I wonder what he was thinking about. He's not frivolous like the boys I knew in high school. Except for that goatee, only a few scraggly hairs ... I can't decide whether it looks silly or stupid.*

Midway through the lecture, the audiovisual equipment malfunctioned. As the TA's worked to fix the problem, the professor fussed with his notes.

"So what do you think of Travis and Park?" asked Elizabeth.

"He's a fast worker when he decides to pay attention to a particular girl. They'll do well together."

"She doesn't like to be alone. I hope he doesn't hurt her."

"Not Travis. He has courtesy as well as charm. His commitments may be a little shallow at times, but he treats his women well."

"What about you?"

"Me? My relationships are more confusing. I left someone at home. She's a senior in high school. Although we never came to a definite conclusion or commitment, I'm not sure that I'm available; however, I am sure I'm not unavailable."

As the professor resumed his lecture, Elizabeth appraised the young freshman beside her: *He's a slow mover. The more skittish the fish, the more valuable the catch.*

Montgomery hung around with Elizabeth that afternoon, and went to dinner with her and her friends.

"Where's Travis?" asked Park.

"He went to the pledge barbecue at the frat."

"Aren't you supposed to be there?" asked Elizabeth.

"I forgot," replied Montgomery with a cat-ate-the-canary grin.

Travis surveyed the scene when he had arrived at the fraternity. *They're here in full force. They all want a good look at us before deciding who to invite and who to refuse. Where's Montgomery? Since he's guaranteed a place, he must not need to be here.*

Travis helped himself to a beer and a couple of hot dogs. Jack Canter and Rip Tilden approached him and asked about his classes.

"Two days a week—Wednesday and Thursday—I'm tied up in class all day. But it's not too bad. The other days I'm finished by lunch. That gives me plenty of time to mess around or get my studying done while everyone else is still in class. My nights are free for dating and having fun. It's really great because I met this girl and things are going well."

"The house is a great place for meeting girls and having fun," said Jack. "There's always a card game or something taking place."

"One huge pleasure house," added Rip. "But you have to be willing to join in."

"How do you sneak girls in?" asked Travis. "The quad layout is great, but when I'm ready for the bed sheet tango, the female has to pass through the common room and everyone knows—she loses the mood."

Jack laughed. "No problem here. That's what fraternity life is all about—this is a private house so nobody knows your business but you. There are plenty of doors and out-of-the-way rooms for whatever activity your mind turns your body to."

Rip smiled. "Absolutely. There are lots of ways to have fun, and most of them happen in the house at one time or another. Being open to new experiences is the key."

Travis grinned. "I hadn't thought much about fraternities, but my roommate was right. Greek life is the best life on campus."

Jack and Rip invited Travis into the house for a private party. In their room, Jack pulled out a water pipe and some marijuana. Travis sat down and smiled. "What a place," he enthused.

Jack set the pipe up, and waved Travis to take the first draw. Travis inhaled deeply, held the smoke in his lungs for several seconds, then exhaled. He leaned back to allow the chemical to make its way through his bloodstream to his brain. In turn, Jack and Rip took their hits off the pipe. In no time at all, the giddiness and artificial hilarity of the drug had taken the three into its grip.

On the patio, the afternoon was giving way to evening. The pledge candidates completed their meals and drinks, their last chances to impress the members coming to a close. As they departed, the pledge committee convened in an empty room to prepare their recommendations for the entire house. Travis was a shoo-in, Montgomery they had already accepted but they planned to force him to quit, and others they took their time reviewing until they had come up with a list of twelve pledges. Cody logged onto the campus Internet, and sent invitations to each of the twelve to come to the house the next night where they would formally meet the brothers, and wait while the house voted on whether to accept them as pledges.

Travis was on the top floor of the house. He was so intoxicated by the drug that he could not figure out how to leave. He blundered into a couple of rooms, but they were empty. Then he burst through another door. A buxom female shape stepped into the shadows, and said, "Who are you?"

Travis giggled. "I'm a new-bee dig-bee."

The shape laughed. "You're high, new-bee dig-bee."

"I'm a sex-bee new-bee dig-bee."

The shape stepped forward. She was dressed only in her underclothing. "Come with me, dig-bee." She led Travis into another room. Closing the door, she pulled his shirt over his head. Travis spun in dizziness. She caught hold of his shorts, and pulled them down to his feet. Travis kicked them off along with his sandals, which he was wearing barefoot. He reached around to her bra clasp, and released the garment. With increasing desire, they tugged each other's remaining clothing off their hips, and their naked bodies fell backwards onto a sofa. Travis was enjoying his time greatly. "What's your name?"

"Janet."

He nuzzled her neck and gave her playful bites.

"Janet, I'm Tra-this."

She laughed to hear his slurred words and made a pun, "Tra-this, try-this ..."

Around midnight, the door to room 3F3 opened quietly. The room was dark. Travis went to his closet, removed his sandals and clothes, and slipped on a pair of shorts. He stepped back into the room and tripped. He caught himself on the wall and giggled.

Montgomery opened his eyes. He had only heard Travis laugh like that on two previous occasions, and both times he had been high from smoking marijuana. "Travis?"

"Montgomery—I was trying not to wake you."

"Where were you tonight?"

"At the frat house—why didn't you come?"

"I had something better to do than to display my soul for the ridicule of all like yesterday."

"They were having a little fun, that's all. I had fun with them today." Travis giggled again.

"You got high."

"How did you guess?"

"You only giggle when you're high."

Travis giggled shrilly. "I reckon I did. I got laid, too."

"You what?"

"Some girl came out of a room wearing nothing and pushed me into a closet. It was great."

This is not like Travis. Travis has an easy-going temperament, he's easily led into many activities, and he's sexually active, but he's never been with one girl while he was dating another, even casually. Travis always focuses on one girl at a time. For that matter, he tried marijuana a couple of times in high school, but he avoids its use because he doesn't like breathing smoke into his lungs. He's a drinker; his parents had supplied him with whatever he wanted as long as he left marijuana and other drugs alone. Travis would never have gone near the fraternity if it hadn't been for me. What have I gotten myself into? If Travis is ruined, it's my fault.

Morning brought e-mails to both boys. Montgomery received an absolution for missing the previous day's grill, and a summons to report to the house at 8:30 p.m. for an interview with the entire fraternity. *I wish there was a way out of it. Will it be a repeat of Wednesday's interview?* His classes seemed to race by.

Travis got an invitation to stop by, meet the brothers and hang out. *Friday! If the weeknights are any indication, the weekend will be a wild blowout!* His class dragged.

The boys decided to head to the fraternity together as Travis had not been given a specific time. They left Somerset Johns shortly after 8:00 p.m. They took the bus to the gymnasium and walked the remaining block and a half to the fraternity house. It was 8:20 p.m. when they arrived.

A notice on the front gate directed them to a side door where they were to enter and wait to be called. They entered the house and sat down in a small lounge. A red-faced, overweight boy was sitting there.

"What's up?" Travis offered.

"They're voting on me now," replied the boy. "I was so nervous; I think I messed up."

"What did they do?" asked Montgomery cautiously.

"They asked a bunch of questions. Some were strange—made no sense. They asked about my GPA in high school. They asked if I was depressed. They asked me to recite the Greek alphabet—I didn't know it was different. I started out A-B-C and they laughed at me. They asked about my psychologicals."

"You, too," said Montgomery. "Did they maul you like they did me?"

"Yep. I think they do everyone that way—it's how they start their hazing."

"Gee, they didn't rate me psychologically," observed Travis.

"You were too busy getting high with them," said Montgomery, a little more sharply than he intended.

"Then you'll get right in," the boy said. "They asked a lot of questions about how I liked to relax—how I had fun. Like they wanted to know if they would feel comfortable with me—would I fit in with their group—be their type of friend: one who would party all night and pee on the street in the morning. I said I was an early riser so I go to bed early. I think that cooked my chances."

"Don't grades and character and responsibility count anymore?" asked Montgomery.

"Nope," said Travis. "Loosen up, buddy, it's okay to have a good time."

"As long as you don't puke in my truck," retorted Montgomery.

Travis reddened in the face as he remembered that incident. "Uh, right, dude. As long as you don't puke in your truck."

The door opened. Rip appeared, greeted Travis, nodded at Montgomery, and summoned the other boy to the front room. "We're ready for you, Colin."

Colin followed Rip out of the room. Two minutes later, he reappeared looking gleeful. "I made it! I'm a pledge!" In his hands was a manual. He waved it around. "This tells all the stuff we have to know. I made it. They said to tell you to come on, Travis."

Colin left the house exulting over his acceptance. Travis went forward to the front of the house. Montgomery was alone. Minutes passed. *Like Wednesday, be here at the appointed time and wait for us to come when we feel like it.* He studied the room. A naked light bulb hung down from the ceiling. The glare did nothing to improve the garish red wallpaper with paisley patterns in black velvet superimposed. The couches and chairs were black leather. There was nothing else in the room. *What do they do in here?*

Fifteen minutes after he left, Travis reappeared. "I'm in: piece of cake. I can't thank you enough, Montgomery, for bringing me to this place. Don't worry, buddy, they're going to take you too. Too much Lee in this place for them to turn you down. They want me upstairs—see you later."

Montgomery took hold of Travis' arm. "What about Park?"

"What about her? We're not engaged or anything. I'll see her tomorrow—buy her some flowers. As a pledge, I have to obey orders." He laughed. "So I have to go upstairs and cater to the brothers."

Rip put his head in the room five minutes later. "Your turn," he stated flatly.

Montgomery followed Rip to the front room. Approximately forty young men sat in the sofas, chairs, standing along the walls, or sitting on the floor. One couch was positioned in the center of the room. Wilson Dole, Cody Spung and two other pledge committee members sat on it. A single, wooden straight-back chair was placed opposing the couch. Cody motioned to Montgomery to sit there.

Cody began the questioning. "Tell us why you want to join Sigma Omicron Beta."

"I've looked forward to joining Sigma Omicron Beta since I decided to come to college. My family—"

Brendon Garrett interrupted, "You want to join because Mama said so? Daddy expects all his offspring to be in the frat?"

Montgomery gulped. *Why the hostility?* "Uh, no, not at all. But the Lees have always been Sigma Omicron Beta men. My Daddy and uncles were SigBees; my cousin Barney as well."

Pete Spivey challenged, "So you think we're obligated to take you."

"No, I thought I would enjoy living in a fraternity. But you don't have to take me."

Brendon said, "Your reaction to your psychologicals showed that you have an attitude problem about this place. What do you have to say about that?"

"I don't have an attitude problem. I was surprised by the interpretation, that's all."

Pete hit hard. "You disagree with what the professionals said, then. Men who have spent their lives dedicated to the field of psychology and you think you know better than them how to interpret test results."

"I don't know better than the experts of psychology; I don't know how to interpret those tests at all. But I do know ME better than anyone else and I know that those results were way off base." Montgomery finished with a firmness that dared anyone else to ask about the tests.

Wilson Dole broke in. "That's not so important anyway, Montgomery. Switch to some other questions, Cody."

Jack Canter asked, "How do you relax?"

Montgomery was relieved. "I like nothing better than to take a telescope and go out into a field and observe the stars."

"Are you a solitary person?"

"No, I enjoy being with people."

"Yet you prefer the stars over people."

"No, my friends and I go out together. We look at the stars, and talk. We listen to music, dance; we do different things together."

"Can you relax with all sorts of people in all sorts of ways?"

"I'm not sure what you're asking."

"Do you party much?"

"I go out with my friends and we have a good time."

"What about others who like to have a good time in different ways than you like to have a good time? Would you party with them? Or do you insist that everyone has to be like you?"

"I would not insist that anyone be like me. People are free to party as they wish—I'm not their judge."

"What if you were at the same party with people doing drugs, for example? Would you party with them?"

Where's this questioning going? "I try to stay away from drugs. I've been around drugs at parties, who hasn't? But they're not for me. I don't drink, either. But I have no problem with people who do, or being around people who do. It's a choice each person has to make."

"What if some brothers in the fraternity do drugs? Would you accept them, or reject them? What if they were doing drugs at a fraternity party? Would you evict them from the house? Make them uncomfortable? Call the police?"

Travis was really gone last night; he had to have been intoxicated for many hours considering the barbecue started at 5:30 p.m. "What's your point?"

Jack snarled, "My point is this: you are intolerant of others, and I do not think you are a good candidate for this house."

Montgomery was devastated. *Why do they keep harping about intolerance? What has made them think that I am intolerant? If I do not want to do drugs, why can't they be tolerant of that? I'm not the one who's being intolerant of others who are different.*

Wilson again interceded. "I think we've finished that line of questioning. Montgomery, what was your GPA in high school?"

"3.72 on a 4.0 scale."

"What's your major?"

"Astronomy. I declared when I applied; it's what I want to do."

"Ever have a girlfriend?" asked Brendon with a mild leer.

"My high school girlfriend is a senior this year. I recently met someone on campus; in fact, she's waiting for me to finish here so we can go to the Bungalow dance."

Brendon whispered to Pete Spivey, "Maybe we were wrong about him."

Cody decided to end the interview. "Is there anything you'd like to tell us before we take a vote?"

"I want to join this fraternity. Y'all's concerns are unwarranted. I'll be a loyal brother to y'all and carry on the traditions that made Sigma Omicron Beta the best fraternity on campus."

Back in the lounge, Montgomery sat down to wait for the vote. *What was the deal in there? They obviously had rehearsed the questions in advance: what to ask and who would ask it. They had made up their minds before I'd gone into the room. What's the point of interviewing someone if you already know what your decision is?*

He did not wait long. Rip summoned him and escorted him back to the front room. Cody spoke, "You have some fine qualities for becoming Sigma Omicron Beta. We also have some concerns about your appropriateness as a fraternity brother. These concerns are a tendency toward solitariness, intolerance of others, and an inability to have fun with persons of differing tastes. During your pledge period, we will be watching you closely to see how well you progress on these concerns. In your interview for induction, we will ask you about these concerns. But I'm pleased to inform you that we have accepted you as a pledge to Sigma Omicron Beta, with some reservations as I have now told you. Congratulations."

Half-hearted applause followed Cody's speech. Montgomery thanked them, took his manual, and left the room. *Should I look for Travis? No, he's a big boy and will have to look after himself. I want to spend my evening with Elizabeth.*

Chapter Three

Greek Studies

SATURDAY MORNING SUNSHINE filtered through the window blinds above Montgomery's head. He rolled over and looked at his clock: 10:30 a.m. He stretched in bed. He had deliberately slept in late having stayed out until 2:30 a.m. The sweetness of Elizabeth's lips were still implanted on his own. Montgomery put his hands behind his head, interlaced his fingers, and lay on his back looking at the ceiling.

What a week! I wonder where Travis is—he's probably at the frat house considering the fast inroads he's making into the inner circle. I wonder if my pledge period will be as rough as the week of rushing. I'd better not pursue a complaint against the pledge committee for stealing my psychologicals; I have no proof. If they had further broadcast the alleged interpretation, Travis would have heard it and told me.

Montgomery yawned, and climbed out of bed. He drew an oversized t-shirt with the sleeves cut out off his chair and over his head. He was wearing the generously sized athletic shorts he usually slept in. He padded into the common area.

His quadmates had been out late as well although Montgomery had been the last one back to the room. Shorts had fallen asleep on one of the couches, and was now half sleeping, half watching Saturday morning cartoons. Cat was drinking a cup of coffee at the table. "Good morning," he greeted Montgomery.

"Hey-y'all," yawned Montgomery. "Any more of that java?"

"Grab a cup and nuke you some. Big night?"

"I went from hell to heaven in a single bound."

"Okay, Superman, I want details."

Montgomery related the tense interview, and then the great time he had at the dance. "She's a dream and a great kisser."

Cat laughed. "Lost your heart already. Those southern girls will do it every time."

Montgomery grinned. "Most of Florida is still the South—everyone talks with a southern accent in my hometown."

"Maybe true in Hicksville, but the bikini babes are on the coasts, and that's a world unto itself. Nothing southern in the beach towns."

"Maybe you're looking in the wrong spots. I can show you places on the beach where you'll think the Civil War was yet to happen."

"Quarter till eleven. I wish those folks would open lunch earlier on Saturday."

"Yeah, I'm hungry too. Let's make a market run after lunch."

Cat pointed at the semi-comatose figure of Shorts. "You want to try to make him pee his pants?"

"What?" asked Montgomery as if he had not heard right.

"Pee his pants. It's a simple trick, but it doesn't always work. You take a glass of warm water and dip his hand in it. Sometimes the person relaxes his sphincter muscle and then wakes up to—well, let's call it an embarrassing moment."

Montgomery laughed. "Let's call it a scientific experiment."

Shorts had the bad timing then to emit a snore. That was all the encouragement the boys needed. Cat grabbed a plastic cup, filled it with water and nuked it. Smothering their laughter, Cat held the cup while Montgomery moved Shorts' arm to place his hand in the water. The boys retreated. Montgomery watched for a few seconds, then went into the bathroom and turned on a faucet.

"Brilliant," whispered Cat. The boys went into Montgomery's room and watched through the cracked door. Suddenly Shorts jumped to his feet and ran for the bathroom. It was too late. He kicked his pants and underwear off and dashed for his room. Cat and Montgomery collapsed in silent laughter.

"Quick, get the cup while I put a video game in so he won't suspect us," breathed Montgomery. Cat dashed out while Montgomery pushed a basketball game into the game player. He found a saved game that he and Travis had been playing and loaded it. Cat came in, threw the cup under Travis' bed, and grabbed a controller.

Returning to the common room, Shorts called out, "Anybody up?"

"In here," yelled Montgomery.

Shorts was very red in the face. "Did you see anything?"

Montgomery replied, "See what? We've been in here with the door closed so the game wouldn't wake anyone."

Shorts stammered, "Not that there was anything to see—I wondered, that's all."

Cat was concentrating very hard on his defense. "Get the others up and we'll go for lunch."

Shorts left the room and banged on rooms one and four. Groggy voices gave him instructions, which he was not inclined to carry out. He returned to Montgomery's room, "They're still sleeping. Only us three."

Montgomery saved the game, then turned off the player. "Let's go then; I'm starved." Shorts saw the twinkle in his eye, but decided not to pursue it.

After eating, the boys hoofed it to the remote parking lot where Montgomery was authorized to leave his truck. Montgomery cranked the engine. "Want to go muddin'?"

Shorts had recovered from his embarrassing moment and hollered, "Let's go!"

Montgomery gunned the engine and peeled out of the parking lot. He headed for a place he knew that was filled with muck and cursed with a high water table. Soon his tires were throwing mud everywhere as the boys spun doughnuts, careened through scrub bush, cabbage palmettos, kudzu, and slash pines. Montgomery parked on a sand bank and hopped out. The other boys followed only to be hit by muck balls hurled by Montgomery's accurate aim. They retaliated and soon no one could tell the difference between the boys, the truck, and the churned up ground.

They collapsed on the ground, laughing. Montgomery got that strange twinkle in his eye again. "Excuse me, I have to take a leak." He jumped through the brush.

Cat tried hard to suppress a grin. "Me too."

Shorts looked suspicious. "Are you guys sure you didn't see anything in the quad?"

"Like what," called out Montgomery from behind the brush.

"Oh, nothing," said Shorts. He was dying to find out if they had seen him hop to the bathroom with a urine-stained crotch, or dash for his room naked from the waist down, but if they had not seen it, he did not want them to know.

Cat returned and made a show of zipping closed his shorts. "That's what I like about the outdoors. Always a convenient bush when you got to go and can't hold it."

"You guys know, don't you," demanded Shorts.

"Know what?" asked Montgomery innocently as he returned.

"Forget it," muttered Shorts.

They headed toward another place Montgomery knew. He stopped at a self-service wash station and cleaned the truck from its coating of muck. He then turned the spray on his friends and washed them off. Cat returned the favor for Montgomery. Then they parked the truck so they could lay in the sun and dry off.

It was close to 4:00 p.m. when they came back to town. Montgomery stopped at the supermarket, and they bought coffee, sports drinks, cokes, snacks, cookies, and peanut butter.

"This ought to deplete the common fund," said Shorts.

"About time we stocked up," said Cat. "One of this and two of that—we never have enough of what we want."

"Too bad the elevator's locked," said Montgomery.

"Don't be too sure of that," smiled Cat.

After hauling the groceries to the room, Montgomery left to return his truck to the parking lot. Cat and Shorts stocked the common room's shelves. By this time, the other quadmates had gotten up and moved about. Travis also had returned.

"Where's Montgomery?" he asked.

"Parking his truck," replied Shorts. "We're meeting him at Jeff Davis for dinner."

"Good," said Travis. "I feel bad for abandoning him last night, but the brothers had asked me to stay for a party. What a group! I was so messed up I spent the night in a lounge on a sofa."

"It wasn't all fun," he added.after noting the incredulous looks on the others' faces. "I had to roll the joints, tend bar, and do other things for them—you know, the pledge has to do all the grunge work."

Red asked, "Travis, why are they being so friendly with you when they are being so nasty with Montgomery? He's the one with the family ties."

"What can I do about it? Maybe it's because I know how to have fun. Anyway, the real pledge work starts Monday. I will only be another pledge getting dumped on. Montgomery will be the one with the advantage."

Cat responded, "Monkey knows how to have fun, ain't that right, Shorts?"

Shorts said, "We went muddin' this afternoon in Monkey's truck."

Travis countered, "See? So why is everyone so concerned for Montgomery? He'll fit into the frat like I do."

Sunday afternoon the boys scattered across the campus while they had leisure time to pursue their interests. The quad was quiet as Montgomery lounged on a sofa and read through his manual. Of great interest to him was the 24-point Greek code presented in the form of an acrostic:

Alpha: apathos	Goodness, Morally Fit,Unquestionable Reputation
Beta: bebaios	Reliable, Dependable
Gamma: gnosis	Knowledgeable
Delta: didache	Learning
Epsilon: egcrateia	Self-Control, Self-Discipline
Zeta: zalos	Zeal, Ardor, Passionate, Striving Earnestly
Eta: agemonia	Leadership
Theta: tharsos	Courageous, Bold

Iota: ilarotase	Cheerful, Glad
Kappa: katakarpos	Productive, Very Fruitful
Lambda: logismos	Rational, Reflective
Mu: makrothumos	Patient, Forbearing, Even-tempered
Nu: napho	Sober, Free from: Excess, Rashness, Confusion
Xye: xenodochone	Showing Hospitality
Omicron: oiktirmos	Compassionate
Pi: pistos	Trustworthy, Faithful
Rho: ratore	Speaking in Public, Advocate
Sigma: sothrios	Rescuing, Saving, Delivering from Danger
Tau: timay	Reverent, Respectful, Showing Honor
Upsilon: ugiase	Healthy, Sound
Phi: philadelphia	Brotherly Affection
Chi: charis	Gracious, Helping
Psi: psallone	Praising, Encouraging
Omega: ophelimos	Useful, Beneficial

There it is from A to Z, or Alpha to Omega. But so far, all those Greeks have shown me is the opposite.

Montgomery studied the organization of the house. *Nine work groups divide the chores: Food, House (repair and maintenance), Cleaning, Yard, Meal Clean-Up, Party, Pledge, Athletics, and Public Relations. An upperclassman led each workgroup: these nine, plus the officers, form the executive committee. The executive committee runs the house although most decisions are made at monthly meetings of the entire house.*

Sanctions for rules violations require a three-fourths vote of the membership. The executive committee may convene a hearing for law-breaking, cheating, theft, lying, failing to come to the aid of a fraternal brother, slovenliness, bringing disrepute upon the fraternity, failing to perform assigned work, and acting contrary to the spirit of fraternal life. That last one's pretty vague. It would be easy to railroad anyone. But with a seventy-five percent majority required, no one would ever be found guilty. Those not abiding by the rules would look out for each other.

Montgomery walked to the refrigerator for a Coke. He popped the tab, and took a drink. *That tastes good. Really, each workgroup head has unlimited power to run his area however he wants. Only the entire fraternity, upon a majority vote, can overturn a decision of a workgroup head. Most decisions of a head will become done deeds before the monthly house meeting could be held. The workgroup heads are virtual dictators.*

(In truth, the workings of the Sigma Omicron Beta house were worse than the manual revealed. For each workgroup head had an informal committee of buddies with whom the real decisions were made and implemented. Thus, the actual workload did not rotate throughout the year, and cliques held the major power and shaped the fraternity to their liking. Major disagreements and undermining of rivals were commonplace as individual brothers vied for power. The pledges were generally too nervous too notice, but most fraternity meetings were filled with tension. Alliances with cliques and individuals were the key to dominance. Thus the overly emphasized attention to how pledges would fit into the fraternity.)

Inside the back cover a loose sheet of paper stuck out. Montgomery pulled this sheet of paper to read it. *Every pledge gets a "supervising brother" who shepherds him through the pledge process, and represents him during fraternity and pledge committee meetings. I get Wilson Dole. Good. He wants me in the fraternity so he'll look out for me. He'll defend me before the pledge committee.*

Scrawled on the paper was a handwritten note:

> *Montgomery, sorry the boys have been treating you roughly; there are some troublemakers in the frat. That's why I had myself assigned as your supervising brother—I'll try to run some interference for you. The normal stuff you'll have to handle on your own, but I won't let them single you out for special treatment of the terrible kind.*
>
> *We should meet and go over some of the manual; I'll show you the important things you have to know. If you're free tomorrow for lunch, let's meet under the clock at the Student Center at 11 a.m. E-mail me to confirm. Wilson.*

Montgomery had just zipped off his confirmation when the phone rang.

"Is this Montgomery? Excellent, this is Rick in the lobby. Two beautiful young ladies are asking for you: a petite, auburn brown eyes and a buxom, shag-cut brunette. You know these girls?"

"Elizabeth and Rose? I know them."

"I'm inviting myself to dinner," said Rick. "Get down here quick. We'll go someplace other than Jeff Davis."

Montgomery hung up the phone and went into the bathroom. Looking in the mirror, he approved his appearance: *no stains on my shirt and shorts, socks, shoes, one last facial check, and I'm out the door and down the stairs.*

Rick immediately sensed the warm affection that was flowing between Montgomery and Elizabeth. Montgomery performed the introductions, "Elizabeth Stuart, Rose Hill—Rick Early."

"Oh, perfect!" Elizabeth cried.

"What's perfect?" asked a confused Rick.

Montgomery laughed. "Another general for the group: Lee, Stuart, Hill, Early, and their other friend is Longstreet. All Civil War generals for the South."

Rick smiled. "Then I belong in this group."

"Definitely," said Elizabeth.

"Definitely," said Rose with more feeling. She had been feeling left out since Park and Elizabeth had found boyfriends so quickly, but now her chances were improving quickly.

"If Travis doesn't blow it with Park, he'll have to change his last name to Jackson," Montgomery said.

"He'd better be careful," replied Rose. "When Park likes a boy, she'll give him every chance, but he'd better pay attention to her or else."

"It's strange," said Montgomery. "I have never known Travis to be attracted to a girl, and see her so little. Usually you would be sick of him hanging around your room. But it seems he spends his free time at the frat house."

"Which is strange for a fraternity," said Rick. "Usually they're standoffish to their pledges; they don't want them around unless they want to haze them or work them. Only when the pledges are inducted are they really welcomed. But in Travis' case, it's like he was already a member in another chapter who transferred here."

"Travis does have a way of becoming familiar within a minute or two of meeting someone," replied Montgomery. "I have seen him get into places with armed security guards for the express purpose of keeping out kids like Travis. But to ignore a girl he likes—that's not Travis."

"Fraternities change people," said Rick. "As you now know, it's not always a positive experience. Sometimes good kids go bad because they get into the wrong frat. Some start partying so much they skip class and do no homework. They figure they'll cram their way through exams. First they go on probation; at the end of the year, they flunk out. As floor advisor, I'm concerned that process has started with Travis."

"I can let you know if he's not studying," said Montgomery. "We'll see how long it takes him to ask me for help."

"Where are we going?" asked Elizabeth in an obvious change of subject.

"The Brasserie," said Rick. "It's a cut above the regular dining hall fare. As a result, they take a bigger bite out of your meal plan credits. But if you're like most students, you bought breakfasts and you don't eat many of them, thus you have extra credits to use before the end of the semester or you lose them. If you're careful, you can afford to eat a little better every so often."

"Works for me," said Montgomery. "I skipped breakfast yesterday and today."

"Can we use our credits for Cokes at the Student Center?" asked Rose.

"Nope," replied Rick. "They have that figured out. They plan on students buying meal credits that won't get used. Student Center food service comes directly out of your student account. What they did was to make it a game. The more you know, the better you play the game, the more you get from your meal credits."

"Somebody should write a book about all the things a freshman should know," said Rose.

"But no one tells," finished Elizabeth.

The quartet crossed a street, walked under an arch, and saw a brick dining hall with colonial paned windows. Rick reached the door and pulled it open as he stood to the side. "General Hill, General Stuart, General Lee, welcome to the Brasserie."

Elizabeth smiled. "Would you please step through the door—give us, please, a table for four."

Rick laughed. "Give the man your student i.d.—the meals are good but are not free."

Rose jumped into the game. "Tell me everything that's good—what choice to make I should."

Elizabeth tapped Montgomery on the arm. "Your turn."

Montgomery stepped into the line, thought a minute, and said, "General Hill, steak from the grill; General Stuart, pork chops fit the bill; General Early, a salad to watch the weight; General Lee is still contemplating his fate."

Elizabeth applauded. Then she carried on, "Come through the line and fill your tray; take all you want—it's the same to pay."

The girls are enjoying this silly game, thought Rick. *When was the last time I was out in mixed company? Too much study, too much work—it's fun to be out with freshmen who are enthusiastic about college life. Rose is lively and pretty; it's been too long since I was on a date.* He quipped, "So much here you want to taste; eat what you take—leave no waste."

This time Rose clapped, and Rick colored slightly. "Meat, vegetable and sweet; which of these makes my heart beat?"

They found a table by a window, and set their trays down as Montgomery took his turn. "Here we are beside the glass; tray on the table and sit on your—"

"Okay," said Elizabeth. "We've had enough of the rhymes." But she was laughing.

Chapter Four

Astronomical Science

WHEN THE 10:20 BELL RANG, Montgomery capped his pen, assembled his books, and made his way out of the classroom, heading for his meeting with Wilson Dole. As he ascended to the portico of the Student Center, he saw the large clock over the doors. *This must be what Wilson meant by meeting "under the clock."*

With a half hour to kill, Montgomery went to the arcade. His favorite game, Space Explorers, was open. Montgomery positioned himself behind the controls, and slipped his student i.d. into the slot. The game read his magnetic code, debited his student account fifty cents for one play, and whirred to life.

Montgomery expertly lifted his rocket ship off its home planet, and sent it speeding through the galaxy. A few deft shots from the ship's front guns blasted a clear path through the first obstacle, an asteroid belt. Montgomery then fired the retro rockets to slow the ship for a docking with a space station. *Refuel now so the ship won't falter at the Omega Galaxy.* Montgomery separated from the station, and headed for the upper left corner on the screen.

Montgomery pushed a button, and a star chart of his current course appeared on the screen. *Hey! Those two errors in naming stars have been corrected; my letter had its effect.* Montgomery returned to the space screen, and resumed his course for a distant galaxy. He dodged vortexes and black holes, slipped through time anomalies, picked up passengers and materials—all the while scoring points and credits for additional ships.

As he was approaching his favorite part of the game, the Eindackiter Galaxy, he felt a tap on his shoulder. Montgomery glanced around and his stomach fell into his abdomen; it was Rip Tilden. "Out of the way, pledge," Rip snarled. He shoved Montgomery aside and took the controls. Rip maneuvered the ship awkwardly to retrace its course, but slipped into a vortex that spun the ship into a nearby planet. It crashed.

Montgomery reached over and took his student i.d. out of the slot.

"What are you doing?" challenged Rip.

"Retrieving my i.d."

"Leave it in—I want to play another game."

"Play on your own dime."

"Didn't I tell you never to question an order?"

"My pledge status doesn't give you the right to steal from me."

"The third thing you need to know, pledge, is that everything you own belongs to me. Hand your card over now."

Montgomery was fired up. "No. What's mine belongs to me, and I don't have to give it to you or anybody else, pledge or no pledge, and if you have a problem with that, we can take it outside."

The arcade fell silent. All over the room machines went dark as untended controls allowed the games to kill their subjects.

Montgomery looked Rip straight in the eyes. "How about it, thief?"

Rip looked around, then said, "You must like to get hurt, don't you, pledge. Wait till you're at the house."

"You're not so brave without your buddies to back you, are you?" Montgomery picked up his notebook and walked off. He glanced over his shoulder before going outside. Rip was standing in the arcade, watching him, with hatred in his eyes.

Wilson was crossing the street when Montgomery came out the door. He waved, and dashed through the traffic to come onto the portico. "Good, good, glad you made it," Wilson greeted. He shook Montgomery's hand.

"I'm glad to see you, too. I just had a run-in with one of your boys."

"Who was that?"

"Rip."

Wilson's face fell. "Tell me what happened."

"There's not much to tell. I was playing an arcade game when Rip came in and took it over."

"You let him have the game, didn't you?"

"Yes, I had no choice. He shoved me out of the way."

"That wasn't necessary. As a pledge, you're bound to give way to him because he's a fraternity brother. This is why I wanted to meet with you—so you wouldn't make any mistakes during your pledge period. Was that all that happened?"

"No. He lost the ship—I was playing Space Explorers—right away. I took my i.d. out of the game to leave the arcade and he demanded that I leave my i.d. so he could keep playing."

"What did you do then?"

"I told him no—my i.d. would give him access to my student account—and I wouldn't let him steal from me. What makes him think I have to give him money whenever he demands it? I told him no, and dared him to a fight which he was too chicken to accept. Then he threatened me, and I came out here."

"Oh, no," moaned Wilson. "This is exactly what I wanted to avoid. You can't antagonize any of those guys—this is bad, really bad."

"I don't understand. So he tells his little group—so what? He probably won't tell them anyway; he won't want to admit that a pledge got the better of him."

"He'll tell them—he'll tell the entire pledge committee. He'll demand blood, and I mean that literally. Come on—we'll go somewhere we can talk without being overheard."

Wilson headed for Bacon's business district. Two blocks down and one block over was a small coffee shop. Its sign read "Maccabees." Inside, Wilson spotted a booth near the rear, which was empty, threaded his way among the tables, and slid into the seat. Montgomery took the opposite side.

"Hardly anyone knows about this place. No one from school ever comes here. I use it for confidential meetings."

"Someone would have to know it was here before coming. It sits back from the street and isn't noticeable unless an observer was at the door."

"Let me tell you about the house," said Wilson. "We are in a struggle for the heart and soul of the frat. Some brothers do not believe in the old ways anymore: a code of honor, personal responsibility, virtue, strong academics, integrity, and a distinct way of life. Some believe that our principles, the Greek Code, are open for interpretation according to one's life situation and personal desires. There are a wide variety of views that are dependent upon the definitions of the words used. Change the definitions, and the code is changed without denying the code, which would upset traditional, fundamental-type persons, or going through a difficult process of amending the code. Redefining words also means that agreement on anything cannot be achieved because opposing sides talk past each other—each believing the other is using their definitions.

"Therefore, brothers like Rip Tilden, Cody Spung, and their pals can do as they please without fear of impeachment. They make a mockery of the societies fraternities were meant to be. Our national leaders fear that if they take a stand, so many brothers would leave the fraternity that it would be bankrupt. So they wink at overt and blatant acts that violate the Greek Code and fraternity rules. You'll find that Rip and company are immoral, drunken cheaters running amok in the house. They corrupt the younger brothers and pledges."

"I noticed. My roommate Travis is under their spell."

"Is that the new pledge they've admitted to their private parties? Every semester they find someone to take into their group; building loyalty by extending privileges pledges are ordinarily denied. The pledges never catch on to what they are doing."

"Travis is a good kid. He'll wake up eventually. But he's easily led. The question is: how much damage will be done before he does wake up?"

"My concern is not your roommate; it's you. Their one ideal for human life is tolerance. Brothers should tolerate any behavior or type of character regardless of what it is. For example, they have this girl they pass from brother to brother. If we could catch her living in a room, we could evict her and that brother. But she moves so often we can't figure out where she is. She has sex with every brother that hides her. In fact, brothers on that network can have intercourse with her anytime they want. They say we should tolerate this lifestyle and not even criticize.

"We're trying to bring accountability to all fraternal brothers, but it's not easy. One problem is the redefining of words. Another problem is that many brothers believe that charging a brother with an infraction is a worse offense than any rule a brother is breaking. But this isn't your concern.

"Cody Spung controls the pledge committee. He and his pals will conduct your training, monitor your conduct, and decide whether to recommend you for admission. Don't make them mad! They have the privilege, ability and personality to hurt you badly if they want. As your supervising brother, I'm supposed to help you with your assignments, but I can't change your assignments. Only Cody can make, alter or revoke an assignment. Montgomery, I've seen them hurt people—physically. Be careful.

"Put up with whatever they dish out. Go along to get along. Once you're in, you can work with us, my allies and me, to bring change. Hazing is a part of fraternity life, Montgomery, suck it up and stick it out. It won't last long. But if you stand up to them, they'll make your life hell. Then they'll drop you. You'll have done it for nothing.

"I looked at your schedule. With the exception of Tuesday, when you have your chemistry lab, you'll report to the house at 4 p.m. to prepare and serve dinner. As of now, your weekends are free. Don't expect this to continue. Ditto your weeknights. But the fraternity isn't allowed to monopolize all your time; it has to allow you to maintain your studies—school rule. Remember, though, what I've told you.

Don't squawk if Cody makes you work at the house 24/7. Grit it out. I'll work with you weekly on the memorization and other studies. Read the first five chapters in the manual and prepare the written exercises. Let's make this time and place our weekly meeting."

Wilson relaxed. "Your cousin Barney is a good friend of mine. Order up, my treat, and tell me about Dallas. Why did he go there and how long will he stay?"

Montgomery studied the menu as he assimilated Wilson's long discourse. *It's a good thing I was called to pledge. Otherwise I'd drop it right now.*

Montgomery's pen slid across white pages, leaving a trail of loops and curves punctuated by dots and slashes, making a record of the political organization of the Greek city-state as well as the dialects of the language. He made notes on the environment, and the common religious beliefs held by the people of the city-states.

The professor wrapped his lecture by assigning copious reading sections in their texts. Montgomery carefully noted the assignments, which were background material for Thursday's lectures. The professor mentioned that the first exam would be Monday, September 23. The freshmen in the class groaned. It was too early for them to think of exams.

Elizabeth placed her hand into Montgomery's as they left the class, causing Montgomery to smile. It was a good, secure feeling. *What an experience college is turning into! One minute on top of the world; the next, the world on top of me.* They decided to brave the heat and mosquitoes and walk back to their dormitories. Montgomery took Elizabeth to her door, kissed her fully and lovingly, and headed back for his quad.

Elizabeth watched him go from inside the door. *Is he the one? Be realistic, Elizabeth. We barely know each other. We're only starting our college education. But he fascinates me in a way I've only read and heard about, but have not yet experienced. It's wonderful and exciting and scary at the same time. He's so intelligent. Will I be able to keep him interested?*

Montgomery wasn't thinking of anything except the kiss they exchanged. *I wish I had nothing to do for the rest of the day except to be with Elizabeth and exchange kisses. My relationship with Judy did nothing to prepare me for anything like this. I need to find a way to tell Judy that she should move on.*

By 4:00 p.m. Montgomery had changed into loose fitting jeans and a polo shirt, and had reported to the kitchen at the Sigma Omicron Beta house. Nervous about the possibility of running into Rip, Cody or one of their cronies, relief washed away his fears when he saw the diminutive figure of the brother who had taken his name at the Cavalcade.

"Call me Gravy—everybody does," announced the short brother. "I run the food committee. Don't worry about hazing in the kitchen; no one wants to mess with a pledge and then eat the food he's prepared—there's too many ways you can get even. As for me, y'all are safe. Preparing a meal for four dozen people is far worse than anything I could do. The kitchen is too busy for the fun." He pronounced this last word as if he considered hazing pledges anything but fun.

Montgomery was put to peeling potatoes and carrots. He focused on his work and ignored the misgivings in his mind. Soon clouds of steam were rising out of the pots in which the vegetables were cooking. After the peeling was done, Montgomery was sent into the dining room to fill the salt and pepper shakers, and sugar bowl. That accomplished, he set the tables for the evening meal: plates, utensils, and cups.

Coming back to the kitchen, he mashed the potatoes as the others finished up with the meat, biscuits, and other accompaniments. He heard the voices of Sigma Omicron Beta brothers as they began assembling in the dining room. Gravy supervised the filling of serving dishes and plates; then he picked up a metal rod and made a rotating motion inside a large metal triangle, banging the rod against each side in turn to produce a loud ringing that called the men to the table.

Gravy motioned to the pledges who picked up the serving dishes and carried them to the tables. The brothers looked up expectantly as Cody Spung stood. "Let's hear our pledges sing our fraternal song."

Montgomery was aghast: *no one said anything about singing a song; the manual had not contained any words or songs or even a mention of a song*. Smiles appeared on the brothers' faces. After a nervous pause, one of the pledges began, "Here's to our beloved Sigma ..." The others joined in.

Montgomery stood there mutely, dumbfounded at this turn of events as the song continued. "Home of the Omicron, We will always sing to Beta, Let the song roll on. We live as Greek, Great learning we seek. Here's to our beloved Sigma, Sigma Ommi Bee."

Cody smiled wickedly. "It seems that one of our pledges failed to learn the song for his first night in the house. My lord Rip, what is the penalty for not knowing the song?"

A nasty leer arose in Rip's face. "My lord Cody, the offending pledge has the option of eating dirt for his supper or taking a shock from the wire."

Cody said serenely, "Mongrel pledge, you have offended the fraternal order of Sigma Omicron Beta by failing to learn our song and to render same upon request. Which penalty do you choose?"

Maybe a shock won't be so bad. "A shock."

"That will be two shocks," said Rip gleefully, "an additional penalty for failing to address your lord master of pledges properly."

"NO!" shouted Wilson.

"Stay out of this, Wilson," warned Cody.

Jack Canter and Brendon Garrett jumped to their feet, grabbed Montgomery and took him down a hall and into a small room. He was forced to sit in a bare chair to which he was strapped. The only other furniture in the room was a table on which a large car battery sat with leads connected to a generator. They attached the leads to Montgomery's wrists. Rip came into the room. "I'll do the honors."

Rip turned a dial on the generator. Jack whistled at the setting, and laughed with Brendon.

It's going to be bad; I should have taken the dirt. Rip moved his hand to the switch, and slowly turned the machine on. A snapping noise ruptured the silence followed by Montgomery's yell. Rip turned the machine off. "You should have given me your card, punk." He turned the machine on again. Montgomery yelled once more. Rip turned the machine off. "This is to make sure you remember the lesson." He struck Montgomery's face with his fist. Montgomery passed out.

An hour and a half later, Montgomery felt someone holding his head and looking into his eyes. "Montgomery, are you okay?" His vision slowly unblurred, and he saw Wilson standing in front of him. He mumbled, "Why didn't you tell me?"

Wilson backed off and began to stutter. "I didn't know they'd use the machine this early. They're not supposed to use such high voltage."

Montgomery was still mumbling half-incoherently. "You're the president. Tell them not to use the shock machine."

"It's not that simple. Cody has complete power over pledges. The president cannot stop the disciplining of pledges by the pledge master."

Montgomery managed one more statement before he passed out again. "The song—why didn't you tell me about the song and give me the words?" He did not hear Wilson's reply, but then, it was not worth the effort to listen.

Montgomery opened his eyes. Wherever he was, it was dark. "Shh," a voice warned. "You're safe, but you have to get out of the house. Wait here." It wasn't Wilson. A door opened and then closed. Montgomery sat up and rubbed his head. A bad headache was pounding his temples. He felt weak from hunger and the shock his body had been through.

The door reopened. The voice came back and helped Montgomery to his feet. They left the room, Montgomery assisted by a small, slender boy who led him to a little used door. He opened it, looked out upon the grounds, was satisfied and hustled Montgomery to a gate behind some bushes. He opened the gate and thrust Montgomery through it.

"They're looking for you," he said urgently. "Go quickly and don't come back until Wednesday. Hopefully they'll have forgotten by then." Montgomery turned to thank his rescuer, but the boy was gone. Montgomery saw movement by the wall, and watched in amazement as the boy scaled the wall and entered an open window.

"He's gone!" someone yelled, and Montgomery started with a jerk. He fled into the night. As he raced through the faculty housing, he heard the carillon begin to chime the 9 o'clock hour. Montgomery gained the campus and remembered that the Astronomy Club was having their first meeting. He veered right and sped along the street that separated the main campus from the business district. He streaked past the bookstore and pounded into the Student Center. He was breathing hard.

"Where's the Astronomy Club?" he panted.

"Upstairs—Room Two," replied a boy curiously.

"Thanks," Montgomery gasped before dashing for the stairs, going up in great bounds to the second floor landing and hurtling down the hall. He found room two, flung the door open, and went inside.

All eyes were on the enactor of the dramatic arrival. Montgomery panted heavily, taking his time to catch his breath. "Sorry—afraid I was late."

"Right on time," smiled a tall brunette dressed in blue jeans, white t-shirt and wearing a scientist's lab coat. "Please have a seat."

Montgomery slid into the nearest available chair. About thirty students were in the room. He put his arms behind his back so no one could see the burn marks.

The tall brunette introduced herself as the president of the club. She introduced the other officers: vice president, secretary. The club ran without money or dues; therefore it did not need a treasurer. The lights dimmed, and photographs of distant space phenomena taken by the Hubble telescope filled a screen.

Montgomery was fascinated by the clear pictures of distant galaxies, clouds of interstellar dust that seemed to be spawning stars, binary star systems, and space travelers—objects of ice and rock moving through space without any apparent origin or destination. He made a mental note when the tall brunette announced that all the pictures were available on the club's campus web site.

Montgomery's headache continued, and his ears began to ring. Still dazed from the shocks, he did not hear much more than the announcement of the next meeting, which was Monday, 9 p.m. on the roof of the Astronomy building. He later remembered volunteering to help run the web site.

Bad as he felt, Montgomery waited to leave the Student Center until a large number of the club members exited. Montgomery squeezed into the middle of the group. He did not want to be spotted, much less caught alone if the pledge committee was out looking for him. Montgomery waited with several of the students until the campus bus arrived at the Student Center. Once he was on the bus, he felt safe.

Montgomery arrived at his dormitory around 11 p.m. He found Travis in their room anxiously waiting for him to come back. "What happened to you?" he yelled as his nervous energy caused him to speak louder than necessary, which was all it took to bring the whole quad into the room.

"Sickbee's little joke," Montgomery said quietly. "A surplus KGB electroshock torture machine."

"Those sick ———", someone cursed.

"I can't believe they would do you that way," said Travis.

"Face it, Travis, those wonderful party friends of yours are sadistic. They like to hurt people." Montgomery faced his roommate and best friend. "They're pulling you into their web of deceit. There's a reason why they're taking such good care of you. You don't know why yet—none of us do. But they have an ulterior motive."

"No, it can't be," said Travis. "They got carried away, that's all."

"Monkey's right," said Cat. "Disassociate from them, Trav, before it's too late."

"Listen to Monkey. What did he do to deserve this?" Red pulled out Montgomery's arm to show the burn mark.

"I'm going to tell them to tone it down. They like me; they'll listen to me," rejoined Travis. Was it indicative of the seriousness of what had taken place, or the pathetic sound of a pledge stating that he would tell the fraternity to stop hazing another pledge, that kept the quadmates from laughing at Travis? Either way, Travis was serious.

"I have a bad headache," said Montgomery. "I'm taking some ibuprofen and going to bed." The other boys filed out to the quadroom. They remained up for over an hour discussing the fraternity, its accumulating record of abuse, and how their two quadmates were mixed up in it.

"Really, Montgomery, I'm sorry," said Travis. "The last week has been a hoot, but I don't like this. Maybe we should drop the pledging. We haven't seen each other less since we were in diapers. Look at me—I have no idea what has happened in my class, and I've been stoned and drunk for the last five nights. Let's drop it, okay?"

Montgomery lay in bed and stared at the ceiling. "I can't make your decisions for you, Travis. I don't think it's good for you to hang out with those guys all the time—they're using you. But you have to decide what you want to do. I'm not going to decide anything tonight; my head hurts too bad."

Travis brought his friend the pain reliever and some water with which to swallow the pills. Montgomery did not bother to undress but pulled a loosely knit blanket over his body. Travis turned out the lights and lay down. He turned on his side, supporting his head with his palm and lower arm, and looked at his friend. *Montgomery has always been loyal to me: either at my side or coming to my rescue. He's a good man. What should I do? Does the price of joining the fraternity include my best friend?*

Chapter Five

Football Frenzy

QUESTIONS SWIRLED through Montgomery's head all night while he slept fitfully and dreamlessly. *Why are the boys of the S.O.B. treating me so badly? I've done nothing to deserve the ferocity with which they pummeled me, or have I? Why does the university allow them to use such a rough method of hazing? Why are they so friendly to Travis? Who's the boy who helped me? Why did he climb the wall to go inside instead of using the door? Is Travis being taken in? Will the fraternity break up my friendship with Travis? Should I drop out? Will that make me a quitter? What did Wilson mean: not this early?*

Twice Montgomery awoke and took another dose of pain reliever. The sight of Travis sleeping in his bed was welcome and reassuring. *Perhaps we'll be back on track. The two of us with Park and Elizabeth—Elizabeth!* Montgomery smiled, recalling her image to his conscious mind.

Light from the sun crept around the curtain, and began to brighten the dark room. Travis woke first, and silently rose, vowing to make up to Montgomery his failure to take his side during the awful week previous. He took his shower, and attended to his personal grooming. He then dressed quietly, and straightened the room, hanging up clothes, putting books on their shelves, and neatly stacking their video games underneath the TV table. He turned off Montgomery's alarm clock so that Montgomery could sleep as late as possible. He then left the room for the dining hall.

Travis took enough food to feed four. He sat down at a table in the far corner of the dining hall where he would not be seen. He took napkins and foil, and wrapped the breakfast food before stuffing it into his pockets, waistband, shirt—wherever he could hold it. He entered the building with abs of steel; he left a pregnant woman. Once clear of the dining hall, he took his shirt off, knotted the neck and arms, and carried all the food inside.

Back in the room, he set everything up on their desks, and then he woke his roommate. "Breakfast," he announced with a wave of his hand. Montgomery lifted his head groggily. The aroma of hot food made his mouth water, as he had not eaten since lunch the day before. Montgomery sat up, mumbled "Thanks," and began to eat.

Travis sat down. "About time I did something for you." He also ate.

The week settled down as the two concentrated on their classes and the girls. Travis was now feeling guilt over his encounter with Janet when he was courting Park. Neither he nor Montgomery went to the frat house except when required for doing work. Montgomery continued on kitchen detail. Travis was assigned to grounds and maintenance. He avoided the pledge committee every time he was there.

The question remained unanswered: would both of them drop their pledging, or one or the other? It seemed as if neither was willing to quit if the other wanted to continue. Montgomery felt it was his fault Travis had started pledging and had almost broken down, and Travis felt he should stand beside Montgomery and not abandon him.

Montgomery saw that Travis was becoming happier as he put the drug usage and sexual encounter behind him. He seemed to like Park sincerely, and she returned his feelings. As Rick Early and Rose Hill had formed a new relationship, it was a merry group of six that ate meals, had dates and enjoyed study breaks together.

Two weeks of classes went by pleasantly, and then the campus took on a new excitement. "This is it," said Rick. "The home opener of the football season is the official start of the campus social season. Everyone will be at a pre-game party Friday night; the trick is to find where the best ones are."

"Are the parties dressy?" asked Park.

"Ready for your debutante?" teased Rick.

"Most girls in Alabama would dress up in a formal gown for a society opener," mentioned Rose. "But that's only to impress their beaus."

"If Rhett and Scarlett should appear, I don't know what I'll wear," laughed Travis. "I do declare, all I have are rags—rags!"

Montgomery chuckled. "This is Florida. In Florida, casual is dressing up. Neither Travis nor I own a tie, much less a suit or sport coat. Wear shorts and a clean top."

"Leave the locations to me," said Travis.

"You think we'll get hung up at the frat?" asked Montgomery.

"I'm not going near the place," responded Travis. "I'm not answering the phone or checking e-mail. I am incommunicado as far as that place is concerned. You cook the meal and run. I'll smuggle something out of the dining hall for you."

"We'll have to leave it to Rick to escort you to the game," said Montgomery. "We have to sit with the fraternity."

Park and Elizabeth were very disappointed to hear that piece of news.

"Will you be free after the game?" asked Park.

Montgomery grimaced. "As long as they don't find another unique way to beat me."

Elizabeth shuddered. "It still makes my blood boil to think of the shocks they gave you. They want to be snooty about whether they will accept you? You could own the place with one simple lawsuit!"

Montgomery dropped his gaze. "It's hard for me to explain how I feel."

"That call business is only a head trip that a few members laid on you, starting with your cousin," said Elizabeth with some heat. "You have no responsibility to have yourself killed because they let some criminals take control."

"She's right," said Rick. "None of us can tell you what to do, or you either, Travis, but Elizabeth is right. Don't pledge because someone is pitching you on being the hero who saves the house; pledge because you like the people and would enjoy being part of their group."

Montgomery argued, "There's more to being a fraternal member than hanging out with buddies. There's a responsibility that is taken on: leadership, character, and virtue. Not everyone is cut out to be part of a fraternity. It takes talent and a call—a call to be the best and use one's gifts in service to the campus. It's not only Sigma Omicron Beta; it's all the fraternities. They've forgotten what they are. They've forgotten what they're supposed to be. So yes, some of us are called to renew the old values and transform the Greek houses back into the models that rose to lead campuses for years before they degenerated into mere social groups."

"But you can't renew until they let you in," countered Rick. "That means running the gamut of the hazing bums who are looking for guys like you so they can drop the black ball on you."

"Drop the black ball?" queried Travis.

"Years ago, when they voted on admitting pledges, everyone had a white ball and a black ball," explained Rick. "They voted in secret. A box was passed around the room, and every member held both balls, about the size of a marble, in one hand. They would put the hand into the box and let one of the balls drop. If one member dropped a black ball, the pledge was terminated. No one ever knew who dropped the black ball. That's where the expression of being blackballed originated. You've been blackballed when you're denied something and you don't know who made the decision or said something fatal to your cause."

"I'll have to tough it out," said Montgomery. "I'll have to pay the price."

"Sounds like you've decided to keep pledging," said Elizabeth. "I'm worried, but I'll support your decision."

Travis squirmed in his seat.

"Again?" asked Park.

"Yeah," said Travis. "It burns and makes everything feel sore. I must be passing a kidney stone or something. I can't empty my bladder and I have a sharp, burning pain when I try."

"Say good night, Travis," said Rick. "You and I need to talk."

The boys rose and bid their girlfriends good night, exchanging kisses and promises for the next day. The boys left the girls' dormitory and began walking back to Somerset Johns.

"Travis," began Rick, "did you say that two weeks ago, during rush week, you had sex with some girl in the frat house?"

Travis was embarrassed. "Yeah," he admitted. "I'm not proud of it now. I was messed up and she came out of nowhere. We were doing it before I was aware of it."

"It wasn't your first time," continued Rick, "was it?"

"No, my first time came when I was fourteen. I came home from playing ball, and a friend of my sister was there but my sister wasn't home, and Mom was at work, and, well—it happened."

"You ever experience something like the pain you have now?"

"No."

"You ever catch an STD?"

"No. I was careful—used condoms and such. I wouldn't date girls who had slept around a lot or had past boyfriends who were questionable as to their standards."

"You mean guys with reputations or who were known to use prostitutes," clarified Rick.

"Yeah."

"So this would be a first experience for you."

"You think I have a sexually-transmitted disease?"

"I'm almost sure of it. What kind of girl is hanging out in a frat house and jumps the bones of any stray boy she sees? Both you and Montgomery know the unsavory characters in that house. Who knows where they have been and whether they were careful? Travis, you have the clap."

Travis paled. "What should I do?"

"Go to the clinic first thing tomorrow. They can run an inexpensive test. If it's positive, they'll give you a penicillin shot. Let's hope that your strain is not resistant."

"What then?" asked Travis in a weak voice.

"They use the stronger drugs—maybe harsh side effects. But worry about that if it comes, but not before. Hopefully you have a simple case, and may this be a lesson to you. I'm not lecturing on your morals, but cautioning you about college life. A lot of young people are free of restraints for the first time, including drinking and drugs. Their judgment becomes impaired and they begin having episodes of casual sex with anyone. They would never have done it if they were sober, but they aren't. Also, lack of sobriety makes them careless—no birth control, no condom, no anything: skin-to-skin. There are other consequences to careless sex than STD's: pregnancy, warts, chafing, and cancer in the long haul, perhaps sterility. If you are going to be sexually active, be smart."

Travis was up at the first light of dawn and out the door to visit the university medical clinic. The nurse took him into an examining room, and had him sit in front of a computer and fill out his medical record. Travis keyed in his personal data, 6' 1", 175#, brown hair, brown eyes, birth date, birth place, vaccinations: measles, polio, TMJ, whooping cough, tetanus; diseases: chicken pox, mumps; family history: prostate cancer, stroke; personal habits: drink alcohol, no smoking, sexually active, rare use of marijuana—nothing else, physically fit, good health. Reason for visit: Travis debated what to type. Finally he keyed: pee pain.

The nurse came into the room, and looked over his shoulder. "We see a lot of that," she said. Travis relaxed. The nurse took out a stethoscope, and wrapped a blood pressure cuff around his upper arm. She took the reading, and entered it into the record. She measured his pulse, and put that in as well. "Open wide," she said, and she inserted the temperature gauge. A beep from a little machine, and the result glowed on the computer screen. She left the room.

Fifteen minutes later the doctor came in. He greeted Travis, and looked at his information on the computer. He looked in the boy's throat and ears, and listened to him breathe. "Stand and drop trou'," the doctor ordered. Travis complied, and the doctor checked for hernia. Travis winced with pain. The doctor smiled.

"No need to run a test on you. This campus is rife with gonorrhea. Be more careful—be smart. Abstinence is recommended as the best health protection, but if you won't refrain, watch who you select. Don't become a regular in here—it could take your life. You hear what I'm saying, boy?"

Travis nodded.

"Good. The nurse will come back and give you a shot in the butt. For good measure, I'm prescribing another shot in two days, and another shot two days after that. If you still have pain in a week, come back immediately."

"Yes, sir," Travis replied.

In a few minutes, the nurse came in with a hypodermic needle and a bottle with a clear liquid. She expertly filled the needle, then pushed the plunger to expel any air. "Turn around and lower your shorts," she ordered. Travis complied. He felt the needle enter his flesh, and the liquid being pushed into the muscle. "You're through," said the nurse. "I'll see you first thing on Monday."

Travis lost no time pulling up his shorts and heading out the door. Back in his room, he told Montgomery, "They were so sure they didn't bother with a test. I go back for two more shots as insurance."

Montgomery nodded as he grabbed his English and chemistry notebooks. "Someone should post a warning sticker on the dog who gave you that memento."

Travis laughed. "Like on a cigarette pack: Warning. Use of this product may result in great pain or other side effects. Known to transmit venereal disease."

Montgomery grinned. "Warning: Use product with extreme care as the lady is a tramp."

Travis guffawed. "Warning: AIDS a-coming. Condom Charlie now."

Montgomery fell on his bed roaring with laughter. "Warning: Rubbing product on inside surfaces may cause inflammation. Beware!"

Travis kept it up as they left their room for class. "Warning: Sniff product for cleanliness before insertion."

The two boys laughed heartily as they left the quad. "What was that all about?" asked Red. No one had a clue.

At the main campus, the boys split for their respective classes. Montgomery entered the English building, headed for the classroom and took a seat. A few minutes later, Park entered and sat next to him. The bell rang. Kyle Appleton, the teaching assistant for the class, began handing out their essays from the first day of class.

Groans of disappointment rose from the seats, as the grades were lower than expected. Both Montgomery and Park received a C. Park looked at her paper with dismay.

"It's full of red marks," she wailed. "Dangling participle, dangling participle, noun/verb agreement, wrong tense, parallelism, period, phrasing, spelling, grammar—what a mess he made of my essay."

"Stilted language, trite expression, dull," read Montgomery. "Anyway you look at it, he wanted to mark us down."

"It's not fair," Park whined.

"Of course it's fair," said Kyle to the class. "You're in college now. Forget all the easy grades you used to get. You must perform on a college level. Not only must your papers be written in standard English with proper spelling, punctuation and grammar; you must write your papers correctly: organized according to the type of paper you are going to write. You must write with crisp, descriptive language that maintains the reader's interest. You must develop a style that will help you sweep the reader through your prose to the end of your work. These papers show you how far you have to go.

"Your next assignment is on this hand-out. Read through the five pages of the report and develop an executive summary that concisely gives the reader the essence of the report in half a page, single-spaced, one inch margins all around, typed paper. Do not shrink the point size of your type—it should approximate what is used on the handout.

"Now, let's look at the technique of writing persuasively. This type of writing is probably the most important for you to master: the art of persuading someone to a course of action. It is an emotional piece; you appeal to the readers' emotions as well as their reason. Here are the features you must include ..."

Montgomery was scribbling notes as fast as he could go. *I'd like to persuade those frat boys to lay off me. Maybe a piece in the campus news-*

paper. Stilted, trite, dull: no chance of publication, much less keeping the readers' interest to the end.

Park sat still, looking at the mistakes on her paper. *I thought my writing was good, but I had no idea how bad I am on the technical points. How can I improve? I've always hoped I could be a successful writer. My high school teachers praised my imagination and composition. I'd like to slap them all silly. How could they let me slide so I'd look like an ignoramus in college? The most damning comment: you may have had something good to say with a pleasing style. But no one will cut through the thicket of errors to see if a rosebush is in the center. Improvement required if you hope to pass.*

Park blinked away a tear. *I was taught to spell phonetically. Fone, kut, sity—all were acceptable in my school system. I need to fix the spell checker on my computer immediately.*

The lecture switched to grammar. Montgomery continued taking detailed notes. Park glanced at his notebook. *I should make copies of his notes. Maybe he could help me cover the better parts of grammar.*

At the close of class, Kyle mentioned that the due date on the summary was Tuesday. "You have much to learn, and a semester is short. Next week we work on term papers. Begin selecting a topic now. Make it something that you're interested in. It can't be a paper that you'll use for another class. Have a good weekend." He picked up his belongings and departed.

As the class broke up, Montgomery headed for the library where he hoped to hole up for an hour before chem class. On his way in, he ran into Wilson. "Montgomery—there you are," said Wilson as if he'd been expecting him. "I wanted to talk to you."

Montgomery blanched. Aside from their weekly sessions, Wilson had kept a low profile when he had been in the house. Montgomery cautiously asked, "What about?"

Wilson drew him into an alcove. "There is some uncertainty in the house about you."

Montgomery raised an eyebrow. "Oh?"

Wilson whispered, "You're too independent minded. Some of the brothers think you need to be broken more. You've got to play ball, Montgomery. Act like you're eager to do anything they ask and take anything they want to dish out. We want you in the house; we really do. Pretend you think like they do."

Montgomery was irritated. "Who is they?"

"Cody, Jack, Rip—those guys."

"Wilson, why don't you stand up to them?"

"See, that's what I mean—you always challenge. You must be more tolerant, Montgomery. The frat is for the college male of an open mind. Of necessity, then, we'll have many brothers who see things different. The point is that, to keep our harmony, we must accept those who think and act different from us."

"What a load of —," said Montgomery loudly. He broke off because the librarian was glaring at him and shhing with her index finger on her lips.

"Wilson," Montgomery lowered his voice, "you talk like we're discussing our favorite ice cream flavors. Those guys are criminals: they mug the pledges, they batter them—what's next? I've been a good boy; I've shown up for my work and kept a low profile. Gravy keeps me out of the dining room so the gang can't get at me. Let's keep it that way."

"Montgomery, you don't understand. Tomorrow you must sit with the frat at the game." Wilson shrugged his shoulders, holding out his hands. "Who knows what they'll plan? Maybe you've made them think they need to make an example of you—I don't know. I try to help you, but you make it so difficult for me."

"Try to help me? By forgetting to tell me I need to memorize a song? Is there anything I'm supposed to know for tomorrow, Wilson?"

"No—at least I don't think so."

"Then I should be okay."

"Remember what I told you. Play ball."

"I'll bring my bat and glove," Montgomery responded with a sarcastic tone which Wilson missed.

"Good boy."

Montgomery watched Wilson leave. *So far he's been more of a hindrance than a help. He won't tell me what I need to know about the house to avoid offending the pledge committee and other brothers. He's supposed to represent me, but he does nothing to stop those guys from their nasty comments and harsh hazing. Our Monday meetings are a waste of time. He reads from the manual for an hour. So far, none of that material has been necessary. I hope the game keeps the brothers so occupied that they won't have time to worry about the pledges.*

The quad met for lunch at Jeff Davis Dining Hall. Montgomery, Cat and Red brought their trays to the table where their quadmates were saving seats for them. The hall was crowded and noisy. The boys were in the midst of a lively discussion over point spreads that had been given for major college games when a piece of Boston Creme pie went flying over their heads.

"FOOD FIGHT!" A mélange of spaghetti, cut fruit, jello, cheese, cold cuts, bread, salad, and cake filled the air. Food Service quickly shut down the food stations and removed all remaining items to the kitchen. Most of the students had dived underneath the tables. Travis rose up to throw something, but Montgomery grabbed his belt and pulled him down. "The last time this happened they were kicked out of school," he spoke into Travis' ear.

Into the maelstrom of food which had landed and been relaunched in retaliation marched the cafeteria manager. A middle-aged woman in her forties of German heritage, she disliked chaos and mess. "Stop this at once," she raged. "Immature children. You are supposed to be adults; act like it! Throwing food like babies. You should be ashamed of yourselves." The activity and noise came to a standstill under the fury of her lecture. A pregnant pause ensued.

Splash! A piece of Boston Creme pie hit the manager across her chest. A volley of jello followed. She retreated as food resumed its flight throughout the room.

"Let's get out of here!" Montgomery yelled to his friends. They nodded, and followed him as he left the table and crawled to the door. Regaining the outdoors, they ran to their dormitory and headed for their quad.

"Wow," said Caveman. "Unbelievable."

"I've heard of ones that were worse," said Red. "Imagine if it had broken out at breakfast: scrambled eggs, grits, waffles, syrup, butter, milk, cereal. It would have closed the hall for the day."

"I'm glad we made it out before the cops came," said Montgomery. "A few years ago they became strict and cracked down. Anyone who starts a fight or retaliates is expelled; simply being there results in probation."

Travis laughed. "Did you see the manager get it? That was awesome—even if it was wrong," he added as he looked at Montgomery's face.

The others laughed too.

"Yeah, but they'll come down on this fight twice as hard because of it," predicted Cat.

"So immature," said Shorts.

"So true," said Travis. "It would never happen here."

"Us? Oh, no," said Red in a funny voice.

"Impossible," said Caveman.

An awkward moment reigned as the boys looked at one another to see who would make the first move. Then the phone rang, and broke the spell.

"Hello?" Red answered the phone. "Travis?" Travis waved his arms and shook his head. Red covered for him. "He's not here now. Sorry. Message? Okay, Pete and Brendon said to come to the house as soon as he gets back. Got it. No, I don't know when to expect him. I'll give him the message." Red hung up the phone, and added, "Not."

"Thanks, Red," said Travis. "I don't want to see those guys today."

"Weren't you guys going to drop out?" asked Red.

"We never decided," said Travis. "Montgomery is sticking it out, and I feel obligated to stay with him and watch his back. Those guys really have it in for him."

"Did they ever say why?" asked Cat.

"No, at least not around me. There's something funny about that place. It's rife with division among the members; they're at cross-purposes but they pretend they have unity and harmony. They have different views about what the fraternity should be and do. It's a wonder the place hasn't split into two fraternities."

Cat replied, "That one is easy to answer: property and money. The group that leaves loses everything to the group that stays. One day they'll have a battle royale and there will be nothing left to fight over."

"Time for class," announced Shorts who had changed his clothes. "I have a one o'clock. Anyone else going?"

The other boys shook their heads. Some were free and the others were cutting class. Travis and Cat left to buy some beer where i.d.'s were not checked. Montgomery said he was going to work on e-mail until his two o'clock, which he planned to attend. Red and Caveman retired for naps.

If only I didn't have to report for kitchen duty this afternoon. I don't want anything to interrupt my plans with Elizabeth after dinner. Montgomery dwelt upon these thoughts as he walked to his class.

When he arrived at the frat house, he stowed his books in a cabinet. "What's our menu? he asked Gravy.

"You're on washing detail as well as cooking today," Gravy replied.

Montgomery grimaced. *There goes my plan for an early arrival at Elizabeth's room. But Wilson will be happy, if no one else.*

"Take these ribs outside to the barbecue pit. Sear both sides, then heat them through. Don't let them dry out. Once the meat is hot, take it off the fire and put it in the Igloo™ chest."

As Montgomery grilled the ribs, Rip and Jack hooted at him from across the yard. With them were three girls, including Janet. Rip said, "Tonight we're entertaining our woman friends so make it perfect. Anything that gets ruined—you know the penalty."

Montgomery's stomach muscles involuntarily tightened. He waved but kept his eyes on the grill. Another burst of laughter receded into the house. *I'd better complete my chores and leave fast.* He put his attention on finishing the meat. He shut the gas off, and closed the grill. He picked up the container and went back to the kitchen.

"Good," his chief said. "We are ready to serve then. Help the others with the dishes."

The pledges picked up the serving dishes and carried them into the dining room. Cloths had been laid, candles lit, and silverware set beside china and crystal goblets. The pledges laid the meal upon the tables. Then chaos broke out. Men and women grabbed for food with their hands. Barbecue sauce went everywhere. Corn on the cob dripped butter on the starched white linen. Montgomery stared in disbelief. *Why would they eat a picnic meal if they planned to set a formal dining table?*

Montgomery turned to go into the kitchen.

Rip Tilden said, "This meat is bad. The pledge ruined it."

Something hit the back of Montgomery's head.

Jack said, "Get the pledge—it's his fault this food is garbage."

Montgomery spun back to be hit be a corncob. Then everyone was yelling and throwing ribs and cobs at him. He hunched down, covering his face with his arms, and retreated from the room.

"Hey! We're not through with you," yelled Rip. He walked into the kitchen. "Back in the dining room, pledge." Rip kicked Montgomery's backside. Montgomery was furious. Without thinking, he whipped around, grabbed Rip's head and plunged it into a huge bowl of chocolate pudding that was waiting to be put into individual serving dishes.

The dining room did not know that Rip was coming out on the losing side of the confrontation. They chanted, "We want the pledge. Bring us the pledge. Justice on the pledge."

The kitchen was quiet. No one knew what to do; pledges do not fight back. The other pledges pulled away from Montgomery, fearing that his punishment would be inflicted on them all.

Gravy saved them. "Well, Rip, if you don't want your buddies to know that you can't handle a simple pledge, you had best go up the back stairs and clean yourself up."

Rip pulled his head out of the bowl. "You've had it now, Mongrel, I'm going to get you good." He charged up the stairs.

Montgomery pulled off the apron he was wearing. "Goodbye. I'd say it was fun, but it wasn't."

"You're not going anywhere," said Gravy. "Now you know why the cooking detail has to help clean up tonight."

"As soon as he washes up, I'm out. Why should I stay knowing he's looking for me?"

"You're not out. He won't dare tell anyone what happened. They'd lose respect for him if they knew. But don't let yourself be caught alone with him. Now help with the dishes."

The double pledge detail made short work of cleaning the dining room and washing the expensive china, crystal and silverware. All had to be done by hand as the items were antiques from the early days of founding the house. The lack of respect for these items appalled Montgomery. "What's next? Smashing the plates like a Greek wedding?"

"Don't give them ideas," said Gravy. "The founders' established this house. They left these treasures to succeeding classes to be passed on as their patrimony. It's a scandal to treat these things so poorly—as the equivalent of paper plates and cups. But the way they talk—the manufacturer did not make each plate complete but glued bits and pieces of fired ceramic together—same for the crystal. The silverware they deny as silver: some say it's pewter, the original silver now corrupted by tin so thoroughly that no one can tell the two apart; some say it's stainless steel that has been shined to gleam like silver, others that the material is of no consequence because everyone is free to decide that truth for themselves, and that they have better eating utensils so we don't need the silverware at all!"

Montgomery wondered, *Is he still talking about place settings? This I do know: Gravy is the only person I respect in the house.* Montgomery hurried with the clean up, and it was over by 7:30 p.m. He began to leave when Gravy pulled him from behind. "Go out the back gate—the one I showed you."

Montgomery looked at the young man with awe. "It was you," he whispered. "You saved me that first night."

Gravy looked directly into Montgomery's eyes. "I have no idea what you're talking about. Use the back gate."

Montgomery nodded: *Don't tell anyone about Gravy's rescue.* "Thanks." Looking around after leaving by the back door, Montgomery noted that he was unobserved, and took advantage of his opportunity to make his escape.

He found the others waiting in the lobby when he returned to Somerset Johns. "What took you so long?" asked Travis.

"I had to help clean up: food fight part two. It was stupid. They plan this meal of barbecued ribs and corn on the cob—foods you eat with your hands. Then they set the dining room with white tablecloths, good china, crystal goblets and silverware—real silver. Then we set the food down, and it's a madhouse. People grabbing food, spilling sauce and butter on the cloths and floor—this in front of their dates! It was like that scene from the movie *Gremlins* when the Dad fed chicken to the gremlin babies. Then Rip and company decided to throw food at me."

"What did you do?" asked Elizabeth.

"I retreated to the kitchen. He came after me, and kicked my behind. So I pushed his head into a huge bowl of chocolate pudding," grinned Montgomery. "He was mad, but the brother in charge of cooking told him to beat it before his friends found out he couldn't handle a pledge."

"Watch your back," said Rick.

"Check," said Montgomery. "Let me wash up and change, and I'll be right down." He raced up the stairs.

"You two need to rethink this fraternity," said Rick. "They need you, but you do not need them, especially not with those yo-yo's running the show."

"I agree," said Park. "You need to spend those pledge hours with me, not those civilization-deprived, overcharged hormones."

"Let's drop the subject," said Travis. "Tonight we are uptown party-hopping. How 'bout them snooks?"

"Have you gone snook fishing?" asked Park.

"Plenty of times. The trick to catching snook is to go at night. Find a good spot where there is a sharp break between light and darkness. Underneath bridges is a prime location. Use fresh shrimp. They don't last long, so keep replacing the bait on the hook. Cast into the water, and work the line from dark to light while the shrimp is wriggling his legs. Snook will snatch the bait on the run. Zing goes the line as the fish rips off 75-100 yards. Then start working him, keeping the line tight. Don't let him loosen the reel because, if he does, he'll spit the hook out. Reel him in, but if he runs again, let him take the line. Be careful, sometimes the fish runs out, then turns and comes straight for the boat. If he can get under the boat or find something to wrap the line around, then he can break free. But keep working him, and he eventually tires. Then bring him to the surface, and net him. They clean well, and they taste good."

"We'll have to go sometime," cooed Park.

"It takes a license, a snook stamp and it has to be in season. Personally, I'd rather go surfing."

Red, Caveman, Cat and Shorts came down the stairs.

Cat smiled. "Travis, you dog, you've been holding out on us."

Travis performed the introductions. "Rose, Park, Elizabeth: my quadmates Red, Caveman, Cat, and Shorts."

Rose asked, "How did you get those names? Unusual, aren't they?"

Cat explained, "My last name is Cattlip. I've always been called Cat. Then one of our quadmates decided he had to give a nickname to everyone. Red because of his red hair, and Caveman because, well, it fits, doesn't it?"

Park took the bait. "But why do they call you (looking at Shorts) Shorts?"

With a straight face, he answered, "My name is Joe Boxer."

The girls burst out laughing. He added, "It is—really. Joseph Addison Boxer: my parents thought it cute; my monogram is jab—J.A.B."

Park said, "Why not uppercut, or roundhouse?"

Joe said, "I have enough names now, thank you anyway."

The four boys went into the night. Travis called after them, "Go to Fizzet Mays first. They have a good band." The boys waved.

Footsteps came clattering down as Montgomery returned to the group. He had taken a quick shower, and put on clean shorts and a pullover shirt. The group set out for their first location, Danswood Manor. Travis explained, "Most of the team lives in Danswood if they're not off campus. We can break up and mingle and see who's there. They'll have a good selection of beverages."

Danswood Manor was the farthest away residence complex in the group. The sun began to set as the three couples arrived. Travis knew someone who was working the door, so they slipped inside with another group without having their i.d.'s checked.

The boys went to the beverage section. Travis picked up two whiskey sours, "This isn't punch, Montgomery."

Montgomery nodded, and selected a cup of wine for Elizabeth and a bottle of flavored water for himself. Rick also selected wine for Rose, and he opened a bottle of beer.

Without their boyfriends, the girls were receiving much attention from unattached males in the crowd. As they made their way back, the boys were aware that many were staring at them.

"Jealous," said Rick.

"Let's move apart," suggested Travis. He gave a cup to Park, and steered her away to another corner of the room. By the far wall, a boy caught his eye and waved him over.

"Dunbar," cried Travis with delight. "What are you doing here?"

"Redshirt freshman. I'm part of the team, except on game days."

"Dunbar is in my study group," Travis explained to Park. "Park Longstreet, Dunbar Edwards."

"Pleased to make your acquaintance," murmured Park. "Why do you wear a red shirt? You aren't wearing one now. Is it like a freshman beanie?"

Dunbar snorted while Travis bit his lip. "Sorry," Dunbar apologized. "A beanie, ha ha ha. Sorry, but redshirt is a sports term. A redshirt is an underclassman who is practicing with the team but not using a year of eligibility—he doesn't play, doesn't dress out for games, isn't allowed on the sidelines or to travel with the team. He uses his redshirt season to learn and train. The word originated because the first redshirts were always on the practice team that the regular players worked against. They would wear red jerseys to distinguish them from the others on the field. The term stuck. Beanies, ha ha ha. Could you picture us, Travis, running around on the field with little propellers twirling on our heads?"

"Human helicopters," Travis replied with a big grin.

"How are the Sick-Bees treating you?" asked Dunbar.

"Not too badly. But they nail my roommate every chance they get."

"No one on the team will have anything to do with them. Coach has warned everyone to stay away. Something bad goes on there—"

Travis finished the sentence for him. "But no one will say what it is."

"It's a mystery," said Park. "Is it true that footballs always bounce with the laces to the magnetic pole?"

"What?" burst out an astonished Dunbar.

"It's not a blonde moment," laughed Travis, "but an obvious change of subject."

Montgomery and Elizabeth had made the acquaintance of a threesome of senior women. They talked about hurricanes: tropical cyclones, university mascots, and drink recipes. This led to a conversation about the hydrologic cycle of south Florida, and the effect on the Everglades ecosystem. They were launching into a debate over efforts to erase invasive plant species when Montgomery spotted Rick waving them to the door.

The three couples reunited.

"Let's go somewhere else before underage alcohol enforcement checks i.d.'s. As a floor advisor, I'd be in big trouble if I got caught," Rick explained.

"We can go to Canfield Slats," suggested Travis. "We can dance there, and they don't serve alcohol."

The three couples walked to the entrance, and paid the $1 per head admission. Inside, couples were dancing to the fast beat of the latest tunes. A disc jockey was spinning CD's. They sat down at a table, except for Travis and Park who went to the dance floor.

Travis led Park through the paces of a frenetic jitterbug, a Texas two-step, the Twist, and a silly parody of the Tango. They came over and sat down, out of breath. Montgomery poured them some Coke out of a pitcher he had picked up at the refreshment station.

"Where did you learn to dance like that?" asked Rick.

"Sock hops, barn dances, goofing around in my room," replied Travis. "It's not difficult if you pay attention to the feet. It's the same as football—you don't get faked out if you watch the feet."

"Travis was the best dancer in our class," added Montgomery. "He's got all the moves, smooth and rhythmic. All the girls wanted to dance with him. The rest of us guys stood by the wall green with jealousy."

"No wonder," said Rose. "Usually the female's dance steps are dictated by avoiding her partner's feet."

"That's why modern dancing was such a blessing," laughed Elizabeth. "When the couple no longer had to hold one another and could break apart, a girl could move as far away as she needed to avoid the elephant stomp."

"The Elephant Stomp," said Travis. "That sounds like a good name for a dance."

"I like it," said Rick. "Now when my partner smacks me and says, 'Just what are you trying to do?' I can answer: the Elephant Stomp."

"There are certain times when an elephant stomp is a good thing," said Travis with a slight leer.

"Keep it clean," Montgomery retorted.

"I don't get it," said Rose.

"Is it true that footballs always bounce with the laces to the magnetic pole?" broke in Park. She and Travis laughed hard. The others stared blankly.

"It's a change of subject," announced Travis. "Park used that line on a friend of mine at Danswood Manor tonight."

"I'll have to remember that," said Elizabeth. "Is it true that footballs always bounce with the laces to the magnetic pole?"

The D.J. was taking a break. He came around the tables taking requests. Travis took out a piece of paper and wrote down several good songs for dancing. The D.J. thanked him, and moved on.

When the D.J. resumed his program, he played a slow number. All three couples went to the floor. While Montgomery and Elizabeth, and Rick and Rose, held each other and slowly stutter-stepped in place, Travis confidently moved Park through the dancing couples, around the floor and back again.

"What was that?" asked Rick.

"A waltz," said Travis.

"You know ballroom, too?" asked an incredulous Rick.

"Arthur Murray and Mama thought it would be good for me." Travis rolled his eyes. "It comes in handy every so often."

The D.J. changed the record to a new song. Travis broke his hold, and moved Park into the Shimmy. The other two couples moved apart and shook their arms and legs to the beat. After more dancing, they returned to their table. They were talking about various dance moves when Travis looked over, and warned Montgomery that Rip Tilden was present.

"Oh, no," said Montgomery, "I don't want to be involved in an altercation."

"Let's go, then," said Elizabeth, beginning to rise.

"Look down, Montgomery," said Travis, "he's looking this way."

"Come on, girls, let's go to the powder room." The three walked together to the women's bathroom. As they passed Rip Tilden, Elizabeth stopped so that their bodies were shielding the boys from Rip's view. Montgomery and Travis took the opportunity to make their escape out the door.

Rick, however, was staring at Rip. *Do I know this guy?*

Rip gained the sense that someone was staring at him. Scanning the room, he saw Rick standing by the table. He held Rick's gaze for a few moments, and then gestured rudely, which was seen by the security men. They promptly ejected Rip from the room. Rip passed within three feet of Montgomery and Travis who were squatting behind the landscaping. Rip muttered something obscene, and walked off.

The boys watched him go. Rick came out of the building, and called their names.

After Rip disappeared, Montgomery and Travis stood, a bit sheepishly, pulling twigs and plant debris out of their hair and brushing themselves off. "Something about that guy is familiar to me," said Rick, "but I can't recall what."

"You see his picture every time you go to the Post Office," said Montgomery.

Rick smiled. "Sarcasm does not become you, Monkey."

"New moon tonight," observed Montgomery.

The girls came out to the boys. "Where to?" asked Park.

"Fizzet Mays," said Travis. "The band should be warmed up and ready to rock."

Montgomery took hold of Elizabeth's hand as the couples walked to their new destination. He mused about the subdued appearance of the stars as they strolled silently.

At Fizzet Mays, Travis ran into Dunbar Edwards. He invited him to sit with the couples. "This is the real brain," Travis told Dunbar as he gestured toward Montgomery. "He's good at everything."

"Maybe he can help me with math," said Dunbar.

"I'd be glad to," replied Montgomery. "Call me."

The time was running toward midnight, and none of the group was dancing. They talked, ate snacks and drank soda, and argued the finer points of alternative, heavy metal and classic rock music. They forgot about football games, classes and most of all, fraternities. Dunbar handicapped the game for the group, and expressed his view that Florida Sawgrass would prevail by two points.

Later, as Montgomery lay in bed, he replayed the past four weeks in his mind. *Tonight was the most pleasant night I've had since coming to college. What will tomorrow bring when Travis and I sit with the fraternity in the stands? Expect something from the pledge committee, Montgomery, instigated by Rip to even the score.*

Montgomery shuddered, remembering the electric shocks he had received. He fell asleep wondering again, *Why did Wilson say that the machine was not to be used "this early"?*

Having slept late, and slowly rising in the morning, the boys got up and dressed in time to eat lunch before heading for the fraternity. The pledges gathered in a side lounge as they heard the brothers moving around the house preparing for the game. Then Pete Spivey came in and said, "Off with those shirts."

"Take this red paint and paint yourselves all over: Face, head, front and back. I'll be back in fifteen minutes."

The pledges began to coat themselves in red. They helped one another coat their backs. When Pete came back, he had a fluorescent yellow with which he painted on each chest a letter: THE SNOOKS! The pledges began to whoop and shout. They were ready to show school and fraternity spirit.

Pete then brought the group into the stadium. The pledges were put at the top of the fraternity's section. Pete told them their job was to stand and cheer the entire game. The house stood and applauded their pledges and taunted the other fraternities.

Travis nudged Montgomery. "Looks like the fire is directed at someone else today."

Montgomery smiled. "This is the way it should be."

"Keep an eye out for Rip."

"Check."

At the kickoff, the pledges hollered support for their team. The brothers kept them screaming at the capacity of their lungs and voice boxes. But there was no threat of punishment if the pledges failed to make enough noise to satisfy whatever arbitrary standard their overseers might set. Indeed, it seemed that another personality had taken hold. The brothers bought cokes and hotdogs for the pledges. Montgomery wondered why the SigBees were being so nice, but Travis said that they should enjoy it while it lasted.

Then Cody brought out a bag of cookies for the pledges. It was the third quarter, and an infusion of quick sugar energy was welcome to the group of pledges who had been roaring all-out for a couple of hours. Each pledge took four or five cookies and passed the bag to the next boy. Travis took half a dozen, and wolfed them down.

Montgomery's throat was dry, so he took his time eating his cookies. He did, though, eat five of them. He drank from a large coke that someone had given him. He saw the pledge committee exchanging winks, smiles and slaps of the hands, but could not figure out why. In about twenty minutes, he knew. He heard the artificially high giggle of Travis which meant he was high. Montgomery could not figure out how Travis could have smoked a joint when he had been in the stands the entire game.

Travis' eyes were lit up with pleasure. "Montgomery, I'm high!" "Me, too," said another pledge; then another. Montgomery was trying to reason out the cause but for some reason his brain was not working like it should and Montgomery thought that was the funniest thing in the world. He opened his mouth and laughed. Suddenly, the whole thing was funny: Travis, him, the pledges, Rip, Jack, Cody, Wilson, the frat, the game, the school, his classes, his dorm, his professors; Montgomery laughed and laughed and laughed. His head was giddy; he was floating on the air. Montgomery felt like he was riding on a cloud looking down at the stadium, and that was funny too. He laughed again.

Travis was guffawing so hard he had fallen onto the concrete floor of the stands. "Montgomery's high," he said through his laughter. He stood up and pushed Montgomery's shoulder with his index finger. "Whoo," he sang. "You're dizzy; you are so dizzy."

Montgomery kept laughing. "So are you. I'm a helium balloon floating above the clouds. I spin round and round to see the ground." Montgomery giggled hysterically.

Travis grinned a big silly smile and hugged his best friend. "Nothing better than good times with my best pal."

"What's going on in the game?"

"Who cares? This party is much better than the game."

Since the pledges first came under the influence of the drug, the people around them had begun giving them funny looks and talking while pointing at them. At first, it was only other students, some of whom cottoned onto the fact that the boys were under the influence of marijuana. Some thought it funny and laughed; a few were jealous and wanted to know how they had done it. Others shook their heads in a bored display of remonstrance; others were outraged.

But as the fourth quarter wound down to the five-minute mark, one of the ushers came up to Wilson and muttered into his ear. Wilson told Cody to get the pledges back to the house because some people had complained to the game's security guards. Cody motioned to the pledges, and sent them off with Pete Spivey to return to the house. The pledges weaved and wobbled their way down the steps and ramps to ground level. Pete led them out the nearest gate, and ran them through the parking lot behind the field house past the athletic offices and classrooms until they reached the fraternity fence. Pete pushed part of it aside, and the pledges plunged through the fence into the safe confines of the house. As they piled up in the lounge, all the pledges roared with laughter over the escape from the stands.

"Travis, is this what it's like to be high?" asked Montgomery.

"Yes, it is—it's a great feeling, isn't it?"

"I should be angry, but all I want to do is laugh. It's made me so silly." Montgomery sat down and closed his eyes.

Travis sat down beside him and put his arm around Montgomery's shoulders. "You are my best bud. I'm glad I was with you when you got high for the first time."

"I thought you didn't like getting high," said Montgomery who was keeping his eyes closed.

"I don't—not at all. I don't like the method because I don't like smoke in my lungs. But here we are. I don't like it because afterward I feel sluggish and dull. It takes quite a while for the dullness to wear off. But here we are. I like to get drunk because afterward, there's the hangover for a day, and then it's done. Pot hangs on and on; it takes the body a long time to get rid of it. But here we are."

Montgomery giggled. "Where are we?"

"We are high. Those SigBees baked it into the cookies. We ate the cookies, ergo we are high. It's a fun feeling while it lasts—so here we are—enjoying our marijuana high. In a couple of hours, it'll wear off."

"Then what?"

"Then you'll be the hungriest you've ever been in your life. By then we can escape the house and chow down somewhere."

"Amazing they didn't turn us over to the cops."

"No, that wasn't part of their plan. Their plan was to lull us into relaxing our guard. When we were having a good time cheering, and not paying attention, then they slipped it to us so we'd look silly to the spectators in the stadium." Travis laughed, shrieking with that high-pitched giggle. "We must have been a sight. But they took us out when they got a warning that the cops were onto us. So all they wanted was to have some fun with us, and they succeeded. You have to admit it was pretty harmless, and we're having fun, too, so it was a good prank."

Montgomery giggled. "Overlooking the fact that we were tricked into taking the drug which violated our persons—I can't get over how everything is so funny when I know it shouldn't be."

He giggled again. "Harmless is in the eye of the beholder. What about the aftereffects?"

Travis now laughed uncontrollably. "Your diet is blown, but once isn't enough to have a lasting effect."

"I wonder what the girls will say."

Travis guffawed. "Montgomery, you have so much to learn. We don't tell them."

"Why not?"

"There's nothing to gain from it; we can only lose or at best, stay even. Let's keep this a secret between the roomies."

Montgomery laughed over and over. "A roomies' secret. A roomies' secret."

Travis kept his silly grin. He closed his eyes, and leaned his head back on the sofa. Soon he was asleep. Not too long afterward, Montgomery's head nodded, then fell upon Travis' shoulder. He, too, was sleeping.

Chapter Six

Pitiful Pledges

JACK CANTER, RIP TILDEN, Brendon Garrett, Pete Spivey and Cody Spung were sprawled upon the sofas of a top floor parlor. Bare-chested to show off the firmness of their flat stomachs, the mass of their pectoral muscles, the veins on their biceps, the "vee" of their upper torso and the triangle of their shoulder muscles, they were dressed in baggy, long shorts and wore sandals or moccasins. Each had a beer bottle in hand, and a dozen and a half empties revealed that the meeting had been underway for two hours.

"This pledge crop is the worst we've ever seen," Jack groused. "Not a promising one in the bunch."

"Wasn't that Travis kid our kind of material?" asked Brendon.

"We got him off to a good start," said Rip. "He even had a turn with Janet his first night." The committee snickered. "But his roommate is that piece of junk Lee, and Travis got tight with him instead of us. We've hardly seen him since the second week of classes."

"What about the others?" Cody asked. "Anyone promising?"

"Only the usual group of light-weights wanting the prestige of belonging to a frat," said Pete.

"Does anyone have a strong character?" asked Cody.

"Only Lee," growled Rip.

"Okay," said Cody. "Let's stall Lee for a time, and dump him at the end of the year. By then, our plans will have come to fruition and we won't have to worry about his family's clout in the house."

"Travis isn't much of a challenge," observed Jack. "He's weak; he won't need much convincing to join us."

"Set him up with Janet," suggested Brendon.

"Too much of a risk," responded Cody. "Janet has served her usefulness. You know what she carries."

"What do we do about these pledges?" asked Pete.

"Let's set up some sessions where we extol the Greek way our way, and see which minds we can subvert. The more that think our way, the better we have it. Brendon, set up a delivery schedule for the pledges. Nobody tells them anything; they're to believe that their errands are part of their hazing."

As they discussed the pledges, Cody's mind was similarly evaluating his committee. *As a graduate student, I've been able to stay in the house long beyond my B.S. degree, but this is my final year. Who'll take over at the end of the year? Of these four, who can handle the responsibilities of grad school and the network?*

"We must fan out across the campus and find promising candidates to take into the house. We need good, dedicated talent to take over. We have to keep the network running."

"You mean recruit pledges?" asked an incredulous Brendon.

"We have taken over the house, and we have almost broken the remaining hold-outs. We have to step up the pressure. We cannot trust to luck anymore. We screen, we recruit, and we have a unified house supporting us."

"If all goes well, we can think of an appropriate way to rid ourselves of that sap Wilson," Rip smacked a fist into his right palm.

"He believes in the fraternal code to this day," observed Jack.

"All the moralists do," Cody opined. "But pluralism is the reality now. Moralists retreat from the postmodern period into the backwardness of medieval fundamentalism. That's their weakness. They can't evolve with progress so they yearn for a time when their moral ideas were enforced by the state. Then, no one could tell the difference between the campus administration and the fraternal officers. They were one and the same. Everyone knew what was expected of them, and they did it. Everyone fit the same mold. That's what they want—no freedom of thought."

Brendon took a long pull from his bottle of beer. "Too bad for them. Life has moved on. We have freedom of thought, and each of us is free to define our ideals as we see fit. Pluralism has brought postmodernism and postmoralism. Under pluralism, there are no morals. It isn't that all morals are accepted; it's that the idea of morals is banished. All we have are lifestyles, all of which are equally acceptable, and tolerance is the order of the day. Do as you please as long as you don't insist on someone else doing as you. If only the moralists would accept our freedom, they'd live among us in peace and contentment. We get drunk and high and stoned; we have no problem if they live next door but don't participate. Why don't moralists understand that all the trouble in the world comes when they judge? Judging brings condemnation, and condemnation sentencing, and sentencing the violence of enforcement. There, my friends, is the cause of all wars."

"Brendon the Philosopher," mocked Rip, "espousing Garrettism."

Brendon gulped the remainder of his bottle, and got up to get another. "Don't knock it; it's a world that made this house, and our place in it, possible."

"Brendon's right," interjected Jack. "What causes the problems in society is that the moralists insist that their interpretations are the only interpretations that are correct. But they hold to ideas thousands of years old—not suitable for a postmodern age. Pluralism says that everybody's interpretations are valid for them; you cannot judge between them. Pluralism cannot judge interpretations because pluralism has done away with evaluating the truth of interpretations altogether. Truth is what you make it. Truth is definitional, not logical or empirical. Take for example—incest. Everyone says incest is wrong. But what is incest? To one man, having his sister would be incest. To another, marrying a sister is acceptable. The moralist decries it based on the Bible, but the Bible itself records men marrying their sisters. The second man denounces incest, but for him, it does not include a sister. Neither's right; neither's wrong. Only that one man's truth differs from another man's truth. Pluralism's strength is in recognizing that both truths exist at the same time."

"That grand speech is what we need to give to the pledges," said Cody. "They can have their truth as long as they buy into our truth. We cannot let them fall into the moralist's truth, though; that would ruin our set-up and our plans. Remember to keep them off-balance; keep their minds off the truth of the moralists by constantly accusing the moralists of intolerance. That simple device keeps the moralists on the defensive, and makes our ideas attractive to the mold of today's college student who hates conflict above all else—his very instinct is to avoid it, and that brings him into our snare." Cody laughed wickedly.

"When should we begin the sessions for the pledges?" asked Pete.

"Day after tomorrow," said Cody.

"What we have here," said Pete, "is a Dirty Dozen."

The pledges looked expectantly at the speaker.

"Alpha, beta, gamma, delta, epsilon," intoned Brendon. He was pointing to each pledge as he spoke. "Zeta, eta, hotdog." He laughed at his own joke. The pledges nervously tittered. They didn't find his joke funny, but they were afraid not to react. The story of Montgomery's experience with the shock machine was known by all the pledges.

"Theta!" Brendon corrected himself. "Iota, Kappa, Lambda, Mongrel." The pledge committee snickered. All the pledges except Travis surreptitiously moved away from Montgomery, the one designated Mongrel.

"Remember your letter," Brendon told the pledges. "It may be useful later."

"Brother Jack," called Pete. "Will you share some culture with our novices?"

Jack Canter stepped forward. "The Greek system for fraternal life is based on the ancient and honorable orders of that ancient land of beauty and nobility. These orders were the Attic, Doric, Ionic, Aeolian and Achaean. These orders maintained an ideal philosophy of life which continue today in the 24 points of honor known as the Greek code."

Jack stepped back and reached into a box. He pulled out a balloon filled with tomato juice and hurled at the pledge tagged Alpha. The balloon burst on impact drenching the boy with the juice. "Alpha!" he projected, "stands for agathon, or goodness. The philosophy of the Greek, the ancient mysteries of antiquity that are known by only a few, and into which you desire to gain admittance, is now being opened to you. The first mystery to understand is the nature of man: Man is innately good."

Montgomery raised his hand.

Jack spoke, "Yes, Mongrel?"

"That is contrary to what I've always understood. My understanding is that man is a sinner—"

Derisive laughter from the pledge committee interrupted Montgomery. "You have been brainwashed by that eastern superstition that destroyed the Golden Age of Greco-Roman civilization," retorted Jack. "You must unlearn everything you were fed in Sunday School. The truth, the real truth, is that man is good—his very nature makes him good. Ergo, you have no need for a savior. Ergo, the uselessness of that superstition, its devotees and its institutions."

"Learn this, and learn it well," said Brendon. "Man is good. Thus, everything he does is good. Since every action of man is good, we must tolerate every action whether we agree with it or not because the action of the good man is always good."

"Why, then," said Montgomery, "does evil exist? If everything is good, evil cannot exist. Yet bad things happen: robberies, neglect, abuse, murder."

"It's very simple," responded an exasperated Pete. "Evil people have been brainwashed by the superstition that they are evil. They do bad things because they are falsely convinced that they are bad. It's the fault of the moralists that evil happens."

Montgomery was astounded. *These are college students? Their logic's faulty; human nature's misunderstood totally.*

"Well said," affirmed Jack. "As members of the fraternal society, we are called to be leaders in revealing the ancient mysteries whose truths are eternal. This place is more than a social hall; it's the storehouse of the true philosophy of life that will bring you success throughout your entire lives. But if you want to gain access to the mysteries, you must not question what you hear, but learn it as gospel. It is this knowledge that will give you an edge and advantage over others in whatever you do."

"Alpha!" shouted Jack. The first boy flinched as he steeled himself for another tomato balloon. "What is the first mystery?"

"Man is innately good."

"Well said," approved Pete. He hurled a balloon at the boy. More tomato juice splattered him and the floor.

"Beta," said Jack. It was Brendon's turn to throw a balloon. On impact it revealed its contents of vinegar. "Beta stands for bebaios, or reliability. Man must rely upon himself: to supply his needs, to determine his fate, to achieve his potential. He does not need a savior, which is a good thing because there are no saviors, no superhuman agents to help, no divine creators for appeal."

"Beta!" shouted Pete. "What is the second mystery?"

"Man must rely upon himself."

"Very good," said Brendon. He threw another balloon of vinegar at the second boy.

"Gamma," said Jack. He grabbed a balloon filled with grape juice. The boy fell backward upon impact. Everyone laughed. "Gamma stands for gnosis, or knowledge. Man already knows; he has the knowledge he needs to live peaceably and well. Man has no need for revelation of secrets known only to superhuman agents and their flunkies."

Then why are we here? thought Montgomery. *If we already know all we need to know, why do y'all need to reveal these so-called mysteries to us?* He gave Travis a poke with his elbow and rolled his eyes. Travis shook his head warningly.

"Gamma!" shouted Brendon. "What is the third mystery?"

"Man already knows all he needs to know."

"Brilliant!" applauded Pete. He threw another balloon at the third boy.

"Delta," said Jack. Brendon lobbed a balloon. Everybody was now curious to see what the next balloon would contain. Milk splattered everywhere. "Delta stands for didache, or learning. Man is a wise animal; he's always learning. The wise man gains knowledge wherever it is found. He learns from every fount of wisdom, the greatest of which is the fount of the fraternal mysteries of Greco-Roman civilization, of which you are drinking today. Learn well."

"You have contradicted yourself," burst out Montgomery before he could think better. "Gamma: Man already knows all he needs to know. Delta: Man is always learning. What for? He already knows; what does he need to learn?"

Jack shook his head sadly. "There's no hope for you. You are such a literalist you cannot appreciate the greater truths of these mysteries. No wonder you are a Mongrel, and a Mongrel you will always be."

Montgomery showed a flash of triumph in his eyes. *Aha! An opponent turns to personal insults when he cannot refute the arguments.* Montgomery quickly removed the flash, though; the memory of pain at the hands of these individuals was near.

Travis was thoughtful. *Are they doing what I think they're doing? Should I do something? But what?*

"Delta!" shouted Pete. "What is the fourth mystery?"

"Man is always learning."

"Good," said Jack. He threw a milk balloon at the boy, who stood to take the full effect of the blast as a reward. The other boys applauded.

"Epsilon," said Jack. Pete threw a balloon full of Thousand Island dressing. "Epsilon stands for encrateia, or discipline. Man needs no discipline; his frustrations come when he does not follow his instincts. The animal Man follows his passions to reach happiness."

The fifth boy stood up. "Epsilon!" he shouted. "Man needs no discipline."

The other boys cheered. The fifth boy grabbed his balloon and broke it over his head.

Brendon, Pete and Jack winked at one another. This was working better than they had planned.

"Zeta," said Jack. The sixth boy received a balloon full of brake fluid in his face, and he hurriedly wiped his face in his shirt. "Zeta stands for zalos, or passion. Man indulges his passions—it is his basic nature. It is the denial of his appetites and urges that twists Man into committing evil acts."

The sixth boy stood and yelled, "Zeta! The sixth mystery is that Man indulges his passions and basic nature." But he turned and protected his face as the brake fluid soaked his back, butt and legs.

"Eta," said Jack. Brendon whipped a balloon full of mayonnaise across the room, nailing the seventh boy on his belt buckle. Ribald laughter followed the result. The seventh boy grinned and winked. "Eta stands for agemonia, or leadership. Your initiation into these mysteries makes you a leader. With a thorough understanding of the beauty of these truths, you will master markets, strategy, women, power, fame and fortune. You will be pre-eminent practitioners admired and envied by millions. You will lead the pack into gaining the desires of your hearts and eyes. The seventh mystery is leading the pack."

The seventh boy stood. "Eta!" he yelled. "The seventh mystery: We lead the pack!" A balloon followed the triumphant statement. The boy reveled in the moment.

"Theta," said Jack. Another balloon, another boy drenched in cane syrup. "The eighth mystery is theta, which stands for tharsos, or courage and boldness. Leaders have courage and boldness, striding confidently into new experiences that are offered to them, and taking advantage of the opportunities that are presented to them. They plunge in; they do not hesitate. They do not question; they gain an opening of their very selves."

The eighth boy stood. "Theta! Leaders are bold!" More syrup followed the first.

"Iota," said Jack. Pete lobbed a balloon filled with raw eggs. It broke across the boy's face; he wiped his face with his hands and then wiped his hands on his shorts. Brendon and Pete snickered. "Iota stands for ilarotase, or cheerfulness. Man is always cheerful when he follows the truths of these mysteries. They bring happiness, contentment and fulfillment. Cheerfulness is the hallmark of the well-developed man. He meets all circumstances of life with great cheer, and uses the aids of cheerfulness freely and steadily. What is alcohol, but cheer in liquid form? What is pot, but the leaf and bud of cheer? And there are many other transferring transformers of cheer. The eighth mystery is that Cheer makes the man."

The ninth boy stood. "Iota! Man freely imbibes of Cheer: the ninth mystery."

"Excellent!" chorused Pete and Brendon. The ninth boy also turned to receive his reward across his back.

"Kappa," said Jack. The tenth boy's eyes grew wide as he recognized the object in Pete's hand not as a balloon, but as a condom. He shrieked as it hit his face. Pete, Brendon and Jack were roaring with laughter. The tenth boy smelled the liquid on his fingers that he had been frantically using to remove the leakage from his face; he realized it was glue. "Glue," he said as he laughed in relief. "Only glue."

"Kappa, the tenth mystery, stands for katakarpos, or fruitful. Man produces fruit of his loins—as often as he can. Man rejects the false straight jacket of the moralist that denies the fruitfulness of man. Man is fruitful."

The tenth boy stood. "Kappa! Fruit of the Loom!"

The room went silent. This was the first time someone had made a mistake. They waited to see how the pledge committee would react.

The boy mumbled, "Slip of the tongue—sorry. Fruit of the loins—Man is fruitful."

"Don't forget it," snapped Jack. He was angry because the mood was broken. Then his countenance changed, and he moved on to Travis.

Lambda," he said. Travis stood up. A balloon of diluted fruit drink soaked his clothes. "Lambda stands for logismos, or rationale. The rationale of these mysteries is that man descended from the apes as the evolutionary process worked across billions of years. Thus, man makes his own standards, determines his own values, and creates his own rationale for living his life, and for the society in which he lives. The lambda mystery is that Man makes his own rationale."

Travis had remained standing. He was bored, not maintaining interest past gamma. He repeated for the room, "Lambda: Man is the maker of his own rationale." Travis sat down right at the moment Jack threw the balloon. It flew over his head. The boys laughed and cheered.

Jack had come to the last teaching point, and Montgomery, to conclude the afternoon's session. "Mongrel," he said in an odd voice, for once free of malice yet still unfriendly, "your letter is mu, standing for macrothumos, or patience. Man does not strive to exceed his grasp; he is content with what he is. The same as we have to be patient and content with what you are: a mongrel, a moralist and a literalist." Jack spat these words with contempt.

Brendon stepped forward. "Let's go over it again! Alpha!"

The first boy stood, "Man is innately good."

"Beta!"

"Man must rely upon himself."

The next boy stood. "Gamma! Man already knows all he needs to know!"

The boys followed in turn. "Delta! Man is always learning."

"Epsilon! Man needs no discipline."

"Zeta! Man indulges his passions and basic nature!"

"Eta! Lead the pack!"

"Theta! Leaders are bold for new experiences!"

"Iota! Man freely imbibes of cheer!"

"Kappa! Man is fruitful as often as possible!"

Travis rose to his feet. "Lambda—Man makes his own rationale."

Montgomery stood up. "Mu, the letter of patience."

Jack sighed and rolled his eyes. "Excellent until the last letter. Remember our work today. Because Mongrel did so poorly, he has to clean the room. The rest are excused."

The pledges left the room, talking and laughing; some pointed back at Montgomery and spoke in low voices. Montgomery left to get rags, buckets and a mop. Travis hung back to help.

"I suppose it's fair," said Montgomery. "They ran out of balloons, so my mess comes in cleaning it up."

"No," said Travis emphatically. "They planned it that way. Didn't you notice that they called all of us by a letter except you? They hurled a name at you, continually, until it was firmly fixed in everyone's mind that you are Mongrel. They hazed everyone but you—like you are too good or snooty to join in the fun. Everybody acted like it was all fun—but you were not included. They are isolating you from the rest of the pledges."

"And I played into their hands when I argued—nobody else did."

"Exactly. You are No-Fun-Mongrel. These guys don't care about a code one way or the other. They want the benefits of belonging to a frat: girls and parties. They aren't deep, and remember, this is Travis saying they aren't deep. I don't have enough water in my pool to drown a rat."

"You'd be surprised."

"With the exception of you, the pledges they took aren't too bright. The question is why? Don't fraternities want the best and the brightest?"

Montgomery started to answer, then said, "This is not the smartest place to be having this conversation. Let's finish and go home."

In the top floor parlor, the pledge committee convened to review their progress.

"What a pitiful group," groused Jack. "Would you believe it? They enjoyed getting struck with the balloons. Only Lee objected to the way we reworked the first twelve letters of the honor code. The others didn't care; they repeated whatever we told them to say."

"Unquestioning idiots," sneered Pete. "It's a wonder they got into the university."

"But useful idiots," mused Cody. "Blind obedience is a good quality in subordinates. Gofers have their places. We already know we're not going to get any management talent out of the group."

"We did better than expected in isolating the Lee kid," said Brendon. "It was a subtle cut—not to balloon him like the others—but it worked. The others left pointing at him and exchanging remarks. After the next session, Lee will have no friends in the house."

"The only question mark," said Cody, "is Travis. What are our prospects?"

"Terrible if he sees what we're doing to Lee. The problem is that if we keep him out the other pledges will resent it. He has to stay part of the group, but then he'll stay tight with Lee. Travis we can win, but we have to do it the way we did at first: invite him to private parties, ply him with drink and drugs, and arrange for trysts in the house. Then he'll think and do whatever we tell him."

"Keep thinking on it," said Cody. "I want a plan in a couple of days."

Down below, Montgomery and Travis finished the clean up; then bolted before anyone could find them and make them do additional work. They decided to go into town and split a pizza for supper. Once there, they found some of their quadmates in a booth: Cat, Red, Caveman and Shorts. The new arrivals squeezed in and grabbed a slice.

Cat waved the waitress over and ordered additional food and drink. Then he asked Montgomery, "What's up?"

"Down," Montgomery responded. Travis laughed. Their friends shot them questioningly looks.

Montgomery elaborated. "We have come from a most interesting lecture at the frat."

"Alpha!" shouted Travis, then at normal volume, "The first person to dump a coke on me gets his butt kicked."

Montgomery again supplied the explanation. "The reward for learning was a bombing with a balloon filled with different substances. Some guys got hit with tomato juice, milk, o.j., mayonnaise, and one was brake fluid."

Travis snickered. "One guy was hit with a condom filled with glue, but it took him a while to figure it out." All the boys laughed.

Montgomery added dryly, "The occasion for this hilarity was teaching us the honor code. But it was inside out: bad was good, wrong was right, ugh. Instead of challenging us to live according to high ideals, they dared us to live by our basest desires. For example, the point that we should be productive and useful in society—they changed that into having sex as often as possible."

Shorts asked, "How does that tie into productive?"

Travis explained, "Think about it. What will sex produce? Be fruitful!"

Cat had a leering grin on his face. "What else?"

Travis laughed. "Being cheerful meant getting messed up and staying messed up—your choice of means."

Red shook his head. "Wow. Those mental midgets must have smoked their brains working on those alterations."

Montgomery smiled ruefully. "They threw out everything that came of higher purposes, and substituted a philosophy of man: you are good, everything you do is good, everything bad is the result of people being told they are bad and acting out that self-image, do what you want, indulge the appetites, you cannot do wrong because you are good—whatever good people do is always good. The traditional language was redefined the way they wanted it—they affirmed the terms which allows them to escape censure for heresy, yet they redefine the terms to mean their heretical ideas."

Red said, "Like George Orwell's book, 1984, in which the government uses doublespeak. The words are familiar, but the meanings are different."

Travis said, "Like that ex-president who tried to weenie out of a lie he was caught telling by saying, 'That depends on what the meaning of 'is' is.'"

Caveman spoke up. "I've always wondered if she —"

Red said, "Not in front of the children, dear."

All the boys laughed.

"What brings you out on such a night as this?" asked Travis.

"Intramurals," said Red. "We want to compete in the rec league for basketball this winter. You guys interested?"

"Yeah," said Travis. "Put me down."

"How about you, Monkey?"

"I'm not that good."

"It's only the rec league. It doesn't matter how good you are; we could use you on the roster. Help us out; it will be fun."

"Okay. But don't count on me to do more than dress out and show up."

"Great," said Cat. "Now all we need are two more players."

"How about Mick?" suggested Montgomery.

Cat shook his head. "Mick was all talk when he moved in: the big man on campus, Mr. Irresistible, and on and on. He ate with us and sat with us in our common room. But now we never see him. Where does he go? What does he do? He's not around. Every once in a while we see him heading for the bathroom, but mostly he keeps to himself. After our first week of classes, he doesn't join into our activities."

Shorts added, "And who is this mysterious roommate from Michigan? Has anyone ever seen him?"

"I'll call him Ghost," mimicked Travis of their initial meeting of Michael Raike.

The boys laughed. The extra pizza arrived, and they began to eat again as Cat ordered more pitchers of Coke. Outside, the stars began to appear in the sky. Montgomery noted the day passing into night, and felt the familiar yearning to be out in the field, observing the heavens. He pulled some money out of his pocket. "Here's my share. I'm going out to see what's happening."

His quadmates regarded him curiously. Travis explained, "Not on the earth—in the sky."

The quadmates were silent. Montgomery excused himself, and headed out the door.

Travis offered additional light. "Every so often he needs some alone time."

Cat said knowingly, "The curse of the introvert."

Red said, "He's been through a lot. There goes one boy whose life is nothing like it was when he arrived on campus several weeks ago. Shy and trusting, even naive, he's fallen in love, he's been tortured and under attack, and he's been involuntarily drugged. The world took notice of him: half applauded, half screamed. He's changed, and he knows it; his problem is that he doesn't know how."

Travis smiled. "Never count Montgomery out. The third strike is called, the catcher has the baseball in his mitt, and he's walking back to the dugout. Now the crowd is screaming, the fans are on their feet, the fielders have their backs to home plate and are looking over the fence, the umpire puts his arm in the air, circling his hand indicating home run, and Montgomery turns around to take his trot around the bases. No one knows how it happens, or why, but Montgomery gets the hit and the run in the end. My roommate has changed, and for the better. However his pledging turns out, he'll emerge a winner.

"Plus you cannot have a more loyal friend. He and I have been friends since diapers. He's pulled me out of so many scrapes that I've lost count. He's always there. Somehow he knows, and he's always there to pull me out of the fire. Don't y'all doubt that he'll be there for y'all; he will be. Maybe that's the gist of the Lee legacy."

"What about the Travis legacy?" asked Shorts.

"I get him to loosen up. Fun and parties is what I'm here for. Didn't I tell y'all where to find the best band the night before our first home football game? Plus I get the girls. The three lovelies were my discovery. So the Travis legacy is to focus on the important things of life."

The boys grinned. "So where are our girls?" teased Shorts.

"Find your own. Or is my quad full of social duds?"

"We should have a party," said Cat. "A mixer."

"Good idea," said Red. "Two weeks from Friday night."

The weeks passed quickly as the quad buzzed with excitement over the party. Special invitations were drawn upon computers, printed and e-mailed to all the girls' dormitories on their end of campus. In no time at all, word had spread to boys' dormitories, which wanted to know where all the girls were going on Friday night. Sunday night the week of the party, Rick stopped in.

"Hey, Rick!" Cat howled with excitement. "Come to see our party plans?"

"Actually, yes. Do y'all have any idea how big y'all's party has become?"

"Talk of the town," grinned Shorts. "How often does a quad party become this famous, and that before the event?"

"Indeed. There will be several hundred people. Your quad isn't big enough to hold your party. Your hall isn't big enough to hold your party. So you can't have it (the boys' faces fell) in your quad.

"So I took the liberty of reserving the lounge in your names. (The boys' faces brightened.) But that requires accountability. You're responsible for security and damage. As this is not an official dorm function, you may not charge for admission or refreshments or anything else connected to the party. You may, however, accept contributions (Rick winked). You're responsible for clean up, including the collection and removal of all litter from the building and grounds. The party is over by 2:00 a.m. You may not have alcohol at your function. Smoking is prohibited in all public spaces, so keep them outside. I'm your official chaperone—don't let me down."

The boys whooped with pleasure. Rick was very popular with the quad since the day he had come to talk to Montgomery. "Bring your little black book," said Red. "This is a mixer—meet lots of girls and have fun."

Rick grinned. "I have an exclusive now, but it's good that you boys are getting the help you need."

"The gimmick," said Cat, "is that an air horn sounds every ten minutes or so. When that happens, you must move to another person. The trick is to leave them wanting more so that they give you their number and ask you to call."

"What happens if people don't change?" asked Rick.

"Oh, that's easy," said Shorts. "We sic Monkey's frat on them. A little shock in the pants, and they'll move." The boys laughed together.

In the few days left, Shorts proved to be a hero as he secured a dispensing fountain and cans of soda syrup and CO2 water. He knew how to set them up, and he put an efficient refreshment station together. Red set up a system for background music. Friday afternoon, the boys rearranged the lounge furniture to create conversation pairs in the rooms.

Montgomery and Travis pitched in and helped. Park, Elizabeth and Rose volunteered to keep the cokes flowing. Rick had secured a short-range radio from campus security in case something got out of hand. Cat brought several disposable air horns—the type that is sold in convenience stores.

Hundreds of young men and women turned out for the mixer. Apparently, they faced the same frustration as the quadmates—how to meet new people of the opposite sex. The format meant that they would keep mixing and not get stuck with someone incompatible, and that they would meet dozens of new persons from whom they could select the ones they wanted to date.

"Did we invite all these people?" Red asked Cat.

"Must have," he responded as he roamed the crowd making sure that no trouble was breaking out.

The air horn kept sounding, and an audible response was heard from the crowd as many considered that they had not had enough time to talk to their new acquaintance. But almost everyone complied with the changes because they had come wanting to meet many new persons.

The boys covered the expenses of soda, cups, napkins and other miscellaneous items from a donation lockbox set on the refreshment table. They had also sold little notebooks and pens at the beginning of the mixer; in fact, they had to make two additional runs to area stores for more. They estimated they had sold, for "donations", five hundred notebooks. Caveman was ecstatic; he was the poorest boy in the quad. "This will keep us in groceries until the end of the semester," he exulted.

Montgomery and Travis were covering the outside. The mixer was so big that the crowd had spilled onto the dormitory's grounds. By this time, campus security had sent a couple cars to the scene to watch and keep things in order. Because there was no alcohol served, and few people had thought to bring any, the evening was successful in keeping problems to a minimum.

Around 1 a.m., the security personnel began to disperse the crowd. Slowly the young people began to break apart, finding the friends with whom they had come, and departing for their homes. The roar of hundreds of conversations began dwindling to dozens. The boys held a short conference on how to end the party at 2 a.m.

They agreed that they would begin closing down the back rooms of the lounge, partitioning off each section as it was cleared of people. At 1:30 a.m., about thirty people remained around the lounge. Montgomery, Travis and Rick were walking their girlfriends home. Three cars pulled up to the curb, and a dozen Sigma Omicron Beta brothers jumped out, heading for the lounge. The security personnel held a short conference, and followed.

"Where's the Mongrel," demanded the lead SigBee.

"Who wants to know?" said Red.

"You look soft to me," threatened the leader. "Get out of my way before you get hurt."

Cat and Caveman came over. "What's the problem?" asked Cat.

"We lost a pledge," said the leader.

"Sorry," replied Cat, "we gave at the office."

Red smothered a laugh. This angered the leader of the group.

"We aim to find our pledge and punish him for not inviting us to his party," said another SigBee. "He has broken another of our rules."

Cat looked the speaker directly in his eyes. "You need to leave."

"Who's going to make us?" demanded the leader.

Cat held up his hand. "Me and my four brothers," he replied as he made a fist.

The leader laughed. "Get a load of this guy," he said to the others. "He wants to fight. Let's teach him a lesson that when Sigma Omicron Beta shows up, we get what we want."

"Who do you think you are—showing up at someone's party uninvited and causing trouble?" asked Red. "You have no right to be here. You're trespassing. Leave now. You may be king in your horror house, but here you're nothing."

"Nobody talks to me that way," growled the leader as he stepped forward to bump chests with Red. He was surprised that Red knocked him backward when their bodies made contact.

The security personnel decided that the confrontation was not going to resolve itself peacefully and stepped in. "The party's over," a sergeant said. "Go back to your fraternity house."

"Tell Mongrel we're looking for him," snarled the leader. "The longer it takes, the worse he'll get it. By the way, we 'll be back."

Cat continued to stare hard directly into the eyes of the leader. "Anytime you think you're man enough," he said, breaking off his stare and turning his back.

The sergeant took hold of the leader's arm. "Move it, now," he commanded. The group of SigBees left the lounge.

Out on the street, they stared at the empty spaces where their cars had been parked. "What happened to our cars?"

A patrol officer said, "No parking zone. The cars were towed."

This brought on an episode of cursing that only ended when the patrol officer threatened to arrest them for rowdiness. The frat boys were fooled by the bluff, and began walking back to their house.

Rip flexed his muscles and pounded his fist into his palm, "That Mongrel will be sorry he ever showed his face on this campus. He'll pay for this, oh how he will pay."

"Watch it, Rip," cautioned Jack. "Cody doesn't want the attention of the authorities. We have to be careful about what we do."

"Cody cannot be everywhere. When I catch that little (he cursed) alone, I will have my revenge, Cody be damned."

Brendon laughed. "I got stoned tonight so I could have fun at a rumble. What say we give the Charlies a bruising?"

"What are you going to do, knock on the door and burst in when they open it?" asked a brother.

"Sounds like a plan to me," said Rip. "We are, after all, the pre-eminent fraternity on campus. It doesn't hurt to give the others a reminder from time to time."

"Let's go!" yelled another brother. The members of Sigma Omicron Beta ran off in search of trouble.

Montgomery, Travis and Rick returned from Alyssa Hawkins. As they had said goodnight, and turned around, Travis stuck his tongue out at Montgomery and moved it around. Montgomery turned bright red and looked at the ground.

Travis laughed heartily. "Welcome to the world of sensuality, my friend. But remember, the tongue is a tease for what comes later."

Montgomery continued to say nothing as they walked along.

Travis said to Rick, "Keep an eye on our Montgomery. He takes a long time to get started, but he's a fast learner, and once he starts, he catches up and then blows by the competition."

Rick retorted, "He would have to have children to overtake you."

Travis grinned. "I do have a certain experience: that is truly said. I'm attracted to the girls I date and conquer, no doubt about that. I like them; they like me. We have fun together. But only Montgomery can make it a spiritual experience with a deep and abiding love. You wait and see; when he finally makes the decision to go all the way, his experience will be far beyond anything you or I can hope to achieve. It must come from all that star-gazing at far-off places that lifts him above the ordinary."

"Then I hope it will be with someone worthy of him, not some 'love him and leave him' chick who seduces him only so she can say that she was the one."

"You missed it!" called out Shorts when he saw the trio come in the door.

"What happened?" asked Rick.

"The S.O.B.'s showed up," said Cat. "Twelve of them. We almost had a fight, but Security broke it up. Then those jerks went outside and Security had towed their cars." Cat laughed and slapped his leg.

"Why were they here?" asked Rick.

"They said they were mad at Monkey for not inviting them to the party," explained Red. "But I think they wanted to cause trouble. They sure have it in for you," he said to Montgomery.

"It was so funny," added Shorts. "The leader tried to intimidate Red by knocking him backward, but Red knocked him backward. They must think that being dorm rats makes us wimps."

"If they come back," Cat said, "they will regret it. If they want a fight, they'll get one."

"Whoa," said Rick. "Chill. You're too old to be settling your differences in the schoolyard. When you were little boys, and you fought, you were pulled apart and sat in the corner. Later, when you were bigger boys, you were suspended from school. But now, you're men in the eyes of the law. You're too old to settle arguments by fighting. If you do, you'll be arrested and charged with battery."

"Assault," corrected Shorts.

"No, battery," responded Rick. "Assault is threatening to beat someone; battery is the actual beating. If you get into a fight with them, all of y'all will be arrested and receive a criminal record for life. That's stupid. Don't fight; call the police."

"We're supposed to let those creeps push us around?" asked an incredulous Cat.

"No, you do what you did tonight," said Rick. "Tell them to leave and then let the cops handle it."

"What if they start it?" demanded Red.

"You're allowed to defend yourself," Rick replied. "But only to defend yourself. You're not allowed to give a beating once you have thwarted the attack."

"In other words, don't do too good of a job," grinned Cat.

"Stop their attack, and walk away," said Rick. "Remember that someone has to believe that the other guy started it."

"Thanks for pooping that party," said Cat sardonically. "Seriously, thanks for thinking that four or five of us can cream a dozen of them."

"You did a great thing tonight," said Rick. "You helped this campus come together and become a true community. Plus, the social life around here has leapt leagues ahead of where it has been. The place looks clean to me. Let's go to bed. Tomorrow, I'm going to nominate you for a commendation. Seriously," he said to their surprised looks.

On the way up the stairs, Montgomery finally spoke. "Thanks, guys."

"We're already a fraternity," Red said. "Give up on them—they're losers."

"I wish I could."

The boys looked at Travis, but Travis only shrugged his shoulders.

In the early hours of the morning, the boys undressed and went to bed. By unspoken agreement, no one was going to stir before noon. At the house of Sigma Omicron Beta, Cody had the dozen brawlers assembled in the lounge with linoleum floor and worn leather couches. "You idiots!" he screamed. "Why did you do such a stupid thing?"

"Those pledges had security at their function," said Brendon. "We couldn't do anything and we wanted to fight."

"So you assault the Charlie house? Do you know that could bring an inquiry? All they have to do is make a complaint. You're lucky the cops weren't called. Fools!"

"We've worked hard to turn this house into the type of place we want; we don't follow the Greek garbage of the past; we do as we please, and that includes a substantial business in illicit merchandise. And you jeopardize that with a stupid fight. Do you remember a concept we call tolerance? That means we don't mix it up with other fraternities. Only moralists and traditionalists are targets; forget the others. How can we keep this fraternity running on our contemporary values if you open it to criticism of its actions? If the administration caught a whiff of what we're doing in this house, we'd lose it all." Cody cursed.

"I'll have to send that fool Wilson over to make amends. That means I'll have to make concessions to gain his cooperation. You jerks really want Mongrel in the house? Your stunt makes it a good possibility." Cody stormed off to make himself a cup of coffee and ponder how to smooth over the debacle.

The fraternal brothers looked at one another. "Is it that bad?" asked one.

"He'll get over it," responded Brendon. "Doggone if I haven't come down from my high. Last one to the bong is a Mongrel." The men whooped and howled as they raced upstairs to their smoking room and stashes and pipes.

Around noon, Montgomery kicked back the covers, got to his feet, and padded into the bathroom. When he came back to the common room, he noticed that Mick's door was ajar. He knocked softly.

"Anyone awake?" There was no answer. Montgomery pulled the door closed. He crossed to the TV, turned on a pregame college football program, popped the lid of a can of Coke, and sat down.

Mick's door burst open. "Who touched my door?"

"Hey, Mick, it's me, Montgomery. I saw it was ajar, so I knocked to see if you were awake."

"Leave my door alone," Mick cursed. "My room is private, nobody touches my things or peeps on me. You moral snoots are all the same: so superior in your attitudes, snooping around other people's lives—stay out or you'll regret it." He slammed the door.

"Tou-chee," said Montgomery to the door.

"What was that about?" inquired a yawning Travis as he entered the common room.

"Tell me; we'll both know," shrugged Montgomery.

"I need a shower. Call me when the beer's cold and the hotdogs steamed."

"Check and check."

Travis went into the bathroom and pulled his shorts off. He reached into the shower and turned on the hot water, waiting for it to come up the pipes so he could adjust the spray before stepping into the unit. He retrieved his shampoo, soap and washcloth from his bin. He felt the stream of water. It was running hot. Travis turned on the cold water, adjusted the knobs and stepped under the spray.

"Wha—ow!" he screamed and jumped out of the shower. He ran into the common room. "Come and see!"

Montgomery looked very surprised. It is not often that your naked roommate comes screaming out of the shower with a demand for a personal inspection of the shower stall. He got up, and went into the bathroom.

"Whoa," he ejected. Then he laughed. He reached into the shower and pulled out a man-sized inflatable vinyl duck. He brought it into the common room. "Travis, you hound."

"It's not mine," a wide-eyed but now laughing Travis said. "How did it get into the shower?"

The door to room four burst open. "Why can't you and your roommate keep your hands off my things," snarled Mick. Both Montgomery and Travis looked shocked at Mick's appearance. His skin was sallow, eyes bloodshot and puffy, hair disheveled, and several week's growth of beard was tangled and uncombed.

Mick grabbed the vinyl duck and retreated to his room, slamming the door.

"What's with him?" asked Travis.

"Tou-chee. Not to be rude, but put some clothes on or take your shower. It feels weird standing in a room with a naked man."

Travis laughed. "It wouldn't if you were naked too," he replied as he snatched at Montgomery's shorts. Montgomery dodged his arm and said, "Not if the whole campus was a nudist colony."

Travis laughed again. "Put that in the suggestion box. Like dress-down Fridays in offices: naked Fridays at Florida Sawgrass University. Think of it: no more lying about one's natural endowments because everything is displayed for inspection. It would be a great boost to everyone's sex life."

"Dream on," replied Montgomery.

The other rooms were still silent. After Travis had showered, and pulled on a clean pair of oversized shorts and a sleeveless t-shirt, he popped the lid on a beer and sat down on the couch. "Who's playing?"

"Southern Cal and Notre Dame; Alabama and LSU; Princeton and Columbia; Georgia and Georgia State; Florida and South Carolina; Miami and Syracuse."

"Flip on the Florida game. Want a brew?"

"Okay."

"What?" said an astonished Travis.

"I said, 'Okay.' I think it's time I tried new things."

Travis retrieved a can of beer for Montgomery from the refrigerator. "If your family ever finds out, they'll blame me forever."

"So who's going to tell them?"

"Like I said last night: you're a fast study."

Montgomery's mouth puckered as the tangy and mildly bitter liquid plucked his taste buds. "You like this stuff?"

"Keep drinking and ask me again when the can is empty."

By now it was 1 p.m. and the other boys were rousting from their dreams. As they joined Montgomery and Travis at the television, they helped themselves to beer and food. Soon a rip-roaring party was underway. They watched the game, discussing the successful party of the night before, yelling for Florida and debating play selection, player substitution and referees' decisions.

Again the door to room four burst open. A wild-eyed Mick stepped into the room. "Can't a man have peace and quiet in his room?" he screamed. "No, the selfish boys have to have it their way. Stay out of my room, or else." Mick slammed his door, and stormed out of the quad.

The six boys looked at one another. For the third time that day, Montgomery said, "Tou-chee."

"Something's not right with that dude," said Cat.

"He looks horrible, whatever it is," observed Travis.

"He couldn't have slept in days," offered Red.

"It's too early to crash and burn," said Shorts. "We're only five weeks into the semester. Nervous breakdowns and failing don't come until the semester's end."

The boys looked at one another. In unison they said, "Tou-chee," and guffawed. They turned their attention back to the television set.

"How's that brew?" Travis asked his roommate.

"Empty."

"Two fresh ones," Travis called to Cat who had gone to the refrigerator.

"So when do y'all go back for more training in the Greek lifestyle?" asked Shorts.

"I could not care less," said Travis.

"Won't they drop y'all for missing y'all's meetings?"

"If I'm lucky."

"What a turnaround from a few weeks ago," observed Red. "You were so devoted to the fun house."

"I found out it's a little house of horrors. I don't need those bums. They need me, but I don't need them."

"What about you, Monkey?" asked Cat.

"Travis is right." Montgomery burped loudly. The boys laughed, including Montgomery.

"So are y'all quitting?" asked Shorts.

"No," said Montgomery, "I have to see it through."

"What about that Rip character?" asked Cat.

"I'll have to deal with him whether I join or not. He's become a personal enemy."

"If he comes back here," said Cat, "all of us will deal with him." The other boys nodded. Even Caveman made a fist and shook it.

"Thanks, y'all, but it will never end unless I take care of him by myself."

"So what happens next?" asked Shorts.

"We keep doing their chores. In a few weeks, we go live in the house for a while. Then they vote, and it's over."

"Then what? You guys move out?" asked Red.

"No, Travis and I talked it over. We're staying here, in or out, for the whole year."

"Awww, I'm touched," mocked Cat.

"You throw better parties," laughed Travis. "Always make a decision by the fundamentals; that's what I was taught."

"Not to mention that our girlfriends are closer," added Montgomery. "But the bottom line is that we don't want to live with those guys."

"Yeah," said Travis. "Sooner or later, it would be our turn with the clap queen."

The boys looked at him questioningly. Montgomery explained that a girl lived in the frat, moving from room to room, handing out sex and gonorrhea liberally. They laughed.

"Isn't that always the way," said Cat. "Fantasies become realities only at a steep price."

"Trust me," said Travis. "She's no fantasy with or without the booby prize."

"Surely somebody in that place goes to the doctor for the all-important penicillin shot," mused Red. "Why wouldn't the Public Health Department move in and inoculate the whole house?"

"Clap is at an epidemic stage on campus," responded Travis. "So I've been told."

"By whom?" demanded Shorts. "What should we know now that we have dozens of girls to date?"

Travis hesitated, then decided to tell them. "I found out about the clap queen the hard way. I had to get some shots from the clinic. The people there told me that it's bad on campus; be careful with whom you sleep."

"Now there's a dumb expression," said Red. "It's not the sleeping that gets us into trouble."

"Maybe that's the problem with Tou-chee," said Shorts.

"Maybe," answered Travis.

Chapter Seven

In-House Hazing

UNDER A CLEAR SKY Montgomery spread a blanket for him and Elizabeth to lie upon, and kindled a fire. It was not a cold night, being the end of September, but they enjoyed watching the flames and listening to the wood pop and crack.

"It's my last night of freedom," said Montgomery. "Tomorrow I move into the House of Horrors."

"If you weren't so stubborn, you'd drop it," Elizabeth responded.

"I can't give up my call."

"Call to what?"

"My call to leadership—to use my talents, my gifts and graces, to restore a declining chapter of a declining fraternity."

"Why not give it up?"

"It's part of the Lee tradition: being Sigma Omicron Beta."

"I can't picture you as an S.O.B."

"When you put it that way ...," Montgomery laughed. They embraced, and exchanged a passionate kiss. Elizabeth murmured with pleasure.

"Look at all the stars," he said, sweeping his hand across the sky. "How many worlds are out there, different from our own and yet built by the same physical laws?"

"Do you believe in space aliens?" she asked.

"No." Montgomery kissed her, then pulled away to lie on his back. "Intelligent life may exist somewhere else in the universe. It's possible because we know that it does exist in one spot. But consider the circumstances needed to support life: a rare one-star solar system—most systems are binary; a planet the right distance from the star ..."

"Does distance make a big difference?"

"Yes. The possible range is very narrow to have the right temperatures so that water exists in all three states, which is essential to proper climate and weather patterns. Life needs an abundance of water, carbon, oxygen and nitrogen, and temperature is essential for the formation of carbon chains which manufacture the basic stuff of life."

Elizabeth placed her lips on his, interrupting his thought. Montgomery responded to her initiative, opening her lips into a deep, passionate exchange.

"So space aliens remain the imagination of supermarket tabloids," she whispered.

"A life-supporting system is a very rare combination only possible statistically given a large enough universe such as this one. If intelligent life did exist, we'd never know it. Light is the fastest moving object in the universe. Nothing can go faster. To come to Earth from another star system would take too many lifetimes—the aliens would never make it."

"Why would they want to? A species intelligent enough to devise a means of travel is intelligent enough to know to stay away. Why come to Earth? We'd blast their spaceship from the sky, put them in a zoo to gawk at them, and slander them with stories about hybrid offspring." Elizabeth laughed softly.

"Any species intelligent enough to come to Earth is too smart to do so."

Elizabeth kissed him in response.

"One reason I love you is the quick way you grasp the heart of any matter."

"I love you for your encyclopedic mind, but more so because you use it without flaunting it. I love your passion for the things that interest you."

"I'm passionate about you." Montgomery kissed her with a long, slow, lingering kiss that remained on their lips long after they pulled their heads apart. The fire died to a hot bed of coals as they remained in the darkness dreaming together of the strange new world they inhabited which was so different from the one they had known a few months ago . . .

Travis looked into the quad. It was empty. "Come on," he mouthed to Park, and he pulled her through the common room by her hand. He opened the door to his bedroom, pulled her in and closed the door. He pulled her into a tight embrace. They kissed passionately. Travis pulled her down onto his bed. "He's out all night."

Park gave herself willingly to Travis. *It's the price of keeping a boyfriend; he's funny, charming, muscular, and attractive—dangerous, yet reassuring. Besides, I enjoy it too.* "Make my eyes roll back."

Travis did every bit of that, and more. Two hours later, she rolled back her head in satisfied pleasure, and fell asleep on his chest.

Travis remained awake, however, in a pensive mood. *What am I heading into? I detest the fraternity; I'm only staying with the pledge program out of loyalty to Montgomery. I've got to watch his back, which is new in my life: to think about more than fun, and do something I don't want to do for noble reasons.*

Then there's Park. I'm enjoying this very much—not the sex, but lying together and being together. What's happened to me? I almost ruined this relationship; is that why I feel so attached to her? But I can't have both Park and the fraternity; he wondered if Montgomery realized the same about Elizabeth?

What am I going to do with my life? I don't have strong interests like Montgomery, and no talent leading to marketable employment. I came to the university to party for four more years, and ride Montgomery's coattails to a degree. Why do all these questions interest me? I'm a lightweight avoiding the serious issues of life; at least I'm supposed to be.

Travis' mind returned to the fraternity. *Living in the house there's no fleeing to safety. Where do I stand with the rough characters there? I'm not a brawler; I never fought at home because no one had been foolish enough to try me.*

He sighed. *I'll do his best, but Montgomery was right: sooner or later Montgomery will have to take care of Rip Tilden himself.*

Travis' clock was flashing 5 a.m. He started which woke the dozing Park. "You've got to go. It's Monday morning."

"One more time," she mumbled.

"We don't have time. I've never turned anyone down before. But please, don't get caught by my quadmates. It'll be too embarrassing for you." *Wow! Have I changed or what? I've never worried about a partner before—I'd want to be caught so I'd look like a big stud in the eyes of my friends.*

Travis pulled on shorts and a t-shirt, then jammed his feet into sandals. Park put her clothes on as she said, "You are someone special. You're blushing!"

Another new experience. "Surf's up. Let's go."

Travis and Montgomery met on their way back to the quad. Montgomery yawned, and Travis found it catching. "Been up all night?"

"We were watching the stars the entire night. We talked about everything and nothing. I've had no sleep. I'd skip English, but we have to be at the frat house by 7 a.m. so there's no point."

"I haven't had any sleep either. You ever lay awake thinking about things?"

"Many times."

"It's a first for me."

"One good thing about the hour: no one's in the showers."

"Let's hit it and head out. We're not gaining anything by waiting."

The roommates quickly showered, shaved, and donned clean clothes. Montgomery grabbed a garbage bag of old clothes and fresh notebooks. Travis smiled at Montgomery's choice of luggage. "Not taking any chances."

"Nothing that I want to keep."

"Tell me again why we are doing this."

"We're on a mission from God."

"That explains your crucifixion."

They left a note for their quadmates explaining that they had reached the in-house phase of pledging, but they would be back as often as possible at unpredictable hours. They tromped down the stairs, out the door, and made their way toward the swamp.

The nervousness that both felt was reflected in their silence as they walked across the predawn campus. A few lights glowed in the windows of the classroom and research buildings. The blocks of faculty housing showed more activity: professors walking, deans cooking breakfast, children grumbling through their preparations for school. To Montgomery and Travis, the scene appeared surreal: something of which they were a part, but knowing that they were a part of it. They had a strange sensation of watching themselves interacting with the domestic scene.

They came to the fraternity's gate, and turned into the yard. They went around to the side of the house where the familiar side entrance appeared with the door ajar. Cautiously they went inside, and went into the pledge room—the linoleum-floored, vinyl or leather sofa furnished lounge. No one was there.

They dropped their belongings onto the floor, and crashed onto different sofas. Both boys fell asleep. When they awoke, the twelve pledges were assembled, and the pledge committee was entering the room.

"First we explain the process: what y'all be going through and what we'll accomplish. For the next five weeks, y'all live in the house, rooming with y'all's supervising brother. He'll be y'all's master; y'all be his servant. Y'all take care of his needs and wishes in addition to y'all's regular duties in the house. Y'all be assembled at whatever hour of the day or night we say. We might test y'all in any number of diverse ways. Or we may have a party together. During this time, we'll test y'all's loyalty to the fraternity.

"We want to know if y'all fit in with us. Those who like to play, work, party and study like we do will become brothers of Sigma Omicron Beta. Be yourselves. Good luck on y'all's conditional acceptance into Sigma Omicron Beta. At the end of the five weeks, we'll interview y'all, and the full house will vote on y'all's acceptance. Because fraternal life is so important to us, even one brother feeling a reservation about y'all will block y'all's acceptance and initiation. So . . . don't make anyone mad.

"At the end of this week is the traditional Sigma Omicron Beta block party. It is open to the entire campus. For that reason, everyone has to work hard to prepare for the party, and to keep the party running smoothly.

"Let's go up to breakfast. Y'all eat y'all's meals with us and participate in all our activities. Y'all are here as our probationary brothers."

It's amazing, thought Montgomery, *that the twelve of us are pledging the fraternity and we have spent little time together. We don't know one another's names.*

As they entered the dining room, the supervising brothers signaled their pledges to sit beside them. Montgomery walked indifferently and sat beside Wilson. Wilson gave him a big smile. "This is it," Wilson whispered in Montgomery's ear, "you're virtually in the house."

Travis entered the dining room; Brendon waved, "Travis! Over here."

Other brothers were coming down the stairs and finding places to sit. Montgomery noticed that most of them greeted Cody and the committee, and sat close to them. A few brothers looked sourly in that direction, and sat on Wilson's side of the room. Montgomery reckoned that 75% of the fraternity was with Cody, and only 25% with Wilson.

Breakfast talk covered the upcoming party.

"Hundreds, maybe a few thousand, attend our block party. It is the event of the fall season," boasted Jack.

"The cops start blocking the streets at 1 p.m. so we can erect the bandstand, and set up refreshment stations," added Pete.

"How late does the party go?" asked one of the pledges.

"Midnight," said Wilson.

"1 a.m.," corrected Cody. "The band shuts down at midnight, but the official end comes at 1 a.m. By then, most everyone has found someone to go home with."

"But private parties continue all night," said Jack.

"That's what I just said," Cody retorted. "However, we'll work all night to dismantle the stands and clean the streets. By sunrise, only the Port-A-Potties will remain as evidence of the party."

"Don't count on having a good time," warned Wilson. "It's hard work for us. We have to keep the refreshment stations supplied—selling cokes is the only way we raise money to pay for the band—we have to maintain crowd control. "

"The band begins at 8 o'clock," Pete said. "Admission is free to the entire campus. It can get wild if a lot of them show up hammered."

"Those Port-A-Potties get messy very quickly," giggled Brendon. "That's why we designate one of our inside bathrooms for the use of our girlfriends."

"That's a privilege you pledges have, also," said Cody. "You may escort any girl into the house to use the designated bathroom."

Montgomery was thinking that the bathroom privilege was decent of them when he noticed Wilson studiously gazing at the ceiling. Montgomery caught Travis' eye; Travis shrugged.

"Our biggest problem is underage drinking," one of the brothers said. "The yu-yu's (Underage Undercover police) cracked down hard with the university several years ago. They were fed up with the rowdiness and vandalism. So we have to keep our party alcohol-free to keep the frat in the clear with the administration."

"Which is why anyone drinking or obviously drunk has to be ejected from the premises," said Wilson. "The last thing we want is the chapter being cited for minor consumption of alcohol."

"We'd rather have major consumption of alcohol," whispered Brendon to Travis.

Travis snickered. "Seems a fellow is more likely to get busted for having a beer than smoking a joint."

Many of the brothers laughed.

"You're right," confirmed Wilson, "but they watch for that, too."

"The important thing is that we stay sober—not even a taste," said a brother from Wilson's side of the dining room. "We enforce the ban and the law. It makes a good impression on the administration that we're responsible."

Travis retorted, "They can't be that stupid. That's like the girl from south Florida who was president of SADD, Students Against Drunk Driving, that flipped her car doing eighty around a tight curve. She was .114 under the influence—dead drunk! Nobody would have expected it from her because she was president of SADD. But it turns out that was a screen—she was really a party alcoholic."

Cody cynically smiled. "Travis, they're not that stupid but they don't want to know. We give them something to keep them happy; they leave us alone so they don't find out different. That happens often—in other places as well as the campus. People deliberately stay ignorant because there's been no trouble. They're happier tolerating existing conditions taking action. That gives us an opportunity to ply our interests without being watched. This opening, we drive a Mack truck through. Remember this in life, and you'll be surprised how much you get away with."

Montgomery's eyes were rolling. *I can't believe what I'm hearing. What's that proverbial Mack truck carrying in its bed? Is something more sinister than crude pranks taking place? Shut up, Montgomery. Don't let your imagination defame their characters because you don't like them.*

When breakfast broke up, Cody told the pledges they were free to attend class and take care of their studies. But, he added, be back for dinner, especially reminding the kitchen workers they were responsible for preparing the meal.

It being Monday, Montgomery headed for The Ring and anthropology class; Travis went to the classroom where all his instruction occurred. "One benefit is that it's not so far to class," remarked Travis.

Montgomery looked around. As they were alone, he said, "Are you rethinking your decision to join?"

Travis snapped back, "No way. No, and no."

Montgomery was peeling potatoes in the kitchen for the evening dinner when Travis came walking through. Gravy immediately drafted Travis to begin boiling the potatoes as he supervised the meat roasting in the huge oven. Two other pledges were at work preparing a dessert and kneading dough for biscuits.

A third pledge was setting the dining room tables. "Where is everybody else?" he grumbled.

"Running errands for the frat," he was told. "We have many deliveries and pick-ups to make during the week. You'll learn more about that after the block party is over."

Montgomery finished the potatoes and began making gravy. *If nothing else, this pledge experience is teaching me how to cook.*

Brothers began filing through the kitchen as the odors filled the house whetting their appetites. "Smells good, Mongrel," said an unknown boy, smacking Montgomery on his butt. Montgomery winced from the sound of the epithet. *The brotherly love being extended apparently has its limits—the hostile attitude toward me has spread through the house.*

Travis turned around and stared at the boy. While butt smacks were common during athletic endeavors, they were unknown in male society at any other time.

Gravy said good-naturedly, "Let us finish, let us finish." He picked up a huge spoon and banged it against a large pot hanging from the ceiling. Additional feet came pounding down the stairs.

The kitchen crew filled the serving dishes, then delivered everything to the tables. That task completed, they sat down in their places. The brothers piled into the food. Montgomery took a few moments to lower his head and give thanks to his Creator. Cody noticed the moment, but he let it pass.

Conversation centered on the upcoming block party. Work crews were assigned to bring the refreshment stations out of storage for clean up and repair. Montgomery was exempted by reason of his chemistry lab. Travis was excused for courier detail.

After dinner, Montgomery and Travis headed for the pledge lounge. They peered through the door; no one was in the lounge. They headed in and sat away from the door so that no one could see them from the hall.

"So far, so good," said Montgomery. "Most of the experience hasn't been too bad—merely work for the frat house. Maybe we misjudged them because the pledge committee has been giving me a hard time. Actually, only one guy has been excessively mean—Rip."

"Maybe. But don't forget your shocking experience. None of them stopped it, either. For that matter, why did they choose you to pick on?"

"If they pick on everyone equally over the next five weeks, it'll show that there's nothing personal against me."

"Cody and company have three-fourths of the house with them. Do we want to associate with these creeps?"

Montgomery sighed. "Expectations are hard to fulfill when they're not one's own."

"Make it easy for yourself—stop trying."

"What's courier duty? I never heard of a fraternity using couriers."

"We get sent around town to deliver packages and envelopes. It must be a means for the frat to raise money. Considering the food they eat, and a residence for fifty men, the dues have to be astronomical unless they have a side business or two."

"Have you gone on courier duty?"

"Not yet. I'm scheduled for tomorrow afternoon." Travis yawned.

"Stop that. You'll put me to sleep."

"If we go upstairs, they'll give us something to do. Let's lie down here for a snooze." Travis stretched out upon a couch and closed his eyes. Montgomery followed his example.

Montgomery was glad for the diversion of chem lab, which would consume his Tuesday afternoon and keep him away from the frat house. The experiments were complicated, and consumed the full three hours so that he and his lab partners, Cat and Red, only left the laboratory as the carillon was chiming the six o'clock hour. He went to dinner with his friends to Jeff Davis Dining Hall.

He was surprised to find Travis waiting for him. "What are you doing here?"

"Courier duty, remember? I've finished my afternoon deliveries and pick-ups, but I also have evening runs. It's the goofiest thing. I deliver packages and envelopes to professors, campus offices, and dormitories. I'm given envelopes or cash in return—most of the packages, especially the dorm deliveries, are C.O.D. Look at this wad of cash." Travis pulled a bulging roll of currency from his pocket. The other three boys' eyes opened wide.

"Wow," whistled Red. "Any idea what it's for?"

"I looked at the packages but they were sealed. I couldn't see inside without leaving evidence of tampering."

Cat asked, "How much do you get for a package?"

"Usually ten to twenty dollars; sometimes only five, sometimes as much as fifty or one hundred, but those deliveries go to campus offices or houses in town."

Cat and Red looked at each other and grinned slyly. Red spoke first. "So tell me, Travis, what product do college kids buy in unmarked packages for ten or twenty dollars?"

Travis looked thunderstruck.

Montgomery spoke, "No way. No way a respected fraternity is running drugs on campus."

Cat remarked, "Forget the 'respected' part. What's your theory?"

"My theory is to ask Wilson about it and find out what he knows."

"I'm testing a theory," Travis said. "That the van won't get a ticket, much less towed, even though I parked illegally."

Following dinner, Travis inspected the windshield. "No ticket even though the meter maid has come by."

A car, whose driver had been emboldened by Travis' blatant parking violation, had parked behind the van. His windshield bore a red parking ticket.

"Curious," said Red.

"Solve the mystery, Sherlock," responded Travis. "I have evening rounds to make."

"Where to?" asked Montgomery.

"Apartments and houses: I reckon they were at work during the day." He jumped into the van and drove off.

Red said. "Monkey, something's not right in that set-up. Be careful."

Cat nodded his head. "What happens when a church stops being a church? Why does a frat stop being a frat, and become a business?"

Montgomery said, "I'm sure there's a reasonable explanation—if I can just figure out what it is."

He walked into the building with his quadmates.

"Are you coming upstairs?" asked Cat.

"Yeah, they think I'm tied up in class so I'm excused from work detail. I'm not going back until late."

Cat and Red laughed. "Let me join, but don't make me be there," Cat teased.

Montgomery reddened, then he laughed. "I'm on a mission from God."

"That explains your crucifixion."

Montgomery looked at his clock in his room. It read 1:30 a.m. He had attacked his studies with a fury so he would not have to take any books or vital notes to the frat house. He had completed all math assignments for the week, chemistry problems and his next two English essays. He completed his reading for anthropology and was halfway done with Western Civilization. He turned his computer off.

The quad was quiet as he let himself out. He walked softly through the halls and down the stairs. He went out the door, walking rapidly, and was back in the house by 2:00 a.m.

The house was dark. Somewhere upstairs a stereo played softly. Montgomery went up the stairs to the third floor bedroom that Wilson shared with two other brothers, Jarett and Steven. Montgomery opened the door quietly and stepped inside. He rolled out his sleeping bag, changed into the gym shorts that he slept in, and crawled into the bag. He pulled his pillow to him and put it under his head.

Montgomery looked out the window. Overhead the stars shone through the fine white crystals of the high cirrus clouds that augured the arrival of a cold front in twenty-four hours. Montgomery found himself thinking about his spiritual condition. *I've changed in the last two months; what changes have been wrought in my spirit? I committed myself to Christ as Lord—am I honoring my commitment? Since I've arrived on campus, I've gone to church every Sunday, but up to now I haven't gotten involved with any church groups or campus ministries. Are my efforts to join the fraternity taking away from time I should spend in the Lord's work?*

Montgomery sighed and closed his eyes. *College is so confusing. My mind is learning facts, but I seem to be unlearning so much else. Politeness, gentility, heritage, dating, friendship, responsibility, leadership: it's all a confusing, swirling mixture in my soul that threatens to become an eddy that will drown me.*

Montgomery stretched as he lay on the floor. Sunshine was creeping into the window. It was seven o'clock. He kicked his way out of his sleeping bag. The other three were still asleep. He changed into shorts and a t-shirt, and headed for the bathroom. Montgomery washed his face, brushed his teeth and attended to his hair. He carefully shaved, preserving those wisps of hair that served as a goatee. He looked into the mirror. A groggy face stared back.

He went down the back stairs to enter the kitchen directly. He greeted Gravy, and asked for his assignment. Gravy set him to frying bacon on a large griddle set into the stove. Montgomery yawned.

"Hi ya pledge," an unfriendly voice said to his back. "You're on courier detail today. That means you're relieved from dinner duty. See me immediately after your last class which is—"

Montgomery turned around. Cody Spung was staring at him. "Uh, math is over at three."

"Right. Be here no later than 3:10 p.m. We have many stops today." Cody strode through the kitchen and entered the dining room.

Montgomery turned back to the bacon. "Gravy, what is courier duty?"

Gravy replied as he worked the kneading machine, "Just what it says: you act as courier. You make pick-ups and deliveries."

"Check. But what do we pick-up and deliver?"

Gravy held his forefinger vertically across his lips. "Don't ask questions. Not here; not now."

"Check." *The mystery deepens. What is this fraternity doing that's so unlike a fraternity? Why is it dangerous to discuss the subject in the kitchen at seven o'clock in the morning?*

That morning Rip Tilden let Montgomery know he was still sore and looking to settle the score. He demanded that Montgomery recite the entire 24-point Greek code backward, not repeating the words in reverse order but pronouncing the syllables as if they were written back to front. For failing to complete this impossible task, Rip emptied a bottle of syrup down his shorts and kicked him for good measure.

As Montgomery rolled on the floor in pain, Wilson bent over and whispered in his ear, "Good boy—don't fight back." Montgomery gritted his teeth as tears of pain stung his eyes, "Obviously I can't fight back."

Rip exchanged high-five slaps of hands with his buddies. He didn't notice Travis' eyes narrowed at him. Travis knelt beside his friend and helped him up. "Go clean up," Travis told Montgomery. "I'll cover for you."

Cody had watched the scene without comment. However, his mind was evaluating the thought that Rip was becoming a liability.

Gravy also watched the scene without comment. His mind was evaluating the possibility that Montgomery might be the catalyst that would break open the secrets of Sigma Omicron Beta.

At 3:15 p.m., Cody Spung handed Montgomery a sheaf of instructions with locations and packages notated in the sequence of a route. Montgomery noted that most of his route involved businesses in town until the evening when it changed to cover dormitories and apartments.

Montgomery looked at the first entry. It was the pizza shop he and his friends patronized. He smiled, took the keys to the van, and went outside. He opened the back of the van, which was filled with cardboard boxes and envelopes. Montgomery examined the delivery label on one of the boxes, then he shook the it. He could not discern what was inside.

Opening the driver's door, Montgomery climbed into the vehicle. He adjusted the seat and mirrors, and buckled his seat belt. He inserted the key into the ignition and turned the motor over. The van fired up. Montgomery smiled. He noted the mileage and amount of gas in the tank pulling out of the driveway.

Four blocks away, Montgomery stopped in front of the pizza shop. He jumped out, went to the back, and located the box for the pizza shop. He walked into the shop, and headed for the counter. The proprietor looked at him expectantly.

"Delivery from Sigma Omicron Beta."

The proprietor grunted. He took the box from Montgomery, and signed for the delivery.

Montgomery turned to go. "Wait," the man said. He pulled an envelope out of his pocket. "This goes back." The man entered his back office and closed the door.

Montgomery looked at the envelope. He held it up to the light. There seemed to be several slips of paper inside. "Curiosity killed the cat," snarled a familiar voice of hate. Montgomery whirled, dodged Rip and dashed out the door, hoping he would not see Rip again.

More deliveries were made, and each was attended with the same procedure: hand over the package, obtain a signature and receive an envelope to return to the frat. As hard as he tried, and Montgomery was much more careful after the run-in with Rip, he could not discern any clues as to the nature of what he was doing.

Montgomery made the last of his business deliveries at 5:30 p.m. He decided not to return to the frat house for dinner. He called Elizabeth on his cell phone. "I'll come by and pick you up. Let's go to the Brasserie."

As they sat down at a table for two, Elizabeth remarked, "I didn't expect to see you during this phase of your pledge period."

"It was Travis who gave me the idea. He skipped the frat and met Cat, Red and me at Jeff Davis last night. So I figured I would do the same—with you."

"But don't they expect you back?"

"Actually—no. They assign afternoon and evening runs so they expect us to stay out until we get done at night."

"How often are you the courier?"

"I don't know—this is my first time."

"I hope it's often—at least twice a week."

"I miss you, too, honey," Montgomery replied, unconscious that he had stepped over a hurdle of romance: the use of pet names.

At the end of dinner, Montgomery took Elizabeth back to her residence. "Want to come with me?"

"Don't ask me that. Ask me if I can."

"Can you come with me?"

Visible disappointment lined her face. "I can't: test tomorrow. I almost wish you hadn't come tonight—you've made me realize how much I miss you and it's only been three days!"

Montgomery longed to be by her side. "I miss you, too," he said with a great lump of a sob caught in his throat. He kissed her goodnight and watched her go into her building. He climbed into the van and looked at his sheet. The first delivery was for—Somerset Johns, third floor, quad F, room 4!

Montgomery reversed course and parked in front of the dorm. He found the envelope that was marked for Michael Raike. He shook it. He heard something slide, but it offered no hint about its nature. Montgomery raced into the building and pounded up the stairs. He ran down the hall to his quad.

"Hey, the monkey's here!" said Shorts.

"Hey y'all," greeted Montgomery.

"For someone living in the frat, you're always popping up here," said Cat.

"Just like a monkey," said Shorts. "When you least expect the critter, he's climbed up the wall and sitting in the window."

Montgomery laughed with his friends. "Actually, I have a delivery for Mick. Is he around?"

Dark looks were exchanged by the quadmates. "Monkey, Mick is in a Tou-chee mood. Be warned," Cat said.

Montgomery nodded, then knocked on the door to room four. A muffled sound of clattering utensils and books came through the door. Then the door swung open. Montgomery was shocked at the sight of Mick, who stared at him in a stupor. Montgomery offered him the package without a word. Similarly, Mick handed him an envelope. The two young men stared at each other for several minutes. Then Mick swung the door closed.

Montgomery turned to find his quadmates as speechless as he was. They heard the sound of paper tearing in Mick's room. "Right, right, good stuff" could be heard in combination with snuffling sounds. Without warning, loud music blasted from the room. Then Mick emerged into the common room.

"Thanks, Monkey; thanks, guys," he said. He had changed into gym shorts, no shirt and headed for the bathroom. Then the quadmates heard the sound of hot water being drawn for a shave.

"A man of many moods," said Shorts. "First anger, then depression, now happy. Go figure."

"I'd like to know what's in these packages I'm delivering," said Montgomery.

Cat slowly drew in his breath with an audible noise. "Be careful, Monkey. Curiosity killed the cat."

"That's the second time today I've heard that."

"All I'm saying is that those guys might not want you to know, and you don't want them to know you're asking questions. They hurt you before; so you know they'll hurt you again. That's all I'm saying."

"All I'm saying," said Red, "is that the less delivering you do, the better off you are."

Caveman ended the conversation by saying, "All I'm saying is that you might want to practice looking dumb if the cops start asking questions. Works for me."

Red looked at his roommate. "All you're saying? That's more than you've said in a week!"

The boys laughed. Montgomery grinned, thanked his friends and returned to his work.

The rest of the night passed in a blur. Montgomery went up steps, down steps, in and out of apartments, buzzed himself in, saw himself out, looked at neat and dirty homes, surprised cats, dueled with dogs, watched the mass of packages dwindle, amassed a large stack of envelopes and cash, and found no more clues to the contents of the packages. At 11:30 p.m. he made the last of his deliveries, and pocketed the last C.O.D. payment. He left the home of a self-proclaimed performance artist who thanked him and invited him to the next performance. Montgomery politely declined.

Montgomery wearily drove the van back to the frat house. After parking in its assigned spot, he took the box with the envelopes and cash into the house. Rip was waiting for him. "It had better all be there," he said with a look that betrayed his hope that it wasn't.

Montgomery yawned. "I'm not a thief," he said with a little too much emphasis on the pronoun.

Rip flushed, and turned on his heel. Over his shoulder he called back, "I'm watching you, Mongrel. You won't last long. First mistake—you're toast."

Montgomery said nothing but stared him down as Rip went up the stairs and into one of the rooms reserved for the pledge committee. *All this over one stinking game of Space Explorers?*

Montgomery climbed the stairs and headed for the bedroom where he slept. The lights were out. He quietly entered the room and unrolled his sleeping bag, changing into his sleeping shorts. He was exhausted from making the rounds. He let his head sink into his pillow and closed his eyes.

"Montgomery? That you?" whispered Wilson.

Montgomery thought of something sarcastic to say, but thought better of it. "It's me."

"Glad you're back. Everything okay?"

Montgomery sat up. "Why wouldn't it be?"

"No reason. Just checking," Wilson said nervously.

"Wilson, what's going on? What's in those packages? Why does everyone pay upon receipt?"

"Don't ask questions."

Montgomery smothered a rising sense of contempt for Wilson. "What's so terrible that no one will talk about it?"

"Not in the house. Later."

"That's the second time today someone has said that. Good night, Wilson."

"I am glad you're sticking it out. We need your kind in the house." Montgomery snorted what he hoped was an inaudible snort. *What we don't need is a wimp like you.*

Chapter Eight

Block Party

AS SATURDAY DAWNED, work details moved over the house and grounds preparing everything for the party that would ensue that night. Outside, the pledges were connecting soda cans to fountain spigots; a large crew assembled the bandstand on the street corner. The party committee drilled the pledges continuously in party procedures. Montgomery was keeping the refreshment stands supplied with fresh cans of coke and fizz. Travis was working crowd control.

Acrid, sweet, pungent smoke began to fill the house several hours before the party officially began. "I thought we were supposed to stay clean and sober," remarked Montgomery.

Travis giggled, "When in Rome ..."

Montgomery looked at him sharply. He prayed that Travis had not succumbed.

Travis grinned. "I'm messing with your mind, dude. Although if it's true a body can catch a secondary high, this is the place to do it. The exhaust is so thick upstairs it's hanging twelve inches off the ceiling."

Wilson came storming down the stairs. "I can't believe it. Those guys know how important it is to be sober for the party. One of these days they'll go too far and the house will wind up on probation."

"Don't get your panties in a knot," Travis said disdainfully. "No one can tell in the dark."

Wilson tried not to show his relief. "It's still not right. They set a bad example for the pledges."

"You're the president of the frat," Travis retorted. "Tell them to stop. Isn't using drugs a rules violation? Order them to cease, or bring them up on charges."

A tic tugged at Wilson's left eye. "I can't do that, don't you see? There's a delicate balance in the frat between us and them. I might lose my office—I don't have enough support to make charges stick. Not to mention the nasty tricks they might do to me."

"Try resigning in protest. Take a stand. Have some integrity."

Wilson pulled himself up. "That's easy for a freshman to say. But when you get to be a junior, you have prospects and need background for your resume. I can't give up being president—it looks too good.

"It's not an issue of integrity, but tolerance. Tolerance is vital in today's society; we can't afford not to have it. I tolerate them, and they tolerate me."

Montgomery spoke impulsively, "So why are you complaining? If you're being tolerant, that is." Travis burst out laughing.

Wilson frowned at Travis. "You're a pledge, aren't you? You can't speak to me like this. How would you like a round on the shock machine? I can use it too."

Travis walked over to Wilson and looked him straight in the eyes. "I'd like to see you try." He walked out of the room.

"Who is that guy?"

Montgomery felt a twinge of anticipatory conscience in his gut as he said, "I don't know. They never introduced us, and they keep us apart."

"You're a bad liar, Montgomery. I'm not incompetent."

Montgomery later confided in Travis that the irony of Wilson's statement must have been lost in the pungent smoke because it entirely escaped Wilson's notice.

By eight o'clock the streets had filled with students anticipating the concert from the highly popular band, *Whale's End*. Travis was in the street, wearing a bright orange armband and carrying a portable radio. Already he had to send two drunken sophomores away.

Montgomery was busy hauling cans of soda and fizz to the stands. The crowd was thirsty, despite the fact that darkness had fallen and the heat of the day had dissipated. Montgomery was sweating and his clothes were soaked. He was wearing a bright lime green armband.

The pledge committee was surveying the crowd from its perch on the roof. They had indulged in the mood enhancement activity of the afternoon and were in high spirits. Cody worked his radio, giving instructions to the brothers and pledges in the crowd.

Loud, metallic chords split the buzz of voices in the air. The band launched into their first set. Travis did a little happy dance in the crowd as he thought, *Great party.* People around him laughed and joined in.

By nine o'clock, Montgomery had already hauled fifty cans of soda and fizz to the various refreshment stands. He estimated that the crowd exceeded a couple thousand. The frat was charging a dollar for a twenty-ounce cup. He took a break and helped himself to a Coke.

"Hey, lover!" called a familiar voice. Elizabeth, Park, Rose and Rick were standing in a group a few feet away.

"We've been looking for you," Elizabeth added.

Montgomery walked over and gave her a long kiss.

"We came to check it out," said Rick. "How's it going?"

"Busy. We're going through Coke cans like diarrhea and toilet paper." Because of the darkness, he missed the strange looks crossing the faces of his friends.

"What's with them?" Rose asked, pointing to a group of eight who were rubbing one another's' shoulders and backs, arms and legs, and chests.

"Ecstasy," replied Rick. "So much for the feared crowd control security at the S.O.B. Block Party." Rose looked puzzled. Rick explained, "It's a drug. It makes their skin extremely sensitive to touch. The rubbing produces pleasurable feelings. All-night raves are notorious for Ecstasy use."

"Why doesn't the fraternity eject them from the party?" asked Park.

Montgomery shrugged. "It's their idea of a good time."

"Have you seen Travis?" asked Park.

"Not since the band started. Look for an orange armband. My break's over—see y'all later." He hurried off.

The three girls and Rick began to move around to find Travis. The music played on. Travis was in the back breaking up a fight between two boys who were hitting on the same girl. Travis sent both of them off the premises. Then he turned around to see another drunken boy relieving himself against the fence. "Hey!" the boy yelled as Travis grabbed him and hauled him out of the yard. "I'm not done yet—" People laughed as the boy's efforts to stop his stream were in vain, and he was spraying his lower legs and shoes as well as the ground around him. Travis took him to the barricade and told him to take off. The boy was finally able to zip his shorts before dashing down the street.

Travis' radio crackled. "That was hilarious," laughed Cody. "Keep up the good work. Come on up when you need a break."

Travis consulted his watch. *Now is as good a time as any.* He made his way through the crowd, nodded at the brothers hanging around the door, and went inside. "Anybody know where Cody is?"

"Upstairs, second floor roof."

Travis made his way up the stairs, and walked around the hallways until he saw an open window. He slipped his body through the window, and landed on a flat roof. He moved around the corner where he saw the committee of Cody, Rip, Jack, Brendon and Pete plus half a dozen other boys seated and watching the party.

"Good command headquarters," Travis remarked as he greeted the guys.

"Travis, welcome to the observation post," Cody smiled and extended his hand. Travis shook it.

"This spot is perfect for watching the crowd," Travis said. "You must see everything from up here."

Jack winked at Travis. "That's right—everything."

The others laughed. Pete pointed to a window three feet away. "Feast your eyes on this," he snickered.

Travis looked where Pete was pointing. It was a brightly lit bathroom in the house. As he stared, the hall door opened and a female walked into the bathroom. She shut the door, and lowered her shorts before sitting on the toilet. The boys laughed uproariously.

"The window's soundproof so they can't hear us," chortled Jack. "Great set-up."

Travis stood there blinking his eyes with his attention riveted upon the seated form. With a great effort he wrenched his head to the side to avert his gaze. "Whoa."

The other boys slapped hands and grinned.

"Welcome to our world," said Cody. "It's a privileged place that only a few can attain."

"You watch girls going to the bathroom all night?" asked Travis in disbelief.

The other boys laughed in response.

Travis sat down. He watched the crowd as he tried to assimilate this new information into his brain. Out of nowhere he heard a soft voice whispering into his ear, but from inside his head, "Depravity."

Travis then saw the girls, and Rick, at one of the refreshment stands.

"Thanks for the tip, y'all," he said quickly. "I need to get back."

"Come whenever you would like some entertainment," said Cody. "You're one of us."

Travis put a big smile on his face, and put out his hand. Cody shook it. Travis left the roof wishing he could talk Montgomery into leaving this place.

Down in the crowd, he greeted the girls and Rick. "I'm on security detail. I bounce the drunks and others to keep the party clean and safe."

"You have a lot of work, then," said Rick. "Drunkenness is common, and many of your attendees are using Ecstasy. Look." Rick pointed out several groups who were rubbing bodies in the telltale manner.

Travis pulled out his radio, and asked Cody for instructions. "Leave them alone unless they get rowdy. If they do, watch out because they can become violent with the strength of ten."

"I can handle it. Ten-four."

"Some party," said Rick.

"Great band, good concept; a little sloppy in the execution with an undercurrent of ... *what was that word?* ... depravity."

"I wouldn't go that far."

"That's because you're not on the roof watching girls go to the bathroom."

Squeals of disgust burst from the girls.

"Okay, I would go that far," Rick said.

"Oh you would, would you?" said a mockingly indignant Rose.

Rick colored. "You know what I meant."

Rose gave him a playful smack.

The others laughed, and the sour mood lifted.

Travis left the group to check on a report of a drunken fight on the back patio.

The girls and Rick decided to leave. Montgomery saw them going, came over and asked if the girls wanted to use the bathroom before they left. All four made gagging motions by opening their mouths, putting their index fingers in and making vomiting noises. Montgomery, baffled, stared stupidly at their retreating backs.

The crowd continued to grow larger as the night progressed. By eleven o'clock, the crowd was packed so tight that one could move around only with difficulty. The party had spilled beyond the barricades and across the entire section of fraternity houses known as "Little Greece." It did not matter: the band was so loud they could be heard across the entire campus. By 11:30, Travis had given up trying to perform any more security. He could not get through the crowd, and the area to cover was too large, anyway.

Similarly, by midnight Montgomery gave up fighting through the crowd to keep the stands replenished with fresh cans of soda and fizz. No one could reach the stands, anyway, to buy additional Cokes. Montgomery found his way back into the house, and went to the front room to flop on a sofa and rest. A few minutes later, Travis found him and flopped down beside him.

"Great party," said Travis.

"If you're not hauling fifty pound cans of coke all night," said a tired Montgomery.

Travis laughed. "You do get the mule jobs."

"Tell me about it. If this keeps up, I won't need to use Shorts' weights. The girls and Rick left early. It was weird: I asked if the girls wanted to use the bathroom before they went, and all four reacted by pretending to vomit."

Travis did not laugh. He leaned over and spoke so only Montgomery could hear him explaining about the private peep show on the roof. Montgomery was disgusted.

"You want anything from the kitchen?" he asked.

"Sure. What do you have?"

"Fried chicken, chips and Coke. The best thing about working kitchen detail is knowing where the leftovers are." In the kitchen, Montgomery filled a tray with food, drink and ice-filled glasses. He balanced the tray on one hand as he opened the door to the front room.

Travis eyed the tray hungrily. "If the astronomy doesn't work out, you can always work as a waiter."

"Chow down, buddy, you've earned it." As the boys began to eat, they swapped stories of what they had seen over the previous four hours of the party. Soon they were laughing, and the stories grew more outrageous as they fluffed and invented to top each other's tales. They were still at it when the band played its last encore.

Most of the crowd remained, clapping their hands for more music and calling out favorite songs. Cody's voice came from the roof announcing that the party was over and requesting that the crowd break up. The students remained for an additional half an hour, but when they saw that the band was not going to play, they began to leave. Police were arriving, and their increasing presence chased the stragglers off the streets. By 2:00 a.m. calm had been restored.

The pledges were given the job of dismantling the stands, storing the parts, and policing the area for litter. They groaned, but set to work. It took a couple of hours to dismantle everything and carry it to storage. Another three hours was spent clearing the area of trash. A huge rented dumpster was filled to overflowing as the sun rose over Bacon. But the grounds and block were clean. The only signs remaining of the party were the bags of trash and the Port-O-Potties, which would be hauled off Monday.

Montgomery went upstairs to take a shower and get cleaned up. When he was finished, he laid down for a nap before church. He awoke at 3 p.m. A stab of guilt went through him.

Travis had slipped off the grounds and gone back to his room to sleep. He planned to meet Park later and spend the day with her.

The pledge committee met at dawn to discuss the party and the potential of their pledges. "Great party," enthused Pete. "We outdid ourselves."

"Did you see the way Travis marched that peeing kid off the property?" Cody laughed. "Travis didn't allow him to finish or zip it; he marched him off with the kid hold his wiener and wetting himself. We've got to pry him away from Mongrel."

"We have a good start," said Jack. "His eyes popped out when he took a good look at the bathroom window. He really is our kind of man at heart; a little encouragement, and he'll be a good lieutenant."

"Do not underestimate the hold Mongrel has over him," cautioned Brendon. "Their Moms took turns nursing them; they drank their milk side by side. That's a hard bond to break."

"But they are nothing like each other," protested Pete. "Travis is shallow: he looks for the next thrill, the next party, the next girl; he has no other interests except for the next wave. Mongrel is deep: head in the stars, philosophical, tradition-bound, spiritual-minded. The way to split them is to snare the one with activities that will repulse the other. Make them think they're different from each other; make them question what makes them friends."

"Good analysis," said Cody. "Who's supervising brother for Travis?"

"I am," said Brendon.

"Work with Pete—that's your assignment between now and mid-November. We want Travis solidly in our fold by the time we put him in the house," said Cody.

"I'll take care of Mongrel," growled Rip.

Cody took his time in replying. "Right, but do it smart: not too violent, not in the house, nothing public. His family wields great clout in the frat. Don't expose us to an investigation, Rip. I mean that." Cody stared hard into the eyes of Rip.

"So who makes it, and who bites the dust?" asked Jack.

"Alpha, Eta and Iota are clearly ins," said Cody. "They did well on their rounds, and really believe in the garbage we fed their minds about the Greek honor code. Zeta and Gamma are possibles: we'll have to see how well they do over the next few weeks. Beta and Theta are zeroes: I don't see how they tie their shoes. Delta, Epsilon and Kappa have latent tendencies to be moralists—according to their psychologicals—so we're well rid of them."

"Do we tell them now?" asked Jack.

"No, we want them to do more work for us first."

The group laughed together.

Pete said, "We have two remaining problems: recruitment for the Spring rush and the stubbornness of the Mongrel in refusing to quit."

Rip snapped, "I said I'd take care of him."

Pete calmly replied, "So you shall. But he's tough; he doesn't give up. Otherwise we'd be rid of him now. We need a second plan, or are we going to take him into the house if he sticks it out?"

"We can't take him into the house. Eventually he'll be a formidable adversary—not like that dolt Wilson. But we can't drop him either. He has to quit on his own. We have no choice but to continue him as a pledge," Cody thought out loud.

"Continue him," interrupted Jack. "Can we do that?"

"Nothing says we can't. We tell him he's not ready to join, but he has potential. We say we're carrying him over as a pledge to the spring semester."

Pete started laughing. "Brilliant! We can give him tasks to complete in preparation for membership."

"I like that idea! He's young, inexperienced and idealistic: that makes him vulnerable to everything we can do to him. We'll destroy his self-image and his confidence by attacking all the areas of his life," enthused Cody.

"First, we tell him he doesn't understand the honor code and he must take a class in moral philosophy with Hinson—Hinson hates moralism," suggested Jack.

"Make him prove his devotion and fitness to the service ideals by making him volunteer in a hospital—say eighty hours," offered Pete.

"Good one," approved Cody.

"How about we make him take counseling afterward," offered Brendon. "To integrate his experience with our concerns about his character and mental deficiencies."

"That will cook his goose," sneered Pete. "How about making him take personal pointers for his social life from one of our leading party men who can get him high?"

"No good," said Cody. "He's too strong for that. But we could hit him about dating women—set him up with some real nutcrackers. Call it a course in interpersonal relations."

"What have we got so far?" asked Pete.

"Class in moral philosophy, community service in hospital, counseling, and interpersonal relations course," repeated Brendon.

"That's good for a start," said Cody.

"Why don't we do the other pledges this way?" asked Pete. "Why drop five pledges and lose their labor cooking, cleaning,and such? Let's carry over all the pledges we don't want so they can keep doing our work for the rest of this semester and the start of next. Let's use the losers to do the work until we have more losers to take their place."

All five men broke into laughter. The meeting over, Rip left in search of Janet. Brendon and Pete headed back to their room in search of sleep. Cody and Jack went downstairs in search of breakfast.

Chapter Nine

K.P. Forever

MONTGOMERY ASSUMED A FAMILIAR POSITION, and picked up a potato. Holding it in his left hand, he applied the potato peeler to the skin. He carefully separated the peel from the tuber with a careful stroke of even pressure as he turned the potato to strip the peel. Montgomery amused himself by seeing how long he could make the strip before it broke off.

Travis strolled in. "On kitchen duty again?"

"Again? When have I been off kitchen duty?"

"Our assignments have become permanent. All I do anymore is run courier errands."

"All I do is peel potatoes."

"Better potatoes than laundry. They assigned Beta to laundry. The dummy washed the colors in hot water with a generous dose of bleach to brighten the colors. The colors brightened all right: now everyone has a rainbow shirt. He did the same thing to a load of blue jeans: it took the blue dye out of the pants which would have been okay except he threw in a few white t-shirts that did not make the last load of whites. The last I heard, they were talking about nailing him to a fence and bleaching him."

"That's not funny. These characters are likely to do it if they think of it."

"I'm not being funny. I've become the confidant of Torquemada and his Inquisition."

The amusement in Montgomery's eyes failed to hide his astonishment. "How do you know about that?"

Travis put on an innocent expression. "Oddest thing in the world. I'm learning something in class."

Gravy bustled into the kitchen. "You're here today," he said to Travis. "We can use the help. Come over here and wash the lettuce. Then fix a huge tossed salad."

Travis came to the sink, turned on the water, and began rinsing the leaves under the water to remove sand and grit as well as tearing off bruised or damaged pieces. Montgomery marveled: *he's helping; before now, he would have left if he didn't have to do it. Travis is changing, and for the better.*

Alpha came in and put on a chef's apron. He prepared to knead the dough and roll out biscuits. "Did everyone recover from the party? I slept until my eight o'clock on Monday."

Montgomery picked up another potato. "I zonked out until three Sunday afternoon. Then I was awake but not aware. I think I went out again about 8 p.m. By the way, I hate those letter names. My name is Montgomery—Montgomery Lee."

Alpha pressed his lips together, but said nothing. Montgomery colored, and returned his attention to the potato. Travis leaned in Montgomery's direction and said, "What a jerk." Montgomery nodded.

As the dinner hour approached, the kitchen became busier. Travis finished the salad, put it into serving bowls and headed upstairs to clean up. Montgomery boiled the potatoes, and then drained them before mashing them and adding milk and butter. Alpha was baking the dinner rolls, and turning them into warming baskets as they came out of the oven. Gravy supervised the production, and tended to the roasting of the pork shoulders.

Dinner was carried into the dining room, which was filled with all the brothers. Conversation was lively and animated after the brothers had heard much praise for the party throughout the campus.

Dessert was chocolate cake. After the brothers finished eating, they scraped their chairs back and headed for their evening pursuits. Montgomery rose to his feet, and headed for the stairs. "Hey,

Montgomery! Come in here for a minute." A voice had come from a small room behind the stairs.

Montgomery walked around. In the room, Alpha, Eta and Iota were gathered around a small table. As he entered the small alcove, Alpha looked up with a friendly grin but malice in his eye. "Strawberry fields: lick the paper."

Montgomery's skin crawled. "No thanks, I'm full from dinner." He backed out of the room, and closed the door as the three wickedly laughed. Montgomery watched through the small window as the three pledges licked their papers.

Montgomery ran up the stairs. He grabbed his notes on Western Civilization, but before he could leave, Cody blocked the doorway. "Why aren't you with the other pledges?"

Montgomery stalled. "Which pledges?"

"We're expanding in your minds in small groups."

"The university expands my mind."

"What we do is more basic."

Montgomery was silent.

Cody maintained his gaze. "Go downstairs to the others. They know what to do."

"If you mean the fools who are under the stairs dropping acid, no thanks. I have a test to study for."

"What we do here is more important than tests. Go downstairs."

"I don't do drugs. I won't do drugs. You go down and join them."

"We can't understand why you hold yourself apart as if you're superior to us. What makes you think you're so hot—because your last name is Lee?"

"Who died and made you king?" Montgomery was beginning to get angry.

"This is your last warning. Play ball."

"As soon as the field is legal."

Cody disappeared. Montgomery moved toward the door, then stopped. *After all I've seen and experienced—it's time to use the back gate.* He went to the window and opened it, climbing onto the roof. He moved around to the side of the house—the grounds were vacant and the way clear. He stuffed his shirt into his shorts, then stuffed his notebook into his shirt. He cautiously hooked his feet over the edge and into the vines growing on the wall. His weight holding, he climbed to the ground and scanned the perimeter. Still seeing no one, he moved surreptitiously to the wall that was screened by vegetation. He opened the gate, and slipped onto the street.

Montgomery made for the athletic building. He went inside and hurried through the corridors. Emerging into the gym, he crossed the floor to exit the building on the far side. Unobservable from the windows of the fraternity house, he made his way across the street and headed through the faculty housing, across the main campus, and caught the bus to residential housing. Soon he had rung Elizabeth's room, and was sitting with her and her roommates.

Elizabeth's eyes opened wide as Montgomery told about being ordered to take a hit of LSD with the three other pledges. "I knew something was up when the pledge Alpha used my name when he had cut me in the kitchen when we were preparing dinner."

"Cut you?" asked Rose.

"Yeah. I told him what my real name was, and he ignored me."

"So friendly," Park remarked sarcastically.

"Check. It's really stupid. They call everyone according to a Greek letter; everyone, that is, except me. They call me Mongrel. It's supposed to be a bad insult to make me mad."

"What letter would you have been?" asked Rose.

"Mu."

Elizabeth burst out laughing. "You got the better end, Mr. Mongrel. Mu like the sound a cow makes? Mongrel is much better than moo. Moooooo—" she imitated a cow lowing.

"Why do they call y'all pledges by letters?" asked Park.

"It's psychological. It leaves us as less than full persons in the organization. It reminds us that we don't belong yet. Our presence is being suffered in their magnanimous gesture of allowing us to be among them while they decide whether we make the grade—a decision that is entirely subjective."

"I don't understand why you bother," said Park. "Who cares? Who needs them?"

"Frats used to be campus leaders. They set an example of becoming a productive member of society: in academics, athletics, service, economy and character. They have fallen away from their purpose; first they degenerated into social organizations and now they are falling to the bottom: the frivolous, the climbers, the barbaric, the losers. The reason I bother is to start a renewal movement to return the fraternity to its original ideals, and to reform the membership to live by those ideals. The ideals are badly corrupted: many do not believe in them, some openly ridicule them, others pay them no mind. But it's important. Campuses are much the poorer without the ideals informing their lives and characters. I want to see that reversed."

"That's not why Travis is there," said Park.

"He's there because of me. But he hates the place and the people."

"What about you?" queried Rose. "Do you hate the place and the people?"

"The place is the people. The building itself is innocuous. I don't like the pledge committee: they're mean and rude. They're the ones who have ruined the fraternity. I haven't met most of the other brothers: I refuse to form an opinion that damns them solely for their association, although they do allow the pledge committee to hold power. Most are confused or unaware. Or they're still terrified from their pledge days and won't confront them. Wilson I don't respect: he's a weenie. He lets them do what they want because he fears them. He pretends that everything is okay when he knows it isn't. He does nothing except what they allow him to do. He justifies this in his mind by saying it's an even trade."

"What does he get out of the trade?" broke in Park.

"He puts president of the S.O.B.'s on his resume," answered Montgomery. They all laughed together.

Rose signaled Park, and the two of them rose. "We need to do some work in the library," said Park. The two girls left the room.

"That was obvious," said Montgomery.

"Who cares?" replied Elizabeth. "The frat uses up your time. I am glad we're alone together."

"Me, too," affirmed Montgomery. He leaned over and kissed her gently. "What were the five Greek dialects in the classical period?"

Elizabeth moved through her notes. "Attic, Doric, Ionic, Thessalonic, and Corinthian. What two city-states fought the Peloponnesian Wars?"

"Sparta and Athens. Sparta won. What two victories by Athens shut the Persians out of Greece?"

"Marathon and Salamis. Which Greek philosopher was sentenced to death as a traitor for his method of questioning everything around him?"

"Socrates. His pupil was Plato, who in turn was the mentor of Aristotle. Whose philosophy guided Western Civilization for one thousand years, and whose philosophy replaced him?"

"Plato's ideas were ascendant until the Crusaders returned from the Holy Land with Aristotle. Aristotle's ideas were the foundation of the Scholastic Movement. Let's run through the major schools of Greek philosophy."

The couple continued going over outlines, notes, reading summaries and sample questions. Time moved along. They finally grew weary, and had confidence that they had a mastery of the knowledge on which they would be tested. They lay down on Elizabeth's bed—Elizabeth in Montgomery's arms. The lateness of the hour caught up with them both, and they fell asleep.

Around midnight, Rose and Park returned to their room. Park motioned for them to be quiet, and pointed at the couple sleeping in each other's arms. Rose pulled a blanket from her closet, and spread it over the two. Then the two girls prepared for bed themselves, and turned the lights out.

Sometime in the middle of the night, Montgomery awoke. It took him several minutes to realize where he was. He regarded the sleeping form of Elizabeth. *It's a sweet thing to have the one I love sleeping next to me. But I have to return to the frat house.* He slipped out of Elizabeth's arms, and off the bed. He lightly kissed her, and silently left the room.

Montgomery jogged through the night air. As he neared the frat house, he felt an impulse—an urge—not to use the back gate or the front entrance. He slipped around to the side, and entered from the gate facing Little Greece. He remained in the shadows until he could see everything in the yard. Since no one was waiting for him, he entered the side door.

Montgomery started up the hall. A hand reached out from an open door, grabbed his shirt, and yanked him inside. A strong hand was clapped over his mouth. "It's me—Travis" identified his assailant in a hoarse whisper. Travis let go, and Montgomery turned around.

"Where have you been?" asked Travis.

"At the girls' place studying with Elizabeth. Why?"

"They looked for you all night. They wanted to use the machine again. They're so upset they've forgotten about Beta ruining the laundry. Good for him; bad for you. What did you do to them?"

"The Alphabets dropped acid tonight. They were in the alcove behind the stairs. I was supposed to join them but I refused. These guys don't know the difference between appropriate and inappropriate hazing. Travis, we have to draw the boundaries, or else we'll be ruined beyond repair."

"Why would they insist on pledges drugging?"

"Per Cody, to expand our minds in a basic way."

Travis thought for several minutes. "Be careful of what you eat and drink. Make sure you know who prepared it and who had access to it before it came to you. I was at a party once where they offered me LSD. I turned it down. That stuff is nasty. It wreaks havoc on the brain—makes changes in personality that could be permanent. Sometimes a person goes crazy; it depends on how one's system reacts to it. It wasn't worth the risk."

"What are they looking for?"

"People who have used acid talk about being opened in their mind and spirit: new ways of seeing things, new understandings, losing fears and inhibitions—things scramble like hearing pictures or seeing sounds. Many think using acid is a spiritual experience—that it opens them to the invisible world around us. Some say that they've seen God or talked to Jesus."

"Sounds like they encountered demons."

"I wouldn't know," Travis tittered. "I'm not religious."

"So the pledges will feel 'opened'—more ready to go along with Cody's program which seems to involve ready access to drugs and sex." Montgomery pondered a few moments. "What Cody has done is to change an institution of culture to one of counter-culture. The next question is why."

"Let it go, Dick Tracy. We have more immediate problems to worry about—like how to get you to Wilson's room before dawn and how to deflect the punishment they plan to inflict."

"Are they still looking for me?"

"They've set a trap in the hall."

"Can I use the back stairs?"

"No, they have a trap there also."

"I used the window to leave."

"That's how you evaded them."

"Why don't I sleep down here?"

"That would give them a legal infraction of procedure to justify punishment. We have to get you upstairs."

"We need a diversion. How about a rock through KA's window courtesy of S.O.B.?"

"You're onto something. But I think an old-fashioned tug on the fire alarm is much more effective; it doesn't involve outsiders. Where did you say the Alphabets were tripping?"

"The alcove behind the stairs. What are you going to do?"

"Smoke a cigar—a big, fat, stinking, cheap stogy that some pledge lit up while tripping and jammed against a heat detector. You get ready to mix in the crowd that rumbles down the stairs. By the time everything is sorted out, you've turned up, all the brothers are around so Cody's boys can't touch you, everyone goes back to bed mad at the pledges who are still flying along and wondering what the stink is about—in more ways than one."

"Check. Thanks, Travis."

"Travis 2, Montgomery 10,004. Here I go."

Montgomery waited a few minutes, then slipped into the front room and crouched behind a sofa. He heard the alcove door open and the sound of a match being lit. Soon the stench of an exceptionally poor cigar was filling the downstairs. The door closed. A few more minutes went by. Montgomery was beginning to tense when a loud horn sounded throughout the house. In ten seconds, boys were stumbling down the stairs, cursing and asking where the fire was.

Montgomery mingled in the crowd that gathered in the front street. In the distance, the firehouse sounded its summons, and the first truck was heard pulling into the street and heading toward the frat. Wilson was running around screaming that the house was burning down. Cody, Jack and Pete stood in a little group watching the proceedings. The trucks arrived and the firemen entered the house to determine the extent of the blaze. In the midst of the confusion, no one saw Rip bring Janet out the side door and escort her to the street.

The fire captain came out of the house, and asked who was in charge. Wilson pompously strode up. "I'm the president of the house."

"Come with me," the captain ordered. The two men entered the house. The loud sounds of an angry captain lecturing a defensive Wilson were heard on the street.

Travis came over to Montgomery. "What's he saying?"

"Near as I can make out, he is citing the house for improper handling of smoking materials—"

"The cigar," whispered Travis.

Montgomery nodded. "— failure of the residents to evacuate completely upon the sounding of the fire alarm—"

"The Alphabets."

Montgomery nodded again. "— failure to maintain fire extinguishers at full strength—"

Travis looked blank. Montgomery shrugged his shoulders, "Maybe he checked while he was in there. He's ordering a full inspection to be conducted as soon as possible, and he wants the building capacity checked. The house might be over its occupancy limit with the pledges sleeping on the floor. Let's volunteer to reduce the overcapacity and go home."

"Excellent idea. But if they know you want to go, they'll make you stay."

The fire truck had stowed its equipment and was pulling away. The captain was writing his report and made Wilson sign it. The boys began to enter the house and go back to bed. Cody came over and conferred with Wilson.

Montgomery and Travis couldn't hear the conference, but caught the gist that the three boys who did not evacuate the building were acting strangely, in the Captain's opinion. Montgomery and Travis went inside and up the stairs.

Montgomery rolled out his sleeping bag, pulled off his shoes and shirt, and slid into the bag before anyone else returned to the room. He closed his eyes and feigned sleep.

Wilson came into the room with his roommates a few minutes later. "Here he is," said Wilson. He kicked Montgomery's body. "Ouch! What is it?" ejected Montgomery in a grouchy voice.

"Where have you been?" demanded Wilson.

"Studying for a test," replied Montgomery, adding to his performance by squinting in the light, stretching his arms and yawning.

"When did you get back?"

"Sometime after midnight—I don't know the exact hour." Montgomery hated dissembling through answers that, while true, were so vague as to deceive.

"Were you here when the alarm went off?"

"Yes, I left with the others." Montgomery was working hard on maintaining a poker face.

"Why didn't I see you?" snapped Wilson.

"I can't answer for your eyesight," said Montgomery, feeling pity and contempt for Wilson at the same time. "The alarm went off, and I was out the door. I must have moved too fast for you, and because my bag was out of your way, you assumed I wasn't here." Montgomery chose his words carefully so as not to tell a straight lie.

"I'm not satisfied," grumbled Wilson.

"Give it up, Wilson," snapped his roommate. "He's a big boy. He can miss curfew if he wants."

"You don't understand," said Wilson.

"Yes, I do," retorted the roommate. "You're scared of Cody. Montgomery can handle himself—leave him be. Stop being a panty-waist: as long as you let Cody jerk your strings, Cody's not going to touch you. Now shut up and go back to bed." The roommate muttered a few curses concerning Wilson.

Montgomery had already closed his eyes pretending to have fallen asleep. *Thank you, God, for the intervention of Travis and now this roommate. I need to become better acquainted with this roommate.*

Montgomery decided to make a quick exit in the morning. He helped prepare breakfast, wolfed down a couple pieces of toast and marmalade, and drank a glass of orange juice. He popped out the back door, strode around front and was out the gate before anyone had done more than sit down in the dining room.

Travis checked the alcove on his way to the dining room. The three pledges were lying on the floor with their feet up on the wall. They had vacant stares and open mouths. Travis watched long enough to see that they were still breathing.

"Y'all come home yet?" Travis asked. There was no response. Travis went to breakfast.

"Wilson," snapped an irritated Cody, "where is that cursed pledge of yours?"

"Cody," snapped an equally irritated Wilson, "why were—are three pledges tripping in the alcove?"

"Very good, Wilson," sneered Cody. "We thought you didn't know the signs."

"I interrogated my pledge last night. He went out to study for a test. He came back after midnight and was asleep in my room when the alarm went off. There's nothing there you can quarrel with."

"The Mongrel disobeyed a direct order. That calls for severe discipline."

"Academics override orders. You know that."

"I decide what overrides orders and what does not."

"Go easy on him," said Wilson.

Travis spit a mouthful of toast onto his plate.

Rip laughed hilariously.

"We won't use the machine," said Cody.

Rip laughed harder.

Wilson looked relieved.

After their afternoon exam, Montgomery and Elizabeth repaired to the Student Center to share a coke and fries. Then they went to the lounge and shot pool for a couple hours. Montgomery showed Elizabeth how to make angle shots and carom shots. When they were through, Montgomery walked Elizabeth back to her dorm.

"I'd like to stay," he said, "but I have to help with dinner. Tomorrow they have something planned for Friday night so I can't come then, either. Saturday's the football game with the frat—I'll try to call you early Saturday night if I can come then or Sunday."

Elizabeth closed her eyes and opened her lips. They exchanged a passionate kiss. Montgomery gave her a full body hug, holding her tightly against him.

"I love you so much," he choked. "You can't possibly know."

"I love you too," she murmured.

They broke apart, and Montgomery watched her receding form until she was no longer in sight. Then he caught the bus back to the main campus. Disembarking at the gym, he headed back to the house. As he came inside, he heard a low whistle. A bag was slipped over his head, and he was carried to the back part of the house. Montgomery had no idea where he was until they had stuffed him into a machine and removed the hood.

He saw Rip giving him an ugly sneer of triumph and then the world went upside down. Through the glass of the front door, he heard the muffled conversation: how much; fifteen minutes; more; half an hour. It took Montgomery many minutes to realize that he was inside a dryer. He was dizzy and nauseous. He would have vomited if the centrifugal force had not kept his stomach contents in place. His vision became double, treble and blurred. The long agony reached an end, and the drum came to a rest.

The perpetrators had left the laundry room. Montgomery kicked the door open and extricated himself. He stumbled to a trashcan and vomited. He collapsed on the floor—too dizzy to remain upright.

Montgomery laid on the floor for over an hour. When he could stand it, he sat up with his back supported by the dryer for another hour. Finally he stood, and wobbled around the room getting his bearings and his balance.

Montgomery left the laundry room, and walked to the front. It was dark outside. Brothers were in the front room watching television. The Alphabets had finished their adventure during the day and vacated the alcove. The dining room was empty. The kitchen was clear except for Gravy who was sitting at a small table working on menus.

"Hi," said Montgomery. He opened the refrigerator and pulled out a can of Coke.

"Have a seat," greeted Gravy, motioning to the chair across from him.

"Thanks."

"You were rolled," stated Gravy evenly.

Montgomery blinked his eyes.

"In the dryer. Better than being nailed to the fence—although they would not have done that—nothing in public, you see."

Montgomery grunted.

"My guess is that they left you in there for a long time—maybe thirty minutes."

"It seemed like thirty hours," gasped Montgomery.

"Sip that drink slowly. Give your body time to reset itself. You're a tough kid—maybe your body isn't sculpted and your muscles aren't hard, but you take what they dish out and then get back up. They can't stand that; it's driving them nuts. You're the hardest challenge this adulterated house has had since it first began going bad. Keep it up; you've got friends in here and I emphasize the plural and I don't include Pinhead Wilson."

Montgomery nervously laughed a little as he stared at Gravy in awe.

"I can't tell you more, but I can keep you in the kitchen." Gravy winked.

"Thanks," said Montgomery. "Thank you."

Montgomery went up the back stairs to Wilson's room. He booted Wilson's computer and logged into his campus e-mail account. There were a few messages from his quadmates about nothing in particular, and a couple of astronomy club notices. Montgomery kicked the floor. He regretted not being able to participate much in the club because the fraternity was using his free time. He shut the computer off.

Montgomery went to the top floor, and entered the fraternity's library. He perused the books that were available on the shelves. Most were old, worn and dirty—relics of an earlier time when the residents were more literary minded. The books included copies of the classics, philosophical works, beginning with Socrates and continuing through John Maynard Keynes and Bertrand Russell, major scientific treatises, scriptures from the world's religions, and histories of everything. The section on Greek culture was the largest: from Homer to studies done in the 1960's. The acquisitions seemed to have stopped during the 1970's. Montgomery could find no book after that time.

Montgomery looked at more books in the stacks. He was surprised to find mystical works by obscure authors, books on wizardry, alchemy treatises, magic books, witchcraft encyclopedias, fortunetelling systems, astrology interpretations, and books on animal sacrifice. He even found volumes related to major cults and secret societies in the United States.

Then Montgomery came across volumes about Sigma Omicron Beta. He pulled a history of S.O.B. off the shelf and sat down on a settee located beneath a window. He opened the book, and began to read.

Downstairs he could hear yelps and things clanging. Montgomery shuddered, and kept reading. Then came the sound of singing, a roar of voices ascending through old chimneys now covered over by the blessing of modern HVAC equipment. The song purported to be a war chant of the Cherokee. Montgomery was surprised to hear it since all things related to American Indians were off-limits according to the dictates of political correctness.

Montgomery looked at his watch. It was eleven p.m. He marked his place in the book and returned it to the shelf. He cautiously made his way downstairs and ran into Delta. "What's up?" Montgomery asked.

"Mohawks."

"Huh?"

"Mohawks. See? (He pointed to his head) You can't tell mine because I wear a buzz cut anyway. Every pledge ...Jack suddenly took inspiration and demanded all pledges be cut to a Mohawk." He tittered. "Reckon they are remaking us in their image."

Montgomery winced as the blasphemous remark boxed his ears. "Have they offered you LSD yet?"

"No, but I'll probably take it," the boy responded nervously.

"Why?"

"I want in. I'll do whatever it takes. How bad could it be? No one has died from it."

"Sometimes they do."

"That's for an overdose. It may even be fun—who knows? Maybe it'll give me what I'm missing—change me so I'm no longer a looker-on, make me more outgoing—a party guy like your friend Travis."

"But it's a crap shoot. If acid changes your personality, the direction of the change is unpredictable. There are better ways of becoming more outgoing than questionable use of drugs."

"I want in. Pete was right—you are a strait-laced killjoy. If you don't want fun in your life, fine—don't have any, but you have no right to say that the rest of us can't have fun. I want in, I'm getting in—why don't you leave? Go stay in a monastery where you'll be happy."

Montgomery continued down the stairs. Kappa was coming up, and Montgomery could see that his mop had been shaved into the Mohawk cut and generously gelled so it would stand up.

"What's up?" Montgomery asked.

"Can't you see?" the boy returned derisively. "Go down and get yours."

Montgomery came into the front room only to be grabbed and taken back to the pledge lounge. There he could see that Travis was getting the haircut. Travis gave him a thumb-up signal.

Then Montgomery was slapped into the chair. He heard the razor taking off his hair down to the scalp. It was over quickly. A couple dozen boys were in the room laughing uproariously. Then they broke into the fake Cherokee war song.

Montgomery looked into a mirror that had been hung to complete the humiliation. He laughed out loud. The others stopped singing. Montgomery laughed again. "Good one," he said to his barbers. "Do I get feathers too?"

He found Travis waiting for him in the hall. "They nailed all of us."

"That's the report I received," said a jubilant Montgomery.

"You're not mad?"

"Buddy, when you've been spun in a dryer for half an hour like I was earlier, a silly haircut's nothing."

"What happened?"

"My punishment for refusing to take the acid. All in all, I got off easy. I found out that they wouldn't nail someone to the fence—too public. Someone might see."

"You amaze me. What's your source—the stars?"

Montgomery laughed. "I don't know what I'm looking forward to more: Park's face when she sees my do, or when I tell her you have one, too."

Travis laughed. "Since you get to show Park, I'm tattling to Elizabeth."

Montgomery smiled mysteriously. "Maybe, maybe."

Friday was a day of deceptive peace. Dinner ran smoothly. Nothing out of the ordinary was said to the pledges. The Alphabets were still in an altered state of mind: joking with one another, sly winks at inside understandings, laughing at ordinary objects like they couldn't figure out what they were, and being absorbed into staring at bright colors. Montgomery figured it was a put-on; nobody would be affected that much by a single dose.

As dinner ended, there was no word on what the pledges should do. Montgomery figured he should stay in the house. Travis was itching to leave for the weekend and skip whatever ordeal the pledge committee had planned. "Remember," he told Montgomery, "I'm planning to bag it as soon as the in-house part is over."

"Check. I'm not ditching tonight's activity. I've found a hiding place where no one ever goes. I'll await the festivities there."

Travis went to change his clothes. The pledge committee was waiting for him. "We have a special place for you tonight," Cody told him. "Get dressed." He pointed to a black robe that looked like a monk's gown.

Travis pulled the robe on. It dropped to his ankles as he pushed his arms through the long sleeves. The cuffs hung halfway down his hands.

"Come along." Travis followed the other men into a small room. "Time to let go." Cody slid a small pill across the table to Travis.

"What is it?" Travis asked.

"Don't ask questions; swallow."

Travis put the pill into his mouth, but secreted it under his tongue. He took a mouthful of water and pretended to swallow the pill. The pledge committee also swallowed a pill.

"The rush will come in about thirty minutes," said Brendon. "This is way cool."

Travis smiled weakly. "Can I rest in the lounge?"

"Good idea. Wait there for us," replied Cody.

Travis left the room and quickly removed the pill from his mouth. He reached a decision: *I'm leaving the frat house tonight*. He went to his room and gathered his clothes, books and notebooks. He collected his personal items and stuffed them into his bag. *I wish I knew where Montgomery was to let him know that I'm leaving. This house and committee are more than I can handle. I want to lose myself in good times and parties, but without the aid of chemicals—no one's going to make me do otherwise. Whatever the fraternity's up to, it's not what a fraternity's for. Even if it has no other purpose than to create a social stratum for class conscious snoots, it should stick to having parties, not pushing drugs.*

Travis hustled down the stairs. A couple of brothers were sitting in the front room playing gin rummy. "Where are you going?" one asked him.

"Away."

"But the function tonight—"

"I'm out, I quit, I'm through," Travis interrupted. "Have an ecstatic time."

"But all pledges have to—you'll forfeit your chance."

"It's over!" Travis shouted. "You may need me, but I don't need you." He spun out the door.

The two men looked at one another in surprise. "Someone had better tell Cody," one said. Neither relished the prospect. "Let's play for it—loser tells," said the other. He dealt a new hand.

Montgomery had found his seat in the library and resumed reading the history of the fraternity. He had reached an interesting chapter on the 1950's when a boy with curly brown hair came into the room. Montgomery gave a start when the boy spoke.

"You've found the refuge. Don't fear—Cody and the gang don't know it's here and would avoid it like a leprosy asylum if they did."

Montgomery scrutinized his visitor. He was tall, about 6' 3", brown eyes, wiry and thin with muscle and sinew stretched across a medium frame, the type usually dubbed a beanpole. The boy sat down in a chair, and his limbs folded up like a surveyor's rule.

"My name is Rusty Mingon. I'm 19, a sophomore, majoring in Communication. Gravy said you'd be up here." *Gravy told me that I had friends in the house. How did he know that? He seems to know everything that goes on in the house.*

"Your friend left tonight. Packed his things; he's gone. Smart move on his part—he couldn't have withstood the pressure. They really thought they could turn him into one of them—a leader and instigator. But that takes too much drugging and other illegal activity.

"They're passing out ecstasy now. It's so you'll let go of your inhibitions. Then they'll have their 'red robe' ceremony. It's the first step of initiation. You don't need to know anything—repeat whatever they say. Oh, do I need to tell you not to take the E pill?"

Montgomery shook his head.

"Good. Gravy said you were smart. Now here's the key: as the ceremony goes on, they'll get more and more into their rush. They'll tune you out as they focus on their pleasures. When the loud music starts, I'll come forward and get you like I want to partner with you—nothing bad or sexual, E users like to touch and rub each other because it makes their skin extra-sensitive and pleasurably tingled by touch. Then we'll get out of there. They won't know we're gone."

"Sounds like a good plan."

"Most of the brothers are good boys seduced by the parties and good times that the pledge committee promises. As you've realized by now, the pledge committee is the real power in the house. They control everything. They seduce the brothers into drugs, then use their need to control them, and thus, the house."

"For want of a nail the kingdom is lost.".

"Cody and his gang believe that the drugs open them to alternative spiritual experiences, and it's a form of worship for them. What they're worshipping, I don't know, but it's not something to try. God has made himself available without drugs, through Jesus Christ, and I don't see how God would reveal himself to someone in a drugged state. One, the druggee is not in his created state, the one God intended for him, and two, the druggee is using drugs to approach God as he wants, not as God specifies. It's an attempt to reach God by human efforts, and therefore, must fail." Rusty drummed his fingers on a book.

"Do you know Jesus Christ as your Lord and Savior, Mr. Lee? Do you believe in your heart that he is risen from the dead?"

"I've been saved since I was a young boy, and Jesus is my risen Lord."

"Trust in his word. Whatever purpose he has for you to pledge this house, trust in him and his word. He'll never fail you nor forsake you."

"Thanks for saying that."

"I believe that Cody is guided by some type of illicit spiritual contact he makes when he's under the influence, especially acid."

"Are you talking about spiritual warfare?"

"Exactly."

"That's out of my league."

"Remember the power of prayer that is made in the name of Jesus."

"I'm amazed to find a Christian in the house."

"Every Paul needs his Barnabus. Go to your room, and get ready. As a pledge you'll wear a black robe. The brothers will be in red robes. We start around nine o'clock. With luck, we'll be out of there by ten."

The red robe ceremony began a short time later. In a darkened, interior room illuminated only by candlelight, the red-robed S.O.B. members chanted and performed different movements and formations. The pledges repeated what was said to them. Montgomery had a scare when the pledges were asked to drink shots of whiskey, remembering the warnings not to eat or drink anything that he could not account for as untampered, but the committee threw his portions into his face. An hour after the ceremony began, a red-robed member pulled him away. They receded into the shadows, and at an opportune moment, slipped out the door. The red robe indicated they should not talk.

Montgomery disrobed, and hugged his benefactor in gratitude. "You're free until tomorrow," Rusty whispered in his ear. "Go forth."

Montgomery took the hint, and left the fraternity house.

"Where's Travis?" The aggravated voice of Cody Spung was heard along the rows of the football stands. "First he disappears last night; now he's missing."

"You!" Cody pointed at Montgomery, "Come here."

Montgomery obediently made his way along the seats.

"Where's Travis?" Cody demanded.

"I don't know," Montgomery truthfully answered.

"He's your friend."

"The last I knew, he was with you. That was last night."

Cody scowled. "Beat it."

Montgomery took Cody at his word. He walked to the stadium exit and headed down the stairs. On the ground, though, he adjusted his course and walked around to where the girls were sitting. He ducked past the usher, and headed up to the top of the stands where the girls were sitting with Rick and Travis.

"Can you squeeze in one more?"

Elizabeth started with delight. "Always."

"Hey, Travis," greeted Montgomery. "Cody's looking for you."

"I hope for his sake he does not find me. Sorry, but I've had it. Last night was the kicker. I left, and I'm not going back."

"It's okay. I'm finding that I have some unknown friends in the house. One of them bailed me out last night."

"Why are you here?" asked Rick.

"Shh," went Elizabeth. "Don't ask why; he's here. That's all that matters."

"Cody told me to get lost," replied Montgomery. "So I did, even if I chose a location other than the one he had in mind."

Montgomery smiled. "I doubt I'll be found before Monday."

Chapter Ten

Black Ball, Blue Ball, White Ball

"WHAT I LIKE ABOUT FLORIDA," said Epsilon as he worked in the kitchen, "is the weather stays nice in the fall. Today is the eleventh of November: sunny skies, eighty degrees, shorts and t-shirt weather. Up north, they bundle up in flannel shirts, long johns, heavy coats, hats, gloves, sweaters and wool socks. Down here, we work on our tans."

Montgomery laughed. "What about our summers? High humidity, ninety plus degrees, mosquitoes the size of small birds, and hurricanes every month."

Epsilon replied good-naturedly, "Very true, but I would rather strip than play like a sheep and wear layers and layers of wool."

Zeta was washing lettuce and chopping carrots and radishes. "Do you know what today is?"

Epsilon replied, "I said it not thirty seconds ago: November 11th."

Montgomery added, "Check. Veterans' Day, or Armistice Day my great-grandpa would say—on the 11th day of the 11th month at the 11th hour, the guns fell silent."

Zeta shook his head vigorously. "Not that, today is the day they decide who gets in."

"Isn't that automatic?" responded Epsilon. "We stuck it out, took all their garbage, recited our lines, wore silly haircuts, did their laundry, cooked their food, cleaned their house, worked their parties, —"

"Took their drugs, played along with their games," added Montgomery. "Shocked by their electric torture, rolled in the dryer, tricked into getting high, —"

"Did their homework, slept in their house, laughed at their jokes," Epsilon resumed, "objected not to being called a letter, sat in their rows at football games, —"

"Splashed with drinks, cursed at, privacy violated, humiliated by bogus psychological evaluations, made their pick-ups and deliveries, —" Montgomery interjected.

"Listened to their lectures —" Epsilon threw in.

"Brainwashed by their philosophies —" Montgomery corrected.

"How can they turn us down now?" finished Epsilon. "We finished the race. All of us, except Lambda, stayed put. We made it. What could they object to?"

Zeta looked worried. "I don't think they want all of us."

Montgomery smiled. "I know they don't want me. But here I am. Let them do what they want; I'm doing what I'm supposed to do. I believe God wants me here. If they have a problem with that, they have a problem with God. If they try to block that, they're blocking God's will. Whatever happens, I'm content knowing that I ran the race like a good athlete and I'm crossing the finish line, whether or not that's into the winner's circle."

Zeta and Epsilon had started at the mention of God.

"You really believe that?" asked Epsilon.

"Yes, I do," replied Montgomery. "Else I would bag it. They aren't worth the trouble that they cause people."

Zeta said, "I need to get in. I can't make the social scene on my own. If I'm in the frat, then I'm somebody. I'm an S.O.B. That should command the respect of males and the attention of females."

Epsilon said, "I did it for the parties. But what Cody and Jack and Pete said about spiritual development in the frat—being open to new experiences and understandings—the SigBees is the best place I can experiment and find that right expression of self. The things we did have helped me toward that goal. I don't believe in the traditional tenets of Greek life; that stuff went out with kerosene lamps. Now I know better. I want to join so I can continue on my way with like-minded persons."

Montgomery had turned his back and was tending the pots on the stove so the two pledges would not see him rolling his eyes. *Why is the historic, resurrected person of Jesus Christ so objectionable to persons seeking spiritual enlightenment? I don't get it.*

Dinner went smoothly. The brothers seemed to have wound up their time of hazing as they were treating the pledges like old friends. Zeta seemed to relax. After dinner, the brothers began to assemble in the front room for the evening's interviews with four of the pledges: Alpha, Theta, Iota and Montgomery. The four were asked to assemble in the pledge lounge. Montgomery noticed that the other three pledges sat apart from him. He lay down and closed his eyes.

The sofa rose up and clattered on the floor. Montgomery opened his eyes. Rip's livid face was inches from his own. "You," he snarled. "You're first."

Montgomery followed Rip into the front room. The set-up was the same as before. Montgomery sat in the central chair, and awaited their proceeding.

Wilson began. "Tell us why you are here."

"Y'all summoned me." A few brothers tittered.

Wilson stammered, "No, no—why you're applying to this house to become a member."

"My family has a long history in this house, this fraternity, particularly in this chapter. We have been, and remain, strong believers in the ideals of campus leadership and character that made up the foundation of the Greek system, and in particular, this denomination of the Greek system. I want to continue in the tradition that has proved beneficial to campus and brother alike.

"This tradition has been under attack by those who would subvert the ideals and remake the system, as well as those who see the Greek ideals as irrelevant, faded glory of a past age and of no use to a post-modern world. Participation in fraternal life has been declining for decades. I want to be part of those who are restoring this great tradition to its vital role in campus society."

A murmur had begun while Montgomery was making this response. Some brothers were exchanging disgusted looks while others looked quizzically at him and themselves.

"Is it your opinion that this chapter is deficient in its practice of the Greek ideals, as you put it?" asked Jack.

"Statistics bear out that this chapter, as well as other Sigma Omicron Beta chapters around the country, has declined in membership, academics and achievement. This chapter reflects the national experience."

Cody knifed in. "Would you say that the reason for this decline is because obedience is lacking among the membership—to the point where not even the pledges feel obliged to obey the orders of the chapter leadership?"

"Certain leaders have issued orders which are illegal and dangerous to life and health. In these cases, the membership and yes, even the pledges, are obligated to refuse to follow the orders to protect and maintain the integrity of the chapter."

"What orders would those be?" asked Brendon.

"Orders to take drugs such as LSD and ecstasy."

Wilson sputtered. "What are you saying—that brothers are using drugs—here in the house? Montgomery, why do you make up these stories?"

Loud laughter erupted in the room; Wilson laughed too. Montgomery sighed: *not only does Wilson not know about the drug problem, he thinks the frat's laughing at his question when in reality they're laughing at him.*

Pete took over. "Since you pledged the house, you've been disciplined on more than one occasion. Would you care to explain why?"

Montgomery's eyes flashed. "Because I would not go along with illegal actions I was ordered to do."

"Such as?"

"Such as taking LSD with three other pledges. That resulted in y'all tumbling me inside the dryer for half an hour." Many of the brothers were now laughing uncontrollably.

Montgomery was getting steamed. "Then there were the times I was set up—no one told me that I had to know something, or gave me the materials to learn. On one of those occasions y'all jolted me with so much electricity I lost consciousness for several hours and had bad headaches and burn marks. I question discipline that risks the life of a human being."

The room was deadly silent. No one spoke or looked at the young pledge blazing with anger.

Wilson broke the silence. "Come on, Montgomery, no one would do that. Cody may be rough at times, but risking your life? That doesn't happen."

Montgomery looked at Wilson with disdain. "You've never heard of a pledge who lost his life because of fraternity hazing? It does happen."

"In other places—not here."

Cody and his gang were smiling: *good ol' Wilson, so naive, so dumb.*

Jack broke into the exchange. "Name the last twelve ideals of Greek life, and explain them."

"Nu: sober, free from use of alcohol and drugs —"

More brothers were now laughing hysterically.

Montgomery ignored it. "Xye: showing hospitality; Omicron: compassionate; Pi: trustworthy and faithful —"

Jack interrupted. "Would you call yourself trustworthy and faithful?"

"Yes. I've prepared dinner six days a week as assigned. I've made the courier rounds as scheduled. All that I was given, I've done. I've been at every scheduled meeting and activity. I've shown myself worthy of the fraternity's trust, and faithful to it. While disagreeing with the actions of members, I haven't disparaged the fraternity itself, or the fraternal life."

"What about the other weekend when you disappeared from the football game and did not return to the house until Monday morning, neglecting your duties?"

"I was ordered to get lost, and I did."

Everyone joined in the laughter. Jack flushed with the anger of embarrassment, but was unable to form a response.

Pete filled in. "Continue with the ideals."

"Rho: public speaking; Sigma: rescuing or delivering; Tau: reverent, respectful —"

Jack interrupted again. "Would you say you have been respectful to your superiors?"

Montgomery looked him directly in the eyes. "Yes."

"Have you been respectful to me?"

"Yes, and no."

"Explain."

"Yes, I have accepted you in your position as a member of the pledge committee. I acknowledged your authority. But no, I have not respected you as a superior. You're not superior to me."

The sharpness of Montgomery's reply took the assembly by surprise.

"How can you say that—you're only a pledge."

"Only a pledge—denied of my basic humanity because I asked to join this organization. Treated harshly and abused badly because y'all assumed privileges that y'all aren't granted by the constitution and rules of the fraternity and this chapter. Y'all superior to me? But then, I'm not watching girls go to the bathroom through an uncurtained window, am I?"

The assembly's laughter had become hollow. Many were looking at the floor, examining their fingernails, or looking out the window. Cody was livid, but said nothing.

Wilson again broke the silence. "Where do you come up with this stuff? I was for you joining the frat, but Montgomery, if you continue to make these baseless charges, I'll have to reconsider my support."

Montgomery was silent. He felt great sorrow for Wilson: *someone who won't admit to the truth—who's unaware of the truth around him—because it would destroy the neat, pleasant world he's set up.*

"Wilson, you have no idea of what goes on around you," said Rusty. "What Montgomery has said—all of it—is true."

Cody snapped out of his trance-like state. "Let's not debate the fraternity in front of the applicant," he said briskly. "Our purpose here is to examine him to see if he's ready to join the house."

Pete took his cue. "Continue with the ideals."

"Upsilon: healthy; Phi: brotherly affection; Chi: gracious and helping; Psi: encouraging; Omega: useful and beneficial."

"Have you lived up to all these qualities as required of a member of Sigma Omicron Beta?"

"Yes."

Jack was going to break in, but stopped after a warning glance from Cody.

Brendon asked, "Do you like girls?"

"What?"

"Do you like girls?"

"Ask my girlfriend."

The pledge committee was thrown for a loss. They had conceived of Montgomery as a nerdy bookworm who spent his time in the library and on the Internet, as someone who was uncomfortable socially, not relating well to others. They did not know what to make of his answer or his relationship.

Pete leered, "Have you —"

"Stop it." This command issued from an unknown boy. Montgomery looked at him. He was big, 6' 2", 260 pounds of hard muscle on a big-boned, wide frame. He looked like a linebacker for a professional football team. He had black hair, thick in an unruly mop.

"Jack Hawkins, Montgomery. Everybody calls me Black Jack, or Blackie."

"It was a simple question," whined Pete.

"You were about to ask him his sexual history which is none of your business. Next y'all want to grill him on his social life when y'all already know the answers. Yes, he enjoys being with others and going out, he likes to go to parties and have a good time, but not like y'all do. Now get on with this interview and get it done."

Rip said, "My objection to this pledge is that he doesn't help brothers in their need. I personally know of a situation in which he refused to help a brother in financial need."

Montgomery said, "You must be referring to the day at the beginning of the semester when you seized my video game at the Student Center and demanded my student i.d. so you could access my account and use my money as you wished. I said it then, and I say it now, that makes you a thief. You have no right to demand money from me, threatening sanctions if I don't comply. I told you then, and I tell you now, that we can settle this between the two of us. But you seem to lack the guts when you have no one to help you."

Deadly silence fell over the group. Gravy sat unnoticed in the background. *What a gutsy performance! The harder they press him, the tougher he becomes.*

Rip said, "Anytime you want, Mongrel."

"The name is Montgomery. Let's go—right now." Montgomery stood up. His nostrils were flaring, his face was flushed and his fists clenched at his side.

"Well, uh, we're busy with these interviews. We, uh, still have three more after you—some other time."

Montgomery sat down, triumph in his eyes. Around the room, brothers were nodding and were impressed that he had stared Rip down. Whispers were heard as brothers commented to one another upon Rip's capitulation.

Brendon tried to rescue the moment. "You mentioned Rho: public speaking. Give evidence of your abilities to speak in public, to maintain poise and get your point across."

"Besides this interview, you mean."

The assembly again erupted in laughter.

Rusty stood up. "I think we've heard enough. I'll escort Montgomery back to the lounge."

When they had left the room, Rusty said, "What a great performance! But I'm afraid you won the battle but lost the war. Cody has too many brothers in his back pocket for you to gain membership. But we'll never forget the inspiration you provided in standing up to him and his thugs—especially as a pledge! Maybe some of the brothers will now have the courage to buck him."

"Then my time has not been wasted."

In the room, Cody said, "Let's vote and get it over."

Rip said, "Wait a minute. I'm not ready to vote. This little twerp is not going to get the better of me. You let him bully you, Cody. He's not an S.O.B. and you know it. Don't lay down and let him get away with it. I say we defer the cursed Mongrel to next semester and lay down some conditions for him to fulfill before we vote."

"That's right. Remember, Cody? We set some conditions for him: course on moral philosophy, interpersonal relations, community service, and counseling," added Brendon.

Black Jack interjected, "Remember? What remember—you 'set' as in past tense? We make the decisions, not the committee."

Cody laughed weakly. "Brendon is referring to some possibilities we had discussed, but nothing was a decision."

Pete jumped in. "Nevertheless, it's a good idea. Many of us have reservations, but the pledge has some support in the room. Okay—let's not vote now. Let him prove himself to us, and if he does, we take him in the spring. Any objections?"

No one objected. Cody's people were willing to support whatever he wanted; the others knew that Montgomery had no chance to win approval now—the deferral gave him another chance and besides, they wanted him to stay with the house because his presence so discomforted Cody and his henchmen.

Cody looked around the room and said, "Done."

Rip left for the next pledge.

Cody filled in the interval, "We like this next pledge. He has a good grounding in the fundamentals of postmodernism. He's not judgmental, he's open to new ideas and experiences, he follows well, he has good business sense and a great sense of humor. He joined willingly in any activity in which we involved him."

Someone asked, "How did he come through his journeys?"

Jack said, "You mean his spiritual awakening?"

Cody said quickly, "He came back with new insights. It was inspirational to us all. People listen to him; we checked around campus and in his dormitory. He speaks well and we believe he'll help us build the fraternal membership."

Rip, knocked and entered the room, bringing Iota in his wake.

Cody said, "Begin by introducing yourself."

Iota responded, "My name is Jupiter Loving. You're laughing; it's okay—I get that all the time. The boys laugh, but the girls melt. They love my name. It's a great icebreaker at parties. And I don't mind telling you that I live up to my name." He smiled.

"My parents were hippies in the sixties. Along the way, they turned pagan as they pursued environmental justice for the trees and plants of the world. Everything has a spirit; they learned how to communicate with the spirits of all living things. When they conceived me, they knew they had a future leader. So they named me for the head god they recognized. Thus I'm Jupiter."

Cody asked, "Who was your supervising brother?"

"I was," said a boy to Cody's right.

"Morgan," said Cody. "Tell us about Jupiter."

"Jupiter is a good man. We had lots of fun while he was staying in my room. He has a quick mind, and a grasp on our way of life, and a persuasive means of communicating it to others. He accepted his role without complaining. He was particularly insightful on spirit matters, as you said earlier. Many times we tripped together and he showed me things I hadn't realized before. He handled his duties well. He showed great promise on the courier route: he brought us additional customers. Always thinking; loyal to the frat. His tests showed he has the aptitude to fit in well."

"Great," said Cody. "Well, if there are no further questions, —"

"I have a question," said Wilson.

Cody turned in shock. "You? What do you want to ask?"

"It has been alleged," said Wilson, "that the pledges were forced to use drugs as part of their hazing-slash-initiation. What do you know about that?"

Jupiter smiled a disarming smile. "I wasn't forced to do anything."

"Good," said Wilson. "Just checking—it's ridiculous to think we would provide drugs to our pledges—like we're some crack house or something."

Smothered laughter hissed throughout the room.

"How do you feel about drugs?" asked Gravy, quickly filling the gap before Cody could stop the interview.

"When used properly, drugs treat many illnesses and deficits in the human body," said Jupiter.

"Don't patronize me, boy," Gravy shot back. "I want a real answer."

Jupiter swallowed. He hadn't realized that there was opposition to the prevailing majority who promoted a lifestyle of recreational drug usage—hedonism run amok. He had happily run amok with the best of the hard-core users.

"Drugs enhance the human consciousness," Jupiter replied. "They take us to levels of awareness we cannot reach on our own. This experience is not for everyone. But for those who are able, they find truths that do not exist in the sober state. These truths, though, are the ones that run the universe. Besides, drugs give pleasure and they're fun. I think everyone should decide for themselves and not attempt to stop others, or force others who want to forgo the experience."

"Very tolerant," observed Cody. "Exactly the kind of attitude that makes a good S.O.B. Jupiter, thank you for your time."

"One more question, if you please," said Gravy. "Jupiter, were you ever put on the shock machine?"

"The what?" Jupiter asked incredulously.

"That is all," Gravy said.

Cody was looking at Gravy with great distaste. After Jupiter left the room, Cody looked at Gravy and said, "Stick to cooking." Gravy said nothing, but dispassionately gazed steadily at Cody. Cody could not hold the gaze, and looked away.

"Do we need to vote?" Jack asked. "I say he's in."

About seventy percent of the room whooped and hollered. In the lounge, Alpha hit Jupiter on the arm and said, "Way to go, buddyrow. You're in."

Jupiter grinned. "As if I didn't know. You and I, we were S.O.B.'s before we came here. This is just a formality."

Rip appeared in the doorway. "Congratulations, Jupiter. You're a member of Sigma Omicron Beta. Alpha, you're next."

Alpha got up, winked at Jupiter and confidently walked out of the room behind Rip. "Congratulations, I hope I make the hat trick," Theta said.

Iota smiled. "Nothing to it. If you partied well and often, you're in. Nothing personal, Mongoose, but you're a zero. That's why you're not getting in."

Montgomery, angry, dazed and confused, said nothing and did not move. *I knew I wouldn't survive the vote, but they continued my candidacy. Why didn't most of the brothers take my beliefs, my work and me seriously? Counseling? Interpersonal relations? They think I'm a defective human being. How dare they! Are they right?*

Alpha was putting on a show-stopping performance in the front room.

"Let's hear your interpretation of your moniker," prompted Pete.

"Alpha: goodness. A Sigma Omicron Beta brother, popularly known as a SigBee, is good by his very nature. He has no need for critical examination of himself for morality because his goodness furnishes his personal morality. His goodness is the basis upon which he thinks, speaks and acts. Good begets good; so, too, the SigBee only can, and does, do good things." Alpha took a little bow.

"How would you respond to those who accuse a Sigma Omicron Beta member of using drugs?" asked Jack.

"If a SigBee uses drugs, say smoking some pot or popping an E pill, it's a good thing. It's good because the person doing it is good, and is only capable of doing good. So if the SigBee does it, it is a good act despite dissenting opinions from moralists or cops. The SigBee should pursue the good even if it is unpopular or proscribed by arbitrary laws made by unenlightened legislatures." Alpha took another bow.

"Why would you make a good S.O.B.?" asked Pete.

"Because I'm good. If I become an S.O.B., as you put it, I can only be a good one, because I have a good nature, and therefore must be good—whatever I am, I can only be a good one." Giggling, "Heh-heh, heh-heh," Alpha peeked around the room. Some brothers looked confused, others were nodding in agreement, and others were disdainful.

"What appeals to you about the fraternal life?" queried Brendon.

"The community lifestyle—living with guys who are of like mind. One is a lonely number—it's no good for riding the E train or unbending straight lines with a lollipop. I like to hear pictures and see sounds. Sigma Omicron Beta is the place that makes it possible. It's where I can do my thing and be myself."

"Are you a crowd pleaser?" asked Jack.

"A toady or brown noser I'm not. But I don't row against the tide. That answer your question?"

"Would you go along with the crowd only to avoid being singled out?" pursued Jack.

"One is the loneliest number. It's the loneliest number underneath the sun—one. I don't like to stand by myself anytime, anyplace, anyhow."

"You have no principles?" suggested Pete.

"Of course I have principles. But I won't insist upon my principles in opposition to others' principles. Prevailing opinion is the means of democracy. Anything else is tyranny and dictatorship."

"Well said!" approved Jack. "Personalities prepared to accept the wishes of the majority and participate without reservation in the majority's ways are the kind of members we need in this house."

"Tell us about a leadership experience you've had," prompted Cody.

"Um, recently I had an interesting experience. I was asked to gather a group of males to undergo an exercise in broadening our minds. I asked each one to join me, and, uh, divided up the assignment so that each one would have an equal share. I, uh, uh, led the group in beginning. I, uh, facilitated the experience and the debriefing. The other two guys and myself were united in enjoying the experience greatly. The other guy really missed out."

"Other guy? You mean one of your assigned persons declined your leadership?" asked one of the brothers.

"Uh, yeah, he was a—a—a real pain. A moralist—you know the type."

"Not really. Why did he decline?"

"He thought he was too good for the rest of us."

"Why do you say that?"

"It was plain from his manner. He thought what we were doing was wrong; rather than being open and tolerant, he judged us."

"So what did you do? How did your leadership handle the recalcitrant person?"

"I let him go. We don't need his kind."

"Wouldn't good leadership be to go after him and convince him to join the group?"

Alpha said nothing.

"You have no answer; then let me try this one: in saying that 'we don't need his kind', are you not being judgmental yourself? You criticize him for judging you, yet you have done the same to him."

Alpha said nothing.

Cody was growing unhappy; he did not like unscripted interviews. He worked hard to prepare every question carefully, assign who would ask it, assign a follow-up question if needed, assign who would take over if the first two persons floundered, and choreograph the 'spontaneous' reactions. The members usually allowed the pledge committee to ask the questions. But now they were jumping in themselves.

Another brother said, "One exercise with two or three persons is not much of a leadership experience. Do you have another that you could tell us about?"

"I led my high school football team in tackles."

"Great! Tell us about it," said Pete.

"I played defensive end. I'm quick, though, and I get around the tackle easily. So, I was able to get to the runner, sometimes the quarterback."

"If you played end, wouldn't you have lined up against the guard?" asked a guy along the front wall.

"Well, uh—sometimes the guard, sometimes the tackle."

"How did you lead the team with your play?" asked another guy.

"It inspired them."

"How?"

"People who are around people who do good are inspired to play better."

"How?" the first guy repeated.

"I don't know. They are."

"Then how is that leadership?" asked the second guy.

"See, I led, they tried to keep up.".

"That's not leadership," snorted another member. "Leadership is talking to the team, before the game, in the huddle, on the sidelines, and in the locker room, telling them to play hard, watch their fundamentals, and that the team can win. Leadership is inspiring talks. Leadership is crafting plans and bringing people into those plans, giving them assignments to execute. Leadership is being spokesman for the group to outsiders. Leadership is criticizing a member of the group who isn't pulling his weight. These and other things are leadership. All you did was an individual achievement in a statistic."

Alpha broke into a sweat.

"Have you made any speeches in public?" asked one of the members who was now questioning the pledge.

"No, well, yes, well—"

"It's a simple question. Have you or haven't you?"

"Define public."

"Public: an open meeting space, outside area, school classroom, church, Scouting, the mall, anywhere people gather who are unrelated to one another. Your audience is composed of individuals who aren't related, and some of whom may be unknown to you. Before a group, standing behind a podium, or some such. Did you ever make a speech to your football team in the locker room?"

"No, I didn't."

"Are you ready to be a fraternity man?" challenged another.

"Yes I am! In fact, I could use a little something right now," Alpha shouted.

"I think we need a sit-back and cool-down," said Cody. "Let's take five. Alpha, for the record, state your name."

"Daniel—Daniel McCabe."

The room broke up. Some of the brothers went out to walk around the yard and dissect what was taking place. Others went to the kitchen for cokes. Daniel headed back to the lounge, but ducked outside the side door to smoke a cigarette. Cody, Jack, Rip, Pete and Brendon were conferring in the middle of the room.

Fifteen minutes later, Cody called the assembly back to order. "We have one more pledge to consider tonight. Rip, will you please summon Theta?"

"Nice try, Cody." Black Jack was standing. "We haven't made a decision on Alpha yet."

"No, we approved him," Cody retorted. "Bad memory got you, Black Jack?"

Cries broke out in the room. Several voices were demanding a vote on Alpha. Others were backing Cody. Wilson decided it was his big moment.

"As president of this chapter, I will rule on this dispute. National rules clearly state that the local chapter has the sole authority for accepting new members, and may do so if the candidates meet the national guidelines plus whatever criteria the local chapter may set. New members must receive a minimum of sixty percent of those present; the local chapter may set the plurality higher if they choose. We go by the sixty percent measure."

"Why are you boring us, Wilson?" demanded Cody.

"There must be a vote. Let's get it on record."

"Fine. All in favor?"

A number of ayes sounded in the room.

"Opposed?" A number of nays came forth.

"Passed," said Cody.

"How can you tell if sixty percent approved membership if you didn't count the votes?" sputtered Wilson. "Cody, do it right."

Cody was not sure that Alpha would receive the sixty percent needed. "I—have—good—ears," he stated slowly and with emphasis on each word.

"What a joint!" exclaimed Rusty to Black Jack. "They only follow their rules when they want to."

Rip led Theta into the room. Theta sat in the chair.

"Tell us your name and your background," started Cody.

"My name is Alan Xavier, and I'm from Miami. My father is Cuban and my mama, she is American—English. I'm studying music and art. My best instruments are piano and tuba, but I can play almost anything."

"Can you play Sunshine in the Rain?" interrupted a boy.

Alan laughed. "Oh, yes, and the ponies too." Other boys laughed.

"Why do you want to join Sigma Omicron Beta?" asked Cody.

"To meet girls," Alan laughed again.

"Have you met any girls?" Jack took over.

"Oh, yes—one." Alan was grinning.

"Who was it?" Jack had caught the infectious grin.

"Her name was Janet. She has a wonderful way of making me feel welcome."

The fraternity exploded with laughter. Tears ran down faces, three or four boys had dropped to their knees pounding the floor, others were leaning against the wall holding their sides, and one ran for the bathroom, laughing hard all the way.

"Mm-hm. Everyone gets to know Janet sooner or later," said Jack with great irony.

"What makes you a good candidate for Sigma Omicron Beta?" asked Pete.

"I can sing, I can dance and I can play musical instruments for the parties. You will always have entertainment as long as I am a member. I like to joke, I like to laugh and I like to perform. You need jokesters, comedians and performers. Everyone is so serious here. You men are so tense—so hard up. Let me loosen the atmosphere. I am 'loony tunes.' You saw that the night we licked strawberries and the night you wore the red robes."

Cody leaned forward, interested. The pledge might have a point.

"Are you a moralist?" demanded Pete.

"What's a moralist?"

"Someone who is fixated on an absolute set of standards of right and wrong without considering the situation, and judges other people by applying those standards to them. Intolerant of people who have different lifestyles, desires and pleasures, especially those they themselves find objectionable. Are you one of those?"

"Oh, no—I couldn't be a moralist. Such a person as you describe is an awful person—terrible, nasty, awful. I couldn't be one of those. What is right? What is wrong? If you do not hurt anybody, who's to say who's right and who's wrong? Is there even such a thing as right and wrong? There's only people who do as they have been brought up in their traditions. So there is no wrong or right. So how can I be such a person saying what is wrong and right when such things do not exist. It is silly, no?"

"I find your attitude commendable," said Cody. "Outstanding."

"Explain your letter," said Brendon.

"My letter?" asked Alan in some confusion.

"You are Theta. What does Theta represent in the Greek system?"

"Oh, yes, my letter name. Theta — theta—I've got it: tharsos. It means courageous and bold."

"Are you tharsos?" asked Jack.

"Oh, yes, I'm very tharsos. The meek and the mild stand at the end of the line. When they get to the buffet, there's nothing left. They're the meek and the mild and the hungry. And as you can see, I'm not hungry."

The fraternity burst into laughter again. Alan was short, 5' 6" with dark brown skin tone and coarse, black hair. He also weighed 190 pounds.

"Are you bold in other ways?" asked Jack.

"Oh, yes, I am bold in many ways. For example, here is the pen you did not know was missing. I just borrowed it." He held out a Mont Blanc knock-off fountain pen. The boys laughed again.

"You see, I told you I will make you laugh."

"Are there any other questions?" asked Cody.

No one spoke. It was the end of a long and exhausting night. Everyone wanted to finish and be done, which worked in Alan's favor. When the vote came, the frat unanimously elected him to the fraternal order, mostly so they wouldn't have to make the meeting longer to fully discuss his candidacy.

Alan joined the other three in the lounge. Rip came to the room and said, "That's it. Three in, one not. The three ins, follow me; I'll show you your new room where you'll move your things tonight and live permanently. Mongrel, get your things and get out!"

Montgomery realized that Rip had no joy in the malice he was displaying, and that he and Rip were unfinished business. But Montgomery was only too happy to bring his residency in the frat house to an end. *It's time to go 'home': back to Somerset Johns, back to Travis, back to Red, Cat and Shorts, back to Rick, back to the quad and meals with people I like, back to the astronomy club, back to Elizabeth—most of all, back to Elizabeth.*

Montgomery raced up the stairs. He pulled out his garbage bag, threw his things inside, and slung the bag over his shoulder. He made tracks down the stairs and out the door. As he looked back, he saw Gravy and Black Jack at the front window looking at him. Montgomery waved his thanks, and sped up the street.

Black Jack spoke first, "He was our best hope."

Gravy countered, "He still is."

Chapter Eleven

Party 101

THE RAUCOUS CELEBRATION that attended the announcement of the pledges who had gained admission to the fraternity was unmarred by the bitterness of those who lost out. It was a Friday blowout. Presided over by Cody, Rip, Jack, Brendon and Pete, the brothers cranked the super-stereo into the screaming decibels range. Morgan Aleppo passed out roach clips with a SOB monogram attached. The roaches passed freely among the crowd. Daniel McCabe, a/k/a Alpha; Jupiter Loving, a/k/a Iota; Alan Xavier, a/k/a Theta; Lance Dubonier, a/k/a Eta; Darrell Ebecker, a/k/a Zeta; and Mansfred Mansfielding, a/k/a Gamma, had been accepted. Along with the marijuana, the young men were sipping whiskey and cokes and ingesting the drug ecstasy so they could release their savagery into high-energy dancing.

Wilson had gone out for the evening. Gravy was sober, sipping on sparkling water, staying in the background and observing the frenetic action. Black Jack, Rusty and a couple of other like-minded brothers, who wanted no part of this social scene, had retired to a private room at the Student Center to analyze the latest admissions, and what it meant to their attempts to reform the house.

Kappa, who was also the Colin that Montgomery and Travis had met on Thursday night of rush week, went into a deep depression upon learning of his rejection. They had been cruel to him, dragging out the questioning, telling him he lacked ego strength to make it as a member of a fraternity, making noises of disgust over his answers to questions about the Greek system, and harping about his commitment made during a "True Love Waits" seminar at his high school. They told him he lacked the ingredients to be a leader among his peers.

Beta was told that he was a zero—that bluntly. However, the pledge committee held out hope if he would continue on with his service—they would deign to allow him to maintain his pledge status while he developed under their tutelage. Meanwhile, they told him, he had a problem with hidden anger that he had to work out. Beta had screamed at them that it was no longer hidden. But he agreed to continue as a pledge.

Delta had confessed that he was an alcoholic having started at age eleven; he had been in a twelve-step program for the last two years. The brothers had sneered at what they thought was misplaced moralism and his lack of control—not over his drinking, but in being steered by the opinions of others. Delta tried to tell them that he had faced the fact that he was powerless over his life, and that submission to a higher power had made the difference. They laughed in his face and kicked him out. Rusty later sent him an e-mail consoling him over his rejection and telling him that Sigma Omicron Beta was no place to be if a recovering alcoholic wanted to remain sober. The pressure to drink and drug to excess was too great.

That left Epsilon, who wanted to be in the frat to continue on his spiritual journey of discovery. He too was continued with the promise that more exciting discoveries could be his if he would continue with his service.

Montgomery sent the committee an e-mail saying that he was working on his assignments, but that left him no time to help out at the frat. The chores of cooking, cleaning, laundry and grounds fell to Beta and Epsilon. These two boys wrangled a room out of the frat so they could live there if they were going to be the servants of four dozen men.

Delta fell off the wagon. Around midnight on the Friday completing admission interviews, he turned up outside the frat, singing an obscene song and displaying his complete contempt for them. The following Tuesday, he woke up in a library bathroom, not remembering a thing. He promptly called his sponsor, and went to meet him.

Kappa-Colin went to see a campus psychiatrist and received a hefty prescription for Prozac. Unfortunately, the Prozac reacted badly to a body that had consumed LSD and ecstasy over several weeks. It was suspected that Kappa had taken LSD again while on the Prozac prescription. He wound up in a hospital in an intensive chemical dependency treatment unit and withdrew from the university.

The new fraternity members melded into the life of the fraternity with ease. They proved to be popular with the house as they continued to make the courier rounds without asking questions. They also helped Beta and Epsilon who were overwhelmed with the workload they had assumed.

Rip was nursing his psychological wounds from the smarting Montgomery had administered. He spent his days concocting fantasies of revenge, biding his time until Montgomery would be vulnerable to his aggression. Rip was afraid of Montgomery, and did not want to run into him unless several of the brothers were with him. He lost much face with the other brothers, the pledge committee, and especially Cody. Cody was still debating whether to jettison Rip.

Elizabeth rejoiced to have her boyfriend back. They delighted in taking long walks, studying together, watching the stars, playing lovers' silly games, and lying together watching old movies or simply talking.

Park was dating Travis, but she was not sure that she welcomed the more serious side of him that emerged from his pledge experience. She was not ready for a deep emotional commitment, and was afraid that Travis would attach too firmly to her when she might want to move on.

Travis was as surprised as everyone else that he had found passion within himself. For what, and where to direct it, he had no idea—he was still reconciling himself to the idea of caring about more than the next party.

Rick fell in love with Rose, and was hoping some day to ask her to marry him. But he played it slow.

Rose fell in love with Rick, and was hoping some day he would ask her to marry him. But she was cautious, not wanting to frighten him off or lead him on. She was also committed to obtaining her degree, and was afraid marriage would sidetrack her from that goal. Rick took her cautiousness to be the old-fashioned charm of reluctance that once marked all Southern women. He loved the fact she was playing hard-to-get.

Mick continued his erratic and mercurial ways. The quad was convinced that he was using drugs and was out-of-control. They also believed that the Michigan roommate did not exist; no one had ever seen him.

Travis poured his energy into his studies and surfing. When he was not with one, he was with the other unless he was with Park. Late November storms came in a series that heaped up big waves every three to four days. When one of those days occurred, Travis called someone in the surfing club or borrowed Montgomery's truck to go to the beach. Park decided she wasn't interested in surfing—she wasn't athletic enough. Travis was disappointed.

The "Party Boys", as the six new admissions had styled themselves, made every effort to prove that they belonged in the fraternity. As the days passed, they showed little interest in their academics as they rarely let a twenty-four hour period pass entirely sober. Deliveries continued, although the pace was slowing with approaching final exams and paper deadlines. However, they were not worried about their exams, for as Daniel McCabe said, "Bad grades do not affect our standing in the frat; besides, we have the Internet for papers, the best cheating techniques for exams, and the means to hack the system to adjust our transcript records if need be." It would take him several semesters to learn the falsity of his opinion.

The football season ended on a promising note as the team won the last two games at home. That left them with a record of five wins, five losses. The quad began practicing for intramural roundball several times a week. It was quickly clear that they had more enthusiasm than talent. But the camaraderie was high; in the few short months of their freshman year, the six young men had drawn together into a close friendship—they were like six brothers: Montgomery, Travis, Cat, Red, Shorts, and Caveman.

Under Shorts' tutelage, Montgomery began lifting weights and made rapid strength gains as he hardened the muscle of his slender body and converted the "freshman fifteen" weight gain into dense muscle mass.

Thanksgiving arrived, and the quad emptied out. No one said anything, but personal property was stowed and locked in the bedrooms. The boys were uncomfortable with Mick's continuing degeneration, and as he planned to stay at the university for the holiday, had no confidence that their property would not disappear. Secretly each cherished a hope that Mick would disappear.

The holiday passed quickly, and Sunday night the quad reassembled in their common room. "All quiet on the Mick front," Red observed.

"Maybe he dropped out," Caveman mumbled.

"From your mouth to God's ears," replied Shorts.

"Has anyone seen the spring schedule?" asked Cat. "What classes will you take?"

"Physics," said Montgomery. "Math 2, Western Civ 2, American Literature, and Moral Philosophy." He grimaced as he mentioned his last class.

"Moral philosophy?" Travis responded. "Why would you take that?"

"It's a condition of being a pledge. I'm supposed to learn how to be politically correct."

"Will your advisor go for it?" asked Cat.

"I think so. It fits into my core requirements."

"I'm in for the physics," said Cat. "How about Red? Stay with the team?"

"Put me down. What time does it meet?"

"Ten a.m. Tuesday, Wednesday and Friday," said Cat. "Now for the lab: Thursday at three okay with y'all?"

"Check," said Montgomery, scribbling on his registration form.

"Fine by me," said Red.

Travis smiled. "I'm sticking with the same regime. No choices, but classes."

"How does that work?" asked Shorts.

Travis explained. "We spend the entire year working on English, literature, history, poly sci, and so forth. When we finish, we'll have thirty-six hours of academic credit that apply to our core requirements. Next year, I can declare a major or continue to take core subjects, but individually like y'all. I'm in a study group—we meet at nights two or three times a week. We have the same classroom every day; only the professors rotate depending upon which subject they're teaching. We get no grades. We earn credit for completing the courses and demonstrating that we've learned the subject. Sometimes the prof gives a test; sometimes we write papers; sometimes we meet with the prof and he talks to us to find out what we know. I like that way the best."

Shorts looked at Travis with wonder. "You like orals the best?"

"I don't have to study for orals. All I have to do is know the subject. We go over everything rather well in the study group. After we've met, the brainy stuff sticks in my head. I wish I could do all four years this way."

Montgomery said, "Don't let the teachers at Sparksburg High hear you say that. They'd die from shock."

Travis laughed. "I never knew how interesting learning could be."

Shorts said, "I can do American Literature and Civ 2 with Monkey; anybody for Freshman English or American History?"

Red said, "History I'm in—say Monday/Thursday eight a.m.?"

Shorts replied, "That early?"

Red said, "It's the only time offered."

Cat said, "I can't go with that. I need the eight a.m.'s for Engineering classes."

Shorts said, "You've decided to declare."

Cat replied, "I might as well. It's what I want to study."

Red replied, "I'm leaning toward law. But I don't want to declare before junior year."

Caveman smiled. "I'm heading toward art, and cartooning. So I'm into art appreciation, art history and the like. I don't suppose I'll have classes with y'all?"

Shorts said, "Not art history! Memorizing paintings and periods and names with odd spellings—no thanks."

Red said, "I'll do art appreciation with you, roomie. It might come in handy later."

Monday morning, before English, Montgomery went to meet with his advisor. Dr. Peterman waved him into his office, and rose to greet him. "Montgomery, how are you? How has your semester gone?"

"Academically, I've had a good term. My GPA, if I do well on exams, should be 3.4 or 3.6."

"That's an excellent start. Even a 3.4 should land you on the Dean's List."

"Thank you, sir."

"What classes are you taking for the Spring?"

"Physics, Math 2, Western Civ 2, and American Literature."

"All good choices. Physics and Math both meet core requirements as well as apply toward an astronomy degree. Finishing the Western Civ gives you continuity and completeness in your core. No one can learn everything; most students pick and choose by whim and end up with a rag-tag, crazy quilt background. That makes the ones who start and follow through in one type of area stand out. It's much better training for the mind in thinking thoroughly.

"American Lit you'll find enjoyable. Be forewarned though: English profs are tough. You'll have to perform highly at the critical level if you hope to have high marks. But a young, dynamic guy like you should have no trouble."

Montgomery grinned. Dr. Peterman was a warm, kind and caring professor who tackled the difficult job of trying to know the dozens of students he advised during the year. He had a genuine affection for this young freshman who was passionate about astronomy and showed much promise for developing a first-rate mind.

"But," Dr. Peterman continued, "you have only mentioned four classes. You must enroll for five classes to maintain progress toward a four-year degree."

Montgomery grimaced. "Moral philosophy."

Dr. Peterman's eyes went up. "Moral philosophy? What made you choose that?"

Montgomery looked at the floor. "It's a condition of joining Sigma Omicron Beta."

Dr. Peterman nodded. "The fraternity you're determined to join. I've never heard of a fraternity demanding that you take certain classes to join. What's this all about?"

"They told me that it was one of the conditions I had to fulfill to be accepted. I pledged; they didn't vote me in or out. They said, 'Not at this time.' Then they gave me four tasks to perform to be considered in the Spring."

"What will they think of next? You're more than qualified to join that rat's nest; oops, excuse me, I shouldn't let my personal feelings out like that. You have the background, personality and social skills to enjoy membership in any of the fraternities. But the time of the Greek fraternities has passed, and the sun is setting upon it. However, you're drawn to it like a moth to a lamp. You'd do as well on campus without the frat life as you will with it. Since I can't dissuade you, think again about Sigma Omicron Beta. It's in serious decline, and there are moral issues regarding its activities. Many of its members are wolves in sheeps' clothing. You can do much better."

"Thank you for your advice, Dr. Peterman."

"They can ruin you. The heavy-set boy Colin? He's been committed to a hospital for treatment. Heavy depression—he put his body and mind on ecstasy and LSD and it broke his mind. His body chemistry may never be straightened out. He may be in a mental facility for the rest of his life. Don't let that happen to you."

"Check," Montgomery replied.

Chapter Twelve

The First Task

MONTGOMERY PUSHED OPEN the wooden-framed glass door, which was lined with a muslin curtain. Inside, a severe looking woman sat behind a large metal desk. The desk was empty except for an anniversary clock, an arrangement of silk roses, two small picture frames and three papers on which the woman was scribbling.

She had long, straight grey hair, which she pulled back into a bun. Her half-moon reading glasses were set in amber-colored plastic. Her skin stretched over her tight frame. If it wasn't for her deep tan and the surfboard sitting in the corner of the room, Montgomery would have thought her a strict schoolmistress. As it was, he didn't know what to make of her.

"Yes?" she asked without looking up.

"I was told that you're the coordinator of volunteers," said Montgomery.

"I am," she replied as she continued to write.

"I'm a new volunteer."

The woman fixed her eyes on Montgomery. He was surprised to see the wrinkled, leathery quality of her skin. "Sit," she said.

"Most people think of the clinical setting as a place for candy stripers to hand out flowers and books. But we play a vital role in the patient's—strike that, we call them clients now—in the client's well being. A hospital is a field, we are a team and the client's health is the score. On the team there are many positions, each as important as the others: doctor, surgeon, specialist, nurse, orderly, social worker, dietitian, technician, radiologist, oncologist, cardiologist, lab worker, pathologist, and many more. But we have a unique role: we tend to the patient's emotional care.

"That's why only serious persons with a light-hearted demeanor need apply. What we do is serious work to be undertaken seriously, but we must do it in a lighthearted manner so that we can bolster the patient's attitude. Do you understand?"

"Yes, ma'am."

The woman gave Montgomery a once-over. "You'll do. What hours can you work?"

"Monday, Wednesday, and Friday, after 4 p.m."

"You must be available on Thursday nights at 7 p.m. for our weekly review. We will be finished by 9 p.m. Let's say you'll work Monday and Wednesday, 4 to 8 p.m., starting next week. Fill out this paperwork, sign the contract and bring it back."

"What's in the contract?"

"You agree that you'll work at the hospital for ten weeks on the agreed upon days and hours, including my weekly sessions. You'll write up a weekly summary of one interaction between yourself and a client, due on Thursday. You'll list out the reasons you have for volunteering, and what issues you would like to work on that involve service to humanity—you know, the interpersonal skills and psychological issues. Welcome to my staff."

"Thank you, ma'am."

"My name is Dorothy Newman. My friends call me Dotty, my enemies dotty Dotty." The woman laughed mirthlessly. "You will call me Ms. Newman."

"Montgomery Lee, ma'am. I'm pleased to make your acquaintance." Montgomery held out his hand, but Dotty did not take hold of it.

"Good day, Mr. Lee. Be here on Monday at 4 p.m. sharp. I grade on punctuality." Again Dotty laughed mirthlessly. Montgomery managed a bare smile, unable to tell whether the woman meant it.

On Monday afternoon, Montgomery presented himself at the hospital. He was nervous: *What's involved in this volunteer work? Probably wheeling people in and out of the hospital, maybe carrying heavy things for the nurses, running errands, that sort of menial chore. But Dotty had made it sound like I'll be a care-giver. Am I able to interact with patients to keep their spirits lifted?*

Dotty reviewed his paperwork, noting that Montgomery had given a religious reason as his motivation for volunteering and also that it was a condition of his joining a fraternity. "Which one?" she asked, and when Montgomery told her Sigma Omicron Beta, she laughed loudly, this time with genuine hilarity.

Dotty highlighted his issues: breaking the ice, appropriate disclosure, and emotional involvement. She pulled out a file, and put his papers into it, then replaced the file in her desk. She examined his attire: a pair of khaki trousers and a white pullover shirt with Florida Sawgrass University embroidered in navy blue on the left breast.

"Keep wearing what you have on." She retrieved an ugly purple, blue and pink flowered top from a cabinet. "Wear this over your clothes. It identifies you as a volunteer. Don't try to fasten it shut like a suit jacket—there are no buttons. Let it hang open."

Montgomery looked at the garment with distaste, but he put it on.

"Go to security and give them this." Dotty handed him a slip, which authorized him to receive a picture i.d. badge for the hospital. "When you are done, report to first floor admissions. They'll break you in."

As Montgomery left Dotty's, he noticed that the surfboard had teeth marks on it and a piece was missing from the side.

Dotty ejected, "Shark," and waved him on his way.

Montgomery reflected that it was probably the shark that got the worst of the encounter as he made his way to the security office.

"A new volunteer," the man at the security desk said. "Have you done this before?"

"No sir."

"Beware the second week. That's when she pounces. You'll be mincemeat by the fourth week, but she's not too bad after that. Stick it out."

Montgomery gave the man a quizzical look. Flash! went the camera. *He did that on purpose. What is it with the people in this hospital?*

The picture came out, the man glued it to a white card, had Montgomery sign the card, imprinted the hospital seal over the photo, and laminated the badge. He punched a hole in the top, and gave Montgomery a clip to wear it with.

"You must display this badge at all times while you are in the hospital."

Montgomery fastened the badge to a side pocket of the flowered top, and made his way to the admissions office.

"Hi, honey," greeted a plump, middle-aged woman. "It's always special to meet a young person who has volunteered to work in the butcher shop." She threw her head back and laughed at her own joke.

"Good afternoon, ma'am."

"Why, thank you. That is so sweet. Sit down here." She patted a chair next to hers.

"Call me Wilkie, everyone does. If you can't call me Wilkie, call me what you want, but don't call me late for supper." She laughed again.

I doubt she's ever been late for any meal.

"Your duties are simple. When you come in, take that cart (she nodded at a cart on wheels) and go around to each floor. We only have two—it's not that hard. Retrieve any books and magazines the people have finished reading, and let them choose something new. Give them a Bible if they ask for one."

In a whisper, she added, "Leave one whether they ask for it or not. We get them by the gross from the Gideons. We're not supposed to hand them out willy-nilly, only upon request, but honey, (she patted Montgomery on the knee) the Lord has requested that every patient, oops! client, receive one." She smiled and laughed at the same time.

"You're supposed to push gift shop purchases: cards, playing cards, games, figurines, and whatever cheap crap we bought off some wrecked truck on the interstate (the woman pealed with laughter again) but you'll find it really angers the clients to have some salesman peddling the wares while they lie in a hospital. So cool it on that, honey. There ain't a danged thing management can do about it—

you're a volunteer; you can't be fired!" She threw her head back and roared with laughter.

"One thing you can't do, and I must stress this very strongly, is to give the clients anything to eat or drink—not even a sip of water, nor a sprinkle of salt for the hash we slop as meals, nor a lemon to suck, a bone to chew or a piece of candy. Do not even wet a washcloth and run it across their lips. Strict orders. What they may have is determined by their condition, and the wrong thing may be fatal. If they ask for anything like that, tell the nurse at the station and let her handle it.

"Another thing to avoid, and I don't have to mention this, but then again, when I don't, some Doctor Kildare who watches TV medical shows goes and does it: don't read the patients' charts. You have no business with their medical info." She patted Montgomery on the knee again. Montgomery squirmed slightly. As a southern male brought up with traditional manners as an inviolable part of his heritage, her familiarity upon meeting him made him uncomfortable.

"One more thing: watch the notices on the doors. Wear a mask when you're supposed to. It's not for your protection, honey, you're a volunteer—if you get sick, we have no obligation to you. (She laughed loudly.) Masks are needed when the client's immune system is vulnerable to infection. We don't want you to kill them with your kindness!" The woman's folds of fat shook with her jolly ho-ho-ho's.

"Be sympathetic, converse with the clients but avoid the inclusive 'we'. Nobody likes that: How are we this morning? The answer is, 'My half is good, but your half looks lousy!' (Wilkie slammed her hand upon her desk) I think I read that in Mad™ magazine years ago.

"Whatever they ask for in way of medical attention, tell the nurse. If they cry, scream bloody murder and run for it! No, no (she gasped for breath), it's okay. Try not to get stuck in a room, though. Don't give medical advice, or make any conclusions for them, or explain anything. Refer them to their physicians. If they want you to provide mental therapy, advise them your billing rate is $300 an hour." Wilkie was slaying herself with her monologue.

"Any questions, honey? No? Then let me answer the one you want to ask. Soak that garish cloth you are wearing in pure bleach for twenty-four hours, rinse and put it through a wash. Trust me on this, honey. It will take most of the color out. I don't know what the fabric designer was on when he put that arrangement together, but it had to be strong!" With more laughter, shaking and panting, she pulled Montgomery out of his chair, spun him around and gave him a push.

"Go to it, Clark Barton," she cried. As Montgomery left with the cart, he could hear her laughter ringing through the front lobby.

Bacon Traditional Medical House was nearly as old as the university. Because the university had no medical school, and the population of the town was small, the hospital itself was small. Despite Wilkie's characterization of it as a "butcher shop", most surgeries were performed elsewhere at major hospitals in the urban centers of Florida. Bacon Traditional was a place that handled routine emergencies such as broken bones and stitching wounds, provided immediate care for heart attack and stroke victims, housed cancer patients undergoing chemotherapy treatments, and provided the in-house care for pneumonia and other common diseases that could not be treated at the patient's home.

Bacon Traditional had fifty patient rooms, semi-private and private. In a pinch, they could handle eighty persons. They had never been pinched during their years of operation. At this time, with Christmas approaching, the hospital was relatively empty. Only two dozen rooms were occupied, and no room had more than one person.

Montgomery quickly made the circuit of both floors, and found that the job was easy. Two hours later, he rode the elevator to the ground floor. He put the cart back in the admissions office and asked Wilkie what to do next.

She laughed. "You like to eat, don't you? Go to supper. The cafeteria serves until 7 p.m. Make sure you get your employee discount." She chortled over a cup of coffee.

Montgomery went to the cafeteria. The selection was meager. He took a tray, and decided upon a jello salad, beef stew over noodles, soggy squash, and chocolate cake. He helped himself to a Coke from the fountain. The checkout girl was in her teens with inch-long nails painted bright pink. She smacked her lips as she chewed her gum.

"I'm a new volunteer," Montgomery said. "Do I get a discount?"

"Yeah, sure, I guess. Go on."

"Go on?"

The girl blew a bubble and popped it with a loud smack. "Yeah, the discount is I don't ring you up. 'Cause I might break a nail." She held them out for Montgomery's admiration.

"Those are the finest nails I've ever seen. No, we wouldn't want to risk breaking one. Have you ever been in a competition? I am sure you'd take Grand Champion."

The girl laughed in an obnoxious way. "You liar, keep talking to me like that and you'll never pay for a meal. Go on."

Montgomery picked up his tray and moved to a table. The squash was terrible, but the stew tolerable if he did not speculate about what species the 'beef' came from. He ate the jello, half the stew, and the cake.

It was only 6:20 p.m.

Montgomery went back to the admissions office to see what he did next. Wilkie looked at him in surprise. "Don't you get it, honey? We're the backwaters—the end of the swamp. An ambulance to ER makes the front page of the Bacon newspaper. You're done. Beat it. Good night. Unless you have some nurse you want to chat up." She roared with laughter.

Montgomery felt guilty about leaving an hour and a half early when he had agreed to four hours of service. He wandered the halls looking for things to do. Finally, he realized that Wilkie was right and he left the hospital at 7 p.m.

At the quad, Travis, Cat and Red had gotten into a chugging contest. Red was the big loser and was hugging the porcelain wondering how he had flushed his brain along with the contents of his stomach.

Cat was sitting on the sofa barely keeping his eyes open, while Travis was on his feet, a little wobbly, but the victor surveying the field of contest.

"Montgomery," Travis said. "Care to challenge me?"

Montgomery grinned. "Travis, you're ripped. I could put you away—I haven't had anything to drink. What time did you guys start?"

A retching noise echoed out of the bathroom.

"Ignore that ignoble noise nottering igsponsibly natural nothing," Travis said. "Four o'clock."

"Didn't y'all eat dinner?"

"No time to tuck in noshable nuptials then knocking down Dippler's ale."

"Let me put you to bed."

Montgomery pushed his roommate into their room. He pulled the covers back on Travis' bed, sat his roommate down, removed his shoes and socks, pulled his shirt off, and swung his legs into the bed. Montgomery threw the sheet over his friend's body.

Travis laid his head upon his pillow. "Thanks, Trav ol' pal—no, I'm Trav—who are you?"

Montgomery laughed. "You'll know in the morning."

"Morning makes Montgomers—hey, you're that Lee helper always aiding ally Travings ..."

Montgomery put their trashcan next to Travis' bed by his pillow. "In case you need it."

Montgomery then pulled Cat off the sofa moving him into his room. Montgomery let Cat slump down upon his bed. He had not been aware of being moved. Montgomery pulled off his sandals, and threw them into his closet.

In the bathroom, Red was kneeling, bare-chested, barefoot and sweating profusely. "Why am I so dumb? I can't handle it like they can!"

"You're the one puking in the bathroom, but on the other hand, the other two have passed out and you're still awake."

"I'm glad you told me that. I'm never doing this again, but I'm glad to know I'm not out for the count." Red leaned over the stool and heaved. "I think it's all out—why won't my stomach calm down?"

"Dry heaves come when you have too much, too fast. They won't last forever. Why don't you go to bed? You're in no danger of vomiting on your sheets or your room."

"Thanks, Monkey. Is this what you do for Travis?"

"All the time."

"Thanks. Maybe we shouldn't call you Monkey—it's not very complimentary, is it?"

"I've grown to like it, but only from y'all—no one other than the quad."

"That fraternity doesn't know what it turned down. They should've let you in and thrown themselves out."

"Thanks," said a sincerely grateful Montgomery, who felt tears come into the corners of his eyes. "That's the nicest thing someone has said to me in a long time."

Wednesday arrived in a rush as the last hours of class dwindled away. Dormitories and apartment buildings clicked with the noises of tens of thousands of keyboards assembling sentences, constructing paragraphs of insightful analysis, scintillating commentary and meaningless blather, depending upon the scholarship of the student. Xerox machines ran hot copying reams of notes taken by attentive students kind enough to take pity on the truant students who spent their term playing and sleeping. The library computer took its semi-annual crash as thousands of students attempted to access its Internet resources at the same time.

Montgomery was finishing his semester on a strong note. He had solid grades moving into his finals, and despite the large amounts of time he had invested in Sigma Omicron Beta and Elizabeth, he had completed his reading assignments, written his English paper and was reviewing his notes for the final exams he would take in Chemistry, Math, Anthropology and Western Civilization.

Travis was on a roll. He met nightly with his study group, then headed over to Park's room. He was looking forward to his last examination of the semester with his different professors. They, too, were pleased with Travis and his performance. He was becoming exhibit A for making the experimental program an alternative for mediocre students making the transition to the collegiate level.

Montgomery was humming as he came into the hospital Wednesday afternoon. He was looking forward to the day of his last final exam when he and Travis would pack for the holidays and head back to the town of their birth.

Wilkie was her usual jolly self as Montgomery took the cart. "We are very light today: only ten beds—all on the first floor. Two auto crashes, three pneumonias, one bad back, one chemo, a who-knows-what, an only-God-knows, and a reindeer accident."

"A what?"

"The man got hit by a reindeer." Wilkie roared with laughter. "I'll let him tell his story."

Montgomery took the cart and headed out. He moved toward the first floor wing of rooms. The first two rooms were empty. The next two were polite but non-talkative. They did not want anything to read. The fifth was asleep. The next two took books and made small talk for five, maybe ten minutes.

Montgomery reached the eighth room and knocked on the door. "Book cart."

"Well, Martha, here's a new one for us," said a well-modulated voice. "A cart that talks. Come in, Mr. Cart, or should I call you Book?"

Montgomery went into the room. "Hello, sir, I'm the volunteer that circulates the book cart in the afternoon. Is there anything you wish to read?"

"Yes, young man, I wish to read tomorrow's newspaper. Would you have that on you?"

"Oh, Ed," his wife lightheartedly scolded, "they haven't printed it yet."

"That's why I wish to read it. Get the scoop on everybody." He laughed.

Montgomery smiled.

"That's what I like to see—a smile. Do you know why I'm in the hospital?"

"No, sir. But I'm all ears."

"Sit down, Montgomery. Let me tell you about the one that got away. 'Water, water everywhere with nary a drop to drink.' Coleridge,

The Rime of the Ancient Mariner. Great verse—you should read it if you haven't already. It describes south Florida. Everyone thinks Everglades, swamps, daily thunderstorms, plenty of water, too much water; not so. The truth is every drop's precious and two or three thirsty mohambas want to put their mitts on it. But the water district sends a couple million gallons a day out of the 'Glades into the ocean. Go figure.

"I'm a farmer, Montgomery. Interesting name, Montgomery. I run livestock on scrubland. It ain't much to look at but the cows and critters like to eat what grows. I make a living. One day I got this great idea to try ostrich farming. It went well, very well. I began to prosper. Today I have eighty birds on the farm laying big eggs that I sell. The meat is good and commands a high price.

"Word gets around that Ed is farming crosses between ducks and giraffes. Now that's farmers having a little bit of fun. But the next thing you know, some joker wants to grow a buffalo, and asks me if I'll keep one on the ranch. I quote a ridiculously high price for keep, and he pays it without dickering. Then he adds another, and another. Now I've got buffalos and ostriches.

"They made an interesting experiment in husbandry; that's animal farming if you're not familiar with the term. You know what? Buffalo and ostriches make great companions. Old MacDonald had some farm!

"Now along comes another great idea. At Christmas time, everyone wants to rent reindeer. I figure they'll mix well with the buffalos and ostriches. I hunt all over the country, way up into Canada too. I find a guy with reindeer, and I buy a dozen—bring 'em back to the ranch and set 'em loose. I put out the word to Santa outfits that I've got the genuine article.

"Then Bradley—a neighbor of mine—decides to play a joke on ol' Ed. He gets a barber pole—who knows where he stole it from—and attaches it to my mailbox with a sign that says 'North Pole'. Well, that's more than a fellow can take, especially after he ran an ad in the paper for used coffins, cheap, and listed my phone number."

"You would not believe the number of phone calls we received," said Martha.

"Skinflints, everyone of them," laughed Ed. "Well, I decided to give Bradley a taste of what he deserves. So I took a couple of reindeer, fixed 'em up with jingle bells and red velvet bridles, put 'em in my truck, and took them over to Bradley's house. I rigged me up a block and tackle, and hoisted those deer onto his roof. Then I drove off and hid and waited for the fun to start.

"Reindeer do not like to stand on roofs. They started stamping and pawing and snorting and bellowing. They made so much noise Bradley is wakened from his mid-day nap. He comes out to see what's making the racket. At that point one of the reindeer decides to leave the roof and make a break for escape. He leaps off the roof. Ed's jaw drops, he says, "Gol' durn, they can fly!" and he runs for the video camera. I fall back, laughing as hard as I can. The reindeer hits the ground, the impact stuns him, and he falls over. I rush out of hiding, because the critters run a grand apiece, to see if he's hurt. That's the moment the other one decides to jump—pack instinct, they can't help theirselves—he lands whomp! Right on my back, knocks me flat, takes the wind out of me, and breaks all my ribs. I'm still laughing so hard the tears are flowing down my face. Bradley comes running out of his house with a portable phone—he's called 911 but not for me—for the first reindeer. EMT responds and they haul me off here so the docs can tape me up to heal. They're afraid I'll puncture a lung, see—

"Bradley's still running around half out of his mind. The animals get to their feet and stagger off. Relax, I tell 'im, get your rifle and bag some deer meat. Montgomery, the deer were hurt bad inside and wouldn't live anyway. But Bradley looks at me like I'm the devil and he says, 'How would I explain that to my grandkids: that Santa ain't coming because I killed two of his reindeer and the sled won't fly!' Did you hear that: killed two of Santa's reindeer and his sled won't fly!"

Ed began laughing and crying from the pain. Montgomery was laughing too. Martha looked severe and tut-tutted, "Ed, stop that. You'll hurt yourself."

Ed said, "Yes, mama," but his eyes danced with delight.

Montgomery said, "That's a great story."

"I've got plenty of 'em but I won't keep you from your rounds. Come back."

"I'll stop in later."

Montgomery covered the last two rooms, and stopped back at the rooms where the patients had been out. With that accomplished, he swung his cart around and headed back for Ed's room.

There was fevered activity as medics, nurses and ER physicians ran in and out of the room. "What happened?" Montgomery asked one of the shift nurses who was watching the activity.

"He coded," the nurse said. In response to Montgomery's puzzled expression, she added, "Code blue—standard hospital lingo for a situation where a patient has stopped breathing, his heart has stopped beating, and/or some other situation where the patient is in immediate danger of dying without swift intervention. He went five minutes ago."

Intense feelings of guilt washed over Montgomery. *Had the excitement Ed felt in telling his story brought on the code blue? Was it my fault?*

Martha stood to the side, crying.

Should I go to her? What would I say? I'm only the volunteer to hand out magazines—I'm not supposed to do much else, am I?

The doctor came out of the room, and went to the new widow. "I'm sorry. It was a massive heart attack unrelated to his injuries. He could have gone at any time, anyplace. You're lucky he died here in the hospital; you'll always have the comfort of knowing he had the best that medical science can offer. It was his time."

Martha thanked the doctor for his efforts. "At least he died laughing. He lived by laughter, and took delight in sharing his laughter with others. That boy was a blessing for him so he could go out laughing."

Montgomery overheard the conversation, but he was not convinced. He turned and wheeled the cart back to the admissions office. Wilkie said, "Wasn't that a good story?" and was surprised to see him burst into tears. She hugged him tight upon learning that the man had died after telling Montgomery his story. "It's not your fault. This happens all the time in a hospital."

Montgomery nodded, wiped his face and said, "Good night." He went into the night, driving his truck into the Glades and stopping at one of his favorite spots for observation. He set his telescope up, and looked through it, but his eyes were unfocused as he thought about what had happened. Eventually he sank to the ground, closed his eyes and began to pray.

The following evening was the time when the volunteer group met for their weekly session with Dotty Newman. Montgomery was punctual, and was surprised to find that the rest of the group was not. He waited fifteen minutes before the next person drifted in. It was a full half-hour before Dotty arrived and the group began.

"We have a new member with us tonight," Dotty began. "Group, may I introduce Montgomery Lee. He began on Monday past. He'll be with us for the next ten weeks. Serianna, present your situation, please."

A mid-thirties woman with beautiful chocolate skin, dark brown eyes, high cheekbones, black wavy hair, and polished fingernails spoke. "The event occurred two weeks before, in the morning, as I was distributing the morning newspapers to the patients' rooms. My issue is whether it's appropriate for volunteers to perform personal services as requested by the patient.

"Mr. B was in bed. He had dropped his hospital gown upon the floor. 'I can never keep those things on,' he said. 'They're so loose they slip off my shoulders. Could you assist me in refastening my gown?' I looked at Mr. B. He was nude, and had arranged his top sheet so that it almost, but not quite, exposed himself.

"I told Mr. B it was not appropriate for me to help a patient dress, but I would summon the orderly who could help him with his problem. He became obnoxious and abusive, accusing me of racism for refusing a white man for a simple act of assistance when he was sure I would readily accept someone of my own race.

"I assured him it was not a question of race; as a female, it was not appropriate for me to be in his room while he is undressed and uncovered. He then asked me if I was uptight and wouldn't I like a peek. In very strong terms I told him he was being inappropriate and I was leaving his room. He then jumped from the bed and started screaming that I had torn the gown from his body—that I had to have a look. He told me—well, the entire hospital he was so loud—to keep my hands to myself and not to touch his ——-, well you get the idea. He made it sound like I was being inappropriate with him.

"I fled the room humiliated over the entire scene. So my question is, Did I do the right thing? or should I have put the gown on the dude to cover him over without looking at him? That would have prevented his performance.

"In thinking about this question, I've thought about our role in the hospital. We're here to help the patients with those little services and helps that they can't do for themselves and that the medical staff is too busy to do for them. I've watered flowers, read books, opened mail, dialed phone calls, retrieved family from the cafeteria, brought toiletries from the hospital shop, and any number of other minor deeds that make the stay more pleasant.

"It would help the hospital staff not to have to deal with this type of behavior. However, we, the volunteers, don't have the training to deal with this situation. Obviously it was not a matter of dressing; it was exhibitionism and perhaps an invitation for more intimate activity.

"Clearly it's not appropriate for volunteers, even though we are unpaid and have no formal connection with the hospital, to have skin to skin contact with patients outside of handshaking, etc. and other forms of greeting that are common between strangers in American society.

"Mr. B was making an opening move of sexual solicitation. So I could not help him without signaling that his advance was welcome. But then, how could I have avoided him making a scene?"

"What were you wearing?" said Dotty.

"I beg your pardon?"

"Your clothes. What did you have on?"

"A dress, neutral color—beige I think. I try to avoid anything more colorful as it clashes with that horrible top."

"Did it button in the front?"

"No, I wouldn't wear a housedress to the hospital."

"No, a supermodel as yourself wouldn't be caught dead in such a mundane outfit," Dotty said with dripping sarcasm. "Makeup?"

"Some eye shadow and liner, lipstick. What has that to do with anything?"

"Shade of lipstick."

"Cherry."

"Aha," Dotty spat.

"Aha what?"

"Bright red lipstick is a provocative sexual come-on, isn't that right, Mr. Lee?"

"Um, um, I wouldn't know," said Montgomery.

"Um, um, I wouldn't know," mocked Dotty. "You are eighteen years old, are you not?"

"Yes, ma'am."

"You are male, are you not?"

"Yes, ma'am."

"Aren't you excited when you see a woman wear red lipstick?"

Montgomery blushed and mumbled, "No, no ma'am, well it depends."

"Depends? Depends on what, Mr. Lee? Which way you're swinging that day?"

Fire flashed in Montgomery's eyes. "Ma'am, that is insulting and uncalled for."

"Insulting and uncalled for," Dotty mocked his words. "So you initiated the sexual advance, Serianna. You still have not acknowledged your secret desire to experience a prostitute's world. So you coyly signal sexual overtures in ways that male patients can't resist. You're divorced with no boyfriend. Your body urges you for satisfaction. Your psychological pathology drives you to find sex for pay—you want the thrill of dabbling in the forbidden, the proscribed. So you come to the hospital where your targets have no means of escape. Deal with it, woman, you're a whore."

"That's ridiculous," sputtered a seventy-year old man. "The gown was on the floor when she entered the room. How could that be a response to her lipstick when the patient had not even seen her yet?"

"Is she giving you a piece of the action, Bertie? Is that why you're sticking up for her?"

Montgomery felt a stabbing pain in his spirit. He was being transported back to that day during rush week when Cody had taken his psychological tests and deliberately twisted his answers to produce a harsh, condemning picture of his self.

"Why are you deliberately twisting the situation to make Miss Serine into a psychological deviant?" he asked Dotty.

"Very good, Mr. Lee," she responded. "We'll take a fifteen minute break."

Montgomery was surprised to see that an hour had already gone by. He walked to the vending machines with Serine to get a coke.

"She was brutal on you."

Serianna smiled. "She does that to everybody."

"Why?"

Serianna laughed. It was a full-bodied laugh, generous, kind and deep. "She's a frustrated counselor stuck in a dead-end job. What she really wants to do is run a program for C.P.E. That's why she makes her volunteers go through this weekly exercise."

"C.P.E.? I've never heard of that."

"Clinical Pastoral Education. It's offered by Chaplain Departments in many hospitals around the country. Chaplains and ministers in training enroll in the program, and work as chaplains in the hospital. C.P.E. is supposed to teach them good interpersonal skills and the spiritual needs of persons in the clinical setting, which is the hospital. As they learn and practice skills needed to minister to persons who are in crisis, they also wind up examining themselves and their reactions to persons in crisis. If they have any weaknesses, these are exposed and they work with the C.P.E. supervisor in overcoming them. The program also tests them to see if they can handle the burdens presented by ministering to folks in crisis."

"What does that have to do with us?"

"C.P.E. programs used to focus on education; training the minister or chaplain for work in the medical arena. If the psychological stuff came up, then they dealt with it. But the programs changed in the late

1980's. Now, they're run by wannabee psychiatrists who see the program as a bastardized form of psychoanalysis. If you don't have any issues when you enlist, they give you some!"

"I don't get how this relates to handing out magazines."

"Didn't she ask you to list your issues when you signed up? For that matter, who asks volunteers to sign a contract? How can they? You give them hours of labor—what is she giving you?"

"A load of crap is what it looks like."

Serianna laughed hard. "You catch on quick, Montgomery."

Montgomery grinned.

"The only one I know who is still doing it right," Serianna continued, "is Henry Marksberry in Cincinnati although he may have retired by now. He keeps the focus on education—the program is to teach. All the others think their job is to play psychotherapist. That's what Dotty plays at. She believes her job is to tear you into pieces, right away, breaking down your ego and your conscience and your values and your ideals and your spirit and your soul. She wants to destroy your psychological make-up."

"Why would she do that?"

"Because she believes it's her job to rebuild you the right way. She believes the only way she can rebuild you is to tear you apart first."

"But no one asked her to do that."

"It doesn't matter to her. She believes she's a top psychoanalyst. She knows best because she has read Freud and Jung. What you believe, think and want doesn't matter to her because she always has a category of psychological deviancy to drop your objections into."

"Why would churches put their ministers through that? Wouldn't they care more about Christ-training and education than the theories of psychologists?"

"You'll have to ask the churches that question."

"No wonder those jerks sent me here. I should have known better; they don't care about community service. They wanted Dotty to break my spirit, or make me give up, and if I don't complete the ten weeks, then I am terminated as a pledge."

"What fraternity are you pledging?"

"Sigma Omicron Beta."

"The S.O.B.'s. They should give Dotty an honorary membership."

They both laughed.

"I'm here to hand out books, not to have an unqualified, uncertified wannabee play with my head. If she tries to make more than that, she can hang-ten on the next wave to Hawaii."

"I'm doing an anthropology study: the hospital as a specialized subculture of American society. I'm writing my dissertation about it." Serianna smiled. "She calls me a whore one more time, she'll have a chapter all to herself: sociological pathologies."

"So the whore jumps on fresh meat the first chance she gets," remarked the acid tongue of Dotty who had stolen up to them unawares.

Serianna smiled wickedly. "You got it."

Dotty's blank look revealed she had not heard Serianna's threat regarding the master's thesis. Serianna and Montgomery burst into laughter and started back to the classroom. With a sudden inspiration, Montgomery grabbed Serianna's hand and held it as they walked.

"If she's going to mess with my mind," said Montgomery, "I'm going to mess with hers."

Serianna laughed deeply. "That's the spirit."

CHAPTER THIRTEEN

THE SECOND TASK

FOLLOWING THANKSGIVING, Montgomery received a notice that his Interpersonal Relations Group had been formed and would meet on Friday at 7 p.m. Montgomery groaned, hoping the group would not take too long because Friday night he wanted to be with Elizabeth.

The head of the group was a female professor in her late forties, extremely thin, who wore tailored trousers, custom shirts, and a long tie. She wore her hair very short—butch style. There were three other members of the group. Each was an undergraduate specializing in women's studies.

"Don't go," said Cat. "Object to the group. Say you had no input in choosing the members."

"Be careful," said Red. "He'll ask us to be in it."

"Why not?" responded Cat. "We'd make a good group. We could sit here in the quad, drink beer and talk about women for an hour, and call it a session."

The boys laughed.

"That's a thought," said Travis.

"What is?" prompted Cat.

"Montgomery should go drunk—whatever they do, he won't care and with luck, won't remember. If they report him to the frat, those guys won't hold it against him!"

The boys laughed again.

"Tell us again what this group is supposed to do," said Red.

"The group is directed to focus on how I relate to women," replied Montgomery. "Every week we talk about a topic or issue of my choosing, and they give me feedback on what they observe. Supposedly, the feedback helps me understand myself better and how to improve the way I relate to women."

"How long do you do this?" asked Red.

"Six weeks. First three before Christmas, last three when the new term starts."

The first Friday night, a warm front from a low-dipping trough brought heavy showers to the campus. Montgomery splashed his way through The Ring to the section of the classroom annex where the Women's Studies Division was housed. He was casually dressed as normal in shorts, t-shirt and sneakers.

He ran inside the building, and shook the excess water from his body. He wiped his feet on the mat in a useless gesture of not mud-dying up the hallway. He moved along until he came to a student lounge where the group was going to meet.

As he came in the door, four heads turned from the conversation they were enjoying.

"Pardon me, is this the Interpersonal Group for Montgomery Lee?"

The oldest woman fixed a piercing gaze upon him. "Are you Mr. Lee?"

"Yes, ma'am, I am."

"Why do you call me ma'am?" she snapped. "Are you trapped in the southern male condescension toward women of all ages?"

"No, ma'am, I am not. I was raised that way—not to condescend—to call women 'ma'am' as a term of respect."

"You don't think I'm a Mammy for you?"

"No, ma'am," said a wary-eyed Montgomery.

"Sit down," barked the woman. "I am Elizabeth Barksdale, faculty adjunct professor for Women's Studies at the university. Three of my students: Alyssa, Marissa, and Clew. Our job is to fix your male-dominant, Neanderthal attitude toward the oppression of women. Got it?"

"Yes, ma'am."

"You will call me Elizabeth. I am your equal, and you will address me as I address you."

"Okay, Elizabeth." Montgomery drew out the word, showing his discomfort at addressing a professor and woman his mother's age by her first name.

"Tonight we will talk about the Garden of Eden. Marissa, give us a run-down of what actually took place during the so-called 'Fall of Man' which, I might note, is a sexist term that excludes one-half of Homo Sapiens."

A honey-blonde girl of average height and slight heaviness spoke. "The female is the central character in the drama that occurs in the center of the Garden of Paradise. Not only does she interact with the antagonist, which the man does not, but she makes the critical decision to obtain the forbidden knowledge which will enable her to achieve goddess status."

The four women smiled. Montgomery wondered: *Do they believe that they're endowed with that status as daughters of Eve?*

Marissa continued, "The snake, a symbol of male oppression and lust, moves for the woman, wishing to wiggle upon her in an effort to defile her. He makes his pitch of seduction for he knows that the woman is the decision-maker for the couple. The man stands dumbly by. Note that this is the pre-Fall status of evolved Homo Sapiens. Even the patriarchal bias of the Biblical writer cannot obscure the leading role of the female.

"The woman decides, the man accepts her decision unquestioningly and joins her. But oh! While goddess status is an obtainable goal for the woman, the man is not a creature made out for such heights. So with her new wisdom, the woman clothes herself so that man will not stare upon her bare body and seek to dominate her out of lust.

"But it is too late. The man got a peek, and in his helplessness, also took a covering so he would not betray his weakness to the woman.

"Then the patriarchal woman-hating god came by. In his anger-filled motivation, he curses woman so that the source of her femininity will always be filled with pain: her ability to give birth. He takes revenge out of his hate by aiding the man in oppressing the woman to an inferior status. He sets the serpent against the woman's children; again, the source of masculinity is hostile to the fruit of femininity."

Clew summed up. "Here it is: the snake of male lust deceives the woman so that males can oppress females using them to satisfy their selfish lust and needs as they desire. The woman, in her natural role as head and decision-maker for the couple, shows her priority in being the one to talk to the snake and to make the decision. She grows in her potential to be a goddess by becoming wise—she knows to cover up or the man will be aroused beyond his capacity to control. Despite the male-snake's intention, she gains—evolves to a better state. The man has no choice but to go along, even though we see he has very little brain to reason with. The woman would have continued in her superior role but for the patriarchal god who comes along and curses her into an inferior state. Males have taken full advantage of the curse to satisfy their lusts and keep women down for thousands of years."

The professor drew her beady eyes upon Montgomery. "What do you say?"

The wheels of Montgomery's mind were rapidly turning in the midst of a dense fog. "Rather unusual interpretation."

"Is it now," said Alyssa. "What's your slant—the usual male view that God put man in charge of woman?"

"It is a fallacy to assume that the results of disobedience that God announced in chapter three of the book of Genesis are what He wills for his creation. The cursed ground that's only worked with great difficulty, the mortality of human flesh, the pain in childbearing, the woman's shift from investing herself into God to investing herself into her husband, and the hatred of snakes are regrettable, dreadful consequences of the sin, which both woman and man committed together in eating of the tree, which God had forbidden. This is not what God wanted, but what came upon humankind as a result of what they had done."

"Oh, really," challenged Alyssa. "He allows it to go on, doesn't He? Why doesn't He stop it?"

"Free will—God gave us free will. Free will means living with the consequences. If God intervened to change or reverse the consequences, then it isn't free will—just an awkward way of achieving a divine, dictated will."

"Free will. Man freely chooses to dominate women, then."

"Careful," urged Marissa.

Montgomery answered, "Some men do. Others don't."

Clew took over. "Isn't in their very nature to oppress women?"

"If they can't help it, why am I here?"

The professor smiled. "He got you there, Clewie dear."

Alyssa resumed, "But don't men use Genesis 3 to justify oppressing women?"

Montgomery said, "Many people, not only men, misread Genesis 3. (The professor thought to herself: *he's sharp and subtle.*) They take it to mean that God wants men to domineer women. But when the entire Bible is read, it's clear that God has a different view for how men and women should relate to each other."

"Don't drag out that tired Ephesians passage about women submitting to men."

"Actually, that's a very good passage to bring out. That's another greatly misused passage because it isn't read properly. There are six subsections: one addressed to wives, one to husbands, one to children, one to parents, one to slaves and one to masters. All six are grouped under the major theme and general principle, which is stated before the subsections: 'Submit to one another in fear of Christ.' So men are to submit to women, and women to men.

"The subsections are addressed to particular persons to add an explanation for them. No man can use the verse, "for the husband is the head of the wife," because it isn't addressed to him; it's addressed to, and is only for, women. As far as men are concerned, that verse doesn't exist. Man's command is to love his wife as dearly as Christ loves the church—to the point of self-sacrifice, which is what the man did in the Garden passage. He sacrificed himself on behalf of his wife, rather than obeying God and risk losing her. If the men of Ephesus were too dense to understand that, they were told to love their wives as they do their own bodies.

"The meaning is this: Man is commanded to sacrifice his desire to rule and domineer, or as you put it, oppress women, if he has such a desire. He's to sacrifice whatever dominance he thinks he's entitled to out of love for his wife, just as Christ sacrificed whatever he was entitled to out of love for humankind. The man who would domineer is checked by the command to sacrifice.

"So the passage that you think condones male oppression actually does the reverse."

Marissa and Clew sat stolidly as they worked out the meaning and implication of Montgomery's interpretation.

Alyssa hissed, "That's why we reject the Bible as male oppression. You men are always able to twist it to your advantage. You're always right because the Bible supports your claims."

"Gee," said Montgomery, "I thought I said that the Bible supports your position."

"That's right, twist it around so you win. The male always has to win the point." Alyssa was beside herself with rage.

The professor's sharp eyes were regarding the person of Montgomery. She looked at his closely shaven head (the hair had not grown much since Montgomery had ditched the Mohawk): half an inch of naturally blond hair, neat sideburns, wispy hairs on the chin, strong green eyes and his slender body. She mused over the strong chin and proportionate nose that combined to make his boyish face attractive and winning.

"Let's move into feedback," she announced. "Marissa, you first."

"The man listened to what we said, but he was not open to understanding our point of view. He was so set in his own opinions that little of what we said made a mark in his male orientation to view women as objects. I resented his obvious efforts to patronize our views. It was probably a clumsy attempt to gain our affection, possibly for future sexual advances."

"Insightful observations," remarked the professor. "Clew, you next."

"Montgomery listened, but I experienced him as closed. His closure left us unable to determine how he was receiving our views. Was he rejecting them? Was he thinking similarly? Was he evaluating his positions? We don't know. Very disconcerting. We need feedback from him if he's to make us feel comfortable in his presence."

"Yes, you have a point. Alyssa?"

"This oppressor is beyond hope. He's so indoctrinated in the methods and thought of male oppression that castration is the only hope for female society. Total mind reprogramming is needed to rid him of his reflex of patriarchal Bible nonsense whenever confronted by truth not his own."

"Perhaps over the edge, but you have a valid basis for holding that opinion."

Clew spoke up. "You're pushing your own issues onto him, Alyssa. His responses were gender-neutral—favoring neither men nor women. Whether or not they actually express his real beliefs we don't know. His manners are old-fashioned—respectful. I don't find that objectionable—it's much better than the alternative 'enlightened' men have chosen: rudeness."

"Your father didn't rape you, Clew. You would see a far different truth if you went through what I went through."

"I'm tired of you using victim status to put down everyone who disagrees with you."

"Stop it," the professor spoke sharply. "We're here to deal with Mr. Lee's issues, not our internal disputes."

The hall clock ticking away punctuated several seconds of silence.

"I'll hold my comments," said the professor. "Mr. Lee, do you have anything to say?"

"No, ma'a—Elizabeth. The opinions are quite unlike anything I've heard before."

The professor smiled grimly. "You will not find tonight a unique experience. Next week at seven."

Montgomery stood, wondering if he should allow the women to

leave first, shake hands, or say goodbye? The four women remained seated. In confusion, Montgomery turned around and gained the hallway, then more from instinct than rational decision, he ran for the door and into the night. He didn't stop running until he arrived at Alyssa Hawkins dormitory and was in the room of the three Alabama women who loved their men and were not tied up in a straitjacket of militant feminism.

Upon arriving in the room, Montgomery grabbed Elizabeth, hugged her tight and kissed her passionately for several minutes. She weakened, and they tumbled back against the wall.

"What's that all about?" asked Park.

"I guess he learned something tonight about interpersonal relations," cracked Travis with a big grin.

Rose looked at Rick. "Next week I'm sending you with him."

"You don't have to," Rick countered as he proceeded with a demonstration for his girlfriend.

"Do we need a hose?" Park asked Travis.

"MMphh," went Travis as he joined Park in mimicking the two couples.

Elizabeth sat down on her bed and pulled Montgomery close to her.

"I love you," he said.

"I love you," she answered.

Travis was feeling a hole in the pit of his bowels. *I can't explain it, but Montgomery and Elizabeth, and Rose and Rick, have something that I don't. I'm jealous—most guys would say that I have the sexiest and prettiest one of the three; I really like her, the sex is great, we're able to arrange some type of privacy three or four times a week, but I don't have with Park what Montgomery has with Elizabeth, and I'm beginning to realize that I'm missing something that I want.*

On the other hand, Park was feeling uncertain with Travis. *He's changing and growing every day. I have what I want: a lightweight party guy to have good times with, a guy with no depth, someone who liked to have a good time and left the thinking to others. That's Travis, or that was Travis; now the bottom's falling out of his personality. He's developing depth—I'm not sure if I like that. Can I hold his interest if he continues to deepen in his character? I'm not sure I want to—I want frivolity and fun, but the man can make my eyes roll back in ways that no one else can. What should I do?*

Rose and Rick wanted to discuss marriage, but each was afraid to raise the subject lest they break up. Rick decided to talk with Montgomery at the end of the evening or sometime the next day. Rose decided to look at bridal dresses with her Mom over the Christmas break.

"What's playing at the campus flick show?" asked Montgomery.

"Five different movies: Cobalt Blue, action-adventure; Casablanca, classic oldie; Huggins the Cuddly Bear, cartoon; Shark Island, romance-adventure; and Greek Pieta, arts film," replied Park.

"Isn't there a sixth movie?" asked Rick.

"Yes, but I don't want to go," said Park.

"Why not?" asked Travis.

"Because—because it's a martial arts film."

"Who's in it?" asked Elizabeth.

"Some Chinese beat-up guy—something Chan, um—let me think."

"Chan—you mean Jackie Chan?" Montgomery suggested.

"Yes. I hate those movies—all you do is watch Asians beat up other Asians, the plots make no sense—if there is a plot—what's so funny?"

The other five were laughing. Travis said, "Hon, we're going to the Jackie Chan film. Trust me—you'll like it."

Park made a face and put on a jacket.

Travis said, "Jackie Chan makes comedies. They're usually cop, spy or detective movies. The martial arts aren't beating people up, but broad comic gags because the stunts involved are unrealistic. The plots are deliberately silly to aid the comic effect. You'll like it—the movies are entertaining and unburdened by a director's social statements or political views."

Park said, "It had better be good."

Travis kissed her. "If it isn't, I'll make it up to you."

Later, as they stood in line, Elizabeth asked Montgomery, "What happened tonight in the group?"

Montgomery laughed. "It's four women and me. Elizabeth Barksdale—"

"The shrew!" cried Rick.

"Who?" said Rose.

"The shrew," repeated Rick. "Tart, sour, severe looking, she hates men. She runs the Women's Studies Department on campus. No man would ever take one of her courses—she's known to fail them for possessing a Y chromosome. Heh-heh-heh-heh-heh. That's funny: the men most obnoxious toward women want you to learn from a Femi-Nazi how to relate to women. Ha-ha-ha."

"What's a femi-nazi?" asked Rose.

"An extreme feminist who hates men and everything male," replied Montgomery. "Someone who is militantly bashing male prerogatives to replace them with equal, but opposite female prerogatives. Someone so extremely feminist that she is unable to have any type of relationship with a male. The term was coined on talk radio."

"Who are the other women?" asked Elizabeth.

"Undergrads: Alyssa, Marissa and Clew. Nobody told me their last names."

"Nobody had to," interjected Rick. "The three witches of Macbeth. Somebody hates you, brother."

"Go figure. They must be slipping if that's all the better they can do."

"Who are the three witches of Macbeth?" asked Elizabeth.

"William Shakespeare opened his tragedy Macbeth with a scene of three witches arranging a meeting," responded Travis. "'When shall we three meet again in thunder, lightning or in rain? When the hurly-burly's done, when the battle's lost and won. That will be ere the set of sun. Where the place? Upon the heath. There to meet with Macbeth. I come, Graymalkin! Paddock calls: anon. Fair is foul, and foul is fair: hover through the fog and filthy air.'"

The other five stared at Travis in astonishment.

"We studied the play," Travis said matter-of-factly. "In class."

"On campus," said Rick, "the three women Montgomery named are known as the three witches of Macbeth—the weird sisters bubbling their cauldrons and speaking their evil spells against all males."

"Come now," said Rose, "y'all are being overly dramatic. They're specializing in women's studies and hold colloquiums once a month to publish their research and discuss their findings. They're quite a feisty group."

"That's putting it mildly," said Montgomery. "The venom they spewed would put pesticide companies out of business."

"Only the male ones, dear," giggled Elizabeth.

"Tell us what happened," said Park eagerly.

"One girl—"

"Never, never, never call them girls," warned Rick.

"One woman," Montgomery corrected himself, "gave a most interesting slant on Genesis 3 from the Bible. The woman was the great heroine, and the rest were villains. Unless the woman said it or did it, it was male oppression. Then they asked what I thought. Then one started in on me, and we talked about Ephesians and the part about wives and husbands. Then the leader—the shrew—told the women to tell me how they perceived me acting. Three different accounts were given that said nothing about me, but revealed much about them. Then the shrew said she would hold her comments. That was it."

"Was it interesting?" asked Elizabeth.

"It was tonight, but if they stick to harping about male oppression, it's going to get old and boring fast. We meet again next week."

"What's your reaction?" asked Rick.

"Look, I'm doing this stuff to get into the frat. That's it. The boys are barking up the wrong tree. They tried to say I'm lousy with women at the last interview, but I told them to tell that to my girlfriend. That shut them up. Why I'm going to this group, I don't know and I don't care. It means nothing to me except rigamarole dreamed up as extended hazing."

"Why don't you tell them to kiss your hairy —" Travis started.

"Here we are at the window," broke in Elizabeth.

"Six for Jackie Chan," said Rick, paying for the tickets from the money he had collected.

"Park's eyes ought to be rolling now like a slot machine in Las Vegas," remarked Elizabeth as she lay in Montgomery's arms on the couch in the quad common room. It was 2 a.m.

"Jackpot!" breathed Montgomery.

They laughed together. By prior arrangement, Park had the room for herself, Rose was staying with Rick because he had a single room as floor advisor, and that left Elizabeth to find a place—which she had decided would be Montgomery's quad, but not in private quarters.

"Do you think Rose —" started Elizabeth.

"I never speculate without data," interrupted Montgomery. "It's very dangerous and the result is more wrong than simply living with not knowing."

"I never thought of it that way."

"It's hard to believe that a male and female would share a room and not become intimate, but then again, here's the two of us—fully clothed."

"Why is that?" Elizabeth laughed. "I'm not giving you an invitation to make a move; I'm merely asking why we're sitting out here like this. Most of our peers would have done it and fallen asleep by now."

"The value in waiting is that we can build deeper levels of intimacy before crossing that line. Without the pressure of sex hanging over us, we're free to develop our relationship in many more ways which is enriching our love far beyond anything Travis and Park have."

"Okay, but when do we cross the line? When do we know our relationship is ready—we've gone to the level and variety of depths that we want?"

"One answer is marriage which I'm definitely not asking you."

"Good. We need more time before considering that."

"Marriage creates a state where the levels of intimacy are deep enough for sex to add, not take away from the relationship," pondered Montgomery. "The missing element is the legal bond so that full trust can be given and acted upon. Under that bond, our fates are welded together into one fate. I can't betray you because that would be to betray myself. That's the point when relationships can safely and beneficially blossom into sexual intercourse."

"Could we reach that point before marriage? Don't misunderstand, I'm not desperate to go to bed; I'm merely wondering if it's possible to reach that point before marriage—since almost nobody waits any longer."

"God doesn't think so. He still asks us to wait for marriage."

"What do you think?"

"I won't deny that I ache for you in the night. If you know how the male body works—"

"I do. Males have an erection every time they enter dream phase in their sleep."

"Right. I love you so much I wake up from that state—well, you know—aching to have you in my arms. But I love you too much to dishonor you by suggesting we have intercourse. I grew up a Christian, and I am trying to live a Christian life. I go to church on Sundays. I don't want to disappoint Christ, my Lord. It's hard, but I love him, too. So I don't and I won't."

"Where did you come from?" asked Elizabeth with wonder in her voice.

"We're having this conversation, and you're wondering where I came from?" Montgomery laughed. He swirled his tongue around her ear.

"You melt me," Elizabeth breathed. "How do you decide what you can and cannot do?"

"I do anything that won't lead into temptation. So we stay out of private quarters, like my room, we keep our clothes on, we keep our hands outside of our clothes, we do not touch each other's genitals even from the outside of our clothing or other hot zones like the breasts, and we maintain enough separation from one another that we do not become overwhelmed by lust for each other."

Elizabeth kissed Montgomery hard.

"Do you ever think you're ready even if God wants you to wait?"

"Obviously my body is ready; it reacts from the slightest touch of your body. But my soul and my spirit are not—my emotions are too tender for me to move ahead of God's plan. Am I disappointing you?"

"No," she murmured. "I, too, am a virgin at the advanced age of eighteen. But sometimes I think I'm ready—for the right person—at the right time."

Montgomery kissed her back. "Let's not rush anything, okay? There's many complications that can arise, emotionally, spiritually, that we want to be sure."

"I love you, General Lee."

"I love you, General Stuart."

The week flew by. Montgomery was glad that this last week of classes was not a series of crises of long-ignored deadlines, but a smooth wrap-up of his first term of college. Besides the interpersonal relations group, he was working twice a week at the hospital and had the Thursday night meetings with his supervisor and the other volunteers.

The night after witnessing the hatchet job Dotty Newman had done on Serianna, Montgomery found himself once more the target of the three witches and the shrew.

"The Taming of the Shrew," said the shrew, "was the attempt of an emasculated male to fulfill the then-extant male fantasy of marrying the Queen of England and restoring male pride wounded over woman's ascendancy to sovereignty. The independent woman, master of her house and kin, sovereign over her domain, is subdued through marriage and male oppressive mistreatment. Clew, you begin."

"The negative portrayal of the independent woman, as rude and unfit for society, reflects the male bias so pervasive in the body of work generally credited to William Shakespeare. Only if she demures in modesty to speak not in male company and to act not without her father's or husband's permission does she win acclamation. Should she be so bold as to speak her mind and make her own decisions, she is branded with the worst cut of the male patriarchal society, she is said to be unmarriageable."

Marissa took up the dissertation. "Kate is loud, she is obnoxious, she is objectionable in every way; refusing to make herself attractive for a man, refusing to learn the domestic skills to make a man happy, and refusing to parade herself in front of males for the purpose of attracting a suitor are depicted as great deficiencies of character. However, the truth is that she is the paradigm of the modern, liberated woman."

Clew took over. "This the medieval-minded man of Elizabethan England found as revolting as the fact of a woman on the throne. Her father is much condescendingly pitied as a fool who did not raise a submissive daughter and now will be stuck with her and, as male tyrants view it, her tart tongue forever. Though the truth is that Kate is the one to be pitied; stuck in a male-domineered society, whereby she is legally the property of her father and must reside with him and his oppressive ideas. The woman's shrewishness is not the fault of her character or personality—it is reflective of the destruction wreaked upon a woman's psyche by men who are unable to understand or tolerate a strong woman."

As Marissa resumed, Montgomery wondered: *Has Alyssa been silenced by the group because of her over the edge hostility of the previous week, or is she in reserve?*

"Of course, men break the spirit of the strong woman. A suitable man is found who marries Kate and carries her home. She attempts to establish herself as the equal of the husband who tortures her by denying her food and comfort until she submits. A year later, the husband takes her back to her father's house and, to the admiration of all who had known her, she is a changed woman, submissive and polite. The husband collects his winnings of a wager he had made that he could tame her, and applause—applause (acid drops of Marissa's sarcasm sizzled in the room) man comes out on top. The truth is that the man cruelly wreaked his violence upon the woman, destroying her femininity and in its place creating an animated mannequin that he may position as his whim wills."

The shrew narrowed her eyes upon Montgomery. "Your comments, Mr. Lee."

"I reckon we need to reclassify The Taming of the Shrew from one of Shakespeare's comedies to one of his tragedies."

"That's exactly the type of comment I'd expect from a male," Alyssa spat. "What seems innocuous and inoffensive is actually an indirect attack upon our views, a typical method of the nasty oppressor. Tragedy? It's a farce! Shakespeare's big joke! Let's all laugh and ridicule a woman who dares to raise herself to the level of men! Let's mock with scathing sarcasm the female human being. She's not a human; she's a nasty, little rodent with a fierce nature and sharp bite: sorex vulgaris. But the vulgarity is that of men who put down women through their oppressive use of language. Sorex vulgaris? I'd like to sorex your vulgaris!"

Montgomery saw Clew suppressing a smile out of the corner of his eye. *Is she a silent ally?*

"You raise the issue of language," he said, hoping to divert the group from further discussion of the play. "It's good to use gender-neutral language although it often becomes impossible to maintain. For example, objections have been made to the use of words like chairman, doorman, fireman and the like. But how do you replace them?

"For the female head of a committee, we changed to chairwoman. But that was less than satisfactory for that emphasized her sex instead of making it irrelevant. The next attempt was chairperson, but even that fell flat as son is a male word, so we contracted to chair. In trying to use gender-neutral language, we have turned the leadership of our committees over to the furniture! I suppose we could use chairper-daughter, but that is awkward, don't you think?

"Even 'female' is troublesome. The word is an inflection of male. Woman is an inflection of man. She is based on he. Person has a son. Heroine derives from hero. I have heard a bishop talk about sheros. He drops the inflection from heroine as a sexist term, but re-inflects the word to make it feminine and the irony escapes him.

"We could reduce the doorman to the door. The door will see you out. The door will hold the door for you. Ask the door to summon a taxi. A tad silly, but serviceable. But you can't change a fireman into a fire. How many fires were injured at the blaze last night? It becomes nonsensical.

"The only way to do it is to drop the sex identification altogether. Use only one set of pronouns for all genders, or at least for both sexes. The woman ate his hamburger with mustard and relish which spilled onto his clothes. He wiped the pants with a hankie, and the woman discarded it into an empty pill bottle he carried in his purse for such an occasion. Or, she emerged from the men's locker room with her jewels securely held by her jockstrap.

"Then we need two separate words to distinguish the sexes with neither derived from the other. Maybe affa for women, and amma for men. For the times when we need a singular word to cover a man or a woman, we could use eeda. The chaireeda, the fire-eeda; an improvement over fires putting themselves out and furniture running meetings."

Alyssa spoke menacingly and softly, "If I had a knife with me ..."

Montgomery smiled. "I'm wearing steel underwear."

"You're enjoying this," said the shrew, not certain whether she approved or disapproved.

Alyssa said, "May I offer feedback?"

The shrew nodded.

"The oppressor's smug attitude is more than off-putting; it's disgusting. With his puny, ineffectual attempts at humor, he reveals his utter lack to comprehend the struggles of women against the oppression of their enemies. He refuses to acknowledge women's rightful place alongside him. He approves of the violence committed against women by ignorant, redneck, traditional males in every way. I say milk him for sperm and cut his buddies off his body." Alyssa was seething like an over hot furnace ready to blow.

Marissa spoke next, "The boy makes sport of important issues in an effort to charm us as he adds his infantile humor to his looks. He assumes that we cannot perceive his purpose, but he has the typical male attitude that we want him to give us sex. Therefore, he continues his efforts, started last week, to throw out hints that he is available—if we are willing to degrade ourselves by making advances toward him. Like all males, his manner here tonight shows he believes himself irresistible."

Clew anchored the feedback portion. "Montgomery is not trying to seduce any of us, Marissa. How can you read that from what he said?"

Marissa snapped, "It's so obvious that I can't understand how you ignore it. He constantly sprays it to all four of us—maybe he thinks he can fulfill the universal male sexual fantasy of having the four of us at the same time."

Clew broke into peals of silvery laughter. "Not Alyssa; he wouldn't risk exposing himself—she'd rip 'em off with her bare hands."

Alyssa rejoindered sarcastically, "Ha—ha—ha."

Clew went on, "What I found most interesting is that Montgomery did not want to discuss our interpretation of The Taming of the Shrew. He most effectively diverted our attention from the play to the question of gender-neutral language. Again, he is a closed book as to revealing his motivation to us. Nevertheless, he shows a remarkable ability to hold his own among the hostility of four women."

Marissa interrupted, "He has to hold his own; he's not getting any from me."

This time the shrew joined Clew in laughing.

"Once again I will hold my comments," the shrew said. "Same time next week."

Montgomery stood, wished the women a pleasant evening and left the room. As he walked along the hallway, he heard footsteps hurrying behind him. It was Clew.

"I love the way you get Alyssa's goat," Clew said breathlessly, "even if I can't show it in the lounge. Keep it up." She blew in Montgomery's ear, then turned and ran back to the lounge.

Montgomery shook his head from side to side, grinning. *What will they think of next?*

Chapter Fourteen

Final Exams

MAILBOXES OPENED the Thursday before finals week disgorged an eight-page booklet listing courses, sections, days and times of scheduled exams. Each exam period was three hours long, Tuesday through Saturday, which made for twenty periods in all.

Montgomery noted that chemistry fell on Tuesday at 1 p.m., Anthropology on Thursday at 8 a.m., Western Civilization on Thursday at 4 p.m., English on Friday at 1 p.m. and Math on Saturday at 8 a.m. He considered it a good spread so his efforts could be evenly spread throughout the week. He wished English was last because he did not need to study for that—English was a simple essay written in class. Kyle Appleton, the T.A. who was Montgomery's instructor, had said they would only have an hour. At 2 p.m. they would be free. Montgomery noted with relief that his exam schedule required no adjustment to his hospital schedule, and he could continue with what he now called the Taming of the Shrews.

Travis had no difficulty with his exam schedule. He simply had to show up at the regular classroom at the regular times. Since study groups did the oral exams, he planned to take a deck of cards and see how much money he could relieve of his classmates' pockets when his group wasn't being examined. Montgomery reminded him that no one carried cash because student i.d.'s were used to purchase everything electronically. Travis was disappointed but still planned to take the cards.

On Monday, Cat and Red sat with Montgomery at the common room table to prep one another as they reviewed their notes. They re-memorized the laws and formulas that they had to know; they reviewed their experiments to remember what they had learned. Travis spent the day with his study group.

Nothing unusual happened at the hospital Monday evening. It was still deserted. Wilkie advised that fewer patients would be in the hospital until January 1. "That's when the after-Christmas discounts kick in," she laughed. "The place will be full."

Montgomery was surprised to find that the lab-teaching assistants were at the front of the room for the chemistry exam. Usually they either sat in the back, or skipped class entirely. "Cheating," said Red. "They'll be watching us for cheating." The class was ordered to sit three seats apart and alternate empty rows with filled rows. "Now we know why we're in this huge room," remarked Cat.

The exam was lengthy. Montgomery realized it would take the three hours allotted to complete the test. Most of it was multiple choice: Montgomery worked his way through the test papers, first answering all the questions to which he knew the answer and then going back through the test to debate the answers to the questions he was not sure of. He found that by working a process of eliminating the definitely wrong answers he could narrow most of the remaining questions to two possibilities. From there, he reasoned his way to the probable answer for each open question.

The last two pages of the exam called for the students to work problems and chemical equations to determine the answers with the admonition to show all their work. Montgomery methodically wrote out his formulas and theorems, step by step. When he was done, he sat back and rubbed his eyes with his fists. He looked at his watch: half an hour to go. Montgomery reviewed his answer sheet to be sure he had properly filled it out, including the section where he gridded his name and student i.d. number. Montgomery remembered the professor's instructions clearly, "You're in college now. It's your responsibility to see that your name is on your paper. Every term I have somebody who forgets. Your answers are scored, but I have no one to credit with the score. I don't run answer sheets twice or guess to whom they belong. If no score comes back with your name, I'll give you a zero for the exam. You're big boys and girls now. Welcome to the adult world."

Montgomery used the remaining minutes to read each question again, and review the answer he had selected. When he was satisfied, he turned in his test paper and answer sheet. That also was something new he learned. "I use my exams anew in subsequent terms," the professor had announced. "Therefore, you will not keep the test questions. I hate to write new questions. If you kept the questions, you would give them to next term's students. That would make me have to write new questions. I'm sure that your brains can figure out why I retain the test papers."

There were only a few minutes remaining for the test. As Montgomery left the room, he glanced at Cat and Red. Both were scribbling away on their papers. He hoped that they would complete the exam before time was out.

The building's bells rang. "Time," announced the professor. A groan went up from the mass of remaining students. There was a shuffling of papers and feet as the students gathered their papers, calculators, and pencils, and massed in the front to drop their tests and answer sheets on top of the piles started by students who finished early.

"How did you do?" Montgomery asked his friends.

"So-so," said Cat. "I think I messed up my equations on the last page."

"I had to race to finish," said Red. "It took me a long time to make my way through the multiple choice."

"You mean multiple guess, don't you," remarked Cat. "I did more guessing than choosing."

Red laughed. "I knew the material, but few of the questions were straightforward. Most of them called on us to apply what we knew to similar but slightly different problems or situations. I hope I got them right, but I don't feel confident."

"What about you, Monkey?" asked Cat.

"I feel I did well, although now I plan to forget everything I know."

"Me, too," said Cat. "It's time to kill some brain cells."

"Maybe one," said Montgomery. "Too much exam week yet to waste my stamina and clarity."

"There's always a sensible one in the crowd," said Cat. "Which I appreciate, by the way."

Red smiled. "Look at how Monkey has loosened up this fall. The Lees may not ever drink, but Monkey has acquired the taste for the finer beverages in life."

"In moderation," said Montgomery, but he loved the way his friends accepted him as one of them.

Tuesday night the quad relaxed over video games, pizza and cokes. Rick stopped in to see how the freshmen were progressing with exams. After getting clobbered in ice hockey twice, he wished them well and continued on his way.

Montgomery talked to Elizabeth twice by phone, but she was deep into studying for an Elementary Psychology exam, and could not spare much time.

Travis went out to meet with his study group.

Caveman demanded silence from all stereos so he could listen to music as he crammed for Music Appreciation. He did not appreciate his quadmates who "helped" him by singing along to the excerpts of symphonies, operas, fugues and quartets.

The quad shut down early. Mick was missing, but nobody missed him. The Michigan roommate continued as a mystery: who was he? where was he?

Wednesday breezed open as strong winds swept the town and campus. Nevertheless, the outside temperature remained warm and demanded nothing more than a windbreaker to cut the wind factor. Students ran back and forth to examination rooms clutching pencils, pens, blue books for writing essays, pencil sharpeners, erasers, notebooks and cram notes. Myriads of t-shirted and blue-jeaned late adolescents sat in hallways with lips moving silently as they attempted to stuff the last crumbs of knowledge into their short-term memory.

The quadmates wore their regular uniform of baggy shorts and oversized t-shirts. Wind chill was not something that necessitated a change in their look. Such considerations were far too serious for something as insignificant as the weather to affect.

Montgomery spent his day reviewing Anthropology. He had plans to spend the evening hours, after he came back from the hospital, with Elizabeth to bone up for Western Civ. It was an uneventful day.

The frat house of Sigma Omicron Beta was in a feverish state of activity. The members were attempting to make up four months of studies in twenty-four to forty-eight hours. It was not their finest hour. The few scholars among the bunch attempted to school their fraternal brothers in the basic points of knowledge, but privately viewed it as a hopeless task. Seminars on undetectable crib notes, the best positioning for copying, and the distribution of answers in multiple-choice tests were given frequently.

As finals week progressed, tensions built in the house and frequent arguments took place, especially between those brothers who finished their exams and wanted to party like it was the end of the world, and those brothers who had exams left to take and wanted a library of silence for the purpose of concentration. It did not help that Gravy and his helpers had to leave off food preparation for their studies; pizza boxes stacked from floor to ceiling were occupying several footprints of the square footage.

The pledge committee had serious work to do. Of the five, only Cody was in the clear. Rip was on the verge of failing three subjects, Pete and Brendon were contending with academic probation from the previous year, and Jack was desperately hacking the computer system to replace his failing grades with positive ones. For two years he had evaded the security programs, but every semester he faced increased, smarter security. There was a rumor on campus that the Computer Science Department had been able to develop artificial intelligence programs that circulated across the Internet like cops searching for escaped felons.

Elizabeth called Montgomery about 1:30 p.m. to report that her psych exam was not difficult and she felt good about doing well. Montgomery praised her for her efforts, and said that he was confident with his progress in Anthropology to do well in it.

As Montgomery was on his way out to the hospital, Caveman morosely swept into the quad.

"How did you do on your exam?"

"Most of the music was unknown; we had to identify periods, composers, themes, and the like. The theory section was written; I did well on that. But the listening part—who knows?"

"You worked hard enough—you must have recognized most of it without realizing it."

"I hope you're right. I guessed at most of it."

Wilkie greeted Montgomery with a ho-ho-ho and a fa-la-la. "We only have two. Be sure to make one mad, or you won't have anything to talk about tomorrow night with the shrinkie dinker." She laughed uncontrollably.

"Shrinkie dinker?"

"Shrinkie dinks," gasped Wilkie. "Kids do them. They color these plastic pieces, then Mom puts them in the oven and they shrink into miniature sizes. Kids love them. Dotty loves to shrink her volunteers down, especially their heads, into miniature sizes, but only after she colors their heads her way. That's why I call her the shrinkie dinker."

"I'll remember that one," said Montgomery as he pushed the cart out the door.

"Merry Christmas," Wilkie called after him.

"A merrier one to you," he returned.

With the work load so light, Montgomery spent thirty or forty minutes in each room talking with the patient, giving the attending family members a chance to go to the cafeteria and eat supper. He enjoyed the volunteer work, although he was already wishing he was done with it so he could go back to his astronomy observations. With the hospital and the Friday night group, he had no time for his hobby or the club.

Thursday he aced both exams. That evening, he was amused as Dotty tried several approaches to break his affable holiday mood. Failing to do that, she threatened him with an adverse report for not cooperating with the process. When he rejoindered that he was only a volunteer, and was not working for a grade or a recommendation, she turned surly and ignored him for the rest of the evening. He shared a good laugh with Serianna in the parking lot over Dotty's frustration.

Montgomery was surprised that his English essay was the most difficult of the exam periods. He discovered that writing under time pressure was not an easy task. He forgot the lesson that Kyle had taught about writing essay exams: Spend the first five - ten minutes organizing your thoughts; roughly outline what you plan to say; save ten minutes for review and rewriting at the end. Montgomery thought that he produced a poor essay; later, he was not surprised when his grade came and revealed that Kyle shared his opinion.

Travis moved triumphantly through the week. Montgomery marveled at how well Travis had adapted to college life and studies under the experimental program. The study group and the oral exams seemed to be the key to his success. The group provided the social atmosphere in which Travis learned best—reading and memorizing were not his strong suits. Travis had never been able to produce under the pressure of written exams, but conversing with his professors, he was relaxed and able to answer questions that showed the knowledge he had gained.

Friday night arrived. The women seemed distracted by the upcoming holidays, and the plans or lack thereof that they had. Clew was frosty and distant, but after the session was over, she privately wished Montgomery Happy Holidays. She again blew in his ear upon taking her leave; Montgomery wondered if she was attracted to him or simply playing with him.

Alyssa spent ten minutes denouncing the male orientation of the holiday: Santa went into the world and received all the acclamation; Mrs. Claus was forgotten at the North Pole and her only fulfillment in life was to bake cookies and greet Santa upon his return with hot cocoa. Montgomery struggled not to laugh.

Alyssa then went on a rant about there being no female reindeer. Montgomery asked her how she knew they were all males. That stumped her. Then she noticed the smug expression on Clew's face. The sparks flew between the two women.

The shrew realized Montgomery was laughing internally at the "cat fight". Montgomery saw her looking at him and realized he had telegraphed his thought. But the shrew let him pass, and tore into the women for disgracing the feminine ideal in front of the male specimen.

Am I a person to them, or a lab rat?

The shrew noted that the group would be in hiatus until the second Friday of January.

Half done! Montgomery gave a whoop of delight when he had escaped the shrew and her three witches of Macbeth.

Saturday, Montgomery took his math exam. He was well prepared, but it was an exhaustive test of methods and theorems, problems and concepts that left him physically and mentally drained. When he arrived back at the quad, Travis asked him when they were leaving. "Later," he said, and crashed upon his bed.

He woke up around seven p.m. In the common room, he could hear the sounds of a party. He walked out of his room to find his quadmates, Travis, Rick, the girls and several other women celebrating Christmas and the end of exams.

Montgomery accepted a cup of punch from Travis. He was thirsty and drank it in a gulp.

"Careful," said Rick. "It's high octane."

Whether Montgomery did not understand, or whether he was cutting loose, he wound up consuming several more cupfuls over the course of three hours. He asked Travis why he felt dizzy, flushed and pleasurable. Travis laughed and said they had better wait for morning before going home. Montgomery realized he was drunk.

This is not so bad, he thought until he woke up Sunday morning with a headache, a dry mouth and a somewhat nauseous feeling. When he shook Travis to ask if he was hung over, Travis mumbled something about tomato juice and sipping water before rolling over and falling asleep again. Montgomery had a drink of water and went back to bed himself.

Sunday afternoon, Rick came into the quad to announce that the boys had to leave by 4 p.m. Montgomery and Travis moved slowly around their room, packing clothes and gifts, and other sundry items that they wanted over the Christmas break. Montgomery retrieved his truck, and they threw their gear into the back.

The boys had taken their leave of their girlfriends the night before. Park's father was arriving Sunday morning to take them back to their Alabama homes. They promised to call each other daily.

Montgomery fired the engine, and pulled away from the curb. What had seemed so strange four months ago was now familiar, and he had the odd sensation of feeling like he was leaving his home to go on a trip, not returning to home in Sparksburg. The boys stopped at a fast food restaurant to buy burgers, fries, and huge cokes to settle their stomachs. As they continued home, Travis used a cell phone to advise both sets of parents that they were underway, at last.

Arriving in Sparksburg, the small town in central Florida where the Lees have lived for generations, Montgomery dropped Travis at his house and headed home. Travis was thoughtful enough to phone the Lee home to let them know Montgomery would arrive in the next five minutes.

As Montgomery pulled into the shaded drive that maneuvered among Spanish oaks, junipers, magnolias and slash pine, his parents and sisters walked onto the front veranda to welcome their son and brother home.

Montgomery pulled into his customary spot under the airplane hangar, which sat screened by hibiscus that the Lees used to shelter their extra cars and farm equipment. Montgomery opened his door and jumped out. He waved as his sisters, 12 and 8, came running to greet him. "Gummy's home!" they cried, using their pet name which they had coined as toddlers because Montgomery was too many syllables for them to master.

Montgomery hugged them both, and walked to the veranda where he greeted his mother with a kiss and a hug. "Welcome home, Son," she said with a lump in her throat. "My goodness, I declare you have grown two or three inches."

Montgomery mumbled, "I hadn't noticed."

His mother turned to the rest of the family. "Don't y'all think he's taller?"

His father shook his hand. "Home for the holidays. Yes, Margaret, I believe he is taller. Let's measure him in the doorway after supper." The doorway was where Mr. Lee made his marks of his children's heights as they grew throughout the years. He used a different color for each. Montgomery, as the first, was black. His most recent mark had been made upon his 17th birthday and stood at 5' 9". Jasmine, age 12, was proud to have crossed to a 5' 1" mark made in green while Forsythia, the youngest at 8, was only 4' 2" recorded in blue and growing very slowly.

The house was decked with greens cut from the trees: sprays of magnolia and pine intermingled with holly and Spanish moss. White miniature lights were the complement to the outdoor decoration. Indoors, Margaret Lee and her daughters had gone all out to provide a festive look for the Christmas season. Every room was decorated with Nativities, sprays of greenery, lights, ornaments and other seasonal decorations. Red candles sat everywhere.

"Supper" consisted of roast duck, country ham, mustard greens, green beans, snow peas, potatos au gratin, cornbread, field peas, and fried okra. Jellies, jams and relishes sat on the sideboard to accompany the meat and vegetables. Apple cider and sweet tea on ice were sweating in great glass pitchers. A red and white tablecloth covered the expansive dining table in the formal room.

Montgomery looked at the spread, and hugged his Mom, "I love you."

"Thank you, dear," she replied. "Your father said you would not be back until today so I waited for this evening for our feast."

"Yeah," Jasmine piped up. "We had to eat cheese sandwiches and baked beans last night 'cause Mama was saving everything for tonight."

The family joined hands around the table. Montgomery automatically bowed his head and closed his eyes, waiting for his father to return thanks. "Shall we let the college boy do it?" he heard his father ask. Then his mother mumbled something. Montgomery opened his eyes. Everyone was looking at him.

"What?"

"You're so different," Jasmine blurted out. "So much—older."

"Son, why don't you 'turn thanks to the Lord," his father said.

Montgomery closed his eyes again. "Sweet Jesus, thank you for reuniting us as a family after being apart. Thank you for providing this food for our table. Thank you for Christmas, and school, and everything I have learned. Thanks for a Mama and Daddy who love me. Thanks for looking out for me. Thanks for watching over my family so I could have this great homecoming. I ask for your blessing for my family and me. Amen."

The food began its circuit around the table as Montgomery's mother jumped to her feet saying, "Something's in her eye".

Forsythia blurted out, "Mama's crying."

Jasmine smacked her younger sister.

"Ow!" Forsythia cried out. "That was uncalled for." Montgomery felt pleasant: *I'm still the same Montgomery who watches the universe through a telescope, lives in the back bedroom on the second floor, and carries the traditions of the Lees upon my shoulders.*

Jasmine looked at her brother with veiled pride. "Tell us about college, Gummy. What's it like?"

"Different. I live on my own, without sisters or bathroom arguments. I have to get myself up and go to school. No mama to rely upon for anything. I have to wash my own clothes. I share a room although Travis is the best roommate a guy could have. It's a tiny room, too. Just enough for two beds and desks. I share a bathroom with seven other guys."

"Good thing there's maid service," Margaret Lee remarked. The family laughed.

"We have a common room together. Usually someone is there at all hours of the day."

"And night," Mama sniffed.

"Not all night," Montgomery replied smiling. "The last owl goes to bed around 3 a.m. and the early birds, the ones with eight o'clock classes, aren't up until six or later. After Thanksgiving, when everyone began cramming and rushing to meet deadlines, no one was getting up until fifteen minutes before class, then throwing some clothes on and running for the bus to main campus."

Forsythia asked, "What are the names of your friends?"

"Travis you know, Red, Cat, Caveman—"

"Caveman?" puzzled Margaret.

"Yeah, 'cause he has long, hairy arms and legs. Then there is Shorts—"

"Shorts?" asked an incredulous Margaret.

"Yeah, his real name is Joe Boxer, but everyone—" Montgomery was interrupted by loud laughter.

"You're making that up," said Forsythia.

"No, I'm not, that's his name."

"Who else?" Forsythia was inquisitive and determined to drag every name out of her brother.

"There's another guy named Mick in the quad, but he wasn't very friendly. He supposedly had a roommate, but nobody ever saw him—not once, not even to meet him."

"Quite a mystery, then," observed Harrison Lee.

"Yes sir. Mick was so touchy by the end of the semester that we think he was using drugs and lost control."

"Did you use drugs, Gummy?" Forsythia was unbearable in her determination to know everything.

"No," said Montgomery, flinching slightly as he remembered the football game when he was tricked into getting high on marijuana. The sharp eyes of Harrison Lee noticed the flinch, and he made a mental note to ask his son later when the two of them were alone.

"Who else do you know?" the impatient eight-year-old demanded.

"The floor advisor Rick, three girls named Park, Rose and Elizabeth (Harrison also noted the glow that crossed Montgomery's face when he mentioned Elizabeth's name, but he was smart enough to know that he must wait until Montgomery decided to tell them about her), Rusty, Black Jack and Gravy from the fraternity house—"

"My gracious," exclaimed his mother. "Doesn't anyone use their Christian name at college?"

"No, ma'am; most everybody has a nickname."

"What's yours?" persisted the eight-year old inquisitor of the Lee clan.

"The quad calls me Monkey, but that's all. Sometimes Elizabeth jokes about us being Civil War generals."

"Why is that?" asked Jasmine.

"Our last names: ours is Lee, for Robert E. Lee; Rick Early, Park Longstreet, Rose Hill, and Elizabeth Stuart."

Harrison Lee roared with laughter. "That's quite a group, Son."

"Yes sir. Travis hangs out with us too. We tell him he has to change his last name to Jackson."

"Did you get good grades?" Forsythia resumed her cross-examination.

Margaret Lee smiled. Thanks to Forsythia, she was finding out the answers she wanted to know without being the interrogator. Thanks to Forsythia, she wasn't getting any nothings, nobody, I don't know and other monosyllabic answers that a teenager, even a college freshman, normally gives to his parents.

"I did okay. A's and B's."

"How many A's and how many B's?"

"I won't know until I receive my report card. Maybe two or three A's and the rest B's."

"That's outstanding," praised Harrison. "I'm very proud of you, Montgomery."

Montgomery beamed.

"Who's your girlfriend?" asked Forsythia in a sing-song voice.

Montgomery turned red in the face, and suddenly needed to eat his vegetables.

Mama came to the rescue. "Why don't you tell your brother about the Christmas play you were in."

Forsythia rose to the bait, and took off on a tangent about her starring role as the Innkeeper's Wife in a play entitled *You Parked Your Donkey Where?*

It was about eleven o'clock when Harrison Lee stoked the fire in the large family room where the Christmas tree reigned over masses of wrapped packages, ribbons and gift bags. Margaret pointed to their son who had fallen asleep ninety minutes ago. "Now's the time," whispered Harrison. "You get the razor; I'll find the shaving cream."

Margaret laughed in her golden tone of love. "Leave the boy alone. We both know those chin hairs look silly, but we have to be silent until he realizes he looks silly."

"Was I that goofy looking in college?"

"Don't ask the question if you don't want to know the answer. But the girls think he's cute."

"It's not his sisters that matter."

"I wasn't talking about his sisters."

"Mrs. Lee, you did a fine job raising your son."

"He has his Daddy's blood."

Montgomery wolfed down his predawn breakfast of bacon, scrambled eggs, toast, grits, and fried squash. He drank two cups of strong coffee as he prepared to go into the woods with his father. It was Christmas Eve. The two men would spend the day hunting deer. Yesterday, Montgomery had taken out his .22 rifle and thoroughly cleaned the bore, trigger mechanism and bullet chamber, polishing the stock and metal.

This morning, he was dressed in camouflage pants, a white t-shirt, orange vest, and camouflage cap. The day would not be cold so it was not necessary to pile on extra layers. He checked his equipment to be sure he had everything he wanted: canteen, binoculars, scope, deer scent, doe bleater, ammunition and knife.

Harrison Lee was out loading their rifles into his pick-up truck. Harrison generally kept a .22 rifle with him, but tended to use a .30-.30. Montgomery admired his father's skill with the .30-.30 but retained a fondness for the .22 with which he had trained up.

Margaret filled two 20 oz. go-cups with the last of the coffee. She kissed her son on the cheek. "Good hunting." Margaret headed back to bed.

Montgomery carried the coffee to the garage.

"Your mother finish her cooking?"

"Yes sir; she went back to y'all's bedroom."

"I'll be right back."

Montgomery grinned. He knew his parents never parted without going through their ritual: two kisses, the second longer than the first, and a confession of love for the other. Montgomery put the coffee into the truck's cup holders and climbed into the passenger side. *I can't wait to be in the woods with Daddy whether we make a kill or not. I've missed spending the day with him.* The father-son deer hunt remains one of the rural South's best-loved traditions; Harrison and Montgomery reveled in it and the close companionship between them that came of it.

Harrison returned to the garage, climbed into the driver's seat and cranked the motor. He backed out of the garage, Montgomery mashed the button on the automatic door valet, and they headed out the driveway.

"Let's try Ocala National Forest," said Harrison. "Several of my colleagues at the courthouse have sighted big bucks around Lake Kerr."

"Excellent," approved Montgomery. Although the companionship was the most important thing, Montgomery had not outgrown the excitement of the multi-pointed buck. He rolled down his window and breathed in the night air. "Mmmm. Fresh pine in the air."

"Rather appropriate for the season. Glad to be home from school?"

"Yes sir. It was fun, it was intense—I was ready for the break."

"You've handled yourself like a man. You went out to a new place and a new situation and took care of yourself. You successfully achieved your goals for the fall term. I'm proud of you."

"Thank you, Daddy. That means a tremendous lot to me. But I missed one goal."

The two men rode in silence for a while. Ahead, the entrance to the National Forest loomed in the dark night that was just beginning to lighten into purples and dark blues. Harrison stopped at the pipe that shot vertically out of the ground and bent horizontal at thirty-six inches of height. Montgomery rolled his window down, opened the pipe hatch, and pulled out the registration book. He dutifully recorded their names, address, truck license plate number, their planned location, the time and date of entry, and estimated time of departure. He shoved the book back into the pipe, and shut the hatch. "We're in the log."

Disembarking at a parking lot, they prepared their rifles, checking that the safety locks were on and slinging them over the shoulders by means of attached straps. They entered the forest on a familiar trail.

Harrison now prompted his son, "What goal did you miss, Montgomery?"

"I didn't make the frat, Daddy." Montgomery's voice was sad and slightly tremulous. He had a profound sense of having disappointed his father.

"Explain that to me again, Son, I don't understand."

"I pledged the first week, and they accepted that. Then they did weird things. Things you'd never heard of. They stole my psychological tests from the university and made up terrible things about me based on those tests. The president of the chapter was supposed to help me, but he was a dolt. He forgot to tell me to memorize a song so, my first night of helping to cook, they hooked to a machine that delivers electric shocks. One guy hates my guts because I wouldn't let him use my student i.d. to play video games with the money in my account. He turned the voltage really high. It knocked me out."

"Son, that's a dangerous man. Did you report him to the university?"

"No sir. I was hoping—I guess I was afraid if I did that would ruin my chances of getting in."

"Go on—what happened next?" Harrison was gently engaging his son to pull out the details of the troubling experience.

"One decent brother rescued me and made sure I got out of the house safely. He helped me several times. Things settled down for a couple of weeks, but then we had the first football game. Wait, the day before that when I served dinner the guy that hates me picked on the part that I cooked, and started a food fight. Since I was their primary target, I retreated into the kitchen."

Montgomery grinned. "This guy ordered me to go back. Then he kicked my butt. So I pushed his head into a huge bowl of chocolate pudding. That was one time I got the best of him. He was going to retaliate, but the brother in charge of the kitchen—he was the one who rescued me from the shock machine—told him to clean himself up before his friends found out I bested him."

"Mm-hm," vocalized Harrison.

"I did it without thinking, Daddy." Montgomery was apologetic. Harrison was a respected attorney with a half dozen associates and a vigorous law practice. Lately the other lawyers in the county had begun talking of putting Harrison up for a Circuit Court Judge slot. Everyone in the county knew why: they would no longer have to contest their cases against him. Montgomery knew that his father had a high regard for the law and thus would take a low view of fighting. But Harrison wanted his son to keep talking, so he remained low-key.

"You were provoked. What happened after that?"

"The next day Travis and I—he pledged with me—went back because we were required to sit with the frat for the football game. At first we were put through normal gags: taking our shirts off and painting our chests so we spelled out 'the snooks' with an exclamation point. We went to the game and were having fun rooting for our team. Then after halftime—" Montgomery broke off his discourse.

Harrison glanced at his son. They had reached a spot where they had found a deer trail, and were constructing a blind several yards away.

"Go on, Son," he calmly urged. "Whatever it is, I want to hear what you have to say."

Montgomery hesitated. *I've never lied or kept anything from Daddy. In high school, when my friends were butting heads with their parents over clothes, haircuts, curfews, morals, habits, sleep, grades and such, when those friends confided in me what they couldn't tell their parents, I always told Daddy everything about me. Daddy never argued; he never lectured. But then, I've never had to tell Daddy that I had been under the influence of marijuana.*

Harrison smiled gently and laid his hand on Montgomery's shoulder. "You and I, we've entered a new relationship now. You're an adult in the eyes of the law. You live on your own, and you make the decisions about how you'll live. I accept that. The time for Daddy to lecture and punish is over. Whatever you've done, you're my son and I'll always love you. You'll make mistakes, no doubt about that, but I raised you to handle yourself and I have complete confidence that you'll make the right decisions and correct your mistakes as you make them."

Tears blinded Montgomery's eyes. *How have I been so fortunate to have such a great Daddy?* "Thank you, sir. I'll always try to be true to your trust."

"You were speaking of halftime."

Montgomery swallowed hoping to remove the big lump in his throat. It did not work. He choked out the words, "They tricked us into getting high by putting marijuana into cookies and passing them out. We didn't know anything was wrong until it was too late."

Harrison was troubled and elated at the same time. He was unhappy that his son had experienced the drug, however involuntary the means, but elated that Montgomery regarded it as a negative experience. "It wasn't your fault, Son. No one holds you responsible."

A wave of relief coursed through Montgomery's mind. "Thank you, sir."

"You're having quite the college try-out. Bogeys are found everywhere, I suppose. It's a shame you ran into so many of them in one place."

"Amen. Next they demolished the honor code. They kept the same language but redefined it completely. Goodness and moral uprightness became we are good by definition so whatever we do is good, no matter how bad it is."

"The university isn't the only place where that nonsense is going on. It's happening in public schools, in churches, and even in courtrooms."

"Now comes the mystery. We're given sealed packages and delivery routes. We drop off the packages, and either receive an envelope to take back to the frat, or the package is C.O.D. and we have to collect cash. Here's the strangest part: all the C.O.D.'s are for small bills, usually ten dollars but sometimes twenty, occasionally fifty, and rarely one hundred."

Harrison drew in his breath sharply. "This went on how often?"

"All the time—every day, in fact. I only went once or twice because they didn't trust me, but until Travis quit, he went several times a week."

"What did you do with the envelopes and cash?"

"I turned them and the delivery sheets into the pledge committee. I don't know what happened after that. It gets stranger, Daddy. I asked some people what we delivered, including the president, Wilson, and each one tells me not to ask questions, especially in the frat house. The pledge committee holds the power in the house. Wilson is a joke. He knows what they're doing, but refuses to do anything."

"It appears shifty and possibly criminal. Leave it alone, Montgomery. If they're doing what I suspect, you're better off not knowing and staying away from it."

"You're thinking drugs?"

Harrison, to divert his son's attention, said, "Rattle the doe bleater so we can bring a buck in our sights."

Montgomery dutifully rattled the can. "Baaa, Baaa" echoed through the trees.

Harrison pulled out his pipe, filled it with tobacco and lit it. He puffed and thought in silence for a long time. Montgomery knew from long association to keep silent when his father was smoking his pipe. He concentrated on looking through the branches of their blind for deer.

"Montgomery, this pledging is a serious business. Did anything else happen to you?"

"Mohawk haircut—that's why mine is so short. I shaved it to a uniform length after the pledging was done to let it grow out again."

"Your mother and I wondered about that."

"Before that, though, we were told to take a hit of LSD. I said no—so they tumbled me in a dryer for half an hour."

Harrison refreshed and relit his pipe in response.

Montgomery agitated the bleat: baaaa, baaaa. He tensed with excitement when he heard stamping on the leaves. Harrison nudged his son. Montgomery made the bleat once more: baaa, baaa. Clomping through the leaves, coming straight toward them, was a magnificent buck. Montgomery counted fourteen points on his head. The buck was fifty yards away. He moved a few yards, then stopped and looked around. His nose was quivering as he searched for the doe's musk that would tell him she was in estrus.

Montgomery sighted the buck through his rifle, but Harrison laid a hand on his arm, which meant to be patient and wait. Over the next half hour, the buck slowly made his way toward them until he was only fifteen yards away. He was facing the blind directly. Neither man moved for the slightest movement would spook the deer.

The buck twisted his head and looked to his side, as he simultaneously smelled the air. Montgomery raised his rifle and sighted the buck. The buck looked down and pawed the ground. He looked up. He snorted. He moved to the side and stopped, sniffing the air. Montgomery felt his Daddy's hand on his shoulder. That was the signal to sight and prepare to fire. The buck took a few steps and stopped again, quivering as he stood in the morning air. Montgomery felt his Daddy tap his leg. That was the signal to remove the safety and fire when the buck presented a good target.

Montgomery slowly worked the safety back so that the release of the trigger would not make a sound. He put his finger on the trigger maintaining his scope on the neck of the deer. He took a deep breath and slowly let it out to calm his excitement. He reminded himself to squeeze the trigger, not pull it. The buck was gorgeous in his winter coat. A full autumn had filled out his shoulders, rib and buttocks.

Montgomery waited for the buck to present the best opportunity. The buck took a step, and Montgomery was satisfied. Crack! The bullet pierced the buck's neck; the impact spread the spinning metal so that it cut the buck's spinal cord—instantly killing the deer. The animal fell over.

Montgomery grinned and shook his father's hand as they stood up and stretched their legs.

"How many points?" asked his father.

"Fourteen," said a jubilant Montgomery.

"Maybe we'll have him mounted."

Montgomery engaged the safety on his rifle.

"You should have done that before you moved," Harrison told him.

"Yes, sir. I forgot," apologized Montgomery.

"Practice until it is instinct," Harrison countered. Montgomery joined his Daddy in repeating the next line he had heard a thousand times, "No apology is equal to the life of a man."

"Yes sir." Montgomery walked over to his buck with his father.

The two men tied the buck's legs, and found a strong branch with which to carry it. They mounted the deer onto the pole, and began hiking to the truck.

Harrison now prodded his son into talking again. "Did Travis take the hit?"

"No sir." Montgomery was emphatic in his answer. "That's why he quit."

"Finish your story, Son. I hope there's not much left."

"That's it. They interviewed us. Half the pledges got in; half did not. Here's another weird thing: three of us were continued as pledges."

"What?" ejected an astonished Harrison.

"Continued. We aren't out, we aren't in, we keep on being pledges."

"I've never heard of a fraternity continuing pledges. What did they tell you? Not at this time?"

"Something like that. They gave me assignments to complete."

"Assignments?" Harrison was dumbfounded.

"Yes sir. I volunteer in a hospital with a supervisor who acts like Sigmund Freud and Carl Jung and Jack the Ripper combined in one badly turned out cloning experiment. She says her job is to break us down so she can rebuild us."

"Your psyche? What do you do there?"

"Hand out magazines."

There was a moment of dead silence.

Then Harrison dropped his end of the deer, falling to the ground and roaring with laughter. It was contagious. Montgomery sat beside his Daddy and laughed with him.

Harrison gasped, "You're making this up."

Montgomery looked directly into his Daddy's eyes. "No sir. Every word I've said is true. It's all true."

Montgomery looked away. "There's more."

"More?"

"Yes sir. I meet with four feminists who snarl at me about male oppression."

"You're smiling. It can't be that bad."

"No sir; it's not. They present a spiel, ask my opinion and then criticize what I say and how I say it. But they are so biased they don't pay any attention to me. Plus, two of them wind up arguing with each other."

"Anything else?"

"I have to take a class in moral philosophy. I have to go for counseling after I finish my hospital work."

"Whatever for?"

"To integrate my experience."

"With what?" Harrison's astonishment kept increasing.

"No one has a clue."

Harrison picked up his end of the deer. Montgomery followed suit.

"Why did they make these assignments?"

"They said it was for me to work on my weaknesses and make me a better fraternity brother when I was admitted. The assignments were related to the psychological evaluation, my chores at the frat and my interviews. But I think the real reason is they want me to quit."

"Did the other two boys receive assignments?"

"No sir. Travis and I think they were continued solely to do the cooking, cleaning and laundry."

"I believe you're right. Who's the leader of the pledge committee?"

"His name is Cody—Cody Spung."

Harrison thought for several minutes. "I haven't heard of any Spungs in the .... But that doesn't mean they aren't involved."

What's Daddy was referring to?

Harrison spoke after another period of silence. "Son, about the fraternity—"

"Yes sir?" Montgomery was listening intently.

"My brothers and I were Sigma men—Sigbees, y'all call us. Your cousin Barney also joined the house. But our family tradition is not a chain on your destiny. You aren't obligated to join this sadly out-of-control with a criminal element fraternity chapter. Do you understand that?" Harrison was speaking with emphasis.

"Yes sir." Montgomery saw the parking lot through the trees. He was glad—the buck was heavy and his shoulder was hurting.

"My advice is that you forget it. But you make your own decision. If you quit, I won't be disappointed. In fact, quite the opposite: I'll be relieved. But you make your own decision." Harrison's mind was working in several directions at once: making plans to check into the backgrounds of the current members, checking with drug enforcement agencies and prosecutors for information about the activities, and assessing the horrendous time his son had received at the hands of the SigBees.

"I'll consider your advice, sir—Daddy. I can't tell you what my decision will be because I don't know myself."

The men reached the truck. Montgomery lowered the tailgate and they slung the deer into the bed.

Harrison looked at his watch. "We'll be home in time for second breakfast."

"Excellent. I'm hungry." Montgomery's stomach growled to prove his point.

As they pulled out of the parking lot, Harrison asked, "How did Travis adjust to college life?"

"Excellent."

"Did he pass his courses?"

"More than that; he excelled. He enrolled in an experimental program that fit him like a well-made glove. You'd be surprised at what he learned."

"Such as?"

"He quotes Shakespeare."

"Travis?"

"Yes sir." Montgomery proudly stated. "He loves the program. He signed up for it again."

"That is surprising. But, as you say, it's excellent."

Ten miles from the Lee home, Travis was riding the fence with his grandfather, checking for places where the fence was broken and making repairs.

Travis' grandfather was listening to Travis talk about his fall, his studies and his experiences.

"To be or not to be, that is the question," Travis quoted. "I found out not to be a fraternity man. It's nonsense—garbage. Contrary to popular opinion, they don't have the best parties or the best girls. I found those on my own."

"Do you ever get tired of breaking hearts," his grandfather teased.

"I think mine is the one breaking."

His grandfather turned in the saddle and squinted at his grandson. *The boy's serious.*

"She was only another girl—my first at college. But then Montgomery started dating her roommate. Typical Montgomery: very shy and slow moving."

"But you caught the bird on the first shot."

Travis blushed. The old man's eyebrows raised.

"No sir. I did catch her, but not on the first shot."

The old man was silent. He knew Travis would fill in the silence.

"We were having fun. She's like me—looking for a good time. But as I watched Montgomery and his girlfriend falling in love, I began to feel empty. I'm missing out on something. I don't know what it is, but Montgomery has it and I don't."

They each inspected several twisted strands of barbed wire.

"I want more," Travis said. "I want to be deeply loved. I need more than a wave, a whiskey and a woman."

"Seek and ye shall find."

"I'm seeking, but will I find?"

The old man watched Travis' eyes eagerly searching his face. He marveled at the great change that had come over the young man. Neither he nor the family had expected Travis to last the first year. They thought the academic demands would be more than he would be willing to meet. But now?

"Ask and it shall be given unto you; knock, and it shall be opened unto you."

"Really?" asked an incredulous Travis.

"Behold, I stand at the door and knock. If any man hears my voice and opens the door, I will come in to him and dine with him, and he with me."

Travis pondered these words. *What Grandpa's telling me is that I'll find what I lacked if I keep looking and asking—when I get back to school, I'll work even harder.*

Two days after Christmas, a yellow mustang convertible pulled into the long drive that led from the highway to the Lee home. The car rolled to a stop in the middle of the asphalt pad. A handsome boy of twenty pocketed his keys and walked to the front door.

Deep chimes resounded in the interior of the two-story house. An interval passed, and then a small girl opened the door.

"Is Montgomery Lee at home?"

The little girl hollered, "Gummy! Front door!"

Montgomery came out of the kitchen, holding a coffee cup and eating a doughnut.

"Rick, hello, great to see you," he mumbled through a mouthful of crumbs. "Come in. Would you like some coffee?"

"A Coke would be welcome, if you have one."

"Check. Forsythia, get my friend a Coke. And bring a glass with ice, too."

The little girl ran to honor her brother's request.

"Let's go into the parlor." Montgomery motioned the way through a glass-encased door, which was normally closed unless Harrison was meeting with clients at home.

The two young men went in and sat down. Forsythia brought the drink for Rick and then left.

"So well behaved," Rick remarked. 'Mine would have stomped my toes for the nerve of asking a favor, and hung around to eavesdrop and be a pest."

"Mama trains them from the cradle. It takes twenty years to produce the Southern Woman. Forsythia is a quick study."

Rick laughed. "My Southern Woman is eighteen. Do I have to wait two years for the completed article?"

"If the answer was yes, you wouldn't be here, would you?"

"You're right. I'm your advisor, but I need your advice. I'm deeply, desperately in love with Rose. I believe she reciprocates my feelings. The problem is neither of us is willing to admit it for fear the other doesn't. So we never talk about it but we desperately wish that we could."

"The elephant in the room."

Rick ejected, "What?"

"You know he's there, you know he doesn't belong there, he's too big to ignore, but you're afraid to mention him for fear the others will deny he's there."

"Exactly. So what do I do?"

"Tell her there's an elephant in the room."

"What if she denies it?"

"How can she? There's an elephant in the room."

"Is it that easy?"

"How should I know? I'm in the first serious relationship of my life. But it should be. She's waiting for your move."

"How do I introduce the subject?"

"Bring it up when the two of you are alone, relaxed and talking. Don't take huge risks. Guys lose their girls because they do something stupid like hand her an engagement ring. The first step is to talk about the elephant. After that, you know what to do with the elephant. Don't try to ride the elephant when you haven't admitted it exists."

"Have you and Elizabeth talked about the elephant?"

"Yes, and we have only a baby elephant. We have a long ways to go before it's full grown."

"I came all this way to talk about Rose, and instead we've talked about elephants."

"Grab your Coke. I'll show you around. Let me introduce you to my folks. Can you spend the day with us?"

Rick spent the day at the Lee home, and wound up staying the night. He and Montgomery talked about his situation several more times, and each time the answer was the same: Tell Rose there's an elephant in the room. Harrison added his approval to the advice. So did Margaret, which clinched the matter for Rick. That night he sent an e-mail to his girlfriend: Sweet Rose, we have an elephant in the room.

Saturday night Montgomery and Travis went out to visit their old haunts from their high school days. They caught up with high school buddies in the back of the overgrown tree farm where the teenagers found the privacy they desired for their nightly exploits.

"Maybe we'll run into Judy so I can break off any understanding we might have had about our relationship," Montgomery hoped.

"It's easy," said Travis. "Tell her you've moved on. It's vague, admits and places no blame, and each side's free."

"But we never agreed that we had anything to move on from."

"Then forget it."

"I feel guilty that she might be spending her senior year waiting for me rather than going to dances and parties with another boy."

"Only you, Montgomery, would concern yourself over such things."

Montgomery and Travis lit a fire with old logs and brush. Several boys collected around the fire, drinking Cokes and beer.

Travis was explaining about the great college parties when one of the boys said, "Good thing you had Montgomery to pull you through your exams."

"Hey!" Travis retorted. "I made it on my own."

"No way," said another. "Next thing you'll claim you know Shakespeare."

To which Travis responded with the famous soliloquy of Hamlet, "To be or not to be."

The first boy gave Travis a playful shove. "You made that up."

Travis shoved him back. "Word for word, that's what the man wrote."

The first boy made to shove Travis, and they broke into a play fight. Several minutes later, they fell to the ground, panting and laughing. Someone handed Travis a fresh beer, and he took a long drink, savoring the coldness and tang as it passed across his taste buds.

Travis spotted Judy's car, and nudged Montgomery. "Now's your chance."

Montgomery deliberated. *I want to and I don't want to. But I might not see her again before returning to school.* He walked toward her car.

As he came through the trees, Montgomery rehearsed what he planned to say. "We left with an elephant in the room. We never made an agreement that we wouldn't see other people, but we never said it was okay. We need to express closure over our relationship. It's not fair for me to expect you to sit out the events of your senior year because I'm in Bacon. I want to banish the elephant: go out with other boys and have a good time." *That sounds noble and I won't have to tell her I'm in love with another girl.*

Montgomery came to the car feeling nervous. The inside was dark and the windows were cloudy. He used the bottom of his t-shirt to clear the glass, but the film was on the inside. He squinted. There were two people in the backseat: Judy and a boy.

Montgomery's face turned bright red, and he left without saying a word.

When he came back to the fire, Travis asked, "Is it over? Did you tell her?"

Montgomery mumbled, "I didn't have to."

Travis observed his red face. In a few moments, he burst out laughing.

Chapter Fifteen

Rush Week Again

THE DORMS REOPENED on the first Monday in January with classes to start on the next day. The excitement of renewing acquaintances with their quadmates and seeing their girlfriends on a daily basis was driving Montgomery and Travis to distraction.

"There's no sense in leaving until after lunch," Montgomery said. "We can't get in until four. The girls won't be back until seven. Even then, they'll have parents to entertain so we won't get to be with them until Tuesday night."

"I almost wish we hadn't gone to Alabama to spend New Year's with them. It has made the last few days more unbearable."

"Poor Travis. I'm surprised you didn't break up with her before Christmas so you could service a filly or two in your hometown."

"I never thought of that. Then I could have had make-up sex when we came back to school."

"You wouldn't have broken up with her because you'd be afraid you couldn't get her back. Face it, Travis, you're falling in love."

"What if I am? I don't have a monopoly on love, do I?"

At the moment of this conversation, Park was sitting in the back seat of Elizabeth's parents' Lincoln Town Car. She was barely paying attention to the conversation flying around her as Rose and Elizabeth talked of the new semester and their plans when they arrived at school. Behind the wheel, Elizabeth's father smoothly steered the automobile along Interstate 75, which he had intersected in Atlanta when they had headed east from Alabama. Elizabeth's mother was the front passenger; she had insisted on accompanying the group so her husband would not have to return alone, but Elizabeth knew the real reason was her mother wanted to meet Montgomery.

Park stared out the window. She really liked Travis: *he's a fun guy. He's sweet and attentive; sexy and muscular: he's buff without needing to lift weights. He's exceptionally excellent as a lover. Is it instinct or did someone teach him?*

The problem is that he's supposed to be as shallow as I am. But he's begun developing into something more, and I'm scared I can't keep up. Plus I don't want to be penned up forever—I'm only a freshman. She flushed as she recalled with guilt the liaisons she had made with former beaus over the Christmas break.

I'm not looking forward to the reunion with Travis. Should I break it off before we become even more entangled? If only there was an easy answer.

Eventually, Montgomery took his leave of his family. He had shaken hands with his father at the breakfast table, who wished him well and reminded him of what he had said about the fraternity. After lunch, he hugged his sisters, kissed his Mama, and with cries of "Bye, Gummy!" in his ears, he drove to the Lewis home to pick up Travis.

Travis waved from the front window, grabbed his gear, and yelled, "I'm going" which received an echo of "Good luck." He threw his things into the truck and climbed into the cab.

They arrived at the quad in time for the questions that their friends were bombarding a pale, brown-haired boy with. He turned out to be the mysterious roommate no one had ever seen. "Where have you been?" they asked. "We went the whole fall term and never saw you—not even a toothbrush or razor to show you were around."

The boy, whose name was Art but had been dubbed Ghost for his invisibility in the fall and the paleness of his skin, replied, "I bombed out in the roommate sweepstakes and spent the fall crashing in the back of a laundromat. The owner let me stay there if I would watch the place at night."

Cat asked, "Why are you here now?"

"I complained to housing, who refunded my money for the fall and moved him for the Spring. Now I can live like a regular student." Ghost noted that his news was welcomed by his quadmates.

"We're glad to meet you," said Montgomery, shaking his hand. "I'm Monkey, this is Travis my roommate, Cat, Shorts, Red, and Caveman. Make yourself at home. Hey y'all, let's help the Ghost clean out Tou-chee's room."

Cheers greeted Montgomery's suggestion. Art was pleased to find how friendly his quadmates were. He said to Montgomery, "You're a friendly bunch. At home it would take us a month to learn names."

"Really?" responded Travis. "Why is that?"

"Midwestern reserve," replied the Ghost.

"None of that here," said Red. "Welcome to the South. Up North, ask a man the time and he walks away. In the mid-Atlantic, ask a man the time and he tells you the time. But here, ask us the time and we'll invite you home to supper."

"But," Montgomery added, "there are some conditions."

"Such as?" prompted the Ghost.

"Answer all questions posed by an adult with 'sir' or 'ma'am'. Yes sir; no ma'am—you get the idea. The second person plural pronoun is y'all; not you guys, you people, or you there."

Travis grinned. "If you don't like fishing, hunting or football, lie and say you do."

Red added, "Grits is an obligatory breakfast food that is eaten for all three meals of the day."

Caveman said, "But don't let these boys pull your leg that chitlins is a southern delicacy." He made a face.

The Ghost could not resist his curiosity. "What are chitlins?"

"Chitlins, known by some barefoot connoisseurs as chitterlings, is the small intestine of a hog which you hope was washed and cleaned thoroughly and completely before it was cooked and served," said Cat. "Sometimes the cook stuffs it with another meat."

"That's when the fun begins," said Shorts. "Are you eating a stuffing or is it the hog's—"

"Leave the man alone, y'all," said Montgomery. "They're playing with your mind. Nobody eats that anymore; it was something poor folks fried because they had to use the whole pig. They couldn't afford to let any of it be wasted."

"They ate everything but the oink," Shorts affirmed.

The boys had a huge garbage bag and began throwing dirty clothes, old papers, torn books, blotter paper, glass vials, shoes, trash, and other sundries into the bag. In about ten minutes they had collected all the personal property and discards of the unlamented Michael Raike.

"What should we do with it?" asked Red.

"This looks like a Rick problem to me," said Cat.

"I volunteer you to take it to him," said Travis.

"I volunteer you to help me since there are several bags," retorted Cat. The two boys hefted the bags and headed down the hall.

The others helped the Ghost to sweep and wash the room.

"A little air freshener, and you can call it home," remarked Shorts.

"Thanks, fellas," said the Ghost. The boys stopped and stared at him. "I mean y'all," corrected the Ghost.

"That's better," said Montgomery.

The boys now turned their attention to the next problem: how to fit the Foosball table that Red brought with him into their crowded common room. This engendered much debate and many trial arrangements before they left everything as it was, turned the long table ninety degrees, and set the Foosball next to it.

"Santa was good to you," observed Caveman.

Red smiled. "I found it on the Internet. Now I'm looking for a good pinball machine."

General frivolity broke out as the boys decided to order in pizza for dinner. By the time darkness fell, a rollicking party was in full swing. The Ghost sighed with contentment that he was installed in his proper home for the coming term. Someone put a war-hero video in the VCR; the boys were playing foosball in a competitive manner and Travis was showing Caveman the inside secrets of playing Dragon-Hunting on the game player. Hard rock played in the background on someone's CD player.

The door opened. The foosball game stopped suddenly. Travis and Caveman came out of the room. Mick was standing in the doorframe. "Thanks for the packing, you ——-" he cursed. He cursed them with an anatomically impossible order, slammed the door and left.

"Anyone for changing the locks?" Cat broke the silence. The boys broke into hearty laughter. They immediately began telling "war stories" about Mick.

"The laundromat never sounded so good," the Ghost remarked.

As the evening wore on, it became evident that Red and Shorts were the best foosball players in the quad. They were consistently on the winning side, and when they teamed together, they were unbeatable. Gradually the noise abated as the boys began to retire to their rooms.

At the sound of a knock on their door, Travis and Montgomery called out, "Come in." The Ghost entered the room wearing a long pair of flannel pants.

"Flannel on the bottom and a rug on top," Travis commented to Montgomery as he viewed the hairy chest of the shirtless Ghost.

Montgomery laughed. "I didn't know spirits had hair."

The Ghost laughed too. "It's nature's balance." He took his hand and brushed the long waves of brown hair off his forehead to reveal the darts of bare skin making inroads across his temples. "I'm already turning shiny up top. I only turned eighteen two months ago."

Travis needled, "At least you have the makings for a toupee whenever you want one." Montgomery and the Ghost laughed.

"I wanted to talk with Monkey. The boys said you pledged a fraternity last term. What was it like?"

"An unmitigated disaster," Travis cut in before Montgomery could speak.

"You have to check it out to understand," said Montgomery. "Are you thinking of rushing?"

"Yeah. I don't know many people from living in the back of a store. I thought it would help me meet people and enjoy the campus better."

"Not a bad thought," said Montgomery. "But you have to be careful which one you select."

"Would you go with me tomorrow night? Most of the houses are having smokers."

"I can't. I've only seen my girlfriend once since finals last term. I plan to spend the whole night with her—stop grinning, Travis, you know what I mean."

"How about Wednesday or Thursday? I could really use your advice."

Montgomery hesitated. "Wednesday, if I don't have to work too late and get back by seven—if not, you'll have to go without me."

"What about you, Travis?"

"The last time I went for the free beer, and it almost cost me my best friend and my sanity. I'll go if we avoid the Sigma Omicron Beta house, but don't ask me to pledge. I don't have what it takes to be a jerky frat member."

"It's a deal," said the Ghost. "Thanks gu—y'all."

"Check," said Montgomery. "And check."

Montgomery was overwhelmed Wednesday night to find the hospital full with visitors and family roaming the halls looking for places to sit. "What's going on?" he asked Wilkie.

Wilkie threw her head back and laughed in her trademark fashion. "After Christmas discount—remember I told you before the holidays? Sick people hold on for one last Christmas—then they let themselves go. They're stacked double-decker in ER; who'll win the bed lottery? Who goes into the night to Fort Meyers? We ought to hold a drawing on the in-house cable channel."

Wilkie roared with laughter. "You have it easy. With all the family, nobody reads. If you're not done by six, I'll assume you were mistaken for a patient and the surgeons are removing your appendix."

Montgomery thought she was mistaken; with all the rooms to visit, it would take him all four hours. But she was right. Since family and friends were camped in every room, no one wanted to talk with him. No one wanted reading material either. They either chatted with family, watched TV or slept. Montgomery did leave a Gideon Bible with each patient. He dropped it on the side table or left it in the bathroom. Nobody objected, but then, nobody saw him leave the Bibles.

It was six o'clock exactly when Montgomery returned the cart to Wilkie's office. "Now shoo! Dotty's on the rampage from some mess-up this morning. Leave before she keeps you here to midnight."

Montgomery did not need telling twice. He vacated the building and ran for his truck. As he fired the engine and pulled out of his space, he saw the figure of Dotty Newman come out of the hospital. He mashed the accelerator and the truck sprinted for the highway. He did not look in his rear view mirror to see if she was trying to flag him down.

Montgomery returned to the quad to change clothes and meet Travis and the Ghost. At seven o'clock, they sallied out to make the rounds of "Little Greece"—the campus name for the row of fraternity houses that marches from the business district of the town past the athletic facilities. Staying well away from Sigma Omicron Beta, which was oddly dark for the evening, they made their way first to Epsilon Alpha Phi.

"How y'all tonight?" greeted an EAP brother.

"How yar is the night?" repeated a puzzled Ghost.

"Very yar," said Travis in a mysterious and deep voice. "A yar night like this calls forth the traveler to seek lodgings in yon monastery. How brew y'all the beer?"

"How blue is the beer?" repeated an increasingly puzzled Ghost.

The EAP brother was rolling his eyes. Travis winked at the boy in a way that the Ghost could not see.

"What's the rush like?" asked Montgomery.

The EAP brother said, "Slow. But we aren't looking to add many pledges."

"Thank you for your time," responded Montgomery. He left the house, pulling the Ghost with him as Travis followed.

Montgomery smiled at the Ghost in a friendly way. "Until you get used to those of us who have southern accents, don't repeat anything we say no matter how strange it sounds. Act like you understand perfectly, and don't say a word. Of course (Montgomery looked at his roommate) it helps if the comic refrains from twisting the words."

"Who me?" asked Travis innocently. "I'm merely a thirsty freshman wanting to wet his whistle."

The next house was more promising. "Omicron Omicron Psi," said Montgomery. "Their reputation is quiet and studious—the nerd's fraternity."

"An oxymoron if there ever was one," said Travis.

"I didn't know you knew that word," retorted Montgomery.

There was no beer at Omicron Omicron Psi, which greatly disappointed Travis. A couple of brothers took the Ghost into a second lounge to promote the fraternity. Montgomery and Travis stood at the front window drinking cherry cokes and talking about their girlfriends.

Fifteen minutes later, the Ghost rejoined the pair. They left the house and walked to the one next door. The Ghost commented that Omicron Omicron Psi had potential but it seemed rather sedate. Their presentation had been marred by several technical glitches in the computer slide program.

"What did you expect?" Travis observed acidly. "Their name says it all: OOPS."

As they approached the front door, it suddenly flew open and four burly men threw another man into the front yard. "Don't come back," he was warned, "or you won't leave in one piece."

Montgomery watched the man in the yard rise to his feet. He recognized the profile—Rip! Montgomery spun around and bent over behind Travis to inspect a bush. However, Rip recognized neither boy as he walked away.

The trio approached the door. "What was that about?" asked Montgomery.

"A SigBee—Sigma Omicron Beta; I hate those guys," said the lead man. "He was trying to sabotage our smoker by spiking our punch with some chemical—probably acid or E." He smiled. "We're not that kind of frat. We don't care where y'all do your drugs—automatic expulsion. But if you're clean, welcome to our house."

The boys shook hands and introduced themselves. "Delta Pi," he said. "Everyone calls me Dell."

"Delta hand," said Travis. "Everyone calls me winner: I had four aces!"

"Don't start with the groaners," complained Montgomery. "Let's check out the house."

Dell led the three on a tour and extolled the features of the Delta house. He pointed out that they were a group of men who wanted to live free from the hazards of campus life: exposure to sexual activity, drunkenness, drugging and other means of excess which mar the pleasantness of most college residences.

"I know who you are," said Travis. "This is the Monk House."

Dell laughed. "Also the No-Fun House, the UnFun house, the Holy Rollers, the Church, and the Christianites. There are some others, but the names are unpronounceable." Dell went on to point out the advantages of living with men who pursued their studies seriously and avidly, as well as relaxing in ways that honored God.

The next house was lit up with loud music piercing the night air. "Make this one the last of the night," yawned Travis. "I'm tired."

The Ghost looked at the letters on the house. "Kappa Kappa ——"

"Korn," Travis interrupted.

"You are tired," said Montgomery. "What is that last letter?"

"Chi," replied the Ghost.

"We'd better skip this one," said Montgomery.

"Why?" asked the Ghost.

"You won't fit in," said Montgomery. "You're a Yankee."

"Yankee," repeated the Ghost with dismay, "nobody has said that in one hundred years. That went out with the nineteenth century."

"Maybe in Michigan, but down here we're still fighting the war. Only the hostilities have ceased."

"What war—the Civil War?"

Travis dropped to one knee laughing. He fell over and pounded the ground with his fist.

"The War of Northern Aggression Against the Southern States. We're still fighting it, defending our honor against the overreaching tyranny of the northern states in regards to their captivity of the Washington government," countered Montgomery. "At least in our heads we're still fighting. Look at the house; what do you see? A rebel flag—the battle flag, which is known as the Southern Cross."

"Wow," said the Ghost.

"Makes you want to retreat to the laundromat, doesn't it?" commented Travis. "It ain't over yet, Yankee, there's more a-coming."

Montgomery said stiffly, "Pride in our southern heritage does not mean we endorse every group that lays claim to it."

"Or every clan that lays claim to it," Travis added with his eyes twinkling.

"What are y'all talking about?" cried an exasperated Ghost.

"Very good!" yelled Travis. "We'll make a rebel of you yet."

Montgomery explained with the same stiff voice, "Kappa Kappa Chi, or K—K—"

"X" Travis interrupted.

"It used to be Kappa," rejoindered Montgomery. "But when political correctness came in, they changed it to a disguised K. Chi as a Greek letter looks like X, but it is pronounced as a hard K. They're still the K—K—K. They hate everybody who isn't white, southern and haters of everybody who isn't white and southern."

"How do they stay on campus?" asked the Ghost.

"Simple," said Travis. "They stay out of trouble so no one notices, they disguise what they need to, and they induct a few tokens to throw the P.C. hounds off the scent."

The Ghost reflected over this information plus the visits they had made. "Y'all know something? There aren't any places worth the effort to join. I don't care for any of these houses we've seen."

Montgomery smiled tolerantly. "Check."

Montgomery checked his e-mail upon returning to the quad. It was quarter till the hour of 10 p.m. One e-mail was from Sigma Omicron Beta reminding him of a pledge meeting Friday night. Montgomery clicked the reply option, returning a message that said he was busy with the assignments and would be unavailable—most likely for weeks.

Montgomery figured that would bring an indignant message from Wilson the next day, and he was right.

"Are you juggling with fire?" Travis asked him.

"Perhaps. But Daddy pointed out to me that they're afraid of my family name, else they'd have dumped me. So I don't have to jump whenever they snap their fingers. I'll go back when I'm ready, and not before." He smiled. "I'm going over to see Elizabeth. Want to come along for Park?"

"No, something's not right between us. I figure to lay low for a few days so she'll be looking for me when I do go."

"Don't wait up."

"Stay all night."

Montgomery smiled. "Not yet, Travis, not yet."

CHAPTER SIXTEEN

THE THIRD TASK

THE BUZZ IN THE CLASSROOM was loud as Montgomery came through the door into the Symposium where Dr. Hinson held his classes on moral philosophy. The first few weeks had been easy, as the professor had laid the foundation for moral philosophy: the evolution of species. Simply put, that the human species had developed standards of behavior in response to evolutionary pressures; the societies who adopted morals that gave them a competitive advantage over other societies displaced those other human societies. The displaced societies either adopted the behavior adaptations or went into extinction. Eventually, a universal set of morals spread across human societies through "social evolution."

Montgomery was revolted by the idea. Brought up in a church where Biblical morals were taught, he believed that the foundation for moral philosophy was the Ten Commandments that the Creator God revealed to Moses upon Mt. Sinai, and that Professor Hinson had backed into the same set of morals by reasoning.

Dr. Hinson had delayed a critique of social evolution for an unspecified future class. What was creating the buzz was that today, in the third week of class, Dr. Hinson was going to present alternate theories of moral philosophy and then demolish them.

The bell rang. Dr. Hinson emerged from the door in the forward wall, accessible only from the faculty offices. All eyes were upon him as he set his briefcase on the table. He picked up a piece of chalk from the blackboard tray and wrote G / O / D on the slate surface in big letters. Next he added an N above the letter O and a T beneath it. The letters now formed the + symbol for addition. Montgomery realized that Dr. Hinson had not formed an addition symbol but a cross. Dr. Hinson laughed merrily at his joke. Montgomery's face flushed red with anger.

"Throughout the history of humanity," Dr. Hinson began his lecture, "people have used religion as the basis of moral philosophy. The philosophy constructed by the Jews has been the most pervasive in the world as well as near-ineradicable over the centuries. You think I speak of the Ten Commandments. No, I do not. The Commandments are a rather mundane collection of dos and don'ts the Jewish tribes learned from other peoples with whom they came into contact during their long centuries of desert migration."

Montgomery was scribbling notes as well as composing questions in the margins of his notebook paper. He thought of what he had learned during his youth group sessions when he was in high school: *First, identify and evaluate the unspoken assumptions. Second, find the premise. Is it supported by evidence, or only by the assumptions? Third, analyze the logic. Have reasoning errors been made? Does the argument lead to absurdity? Fourth, have factual errors been made? Fifth, is the conclusion sound? In his first five sentences, Dr. Hinson's made no less than two factual errors, four unsupported premises, and three unspoken assumptions.*

"The philosophy of which I speak is that a Being, not higher than the highest achievement of carbon-based evolution but of a different essence and nature—a God, if you will—created the material world and formed all the life in it. For moral philosophy, this Divine Being becomes the source and author of human morals, not merely for the society that worships Him, but universally for all humankind, and possibly the animals as well."

Dr. Hinson glanced around the room. A few heads were nodding, many shiny pairs of eyes were looking back, and some faces had quizzical expressions.

"The key to a God-basis for deriving standards for human behavior is to determine what pleases and offends the God. When the history of a religion is constructed, it is found that a process of trial and error determined the moral standards. Natural disasters and great calamities resulted in the devastated societies looking for the errors of omission or commission that offended the God. When generally agreement was reached on what the offense was, a moral value was 'discovered' and spread through cooperation and coercion."

Dr. Hinson was smirking to himself on the inside. *When they are this young, one can serve them any tripe and they will eat it as awesome truth.* This was Dr. Hinson's favorite part of his course: smashing the religious ideas of young minds and giving them a humanist philosophy to replace them.

"For example, a great flood wipes out most of the village. Only a few survive and return to rebuild. Those who do discover that the precious jewels that adorned their idol had been taken before the flood. The God is angry over their loss; therefore, the villagers decide that stealing is morally wrong. Or they find out that the sacrifices had been diverted for human consumption; again, the stealing brought the disaster, therefore it is morally wrong.

"Suppose that a man killed his neighbor over a boundary dispute. That man goes to worship in a temple. An earthquake shakes the region. When the villagers come to the temple, they find that the idol fell over and killed the murderer. Clearly, the God punishes murderers; it is morally wrong. Adulterers die from sexually transmitted disease. The God is punishing the adulterers; it is morally wrong.

"In the case of the Jewish God, we have a different idea that takes hold. Morals are not divined (Dr. Hinson grinned at his pun; the students were too busy taking notes to notice) from disasters and rooted in a system of appeasement of the God. The God reveals his character to the people; they must become like Him if they are to receive His blessing. Therefore, the effort goes forth to determine exactly who that God is and what He is like. Not surprisingly, certain 'special' persons encounter the God, and reveal to the people the necessary morals. The monopoly on the God, and the privilege of setting the morals, falls to one or a few individuals who then impose their way upon the entire people. For the Jews, the man was Moses, and thus began the long history of Judaism & Christianity proclaiming their superior morals and forcing these morals upon all peoples everywhere."

Montgomery was aghast. *How could a university professor be so wrong? Is his belief in evolution causing him to deny God the Creator? Does one mistaken belief bring so many repercussions in a person's philosophical system? Why does his reasoning ignore known facts? Does Dr. Hinson hold pet theories that he forces his logic, reasoning and facts into serving no matter how strained?*

"The right to impose these morals is based upon the God being the Creator. He made it; therefore, he may tell it how it will live. He made it; therefore, if he's not pleased, he may destroy it. The so-called created has no autonomy of their own; they're endowed with no rights. The Creator bestows the breath of life, but it has a mortgage on it, and the Creator may repossess it whenever he wishes upon the merest whim. Such philosophy is devastating to freedom, but overpowering in providing control over people as long as they believe.

"Our time is almost expired. As a starting point for critique, know that the religion-based moral philosophy fails to pass the test of truth because the world's religions have philosophies that differ. They are not 100% in agreement which proves that none of them were revealed by a Divine Being—the God; they were the products of human cultures. As such, we must look elsewhere than 'God said so' for our morals."

Half the class applauded as Dr. Hinson completed his lecture for the period.

"Your first paper is due in two weeks: research and describe a religion-based moral philosophy. Then critique it. Good day." Dr. Hinson shut his briefcase, and left the room. A loud buzz broke out.

"So brilliant ..." "... wrong about God ..." "... thought all religions were the same ..." "... see the faces of those twerps who still believe in God ..." "... evolution destroyed religion long ago ..." "... ask my minister ..." "... shows up the superstitions of long ago ..." "... and today ..." "... thought the Ten Commandments were given to Moses ... never realized he borrowed them from other cultures ..." "... exposed the absurdity of a Creator God ..." "... a God like the Jewish-Christian God is not one worthy of worshipping ... imagine, killing a living thing because he is not pleased ..." "... not say that ..." "... he did ..." "... if he's right, then morals are accidents of history ..." "... means we're free to make our own ..."

On the other side of the door, Dr. Hinson was listening to fragments of student conversations and splitting his face with an ear-to-ear grin: *the little lambs following me to the slaughter.*

Later, Montgomery tried to explain to Elizabeth how he constructed a moral philosophy. "The professor said that religiously-derived morals in the Jewish-Christian tradition are based upon the Creator's ownership rights in his creatures: the Creator makes a creature with free will, but then imposes upon the creature external rules from his power to create, and by implication, to destroy. But that's not it. He's wrong. He says that God manipulates us to obey his moral code by blessing us if we obey, and cursing us if we don't. He's wrong. The key problem is this: he has judged Christian morals as inappropriate for humankind, and based upon that, judged the Creator God who gave us the morals."

"But that's backward, isn't it? How can you judge anyone's set of morals, Christian and non-Christian alike, until you have determined the basis—the foundation—of your moral philosophy?"

"Exactly, he's conducting a supposedly unbiased examination of moral foundations, but he has already determined which morals are right and which morals are wrong. What purports to be fair is slanted because he considers each type of philosophy, not on its own terms, but by the terms of his predetermined philosophy. Before comparing the different philosophies, we must first understand them and their merits and faults as they present themselves. Then we can look for ways to validate them as truth. Dr. Hinson measures moral philosophies by how well they agree with what he believes: he validates them where they agree, and faults them where they don't."

"That isn't sound scholarship, is it? How can anyone predetermine truth? Isn't truth what you arrive at? It's not where you start in making an intellectual inquiry. What throws Hinson off?"

"The unspoken assumption."

"Huh?"

"The unspoken assumption," Montgomery repeated. "His lectures contain unspoken assumptions he has made. He never states them, so they never receive critical scrutiny. But they're crucial to what he's presenting. One, he assumes that there is no God. Two, which follows from one, all moral philosophy is the product of human thinking."

"So he trashes everything we learned in Sunday School and Church."

"Check. Now how do I write a paper and say that?"

"Honey, if you do that, save yourself the trouble and write a huge red F on a blank sheet of paper and turn it in."

"You don't think he wants us to use our minds and say what we believe, inquiring into the religious-based moral philosophy and supporting our conclusions?"

"Not if your conclusions differ from his opinions. We're undergraduates. They're professors. They don't care what we think. They want us to regurgitate what they've fed us. What you make of it keep to yourself unless it is unabashed admiration for what they've said."

"How do I maintain my integrity?"

"You're not compromised; you're demonstrating that you listened to him, and understand what he said."

Elizabeth read in his earnest eyes the internal struggle over the truth he knew, and the desire to propound it, versus the knowledge that the professor was not seeking a debate and would not respect his writing because he was only an undergraduate student, and a freshman at that. Her heart beat a little quicker as she pondered how attractive he was, with his blond hair growing out, those green passionate eyes, neat sideburns and scruffy chin hairs. "Why are you taking this course?"

"It's a requirement for me to join the fraternity."

"The frat—of course. Why does a pledge need to learn moral philosophy to join a house rampant with drunkenness, drugging and sexual encounters?"

"I don't know. They called me a moralist. They don't want me to join. Maybe the course is to confuse me so I don't know what to believe or maybe they think with my strong moral character that I won't be able to complete the course."

"Maybe, to them, it's a big joke."

"That could be, or they made it up on the spot. Whatever the reason, it's going to backfire on them. By the time I'm done, I'm going to eat their lunch if they put that moralist tag on me. I'll make a case for the moral values that God set for all humankind that's so strong and natural and reasonable they 'll slink with shame into the cracks in the walls."

Rose brought the medium-sized box to her room the day it arrived through the campus mail. Her roommates gathered around her as she regarded the bright red wrapping paper and pink ribbon. A small card had merely read: For Rose.

"No name?" said an unbelieving Park.

"Who else could it be?" retorted Elizabeth. "Duh."

Rose shook her head. "I don't know."

"Open it," squealed Park.

Rose slowly pulled the ribbon and bow off the package. She then carefully peeled the taped ends open, and pulled the paper out removing the folds. She sat and held it on her lap. The suspense snapped in the air as starched canvas flaps in the wind.

"Good things come in bright packages," said Elizabeth. "Go on—let's see what's inside."

Rose nodded, and ran her hand between the edges of the paper, separating the last piece of tape from the paper. She opened the paper and stared at the box. "Bertie's Ceramics" read the gold lettering on the cream cardboard. Rose pulled the top, which sat, snugly around the bottom of the box. With a last whoosh, the box separated. Green crepe paper rustled into the exposed opening. Rose parted the crepe paper sheet by sheet. At last, it was all brushed back over the sides of the box. Inside a white ceramic figurine shone in the light. Rose pulled it out.

"What an odd gift," said Park.

"There's a meaning attached," said Elizabeth. "Is there any writing in the box?"

Rose shook her head. She looked the figurine over. "No writing—no message."

"It's a mystery," Park exclaimed. "That's a clue."

"Okay, genius," Elizabeth said wryly, "What does an elephant mean?"

Park looked at the figurine carefully. "Look at the mouth. It's open; the elephant's talking."

Elizabeth said, "And what does a talking elephant signify?"

"It means," said Rose, "we need to talk about the elephant in the room." She burst into tears.

Elizabeth and Park exchanged puzzled looks as they sat on either side of their friend to comfort her.

Elizabeth said, "What is it, Rose? What's bothering you?"

"The invisible elephant," said Rose.

"Honey, you're making no sense," cried Park. "Speak English."

"The invisible elephant in the room," elaborated Rose. "He's so big everyone's aware of his presence, but no one will talk about him for fear the others will say he's crazy. So they go around pretending the elephant isn't there. Now the elephant can be seen; we have to talk about him." Her tears flowed.

"This is bad—" prompted Park.

"I did not come to college to husband-hunt," said Rose. "I want a degree, a real degree like mechanical engineering or chemistry or mathematician."

"I still don't get the elephant," said a confused Park.

"Silly, it's a sweetheart gift," said an astute Elizabeth. "What's the king of all elephants when it comes to having conversations with sweethearts?"

"If you are so smart, Einstein, then you tell me," countered Park.

"Rick sent Rose the talking elephant to mean that they need to talk about the seriousness of their relationship. To engage or not to engage, that is the question," explained Elizabeth.

"Another riddle," snapped Park. "Spit it out."

"I've been dreading this for weeks," said Rose. "He wants to talk about marriage."

Park stopped in mid-squeal when she realized that Rose had not said this in the happiest of voices.

"That's good, isn't it?" Park asked. "You love him, he loves you, you don't love him—" Park changed as she watched Rose shake her head.

"I understand," said Elizabeth. "He makes you very happy. You two are deeply in love, but you're afraid of what that means. You want to talk about marriage, but you don't want to talk because you're afraid he'll break up because he's not ready for marriage. But you're even more afraid that he'll ask you to marry him because you're not sure that you're ready for marriage. But you can't stand the tension of not talking about it, so you really want to talk about it. But you also fear that you and he will agree upon marriage, and you're afraid that you won't finish your degree as you want. Yet you're afraid that if you avoid the subject, you 'll miss out on the greatest thing in your life. You're torn in many directions. Going in any one of them would be better, yet you fear turning your back on the others. So you want to go on in uncertainty because you're afraid of what certainty will do. But now you must decide—because he has said, 'We need to talk."

Rose nodded her head as her tears again ran over her eyelids.

Park said nothing but was thanking her lucky stars she was shallow and only wanted good times and sex. Elizabeth's explanation made no sense to Park.

"Time to face the executioner," said Elizabeth. "The sooner you get it over with, the sooner you'll feel better." Elizabeth picked up the phone and held it out.

Rose said, "I don't know what to say. I've been avoiding this conversation ever since we got back from the holidays."

Park finally found something to offer, "Don't say anything. He sent the elephant; let him do the talking."

Across the campus, the telephone in room 3B1 rapidly vibrated a small pin against a metallic dome inside its box. Five times it made its motion, and paused. The sixth time, it was cut in mid-ring: "Hello, hang on a minute." The handset was set on a table. The sound of plastic bags settling on a horizontal surface signaled that the arms of the answerer were now free.

"Hello, Rick Early speaking. Whom do I have the pleasure of answering?"

Silence on a deadened line communicated the message that the caller had hung up. Rick shrugged his shoulders and replaced the handset. He went into the bathroom. The small pin began its series of vibrations again.

Rick came dashing out of the bathroom; his shorts around his ankles. He picked up the handset just as the caller hung up. He shook his head, pulled up his clothes and headed back to the bathroom.

When he returned to his room, the small pin started up its ringing. Rick walked over and looked at his phone. He picked up the handset, "Rick Early speaking. Say something—anything." The phone went dead.

Rick was exasperated. *Whoever was playing this joke did not have the imagination of a …* Rick thought of someone who would be nervous about calling. Since he had talked with Montgomery, Rick had tried to bring up the subject of their relationship with Rose. She would shy away. Then he would lose his nerve for fear of losing her. Over and over he went through the steps. Finally he thought of sending her the elephant. Now he was committed to bring it up, he could not chicken out, and she could not avoid it; he had to explain the elephant.

Rick picked up the phone and dialed Rose's room. "Rick Early on the line. Is Rose available?"

"Let me ask her," said Park, and then she slapped her forehead. She handed the phone to Rose as she mouthed the word, "Sorry."

"Hello?" asked Rose. "Rick—so nice of you to call." She felt awkward and stupid; her tears filled her eyes.

"Let's end the tap dance, honey."

| RUSH WEEK |

Dunbar Edwards looked at the clock on the library wall. It read 10:45 p.m. He yawned. The study group had been meeting for the last three hours. He was ready to call it a night.

"What's left?" a pink-cheeked girl asked.

"The effect of the Renaissance in moving Western Civilization from the Medieval period into the Modern period," said another girl.

"Can we let it go until next time?" said Dunbar. "I'm exhausted."

"Let's catalog the differences between the two periods and end there," suggested Travis. The group adopted his suggestion. "The major differences were the separation of the church from the state; the switch to a scientific understanding of the universe, in which things behaved according to fixed, natural laws instead of the pre-scientific view whereby a divine decree established the course of individual objects; reason replaced faith as the basis for inquiring about the universe; empirical observation rather than revelation was the basis for constructing one's worldview; individual liberties became the ideal rather than a fixed order to society; nationalism rose to replace two ideological loyalties: the church as political entity and the feudal estate. Ironically, what aided the kings in establishing a strong, central state ultimately undermined their role as the authoritarian power of the strong, central state as that power dissolved to the masses under democratic ideals."

"Stop!" said Dunbar. "That's a great catalog. Good night."

The group began pulling books, papers, notebooks and other academic paraphernalia into neat piles, which they stuffed, into their book bags.

"I don't know what we would do without you, Travis," said the pink-faced girl. "You have really been the mainstay for our group."

"She's right," confirmed Dunbar. "I'm glad we have a brain among us."

Travis reddened. "I'm no brain," he mumbled. "It's interesting so I remember it, that's all."

"You're too modest," said the pink-faced girl. "You understand everything and connect it together in coherent understandings and construction of theories. I can memorize facts, but I can't put them together into theories. You see the patterns that I miss. You draw the conclusions, which I stop short of finding. You're a great thinker."

"You have me mistaken for someone else—like my roommate. But thanks for the compliments."

As Travis left the room, Dunbar caught up to him. "Can I talk to you, Travis?"

"Sure—what's up?"

"What's been going on between you and Park? I know it's a personal subject, but—well—"

"The answer to your question is not much. She and I are drifting apart. I don't know why. I wish we were getting closer like my roommate and his girlfriend. Why do you ask?"

"Well—" Dunbar looked at the ground, embarrassed. "It's ... It's like this. She comes over to the dorm and hangs out. She throws out these hints like she wants to get friendly. But I don't want to cut in on you. So what should I do?"

Travis found the news disconcerting. "It's like this, Dunbar. If Park and I have something, she won't go out with you. If she does, then she and I are over. So ask her for a date; then we'll both know."

"You don't sound very happy."

"I'm not. I like Park. I would like — maybe I want something between us that she doesn't. Maybe I'm ready to love her, but she's not ready to love me. Anyhow, I'm better off to know. If it's time to move on, I need to move on; so there's no hard feelings, Dunbar. Go ahead—see what she does."

"Thanks, Travis; you're a real pal."

Montgomery was spending hours in the library researching religions to find a philosophy he could describe and critique. "The problem," he told Elizabeth, "with writing on the Jewish-Christian moral basis is that it is rooted in creation theology. God the Creator made homo sapiens to be like him for the earth. We were made in his image; therefore, we were made to be like him—not in being divine with superhuman powers, or to be worshipped and glorified—but in our wisdom to take care of creation on his behalf. His moral standards reveal who he is, and therefore what we should be. If we don't keep his moral standards, we're not being human—we're being something less than human."

"Doesn't Dr. Hinson have the same problem when he avers his theory that morals evolved as humans evolved? He has to go back to a theory on how the earth and its creatures came to be—then he develops his moral philosophy."

"True, but I'm supposed to write a paper on moral philosophy; if I go to the creation versus evolution issue, I'll have to write a book to settle that issue before I can go on to write a paper."

"I think, based upon your research, you should describe the moral philosophy of Islam: submission to Allah. Then critique it. You've accomplished the assignment. You've avoided the problem of bucking the biased professor's pet theory if you assert your own. Save your arguments for later in the course."

Montgomery looked at her with warmth and desire in his eyes. "You're a genius." He leaned over, and their lips met in a long and lingering kiss.

An impatient pencil tapped on the carousel where he and Elizabeth were working. A fifty-ish matron wearing a blue printed dress, black pumps and half-moon glasses on a chain harrumphed as they looked up. "You may study the books, but not each other," she said in an offended tone, and she clomped off. The couple burst out laughing.

"Experts on ancient societies, ancient writings, ancient customs and cultures, and ancient archeology, especially those who specialize in the Middle East, or the Near East, have proven that the book popularly called "The Bible" is not a historical record." Dr. Hinson surveyed his class. Most were taking notes, a few looked bored, and a few seemed offended. "Not only did most of the events recorded never take place, but most of the people are fictional as well."

Montgomery bit the end of his pen to keep from reacting to the misleading presentation the professor was making. He knew that many scholars did doubt the Bible's record of history, but that many others upheld the history in the Bible. He also knew that archeology had confirmed the existence of many persons, cities, lands and events mentioned in the Bible. Further, that archeology had never disproven the existence of any person, city, land or event. Nevertheless, he gritted his teeth and took notes on what the professor was propounding.

"But we need not concern ourselves with that. Even knowing the Bible as mythology, and knowing that persons like Moses are mythological figures along the lines of Hercules in Greek mythology, the Bible still records the ideas of morality that the Jewish people developed, and insisted everybody follow.

"Those ideas of morality were based upon an idea of ritual purity. Doing certain things would violate one's purity—thus they were forbidden. Proscriptions were applied to sexuality, food, bodily functions, and the like. The question is why. It's a complex question that delves into the historical development of national consciousness ..." The professor droned on.

Montgomery fought the urge to fall asleep as the professor meandered through an exposition of Israelite history. *Amazing, the Bible is mythology when it asserts moral values, thus making them a subjective set formed from human thinking and not binding upon anyone who doesn't agree with them, but it can be used as history when providing an explanation to deny the moral values as God's revelation to humanity.*

He was glad when the period came to an end. As he rose to go, he saw a familiar figure rise out of the back of the room and vanish through the rear door. *That's odd. What's he doing here?*

Montgomery caught the bus back to the residence halls. As he joined his quadmates in the dining hall, Red mentioned that Montgomery had received several phone calls from a man named Wilson. "He said it was urgent."

Montgomery groaned. "The semester has been sweet. But I reckon that's over. It's time to face the buzz mill and undergo another period of torture. The SigBees are massing for a stinging."

"We are sympathetic," said Cat, "but then, this is a choice you're making. You don't have to go back."

"I can't explain it," said a morose Montgomery. "I'm compelled to go through with it. Why do you think I went to that women's group? Why have I worked in the hospital with the pseudo-psycho supervisor? What other reason for taking a class on moral philosophy that has provided no clear thinking about right and wrong? Quite the opposite, the professor delights in muddying the waters. All this garbage has been to satisfy the demands of the frat. Do you think, because I haven't been to the house, that I've forgotten about it? To the contrary, I never stop thinking about it. I'm determined to get in; I won't give up. Then I'll press for reforms to return the house to its original purpose as a society of campus leaders and role models excelling in character and leadership. I've joined the battle; the victory's obtainable, but not in sight. It's not the time to give up."

Travis said, "I've never known you to be so stubborn."

"I've never faced stiff opposition before now."

Chapter Seventeen

Greek Inquisition

"WE'RE VERY DISAPPOINTED IN YOU," harrumphed a grumpy Wilson.

Montgomery peered at the face of the stocky junior. Already lines were apparent across Wilson's brow. His eyes were somewhat bloodshot, and roamed around his sockets as he avoided Montgomery's direct stare. He hadn't shaved in three days; his normally neat haircut was growing out in a haphazard way.

"Where have you been? You belong at the house. You have precious little support as it goes; you're losing the undecided and wavering."

Montgomery was impassive.

"You belong in the kitchen; you neglect your assignments. The rituals, the male bonding, the camaraderie: you miss it all. Are you quitting?"

Montgomery did not move. He let the pressure of the silence grow.

"Have you nothing to say?"

Montgomery did not speak.

Wilson became more agitated. "What does your silence mean? Say something—anything."

"Why are you here?"

"Why am I here? To talk to you."

"Why have you come to talk to me?"

"I'm your supervising brother."

Closing his eyes, Montgomery sighed. *I've been dreading this moment. Should I put Wilson off or confront him? The longer I delay, the worse it will be.*

"Supervising brother?" Montgomery raised the pitch of his voice to indicate that the concept was very much in question. "Supervising what? Electrocution? Acid trips? Drug parties? The courier business which no one will talk about? Crusty women carrying venereal diseases moving from room to room? Peep shows into women's bathrooms? Lack of respect for the traditions of the place you represent?"

Wilson started to say something, but quailed at the fury moving across Montgomery's face.

"Wilson, you're being used by Cody and his gang. You let it happen; you abet his operation. I don't know what he's turned the fraternity into, but I have a strong hunch it's illegal. So does my Dad."

"Harrison Lee? What does he know about us?" A worried Wilson was green around the gills.

"Only what happened to me last fall."

"Not good," Wilson moaned. "Not good, not good, not good."

"I don't know what your problem is, but you're pathetic. Where's your self-respect, man? You made a deal with the devil. Get your soul back. Resign. Stop pretending to be a big man with clout. You're a joke. Everyone knows you're a puppet for Cody. Have you no principles?"

Wilson slumped back in the booth he and Montgomery were sharing at the in-town restaurant where they had met last fall.

"Why did Cody send you to talk to me?" Montgomery demanded.

Wilson shifted his eyes. "What makes you think Cody sent me?"

Montgomery was silent.

Wilson flailed at the old, tired leather of the booth in an effort to pull himself up. He failed. To Montgomery, he was like a puppy scratching at the gate of his pen.

"He wants to see you," Wilson said in a low voice. "But not formally. If you come to the house, he can 'accidentally' run into you."

"Why does he want to see me?"

"I don't know. Honestly, I don't. The best I can tell you is that he's worried about something."

"Tell me about the new pledges."

"We have a small, but select group. There's Nu, —"

"Cut it out. Don't you know their names?"

Wilson moved his eyes upward as if he could see the names written inside his brain. "Um, Byron Mueller, Cleveland Ivers, Joshua Plintz, Mick Raike—"

"Who? Did you say Mick Raike?"

"Right. Great find according to Cody."

"It figures," muttered Montgomery.

"Pardon?"

"Nothing. He was in my quad last semester. He fell apart as the semester progressed. In fact, he was evicted when this term began. The quad suspected he was deeply into drugs."

Wilson shrugged. "The committee thought he had potential for leadership."

"Who are the others?"

"Colin Beavers, and Damon Eagleford. We skipped the traditional rush. We spent much time going through dormitories recruiting the type of man that we want. We shouldn't have the problem we had before. We screened out the undesirables by focusing on recruiting the ones who had the characteristics we wanted. They should have an easy pass into our ranks."

"What are the hazing plans?"

"The normal stunts: peanut butter in the hair, drinking contest, chores and grunt work, red robe ceremony, sing the songs, really tame fun."

"Not that you would know," Montgomery observed sardonically.

Wilson flinched. "Why don't you respect me?"

"You don't respect yourself. Grab the check. I'm going."

"What do I tell Cody?" whined Wilson.

"Leave the house or you call the cops. As for me, I was sent to accomplish four tasks. One is finished, one is almost finished, one is underway, and one is dependent on finishing the second. That was my assignment, not cooking wieners for weenies and wastrels. I'll come to the house at a time of my choosing, not theirs."

Montgomery rose to leave. "And, if Cody wants to see me, he can call me himself—not send his flunky."

Friday night arrived. At seven o'clock, Rick and Montgomery left Somerset Johns to pick up Rose and Elizabeth. The foursome left the campus in Rick's car and headed for a bowling alley. Somewhere along the way, they decided to compete as men vs. women. Since none of the four were regular bowlers, there was no advantage to either side.

After the foursome departed the girls' room, Dunbar Edwards arrived to pick up Park. "Where would you like to go?"

"Somewhere we can dance."

"I know the very place." They headed off campus to a private club that Dunbar knew of and could gain access to. Dunbar had secured a bottle of blackberry schnapps. They enjoyed several swallows along the way.

Travis was at a loss to know what to do with himself. He felt very lonely; he wished the old Travis would come back so he could forget about Park and go look for a party. The quadmates were dispersed across the campus; some had headed to classmates' parties, some had gone away overnight, and others had activities in which they were involved. Travis felt some pangs of envy for Montgomery's astronomy club; it was something his roommate could turn to as he wanted and find someone to share an evening. Surfing was dependent upon the weather stirring up the waves. When it was calm, the surfing club was non-existent.

Travis was determined to find something to do. He was not going to sit in the quad and watch TV. He had not done that since pre-puberty. He washed his face, changed his shirt and headed into the night. He walked aimlessly eventually arriving at the main campus. *The*

SigBees are jerks, but I almost wish I was back in the fall when the pledge activities had kept me busy.

Travis wandered across the campus. The buildings were dark. The theater was empty: no plays or concerts on the schedule. He did not want to go down fraternity row. He definitely was not interested in that lifestyle.

It was close to 8 p.m. when Travis saw the welcome lights of the student center. He decided to play some video games, or maybe find a game of pool.

The building was mostly deserted. *Few losers like me drifting around. I wish I was home. Why did I start reading Shakespeare and thinking about the natural rights of humans and the nature of liberty? But I enjoy it. I find it interesting, and stimulating. Why does the intellectual me have to smother the party me? What did I do to Park to make her pull away? All I wanted was more depth to our relationship—like Montgomery and Elizabeth.*

Travis went to the room where the video games were housed. He found a cord strung across the entrance with a sign, "Closed for repairs." He hung his head and kicked the wall. *Why do I feel so bad? Why do I feel so depressed on this Friday night? I don't even feel like getting drunk.*

Travis decided to get something to eat. As he went toward the small cafe, he heard laughter from the second floor. On a whim, he decided to go upstairs and see what was happening. He could hear someone speaking, and then more laughing. *Maybe this is promising.*

Travis moved down the hall toward an open door where light and laughter were spilling into the hall. He stopped opposite the doorway. About fifty students sat on the floor, watching a man in his thirties doing impressions and magic tricks. They were laughing and enjoying the show. There were several older adults as well. They looked like faculty members.

One of them saw him standing there, and beckoned him to come in. Travis hesitated. But now heads were turning to look at him, and several voices were urging him to come in. *Why not? The show's funny and it would cause the evening to pass in a tolerable fashion. It won't be a life-changing decision to go in.*

Travis entered the room and sat down. The man went on with his show.

POW! "I love the sound of wooden pins knocking against the cinder block ends of the alleys," enthused Montgomery.

Elizabeth made a face. "Strike again. Spare me."

Montgomery groaned. "Want to split?"

"No and no."

The couples were in the midst of their second game. Because Montgomery was hot and bowling well, the men had won the first game and were ahead in the middle of the second. Rose went up to the ball return and picked up the ball she was using.

Rick sat on the bench watching her. She carefully aligned herself on the lane and held her ball out. She took three short steps as she swung the ball back, and slid on her right foot as she laid the ball on the alley with her forward motion. The ball seemed to sit where she put it. Slowly it gathered speed as it rolled down the hard-waxed surface. The ball kissed the front pins, which tumbled over from the contact. When it was done, all the pins were down.

Rose jumped with delight and clapped her hands.

Rick rose from his place, and watched the machine reset the pins. He picked up his ball, and took his place on the lane. He leaned over, began his motion and hurled the ball down the alley. The force of his throw was so great that the ball went through the pins leaving a classic 7—10 pin split. "Just get one," Montgomery advised.

But Rick was competitive, and tried for both. He threw a crazy spinner down the lane, hoping the spin would hold the ball on the edge of the gutter long enough for the ball to kick the seven pin against the ten pin. Unfortunately, the spin carried the ball into the left gutter, out of the gutter and into the next lane. Rick turned bright red and retrieved his ball as he apologized to the people using that lane.

Elizabeth now took to the lane. She held her ball up, and let it fly. It made two bounces on the floor and rolled down the lane. She had knocked over six pins. Elizabeth smiled, and waited for her ball to come back. She aimed it again, and let it fly. The ball landed on the lane and skidded into the right gutter. Elizabeth walked back to the bench smiling.

Montgomery took his turn. He took his ball, and delivered another strike. Rose matched him, and it was Rick's turn again. Once more he overcompensated and hurled the ball through the pins. However, he was able to score nine with his second throw.

Elizabeth continued her unorthodox throwing motion. While she was not making strikes or spares, she was steadily scoring sixes, sevens and eights. Montgomery continued to score well. Rose kept stride, and Rick became more inconsistent as the evening progressed.

At the end of three games, the score stood men, 2 games; women, 1 game (the last). They completed the frames and removed their rented shoes. The balls were replaced in the racks.

"Where now?" asked Elizabeth.

"Let's get some french fries and Cokes," suggested Montgomery.

Rose and Rick assented, and the couples went into the night to find a Fry Shack.

The women held a table on the outdoor patio while the men went to purchase the spuds and the Cokes. They carried the refreshments over to the table.

"Beautiful night out," observed Elizabeth. "One thing about dating a star gazer: I've learned to appreciate the beauty of the night sky."

"No wind," approved Rose. "It's the end of February, and there's no wind. Makes it seasonable and pleasant to sit outside."

"So Rick," Montgomery said, "seen any elephants lately?"

Under the table, Elizabeth kicked his leg.

"Not anything to talk about," Rick responded.

"Fascinating creatures, elephants. Did you know they mate for life?"

"Really," said Elizabeth in an icy tone. "Do tell."

"It's a long and slow courting dance," replied Montgomery. "The male trumpets to announce his love, stomps the ground and strides around the herd. The female ignores him. The male continues to trumpet and stomp until the female trumpets out a plaintive note. Then the male drops to his knees, and begins to swish the dust with his trunk. The female gives him a plain, intimidating stare. The male rises to his feet and begins to stomp."

"You're making this up," said Rose.

"No, I swear, it's true. The charade goes on for days: male trumpeting, sign of submission; the female making out like she wishes he would go away, and she'll whip his butt if he tries to come near."

"I can relate," said Rick. "He doesn't know what kind of reception he's really getting, and the state of confusion goes on for days and weeks while the suspense becomes heavier than the elephant."

"Maybe," said Elizabeth, "the big dummy doesn't sense that the female's silence means she doesn't want to talk to him about mating dances."

"Maybe," said Montgomery, "what the elephants need is for their friends to leave them alone so they can talk about mating dances."

"Maybe—," began Elizabeth, but she stopped speaking when she felt Rose's hand on her arm.

"Go on, please," Rose said softly. "He's right about the elephants."

Elizabeth rose to her feet. "My dear sister of the better sex, I wish you hadn't said that in the hearing of my bull elephant. He'll strut in pride for weeks."

"Leave them alone," Montgomery interjected, "before they lose their nerve."

Montgomery and Elizabeth strolled off to the other end of the parking lot. Rick and Rose faced each other nervously.

"I have waited for this moment ..." Rick paused to think of what to say. "You are the ... no—I've fallen deeply in love with you. I'm miserable that I may not spend my life with you. I'll do anything you say, go anywhere you want, support you however you want, you may do whatever you want to do, but say that you'll do it together with me. Finish college, have a career or stay at home. It doesn't matter. All that matters is that we join our lives together. That's what I want. You're the most beautiful girl in the world. Say that you'll marry me. At least say that you'll talk about it. Please don't turn me away."

Rose had begun crying as these words rushed from Rick's mouth. "I've been dreading this talk; I've been so torn. I've been afraid of losing you, yet I've been afraid of losing my dream of earning my degree. I've worried about not being ready for marriage. I've worried about you not being ready for marriage. I've wondered what that means for the two of us, and if that is what I really want."

Rose took Rick's hands into hers. "But now I feel the greatest peace as the subject is finally between us. I'm not torn; I know what I want. Mr. Rick Early, will you marry me?"

Rick smiled as the air rushing from his lungs was shaped into carrying the sound of Yes. He leaped across the table into Rose's arms. They hugged and exchanged a passionate kiss.

Travis had watched the man perform the simplest tricks with great fascination. Until he had begun laughing with the group over the tricks that anybody knew how to do, he had not realized how tense he had been.

The man had pulled a fake rabbit from a top hat, did card tricks, changed the color of scarves, turned wands into flowers, and many other stunts. At last he arrived at his grand finale: "Ladies and gentlemen, I will demonstrate for you the most amazing, the most awesome, inspiring, tremendous feat of power and skill that the world has ever known. Nothing you have ever experienced in your life will prepare you for this feat. You have never seen anything top it, and you never will. For the rest of your life, nothing that you experience will ever be greater than what I am about to reveal."

The man unfolded a small table and set it down. "What you are about to see will cause you to forget my name. I am a nobody. You will remember the name you are about to hear because it is unforgettable."

Travis got up on his knees to see better. He was being pulled in by the man's build-up.

The man pulled out a stone the size of a bowling ball. It had a hole in one side. "What you see is a stone—a very hard stone." He set it on the table. The man now removed a small doll from his pocket: "Here is a dead man. I will seal him inside the stone."

The man placed the doll into the stone. He brought out a much smaller stone that sealed the hole completely—a perfect fit with the opening. He took a bottle of glue, and glued the piece to the stone.

"A tomb!" he cried with a strange, excited look in his eyes. "A tomb forever sealed that cannot be broken into. You! (He pointed to Travis) With the muscles—come here."

Travis got up. All eyes were upon the two.

"Open this stone," commanded the man.

Travis took the stone and tried to pull the piece away. He could not. He tried to find a crack so he could pry it out. Nothing doing. Travis shook the stone so the piece would fall out. The piece remained where it was. Travis looked at the man.

"Perhaps you could smash it," suggested the excited showman. He handed Travis a fifty-pound sledgehammer. Travis put the stone on the floor. He hefted the hammer to his shoulder. With a loud yell, Travis conducted a complete circle of a swing with his arms and the hammer handle fully extended. The hammer's head hit the stone and bounced off.

"You lost your doll, mister."

"Do you think so?" cried the man. "Let's see. Three days should do it—ONE, TWO, THREE!" As the man shouted three, there was a blinding flash of light in the room. The glued piece fell off the stone.

As he looked into the opening, Travis thought: *this is some trick—not the greatest I've ever seen, but certainly dramatic and without an obvious explanation*. "It's empty. Your doll's gone. The stone is empty."

Travis waited, expecting the man to produce the doll from a pocket or his hat. The man did neither. He looked directly into Travis' eyes. "Why do you seek the living among the dead. He is not here; he has risen as he said."

The man took off his coat and handed it to Travis. "Search for yourself; he isn't there." Travis pulled out scarves, jacks, balls, cards, silver rings, feathers, bands and sundry other objects for magical illusions.

He felt every pocket, then the lining of the coat. Travis did not find a doll.

The man let Travis examine his hat—no doll. He pulled his pants pockets inside out—no doll. He removed his shoes. He dumped out his bag of tricks. He emptied his prop boxes. Travis went through everything carefully—no doll. Travis searched everywhere and everything in the room he thought might contain the doll. He found nothing. He spent several minutes groping inside the stone hoping to find a trap door—nothing.

"What's this about?" asked a confused Travis.

"He has risen as he said," the man explained cryptically. "He has gone ahead of you, but now he waits for you. The tomb is empty, believe it, son, the tomb—is—empty."

"Yeah, I can see that. Great trick. So what?"

"What did you come here to see? Whom are you seeking?"

"I am not seeking anyone, sir. I wandered up from the game room."

"What did you come here to see?"

Travis began to feel uneasy. All the tension returned to his muscles and flesh. He felt the corner of his left eye twitch. "I heard the laughter, and thought I'd check it out. I came to see why everyone was laughing."

"And why are they laughing?"

"You put on a good show."

"A show? A show? Did you find the body?"

Travis suddenly thought the man was unbalanced. The rest of the room was quiet; absorbed in the drama between him and the showman.

"Sir, it was a doll—only a doll. Amazing trick; I doubt anyone can explain how you pulled it off. The best part is that you did something with the doll that—where did you put it?"

"Do you seek the doll?" the man asked softly.

"Sir, per your instructions I spent several minutes looking for it."

"Yes, yes, son, you looked for it. But do you seek him?" the man asked with an intensity that spoke of a high fever or insanity.

"I don't know him. How can I seek someone whom I do not know?"

The man laughed a high-pitched cackle as triumph gleamed in his eyes. "But you shall, Travis Lewis, you shall."

Travis started at the sound of his name. He scanned the room. *Perfect strangers, all: no one knows me, and I know none of them. There's no chance that this strange, manic man could have known my name. I came to the room on a whim, so no one could have tipped the man off in advance.*

"The wind blows where it wishes and you hear the sound of it, but do not know where it comes from and where it is going; so, too, the Spirit of the Living God. He speaks what he wishes to whom he wishes, and he told me to be on the lookout tonight for a boy named Travis Lewis who is seeking meaning in life—who is desperate for a deep relationship with someone who cares about the great issues and the little things in life. Most of all, he said that Mr. Travis Lewis is seeking One who would love him deeply and completely—One who would be his forever." The man was speaking hoarsely in a whisper.

"That, Travis Lewis, is the One you seek. But you cannot find him in a tomb; he is not among the dead. He has risen as he said he would. So naturally, he took his body with him." The man suddenly had changed to his natural speaking voice. His strange demeanor faded away.

Then Travis got it. He understood. "You're talking about Jesus."

In a small upstairs room of the Sigma Omicron Beta house, Cody Spung had buttonholed Wilson Dole and was giving him the third-degree. "Why won't he come?"

Wilson mumbled, "Because he's busy with the assignments."

"That's no excuse. For a simple meeting?" Cody looked ominous.

"He refused to come. He won't listen; he won't help."

"You-are-a-brother. You-are-supervising-him. He-is-a-pledge. You-are-the-president. You-summon-him-to-the-house."

"He won't come. He's very stubborn. He said that he wouldn't come before he was ready. I couldn't convince him." Wilson looked apologetic. "Honestly, Cody, if you had seen him: fire in his eyes, fury in his voice; he's a power to reckon with."

"Him?" Cody laughed in astonishment and cursed, "He's a stupid pledge. We know he has a brass set; he proved that last fall. But where he gets the arrogance to dictate to the chapter the terms and conditions of his pledge period—"

"Hang the pledge period," Wilson cursed. Now Cody stared in astonishment at the man he had driven to a nervous breakdown. "He has something—I don't know what—that puts him in a superior position. Be careful or he'll string you out to dry. You know what he said I should do? Tell you to leave the house or call the cops."

"You idiot," Cody cursed. "What did I tell you? Don't let on that I want him over here. Why did you tell him?"

"He figured it out. He's a smart kid."

"Put me out or call the cops. His old man's nosing around in my background, asking questions, and has a private detective looking into the frat, and he says to put me out or call the cops. Our pledge needs to be put in his place, Wilson."

"I don't want to know anything. Leave me out of it. He said if you want to speak to him, you need to call him yourself."

Cody thought for a moment. *Normally, I have subordinates summon others to meetings—that puts me in the superior position. If I had simply called him, we'd be in equal positions. But to call him now—he's in the superior position; I, Cody, have capitulated to his demand.*

Cody put on a calm exterior. "Thanks, Wilson, you did the best you could do. That's one tough kid. Forget about it. Maybe I will call him."

Without saying another word, Wilson went back to his room, locked the door, and sobbed into his pillow. *I'm trapped with no way out; I can't last much longer as president.*

Cody reflected upon his difficulty. *I have to find out what Harrison Lee is doing. How can I approach the man's son to get him to reveal why his father's investigating and how much he knows?*

"They needed to talk," Montgomery was explaining to Elizabeth. "They kept avoiding the subject and it was driving them both crazy. All I did was give a little spark to start the conversation."

"But it's their business, not yours. Who are you to decide when they should discuss certain subjects in their relationship? What if one of them didn't want to talk? Did you think how harmful that could be?"

"They are at the point of no return. They must go forward or fall apart. Rick has wanted to talk to her about marriage for months. She gives all the signals that she's ready to discuss the subject."

"What signals are those? I'd like to know so I don't accidentally send you those signals."

"It's the combination of hundreds of things. It's hard to put into words."

"Men are so intuitive," Elizabeth remarked acidly. "They know, but they can't explain how. You should mind your own beeswax."

"Yes dear."

"Don't patronize me." She pulled away from Montgomery.

"They're calling us back. Are you coming?"

"Only to keep an eye on you."

The happy faces of Rose and Rick told the other couple that the issue had been resolved into an engagement. Montgomery congratulated them enthusiastically. Elizabeth mustered some wishes for happiness and fumbled with her jacket.

"We had a quarrel," Montgomery said quietly.

"Let's go back to campus," said Elizabeth.

The ride back was strained. Montgomery observed Elizabeth was sulking, and her foul mood increased in intensity because things had worked out between Rick and Rose, and they were grateful that Montgomery had steered the conversation for them. That made him right.

Rick and Rose decided to stroll around campus. Elizabeth left Montgomery at the door. She flounced up the stairs to her room. Montgomery watched her go with a sick feeling in the pit of his stomach. *How did this crisis in our relationship erupt?*

He decided to go back to his room. As he came in the door, he ran into Cat and Red who were coming back from a party. At their urging, he went out for pizza. When they returned, it was close to midnight.

Montgomery decided to make an early night of this Friday. In their room, Travis was sitting on his bed absorbed in reading a book. Montgomery was so distracted by his quarrel with Elizabeth that he failed to notice how odd that was.

"Hey, roomie," Travis said.

"Hey, Trav." Montgomery went into his closet and stripped off his clothes. He pulled on the oversized shorts that he slept in.

"You're back a little early."

"Rick and Rose are engaged and Elizabeth and I had a fight about it. In fact, I would have been back earlier but Cat and Red dragged me off for pizza."

"Oh." Travis went back to his reading.

Montgomery went to his bed and pulled back the cover. "What are you doing? Did you find anything interesting tonight?"

Travis smiled a dazzling, bright grin. "I believe I did."

Montgomery was tired. He lay down and closed his eyes. "What was it?"

"I was bored and lonely but had nothing I wanted to do. I went out and wound up in the Student Center. There, this guy was doing magic tricks so I joined the group that was watching. They were all having a good time. Most of his tricks were lame; a kid could explain it. Then he pulled this amazing stunt."

Montgomery mumbled something to show that he was still listening.

"He glued this doll inside a stone. Then he built up the suspense with some mumbo-jumbo. After he counted down three—two—one, he set off a flash and the stone cracked open. The doll was gone." Travis' eyes had grown shiny from recalling the deed.

"He palmed it, or had a secret compartment or some other trick for concealment after he distracted your eyes."

"But I searched everything: the props, the room, his clothes—no doll. Then he explained his purpose of doing the trick. 'The tomb is empty,' he said."

"Weird," the almost sleeping Montgomery replied.

"Truth," Travis countered. "He was telling the truth. I never knew before."

"Never knew what?" asked Montgomery who was fading out.

"That Jesus Christ rose from the dead."

It took a few moments for the boy's words to register in Montgomery's mind.

"What?" he burst out, sitting up straight. "Did you just say that Jesus Christ rose from the dead?"

"Yes. Is that news to you?"

"No. But I thought you didn't care."

"I never knew. There's lots of things I never knew. I didn't know he was God's Son. I didn't know God cared so much about me. I didn't know his Son became a man and lived a human life. I didn't know he died, not for his faults or crimes, but because of mine. I didn't know he did this from love. I never knew he loved me enough to die for me. I've never known such love before. I've always been the party man—looking for good times through pleasing my flesh. I never realized how much he wanted me to stay sober and keep my pants zipped so he could talk to me."

"Wow. You've had quite a night."

"I was jealous of you and Elizabeth. I wanted to be loved like she loved you. Park was shallow—as shallow as me. I felt alone tonight; alone and lost and desperate for love—I wanted someone to know who I am, where I am, and to care. Now I'm no longer alone; I'll never be alone again. He cares for me, and about me. It's the greatest feeling in the world. I've been saved."

"Did you pray the sinner's prayer?"

"I don't know what that is. I told him I was sorry for the lousy way I was living my life, and asked him to forgive me for not knowing who he was. I told him how much I appreciated that he cared for me, and asked him to share my life. I told him I was sorry for all the wrong things I'd done, and that I'd let him show me how to act in the future. He told me that he knew I was sorry, and that he had removed my sin by dying on the cross. He told me that he would always be with me, and I'd never be lonely again or feel unloved. He told me he loved me, and I felt all the empty places in my life fill up. It's the greatest feeling in the world, Montgomery. This is what I've been looking forever since we came to college. My studies showed me I was missing something; He showed me that I was missing him. It's like a dream, but it's real: Jesus, the real Lord, Jesus Christ. He's better than sex—no more flings for me. The feeling of belonging to Christ is much better than sex."

"When's your baptism?" said Montgomery jokingly.

"Sunday. Will you come?" Travis asked earnestly.

"Check," said Montgomery who again was feeling great awe over hearing Travis speak about the Lord.

"Do you mind if I stay up and keep the light on? I'm reading about His life. I want to learn everything."

"Check; stay up as late as you like," said Montgomery, who fell back and was asleep before his head hit the pillow.

Montgomery looked at his clock when he opened his eyes. It read 10:30 a.m. He rolled over. He did not feel refreshed from his belabored night's sleep. Travis was in the clothes he had been wearing the night before. The desk lamp was on. *He's been reading all night.* Montgomery remembered their previous conversation. *No one's going to believe it in Sparksburg. Travis being saved, yes; Travis reading all night, no.*

Montgomery slumped as he recalled the argument with Elizabeth. *Maybe she's in a better mood.* He went out to the telephone to call her.

Elizabeth was still angry with Montgomery, angrier than she had ever been. What had steamed her was the fact that Montgomery did not obey her signals to be quiet. She did not care about what he had done; she was mad because he did it after she told him not to.

"What do you want," she snapped at him.

"I was hoping we could patch up our argument."

"What's done is done."

"Check."

"Why do you always say that stupid word?"

Montgomery felt like a mule had kicked him in the stomach. He was overwhelmed with sadness; then anger struck him with lightning-like quickness. "Does that bother you? What other little customs of mine do you find offensive?"

Elizabeth felt icy fear slice through her. She did not want to lose this man. She could not stop, though. "It will take me the day to catalog the list," she shot back.

Montgomery seethed. "I'll leave you to it," he said, and hung up the phone. He kicked the wall.

Elizabeth replaced the handset in the cradle. She burst into tears.

"Why, what's wrong?" said Park who had come in the door from her date with Dunbar.

"I love that man," cried Elizabeth. "Why do I want to control him?"

"Because you love him," replied Park. "It's the feminine instinct to try to improve our men. Wherever he doesn't measure up to Daddy, that's where you work on him. The better ones resist, of course."

"Poppycock. Women do not try to turn their men into their fathers. That attitude went out with the notion that women must stay at home, raise the kids, have dinner on the table at six, and be ready by ten for sex."

"You have deep feelings for him," broke in Rose. "You're afraid he doesn't reciprocate. You turn a minor dispute into a major argument. To love you he must do as you say. But that would make him a robot. For you to love him he mustn't do as you say. Welcome to my world. I only escaped last night."

"How did you escape?" asked Elizabeth.

"When I was forced to confront the feelings I had for Rick in the face of the feelings that he had for me, all the confusion and conflict went away. I knew; somehow I knew that he was the one for me. That everything else would work out. That he loved me so much he would let me achieve my goals and would cheer me on. I had peace."

"We're not ready for that peace."

"The perfect couple has a few flaws," observed Park.

"What's that supposed to mean?" snapped Elizabeth.

"You had your relationship perfect—everything worked to a mutual understanding," replied Park. "All love, perfect unity and harmony. He's a hero; you a goddess. Now y'all are only human. Misunderstandings arise. Tempers flare. Y'all aren't perfect after all."

Elizabeth was about to unload on Park. But she calmed herself and said, "You're right. We aren't perfect, and we don't have a mutual understanding about everything."

"Let it go," said Rose. "What's more important: being right or being with him?"

Elizabeth smiled bitterly. "At the moment I have neither."

Montgomery rousted his roommate from his reading. "Let's go."

"Where to?"

"I don't care—anywhere,"

Travis looked at him carefully. "I'm sorry."

"About what?"

"Your fight with Elizabeth. Sweat it out, Montgomery. Let her calm down; then you can talk with her. As long as they're angry, you're still in the game. It's when they're matter-of-fact that you know the relationship is over."

"Let's blow this town."

"Let's go to the beach. I'll teach you to surf on baby waves. That'll take your mind off girlfriend troubles."

The two boys departed for a welcome respite from the campus and their studies.

Across campus in the Sigma Omicron Beta house, Cody Spung began to lay careful plans to take down Montgomery Lee. There were a number of steps: disallow his completed assignments as inadequate requiring more work, attack his self-image as upright and idealistic, force him to betray his morals, disrupt his friendships to isolate him, put him in the frat house to disrupt his senses, sleep and habits, falsify communications to strain his relationship with his father, and hurt him. This last step particularly satisfied Rip.

"You're foolish," said Jack. "We should lay off the kid. He's forgotten about us; we should forget about him. He won't come back. We're rid of him. Wasn't that the plan?"

"It was before his old man started nosing around," countered Cody. "Now we've got to get a hold over him so he can derail the attorney before we land in jail."

"His Daddy, his morals and his friendships: those are his strengths," observed Pete. "What possible purpose would it serve to hit him there?"

"Always attack the strengths," responded Cody. "It throws the victim into self-doubt. Then it's 'Katy bar the door.' When he doubts himself, he's through. We'll mold him into our image, corrupt the little dipstick, and sabotage Daddy's inquiry. Only the stupid and inexperienced attack the weaknesses, Pete. That's where his guard will be the strongest."

Unaware of his own weakness within, Cody did not realize that a different SigBee had overheard this conversation, and was now sending an untraceable e-mail to Montgomery Lee: *Attack of the SigBees: Be on guard for direct attack on friendships, morals and your father. The soldiers are sharpening their stingers. Above all else, never doubt yourself.*

Later that afternoon, Mick Raike visited his former quadmates and apologized for his mean behavior when the semester first began. He apologized to the Ghost for not allowing him to live in the room. He apologized for how bad he had been during the fall term.

"How did you pull through?" asked a curious Red.

"Probation. I have to pull a two point oh this term or I flunk out. But the frat will help me there."

"You joined a fraternity?"

"I'm pledging—Sigma Omicron Beta."

"Really," said a suspicious Cat. "Why them?"

"They recruited me. They told me I had much potential to be a leader in the house. The leadership is graduating this year; they lack the members who are capable of continuing their winning ways. Besides me, they recruited five other boys to train and take over."

"You dried out then," suggested Shorts.

"They've taught me how to have my fun without destroying my life. I get more out of less without compromising the rest."

"Sounds like a commercial for light beer," said the Ghost.

Cat looked dubious. "So Mick, what brought this on? Why show up with the apologies? Since you are getting more fun out of less drugging, you can't be in a twelve-step program. Why us? Why now?"

Mick felt sweat on the palms of his hands. "Since I put my act together, it's been on my mind that I treated y'all less than fairly. Today I had the time and inclination to remedy that. I brought a peace offering: look." Mick opened a paper sack he had carried with him. "Cookies—from our kitchen. The brothers have an excellent secret recipe. Try some."

Cat intercepted the offering. "Thanks, Mick. Anything else?"

Mick felt cold sweat dripping from his armpits onto his sides. "Uh, yeah. Our special mix of spiced tea. The brothers said it was a special favorite of Montgomery when he was living there. Maybe you'll want to save it for him."

Shorts took the tea mix, thinking: *maybe you're being too obvious.*

Mick then revealed his piece de resistance: sugar cubes. "It seems dumb, but I was putting the other items in the bag when I saw the box and put it in. Y'all drink coffee, thus I figured y'all could use it."

"Why wait for coffee?" spoke Caveman. "Let's pop a sugar cube now." He grabbed the box, opened the lid, held it out to Mick, and growled, "You first."

"Um, (beads of sweat appeared on Mick's forehead), I don't care for any."

Caveman walked to the bathroom and flushed the contents of the box down the toilet. He returned to the common room, grabbed Mick by the front of the shirt, and hoisted him into the air. "Too obvious. Don't come back—ever." He dropped Mick onto the floor.

Mick jumped up. A furious tirade of obscenities did not mask the fear he was feeling. He went out the door, slamming it in his haste.

Cat spoke first. "Caveman, we haven't seen that much emotion out of you since the day we moved in."

"He was after Monkey. We were unimportant casualties. I may not say much, but I'm not stupid. It was amateurish, clumsy and transparent. These peace offerings are drugged. I figure pot in the cookies, acid on the sugar, and something that the taste of spices covers in the tea."

"I'll send the tea mix after the sugar," said Shorts.

"What about the cookies?" asked Cat. "We can't flush them down the toilet."

"Yes, we can" said Caveman. "A few at a time."

"Do we have to?" said Red. "After all, it's not hard stuff; some of us like a toot now and then."

"The cookies came from the S.O.B.'s," growled Caveman. "You don't know what's in them. My guess was that—a guess. You want to get high, buy your own weed. Then you'll know exactly what you're getting."

"I reckon you're right," said a sad Red. "Do it so the temptation is gone."

"You've been on campus since mid-August and you've never smoked weed," said a surprised Caveman. "I thought you were clean."

"I am," replied Red. "Well, most of the time. I haven't smoked any pot because y'all haven't—we get drunk instead. But I would from time to time if anyone else did. I like the feeling—not everyday, not every weekend. But every so often, I do."

The boys were letting this revelation sink in as the sound of flushing continued from the bathroom. Cat took the cookies to Shorts, who dispatched them as Caveman had prescribed. Then a frenzied conversation broke out centering on the visit, its intended target, and whether they should tell him.

"He's got to know," averred Caveman, Red and Shorts.

"It will make no difference—what's the point?" countered Cat and the Ghost.

In the end, they decided they would wait and see when their quadmates returned from the beach.

Sunday morning, the quad hummed with activity as the boys rummaged through their closets looking for their best garments. They had decided to attend Travis' baptism in support of this meaningful event in his life.

"You've changed," said Shorts as he and Travis waited for the others in the common room. "Of all the guys in the quad, you had to be the least likely to get religious and be dunked in a pool."

Travis laughed. "I only regret it took me to age nineteen to find Jesus and realize what it means to live daily in his love. Any chance I can persuade you to join me?"

Shorts smiled. "I'm not religious."

"Neither was I."

"It's not my time."

"Don't wait till it is, Joseph. Don't wait till it's too late. You're missing out on the greatest thing in the world—the love of God from daily fellowship. Jesus is better than sex."

Shorts grinned, "That's saying something because I've heard your girlfriend moan in your room."

Travis flushed red with embarrassment. "Two days ago I would have been flattered beyond belief to hear you say that. Now it's painful to me to think how I have lived."

"Sincerity is the mark of authenticity. You mean what you say. Someday a lucky woman will snag you and find pleasures unknown to most of womankind."

"The love, Joseph, that's the key. Because God loves me, I can love too: Jesus, my friends, and one day, a wife. Love will be the greatest prize I can offer, not skill in bringing orgasm."

Red and Caveman emerged from their room. Caveman was dressed in khakis and a sport shirt, but Red's best clothing was blue jeans and a pullover jersey.

"Maybe I shouldn't go," said Red.

"Nonsense," said Travis. "They won't care how you look."

The others soon finished their preparations, and the group sallied forth. They walked into town, and found the church where Travis had arranged for a baptism. The church was packed, but seats had been saved for the seven boys.

Travis was surprised to find his grandfather, parents and other family members at the church. Of greater surprise was the presence of Montgomery's parents and two sisters. His grandfather drew him aside.

"I was against you coming to the university. I thought you'd waste your time and your Daddy's money. You surprised me, boy. I'm so doggone proud of you—" He broke off as tears filled his eyes. He gave Travis a strong bear hug.

"Montgomery always said there was more to you than meets the eye," Harrison Lee told Travis. "He said you were solid down deep; we had to wait until you plumbed your depths. He was right. You are one fine young man and I am proud to know you. May I shake your hand."

Travis flushed red with embarrassment and pride. He had always regarded Montgomery's Daddy as a prince among men; too lofty for an ordinary boy like him. The words of Harrison Lee gave Travis recognition as a young man worth reckoning. He felt that he had been awarded a medal. The thane of the Florida Lees had pronounced him a peer, and a fit companion for the thane's son.

The boys settled into their seats for the service. Upon its conclusion, the company and congregation departed for a nearby river. The minister waded into the water about waist high. Travis followed him in foot thongs and a white robe.

"Travis Lewis, in the name of Jesus Christ, I ask you to affirm your decision that you have made to be a disciple of Jesus. Do you repent of your sins, and renounce the forces of evil that have guided your steps before this day?"

Travis answered in a firm voice, "I do."

"Travis, do you in the presence of these people and the angels of God, confess your belief in Jesus Christ as the Son of God, that he was crucified, and laid into a tomb a dead man, but on the third day of his entombment, his life re-entered his body, and he rose up, alive forevermore?"

Travis answered firmly, "I do."

"Travis, do you intend this day to live a new life in Christ, free from sin and doubts, to be obedient to his commands, and to acknowledge him as Lord?"

Travis answered more firmly, "I do."

"Travis, do you receive this day the gift of the Holy Spirit that the Lord Jesus Christ promised to his followers when he ascended into heaven?"

Travis' voice caught. He whispered, "Yes, please."

The minister laughed. To the assembly he said, "That was affirmative if you did not hear his response."

"Travis Lewis, in the name of Jesus Christ, will you be baptized this day into the fellowship of saints?"

"Do it now—I can't wait any longer."

The minister laughed again. He turned Travis to the side so that his left arm was across Travis' upper back. He pulled a white handkerchief from his pocket, and placed it over Travis' nose and mouth with his hand resting on top.

In a loud voice, the minister proclaimed, "Travis Dalton Lewis, I baptize you in the name of the Father, the Son and the Holy Ghost."

He whispered to Travis, "Hold your breath—now."

With his right hand the minister bent Travis backward as he lowered his left arm toward the water. Kerplosh! The bent-back form of Travis disappeared beneath the surface. In an instant, the minister was using his left arm to reverse the motion using the buoyancy of the water to provide lift to Travis' upper body to raise him erect.

"Amen." The minister then asked Travis to kneel in the waters. He placed his hands on Travis' head. He cued the crowd, and two elders of the church as well as Travis' grandfather and Harrison Lee entered the water and placed their hands on Travis' head.

"Receive the Holy Spirit through the laying-on of hands," the minister proclaimed.

Travis would always swear afterward this moment brought a large gust of wind across the river. The others said it had started blowing before then. To Travis, however, the gust was the Holy Spirit coming across the waters to light upon him and change him from a goofball boy into a solid man of God. He was overwhelmed with emotion.

The minister leaned over and spoke in his ear. "The Lord keep you and bless you, The Lord make his face to shine upon you, and give you peace. Let's go to the shore."

The group waded ashore. The assembly was clapping and cheering. It surged forward in a line to congratulate Travis and welcome him to the community of believers. Travis was overwhelmed. Men shook his hand, women hugged him, girls kissed his cheek, and his quadmates pounded his arm. Montgomery hugged him with tears in his eyes, but — that was Montgomery. He was an emotional boy.

The two families went to dinner together. They had a great feast in Bacon's best restaurant. Travis' grandfather and Harrison Lee became involved in a deep discussion about Travis' prospects. Travis' grandfather mentioned sadly that he was afraid Travis would not be taking over the farm as he had hoped. Harrison said the world lay at Travis' feet, but that did not mean he would be walking around it. Travis and Montgomery seemed to be seven again at a birthday party for Travis. The joy was contagious. Not until the end did Montgomery realize someone was missing: Elizabeth.

That night, Travis and Montgomery began the first of their nightly devotions together before turning out the lights for sleep. Montgomery's spirit was bolstered as he realized that he had been slack in keeping his quiet time a daily habit. He was emboldened to dream great dreams for following the footsteps of other great apostles. He thanked God for providing him with a roommate with whom he could keep accountability.

Monday Montgomery headed to his American Literature class with Shorts. They were heading into their last week of class before Spring Break. Montgomery noted the assignment of reading Huckleberry Finn over Spring Break, and preparing ten pages double-spaced detailing the commentary Mark Twain had incorporated into his novel about race relations in mid-nineteenth century America. Following Spring Break, the class would begin its work on the short story in American letters by taking up the body of work by Edgar Allen Poe.

Coming out of class, Montgomery separated from Shorts. He went out the door into the center of The Ring. Looming ahead were three young men: Pete Spivey, Brendon Garrett, and Jack Canter. They surrounded Montgomery quickly.

"What do you want?" Montgomery asked stiffly.

"To talk to you," Jack answered.

"What about?"

"Stuff."

"Make it quick. You have five minutes."

"Let's go to the house," suggested Brendon.

"Nothing doing," said Montgomery. "Do it here."

"You little punk," cursed Pete. "As long as you remain our pledge, you will do as we say, or else—"

"Else what?" said Montgomery quietly. "I'm not playing your games. Lay a hand on me, and I'll file charges of battery. Detain me, and the charges will be kidnapping. As Scarface says, 'That's a Federal rap.' I won't ask you again why you seek to talk to me."

"Listen, smart mouth lawyer's kid," Pete sneered, "you don't frighten us. You think your old man's going to scare us, investigating our backgrounds, talking to district and national headquarters—"

"Pete!" cried Jack sharply. "Shut up!"

Montgomery's eyes flashed like lightning through the night sky. "So that's what this is about. I had no idea. Thanks for the tip. Here's one for you: Tell Cody I don't talk to flunkies." Montgomery began to part the shoulders of Jack and Brendon to leave when Pete smacked the back of his head. Montgomery whirled around and hit Pete with a roundhouse on his left cheek. Pete staggered to the side and fell over. The second member of the committee had found out that Montgomery could give at least as good as he got.

"Next time, I won't avoid your jaw."

Pete unleashed a vicious stream of profanity.

Montgomery retorted, "Why do y'all travel in groups? Can't take anyone one-on-one?"

The eyes of all three men turned dark with hatred as Montgomery walked away.

"I'll take care of the punk," said Pete.

"Yeah, I noticed," said Brendon. "Be sure to tell Cody you were the one who messed it up—blurting out the fact we know his old man's poking around. We were supposed to find out what he knows and what he has told; not tell him what we know."

"Do you want a piece of me?" demanded Pete.

"No, I refuse the sloppy seconds," snarled Brendon.

"Cut it out, you two," ordered Jack. "This plays right into the punk's hands. We must stay together." It was a surly threesome that ascended the front porch of the Sigma Omicron Beta house in silence.

The next day, Montgomery turned in his moral philosophy class to see a student who was asking a question, and he spotted Cody Spung sitting in the rear. As the period ended, Montgomery went forward to ask the professor a question. He engaged the professor in five minutes of conversation as the Symposium room emptied. He bade the professor goodbye, then turned and acted surprised. "Cody? What are you doing here?"

"You and I need to talk."

"I'm hungry. You buying lunch?"

Cody admired Montgomery's hubris, especially in maneuvering him toward buying lunch. *If I refuse, I look cheap; if I accept, he's one-up.* "I'm short of cash. Let's split the check."

They walked from The Ring through the swamp to the Jeff Davis dining hall. Cody again admired Montgomery's hubris in forcing the interview on Montgomery's turf with his friends and classmates around them as well as conducting it in a public place. *Dr. Frankenstein,* Cody asked himself, *did you create this monster? This is not the same boy who came to the university planning to pledge a frat. Wilson's right, he's developed some internal steel. I can almost feel power radiating from him.* Cody shuddered. *Get a grip, this is only a freshman—a boy. Take him down, and do it slowly: enjoy the pain.*

Each took a tray, and filled it with lunch items. Montgomery selected beef stew and a generous selection of french bread with butter. He supplemented his entree with a fresh salad and ended with carrot cake. Cody went for the grill and ordered a cheeseburger and fries. Both took Cokes.

Cody found a table for the two of them where no one could distract them. Montgomery sat, bowed his head and verbally gave thanks for his meal. Again Cody was forced to admire the hubris: *no request for permission, he goes ahead forcing me to wait for him to finish. He's maintaining the upper hand.*

Montgomery glanced at Cody's face as he picked up his spoon and began to eat.

Cody stewed over beginning conversation. *Should I accept the challenge to see who has to break the silence? I don't want to refuse the challenge, but he has the advantage. He can be silent the whole time, and I lose because this is my meeting. If nothing's said, the kid has outmaneuvered the master.*

"We are puzzled by your absence. Is something wrong? Maybe I can help you through some problem at the house," Cody opened.

Montgomery snorted in his stew. He noted with pleasure that Cody was being very nice; instantly his guard went up. "Nothing's wrong; I'm busy. You gave me a heavy workload on top of my classes. No time for fraternity pastimes."

"We got off to a bad start in the Fall. I was overly influenced by that wretched Rip into seeing you in a bad light. He's a bad one, that Rip. You have excellent prospects. Let's work together, and I can assure you a smooth path into membership during our Spring initiations."

"I've done so much work already. What do you have in mind?"

"Cooperation," said Cody briskly thinking that Montgomery had taken the bait. "Exchange of information. I tell you how to circumvent the pledge process; you tell me what interested parties know about our activities. You've noticed that we carry on a lucrative sideline that enables us to live like kings."

"I've noticed. Perhaps you should say, 'We live like kingpins.'"

"That's exactly what I'm talking about." Cody slapped the table with the palm of his hand. "You're way above the average freshman.

You surpass most sophomores and stack up well against any junior on campus. You know what we do."

"No, I don't. I suspect y'all are trafficking in narcotics, and using the pledges as runners. But I don't know a thing."

He's good. "Once you're in the frat, we can be more open with you. You have great potential. This is my last year. Come June, I'm out. I need a far-sighted, intelligent man like myself to take over. Jack will provide interim leadership, but none of the boys have the qualities I do. You may be the one."

Montgomery gagged on a piece of lettuce, and spent many seconds coughing it out of his throat and appeasing the insulted membranes. "Sorry. Your vision took my breath away."

"Of course," Cody said casually, "certain inquiries could shut the whole thing down. The network would be maintained, but fronting through the chapter would have to stop. That would cause your opportunity to disappear."

Montgomery grinned. "I had no idea Daddy was researching your background until Pete spilled the beans yesterday. I'll have to ask him what he found. Not that he tells me; I'm an astronomer. Matters of law are his bailiwick."

Cody regarded the grinning face opposite him with distaste. "Use your influence to get him to stop. Then your potential has no limit."

"Whatever do you have to be worried about?"

"Exactly!" cried Cody, slapping the table with his palm. "Nothing at all. So there's no need to waste everyone's time."

Montgomery set his fork on his tray. He engaged Cody's eyes, and bore in with his own. "Daddy doesn't discuss his business with me. If you have a concern, take it up with him."

"What has he told you?"

"Nothing."

"Play ball with us."

"Strike three."

"I don't get strikes; I'm the umpire."

"The umpire? He's the first one fired when the league does poorly. I'll join my quadmates to eat my cake." He picked up his tray; then he set it down again.

"Did I tell you about Travis? (Cody winced) He was saved Friday night and was baptized Sunday." Montgomery walked off laughing with his pie and fork.

Cody cursed loudly. *He's very good. He ends with a bombshell simultaneously reminding me of a failure—a contest even that he won—and he leaves me with his dishes to return like I'm his servant. He has one-upped me through this whole encounter. It's time to take him down.*

Chapter Eighteen

Trial by Fire

WEDNESDAY MONTGOMERY BREEZED into the kitchen of Sigma Omicron Beta, picked up an apron and potato peeler, and set to the mountain of potatoes heaped on the kitchen counter next to the sink. He greeted the brother who supervised the kitchen crew and whistled happily.

"What brought you back?" asked Gravy.

"I finished my hospital work. Some brothers think I was shirking my duties. With the coming of Spring Break, I had some free time today so I came over to help. You do need help, don't you?"

"Do we ever! This new recruiting approach has brought me nothing but prima donnas whom the pledge committee is enabling in their stuck-up attitude. I can hardly get them to do anything. Then when they do want to work, they're high or tripping. No good at all—the kitchen is a dangerous place for people under the influence: too many sharp instruments, hot surfaces, and mechanical blades. I've had to make do with the two boys that were deferred with you: Howard Libbell and Mark Matthews."

"They stuck it out?"

"Yes, they want to get in. Unfortunately there's no depth to them. Cody considers the concept of deferral a brilliant stroke of his mad genius. He has no intention of admitting them; he has every intention of working them until they catch on and quit."

"I have returned to the fray. I'm determined to overcome their opposition so we can clean house. So far, I've produced good reports from the saboteurs: the shrew and dotty Dotty. I'm working hard in moral philosophy and it's not changing my values. They'll be disappointed that I've done so well."

"I'm glad you're hanging tough. Many brothers don't like the atmosphere and changes in the house that Cody engineered. But they're scared. They need a leader to rally them. I believe you're that man."

Montgomery blushed. "Travis was saved last week. He was baptized Sunday."

"Wow! What brought that on?"

"He broke up with Park. It was a rotten break-up, too. A classmate from his study group asked his permission to ask her out. What could he do but say yes and hope she would turn the dude down. But she went out with him. Rick and I went out with the other girls, which left Travis alone Friday night. He wandered into a campus meeting of Jesus Jesus, and gave his heart and soul to the Lord."

"I never would have thought it."

"No one gives Travis much credit, but he's deep—very deep. The university and especially that experimental program was the best thing that has happened for him. He was put into a different type of learning program perfectly suited to his personality. He began learning things and started thinking about more important things than the next wave or girl. More and more of the real Travis began to emerge. With that, he realized he was searching for something meaningful and deep to commit his life to. Salvation was bound to happen. It was a question of when."

"Congratulate him for me, will you?" I have my hands full at the house or I would go see him personally."

"The only thing he lost was Park; she grew increasingly uncomfortable the more depth he showed. It's a shame but for the best.

"Where are the others?" Montgomery asked.

"Special pledge meeting for the new pledges only. Libbell and Matthews are making deliveries."

"Ah, yes. We mustn't interrupt the deliveries."

Gravy smiled. "You upset Cody yesterday. It's not easy to do that."

"Serves him right—fishing for information. If Daddy is looking into some things, what business is that of Cody's? It's nothing that I need to know, or Daddy would have told me. I have no idea. Cody made nice for nothing; that must have got his goat."

"The way he views the world, you one-upped him yesterday—several times. He's looking to get even."

"I received the warning. Whatever he's doing, someone's getting close enough to make him nervous. He even disavowed Rip. Cody must be ready to throw Rip to the dogs."

The two men continued the kitchen work. Montgomery chopped the potatoes into fries, and began filling the deep fryer baskets. Then he went to work steaming vegetables and preparing bread. Gravy was broiling steaks and finishing the chocolate cake for dessert.

At the designated hour, Montgomery helped Gravy serve the food to the tables. He noted that some of the other brothers also helped bring dinner from the kitchen. He noted with amusement the startled looks of Cody and company when they saw him assisting Gravy. As they began to eat, Montgomery went back into the kitchen and served himself from the leftovers.

When Montgomery finished eating, he began washing the pots and utensils used for the meal. He had most of the job done when Gravy came back into the kitchen for the cake. Montgomery winked and kept on washing. When he finished, he wiped his hands and went upstairs to the fraternity library. He did not take his customary seat, but moved a chair to the back shelf and sat behind it. He pulled a random book off the shelf and perused it.

The book explained the rituals of the frat. Montgomery skipped to the chapter on the red robe ceremony. As he began to read, he was fascinated by the original ceremony and how far the current version deviated from the standard.

Two floors down, an emergency meeting of the pledge committee got underway.

"I don't know how he did it, but he reversed the situation on you," Jack said to Cody. "He now enters the house as the conquering hero. We're losing the membership. We have to get rid of him. Let's terminate him and be done with it."

"Too late," Brendon replied. "We've already lost. We have to keep him in the game until we can turn it around and beat him."

Pete touched the sore bruise on his cheek. "I'm for that."

"Get in line," growled Rip.

"What have we found out?" asked Cody.

"Solid grades in all his classes," said Brendon. "He's tight with his quadmates, who despise Raike, by the way. That was a terrible move—they saw right through him. They flushed all the goodies down the john."

"The shrew and Dotty gave him good marks," said Jack. "No openings there. He's been cagey in moral philosophy; he does his assignments in ways that he doesn't have to reveal his rigid repressed sexuality."

"Hmm," mused Cody. "He mentioned a girlfriend last fall. What's happened with her?"

"True love," said Jack. "But they had a fight over the weekend and it's not patched up. Do you think we might try something there?"

"It's worth a shot," said Cody. "Find out what the spat was over. Then we can try to exploit it. We need to strike him hard."

"If he's back in the house, why don't we put him on the machine?" said Rip.

"The machine is gone," Cody replied. "Too risky to have it in the house. Besides, our goal is not to make him quit; our goal is to discredit him in the eyes of our fraternal brothers. Physical punishment won't accomplish that; we must force him into a mental breakdown like that nimknocker Wilson."

"If he's in love, and we can get that girl all worked up to dump him, that will cause an opening," offered Brendon.

"That's our first objective," confirmed Cody. "Find his vulnerability."

"He's a do-gooder," said Jack. "If he thinks he can rescue Mick from our clutches, and get him off drugs, he'll open himself to emotional and spiritual whiplash as the junkie works him over. We should get Raike drugged up and keep him there; then throw the two together as often as possible. We can plant suggestions with Raike to be tossed at the punk. We can exploit his impulse to rescue the lost."

"That will destroy Raike, though," objected Brendon. "He almost went last semester. You know we keep him on a strict limit. If his body holds together, his mind will give out. He'll be ruined for life."

"Who cares?" said Cody. "Every cause demands sacrifice, and every war has losses. He's nothing but a soldier anyway; he'll never make an officer—he doesn't have the talent. Jack, get started on that right away. Break out the best we have—let's go with speedballs.

"Brendon, find out about the girl. I want a full report tomorrow evening. Meanwhile, we lay low. Stay out of his way. Right after Spring Break, we launch a full assault. As for me, I need to look into some matters and will be gone until tomorrow night. Be careful."

As Cody left, Jack and Brendon headed downstairs. Pete and Rip's eyes met and agreed on the same thought: *with Cody gone, we can jump the punk and give him a pounding.* They discussed possible ambushes before exiting into the hallway to join Jack and Brendon.

It was that moment that Montgomery chose to descend the stairs to make his way back to his quad. He met Pete and Rip in the hall on the third floor landing. Rip shoved him, and Pete caught him from behind.

"Pay back time," announced Rip. He swung a left hook toward Montgomery's jaw. Montgomery ducked, but grunted "oof" as Pete connected with his kidney from the rear. Rip kicked at Montgomery's knee, but he sidestepped the blow. However, Pete took the opportunity to hit him in his laterals.

Montgomery felt another blow upon his back. Instinctively, he fell forward tying Rip up in his body. He grabbed Rip's shirt and swung him around. Pete had been aiming a blow at the back of Montgomery's head. Instead, Rip caught the blow's force. His head jerked forward, then snapped back. His eyes turned glassy and the pupils rotated upward. His eyelids closed, and he slumped. Montgomery let go and let his face crash to the floor. Rip would have to wake up before discovering that his nose was broken.

Montgomery stepped over Rip toward Pete. Taking Pete by surprise, Montgomery popped him hard in his right eye. Pete staggered back toward the stairs. Montgomery followed with a hard hit to his left eye. Pete wobbled back and forth as bright stars clouded his vision. He weakly lashed out with his knee. Montgomery caught his leg and drove him backward into the wall. Pete stood a moment longer; then he toppled down the stairs.

On the floor below, three brothers and a pledge witnessed Pete's tumbling body slide to a heap on the lower landing. They looked up and saw Montgomery watching Pete go and licking the blood off his fist where the skin had split from the force of his blows.

"Get him," cried one, and they pounded up the stairs. Montgomery sprinted down the hall for the back staircase. He did not bother to take the steps; he leaped from landing to landing until he went flying through the kitchen, into the dining room, through the front of the house, out the door, through the gate and across the street into the maze of faculty housing.

The pursuing quartet gave up the chase at the front gate. By now the whole house was in an uproar. Jack went to the kitchen for ice. Gravy was at the table pretending to be so absorbed in his reading that he did not notice the commotion. Jack prepared two compresses and went to tend to Pete. Brendon waved smelling salts under Rip's demolished nose, which made the sting many times worse. Rip woke up as Brendon hauled him to his feet to take him to the hospital.

"You stupid idiot," he cursed. "Cody said no rough stuff. Now you know why."

"I'm going to get that punk," Rip cursed. "One day, when he's not looking, —"

"His Daddy owns the legal system, imbecile," cursed Brendon. "Go ahead, one of two things will happen: he beats you even worse, or you go to prison for a long time."

"When I get him," Rip cursed a long, vile, profane obscenity, "it will be worth it."

"There won't be enough left of you to celebrate."

Jack was also giving the what-for to Pete. "One would suppose a man smart enough for college would learn from his mistake the first time. Don't try to take the boy—he's fast, wily and packs a powerful wallop—which you could see if you hadn't tried to take him, and in the house! Your eyes will be closed come morning. What a pretty picture! But this is nothing compared to when Cody gets ahold of you."

Pete cursed weakly.

"You're aptly named. Get to bed and try to fall asleep before the headaches come. Stupid!"

Montgomery slowed to a walk and caught his breath when he reached campus. He headed for the nearest bus stop, and took the bus back to the dorm. When he reached his quad, he found a party was in progress. Travis was the life of the party. He was doing imitations of well-known personalities on and off campus.

Cat blanched at the sight of Montgomery and said, "Where were you? At the gym?"

"Another fight with the SigBees."

"How many does that make?"

"Three, I think. Two of them jumped me in the house, but I had the better of them."

Red asked, "Why did you go there?"

"To let them know I'm still around. They're afraid of me; I don't know why. Cody pumped me for information yesterday. I went to rattle their cage."

Cat remarked, "I'd say you did."

Montgomery took a beer from the refrigerator, opened the bottle and took a long draught. "Whew! That tastes good."

Travis laughed. "My roommate: Montgomery Ah-Lee." He began doing another impression as the boys burst into belly laughs.

As the night drew into the early morning hours, two figures slipped across the remote parking lot where freshman were required to keep their vehicles. With a small beam from a mini-flashlight, they moved along the rows of cars and trucks surveiling the license tags for the Florida Space Shuttle tag that would betray Montgomery's ownership.

"Here it is," whispered one.

"Check the numbers and be sure," said the other.

The first figure mumbled a combination of letters and numbers.

"This is it," confirmed the second. He slipped to the chest fastened behind the cab window to the sidewalls of the bed. He lifted the cover. "The fool doesn't keep it locked." His companion looked around. Satisfied that no one was looking, he pulled a small bag out of his pocket and put it in the chest. The other one removed a glass tube from his jacket and placed it beside the bag. He dropped the lid.

"Quiet," urged his accomplice. They looked around, then knelt and made a quick pace for the street and the safety of the shadows.

Thursday was uneventful for Montgomery. He was feeling bad, though, because he and Elizabeth were still feuding. Monday she had deliberately taken a seat across the room from where they usually sat together for Western Civilization. Thursday he went to class early and waited for her to arrive. He waved to her to come over, but she went and sat apart. Montgomery put his head into a book, feeling that the class had seen his humiliation of being spurned. *I wish we could make up, but I don't know how. Maybe we've broken up and I don't know it.*

He returned to the dorm at four to finish an English essay before having dinner with his quadmates. He found Travis waiting for him.

"What's up?"

"This," Travis said grimly as he pulled a small plastic bag filled with dried green leaves and a bong from his desk drawer.

"Where did that come from?"

"It's not mine,"

"Check. You don't like it."

"Right. But why did I find it in the cargo box on your truck?"

"I didn't put it there."

"Who did?"

"Persons unknown to me who mistook my truck for someone else's. You know I don't keep the box locked."

"Right. I went to borrow some fishing line and tackle for a project. Weed is what I found. I cut out of class an hour early so I could talk to you. Why was it there?"

"It isn't mine. Someone must have mistaken my truck for someone else's."

There was a knock on their door. "Monkey, phone."

Montgomery went out and picked up the phone. "Hello?"

"Montgomery Lee?"

"Sir?"

"Sergeant Hillsworth, Bacon Police Department. I would like to speak with you concerning some information we received. Will you come down to the lobby," he said with a tone that was an order, not a request.

"Yes, sir." Montgomery popped his head into his room. "The cops want to talk to me. I don't like this."

"Me neither," Travis said. "This might be a set-up."

In the lobby, Montgomery found more than Sergeant Hillsworth, there were two additional officers. The sergeant took the lead. "We've received information that contraband may be stored in your vehicle. What do you know about that?"

"Nothing, sir."

"Are you sure? If there's something you need to tell me, tell me now before you have to tell me."

"I have no contraband in my vehicle—to the best of my knowledge."

"Right," sighed the sergeant. "Let's take a ride."

Montgomery walked with the police officers and got into the right hand passenger seat of Sergeant Hillsworth's vehicle. The sergeant climbed in, and cranked the engine. "It happens all the time, son," he said in a kind voice. "A kid comes to college and plays around with drugs—curious to see what it's like. But you get caught, and there are consequences. Make this easy on yourself. Tell me what I'm going to find."

"Nothing that was put in my truck by me," Montgomery said stiffly.

They arrived at the parking lot. There were already four officers and a dog at Montgomery's vehicle.

"Do I have your permission to search your vehicle?" the sergeant asked Montgomery.

"Not before I talk to my father."

"No phone calls," said the sergeant. "You don't need to speak to your old man who can't tell you beans anyway. This is a search; you're not under arrest. Do I have your permission to search your vehicle?"

"Not before I talk to my father."

"Use the dog," the sergeant said curtly.

The dog sniffed around the truck paying attention to the side panels, wheel wells and other cavities where contraband might be hidden. He made no signal. The handler then put the dog into the bed. The dog sniffed at the cargo box and sat down.

The sergeant smiled. "Kid, this is your last chance to level with me and possibly receive lenient treatment. Tell me what's in the box."

Montgomery said nothing.

The sergeant scowled. "You should cooperate, kid. Do I have your permission to search the locker?"

"Not before I talk to my father."

"I don't need your permission," the sergeant informed Montgomery. "The dog's reaction at the box gives me probable cause for a search." He turned to an officer. "Open the box."

Two officers opened the box and removed all the contents: a pair of blue jeans, a pair of athletic shorts, swimming trunks, two t-shirts with the sleeves ripped out, two spools of fishing line, several lures and sinkers, two screwdrivers, pliers and a crescent wrench. The dog sniffed at a t-shirt and sat down.

"Nothing there, Clete," said one of the officers.

"Nothing?"

"Nothing."

"The dog hit on something." The sergeant spoke to Montgomery. "You're coming with me. I'll get it out of you if it takes all night."

"Uh, Clete?" spoke another uniformed officer. "Can I have a conference with you?"

The two men stood aside. "Do you know whose kid that is?" the uniform asked.

"Someone whose kid likes to get high."

"I take that as a no."

"What are you getting at?"

"That's Harrison Lee's kid. It's exceedingly doubtful he's mixed up in any drug use—even to try a puff at a party—and much more remote is the possibility that he's guilty of possession. You act like you want to stick him with 'intent to sell'. Do that, and you won't have enough of a reputation to work as a security guard at Wal-Mart."

The sergeant considered this new information. "What do you think?"

"Fraternity prank. It happens occasionally. Plant something incriminating, and make an anonymous phone call to the cops. That is why we're here, isn't it?"

The sergeant walked back to the vehicle. "It appears that the situation is a joke of some kind. Put your things back into your locker, son. Do you know anyone who might be pulling a prank on you?"

Montgomery said innocently, "I'm a pledge at Sigma Omicron Beta."

The sergeant wrote that down in his notebook. "We'll follow that up."

"Am I no longer under suspicion?"

"No," replied the sergeant.

"Good. Then come back to my room. My roommate found the drugs earlier. He'll give them to you." Montgomery walked back to the police cruiser.

"Just like his old man," said the officer to the sergeant.

Cody grinned with delight. "You planted marijuana in his truck and called the cops? Brilliant! Even if the cops don't go for it, he won't be swaggering around here like he's king of the dung heap. That's smart thinking, Brendon. It repairs the damage the two dunderheads caused, and advances our plan."

"Some of the guys are mad at him for beating up two brothers," reported Jack. "They think he started it since our guys took the worst of the beating."

"Even better," grinned Cody. "Stupidity can be salvaged." Then he scowled, "But if they try it again, against orders, I will not hold back. There will be no mercy." Cody softened his features. "Tell me about his girlfriend."

"Her name is Elizabeth; one of three southern belles from Alabama. They look the part; they act the part. One girl dated the roommate in the fall, but broke up with him when they returned to school. She's rather loose and has moved on to a football player. She has real potential as a 'little sister' in the house—shallow but smart. Maybe we could take the football player in—" Brendon reported.

"Maybe she has moved on by then," interrupted Cody. "Forget her; tell me about Elizabeth."

"Smart girl: she knows what she wants and moves to get it. They met through the roommate. They went out together as a group and the two developed feelings for one another. She managed to turn up in one of his fall classes; he doesn't know it but that was a deliberate move on her part."

"She set her sights on him. Interesting. She bagged him."

"They grew tight," said Brendon.

"They fell in love," said Cody. "How compatible are they?"

"Nobody cares about that star-gazing habit. But here's the thing: whoever is with him always goes along when he tugs out his telescope. The girlfriend is no different."

"What do they do?"

"They sit and talk while he looks around the universe. When he sees something interesting, he'll have her look through the glass."

"He's every girl's dream. He'll sit all night and talk. All they have to do is look through a tube once an hour for maybe ten seconds."

"I couldn't find out anything about his abilities in the sack. He must be a private sort—never says anything."

"Don't overlook the possibility that he's a virgin. What about her?"

"I drew a blank. That's hard information unless they become notorious."

"What do you mean?" asked Jack.

"Two years ago when we were freshman," replied Brendon, "a girl in Alyssa Hawkins was giving it up on a regular basis, but no one knew because girls keep their secrets. Then one day she and her boyfriend were going so hard they fell out the door into the hall. The entire floor came out to watch. An act like that is impossible to keep under a lid. Everyone found out."

"Elizabeth is not the village madam," Cody summed up. "Maybe we could plant some rumors to the contrary. He gets up in arms, confronts her, she defends her honor, he gets dumped and blames himself."

"Here's the kicker," added Brendon. "Currently they are having a fight. She did not sit by him in class either day this week."

"What's the fight about?"

"He did something she told him not to do."

"I would expect that from him. But she did not take it well ..."

"Not at all," grinned Brendon.

"On the other hand, as long as they are on the outs with each other," mused Cody, "the value of disrupting the relationship is limited. They've already done that themselves. It hasn't affected him, though."

"Because he doesn't think the relationship is over," supplied Jack. "He thinks he'll fix things as soon as she gets over her fit—classic male response. We could roil the waters to a greater degree—we could send her dead flowers with an apology."

"Too clumsy," argued Brendon. "That's what went wrong with Mick. She would see through it at once, or she would call him to complain. He'd deny it, and the two of them would figure it out. Instead of breaking them up, it would bring them back together. What we need to do is feed him relationship advice that furthers the conflict. Could we use Mick for that?"

"Not in time," countered Jack. "He won't be ready until next week, but that's the breaks. The two lovebirds won't part for a week without reconciling."

"Anything else?" Cody asked. Brendon shook his head. Cody gave his analysis, "I don't see where we could disrupt the relationship before the break. We'll have to hope that the quarrel deepens, and wait for an opportunity. Maintain surveillance for new developments, Brendon."

"What did you find out from your trip?" asked Jack.

"Later, men." Cody was final and dismissing with this word.

Chapter Nineteen

Spring Break

TRAVIS TALKED MONTGOMERY into cruising the Atlantic coast for good waves over Spring break. They wound up on the Outer Banks of North Carolina. At Coquina State Park south of Nag's Head, there were good waves sweeping in as the winds of ocean storms pushed their energy through the surface of the water.

They had stopped in Sparksburg to pick up clothes and pay their obligatory respects to their families. They stopped at a famous sports shop in Cocoa Beach for Montgomery to buy a wet suit and a beginner board. Then they pushed northward, monitoring the beaches and weather. They set up camp when they decided to spend their holiday on the Outer Banks.

The weather being raw, Montgomery built a fire in the lee of the sand dune where they had pitched their tent. Travis made coffee, Montgomery mixed a poor man's stew, and the boys settled into supper. As the flames died to a bed of glowing coals, Travis schooled Montgomery in the basics of surfing. Montgomery lay on his back and watched the stars overhead. He found that his location, jutting out into the sea with less artificial light from developed civilization, enabled the sky to blaze into a spangled relief. He loved it.

The next day, after an early breakfast of sausage and scrambled eggs, the two boys took their boards and went over the dunes to the beach. The sea was heavy, pounding the shore with four and five footers. Travis' eyes glowed as he raced for the surf. Montgomery followed. Few people had yet ventured out.

As the morning progressed, the sun made its appearance, and warmed the air and sand. The boys took a breather, peeled off their wet suits, stretched a blanket on the sand, and lay down to dry off. A little ways down the sand, a group of young people began singing to the accompaniment of two guitars.

"What's that?" queried Travis, sitting up and looking across a stretch of sand, gravel and sea debris.

Montgomery lay still with his eyes closed. "Sounds like music," he murmured, half asleep. "Awesome God, maybe, or ... " He dropped off.

"I'll go check it out." Travis walked through the breakers to get a closer look. As he approached the group, several waved at him to join them.

Nine young adults, ages eighteen to twenty-three were standing with their backs to the wind along with a man in his thirties. They were gathered on the beach in worship to celebrate their love for the Lord. They were dressed in swimwear and cover-ups; a couple wore t-shirts that read, "Surfers for Christ".

"Surfers for Christ?" observed Travis. "What's that?"

"We love to surf and we love Jesus Christ," a young man explained. "When we finish here, we're going to take to the waves in celebration of the awesome Creator who makes wind and wave."

"May I join you? I love to surf and it was one week and two days ago that I met Jesus and was saved. My friend is over there where our boards are. We came up for Spring break. We go to Florida Sawgrass. I'm new to Christ and he's new to surfing. I've surfed all my life and he's been a Christian all his life. Some combination, huh?"

The group insisted that they join them. Travis jogged down the beach, woke Montgomery up, and the two picked up their things and joined the group who had begun singing again. After a few bars, Montgomery picked up the song and joined in.

Then the older man motioned for everyone to be quiet. He brought out his Bible, and turned to Mark 4.35-41:

As it was becoming late in the day, he said to them, "We should be going to the other side." They sent the crowd away, then they took him with them in the boat, and other boats were with him. A great rushing of wind broke out and threw the waves over the boat causing the boat to be full of water. He was sleeping upon the cushion in the stern. They roused him and said, "Teacher, is it no concern of yours that we are perishing?" After he was awake, he rebuked the wind and said to the sea, "Silence, and stay silent." The wind dropped and a great calm occurred. He said to them, "Why are you cowardly? Do you still have no faith?" They were frightened at this and said to one another, "Who then is this man that even the wind and the sea obey him?"

The speaker turned out to be Pastor Mark, and the group was from the University of North Carolina on their Spring Break. Pastor Mark laughed at the group's faces because the wind and waves falling calm was the last thing they wanted. But he taught a good lesson about the Lord being the master of the earth and the powerful forces that fill it—forces that will humble and break a human being into pieces. Then he moved on to speak of the need for faith. Even when it seems like the Lord is sleeping, the wind and the waves cannot overwhelm him and they cannot destroy him. He is always more powerful than they. By implication, Pastor Mark continued, those who are with the Lord need to fear nothing. He who gives life and cannot be taken unaware by death can preserve life in any circumstances whether or not it seems he is conscious of the situation.

"Those who are with him need not fear; he is more than able to preserve their lives. We who are with him need not fear; he will sustain our lives. But the wind and the waves are also symbols of the forces of evil that suddenly broke out against the boat and its company. They made a surprise attack against the Lord hoping to catch him unaware, vulnerable and weak. They were wrong. Even in his sleep, the Lord is more powerful than the evil in the world. They could not hurt him. He wondered why his disciples could not understand this. We should remember this in those times when great evil suddenly breaks out against us. The Lord says to us, 'Are you cowardly? Or do you have faith in me?' He will rescue; he will save. At the sound of his voice, evil must obey and be silent. That gives us great hope as we negotiate the shoals of this world. Amen."

The group whooped and cheered and broke into a song of praise. Then they grabbed their boards and headed for the ocean. Travis and Montgomery joined them, and spent the rest of the day with them. They accepted their invitation to supper, and passed an enjoyable evening talking, sharing and listening to music. Late that night they returned to their campsite. The group had invited them to join them again the next day, and they promised to do so.

Elizabeth was not enjoying her spring break. The girls had stayed in Florida because their families had deemed it less expensive than chauffeuring them home and back to school. Elizabeth had been morose since Friday afternoon when classes ceased and the campus emptied. The girls had packed and departed for Fort Myers where they were going to spend the week.

"Geriatric city," groaned Elizabeth. She screamed out the window, "Where's the fresh meat?"

"You've got it bad, honey," said Park. "Why wouldn't you talk to him before we left?"

"Pride," chimed in Rose. "No, stow it, Elizabeth, I'm going to have my say. You're mad because Montgomery ignored you and went ahead with butting into Rick's and my business. But we needed that. He was a good friend to risk our friendship to poke us into resolving a big question that was bothering us both. You think you're trying to control him; at least, that's what you said. But that's not it at all."

Rose took a long breath. "You're used to being right—all the time. What bothers you is that he was right and you weren't. So your bruised pride asserts itself by saying the issue is he ignored your wishes. You subconsciously know you're lying to yourself so you say you're trying to control him—an admission that you realize maybe you aren't in the right.

"You won't see him and you won't talk to him because you're afraid you'll break and apologize and your pride won't allow that to happen—so you avoid him. You refuse to talk to him. Good for you. He can live his life in peace and you can be miserable and mean and make your roommates miserable. Why don't you call him? If you want to sulk with your pride, at least break up and get it over with. If you want to let love reign over your pride, make up and get it over with. Either way, call him now. Then we can all relax."

"Thank you, Mrs. Freud," Elizabeth spat. She harrumphed to her bedroom.

"Can you believe it? What's happened to her?" Park asked in a low voice. "She's never been like this before."

"She's never loved like this before. It's hard for her to admit defeat."

"Let's not hang around here all day. I'm tired of the beach; it makes me think of old cotton, moldy leather and jars of tobacco spit. Let's go shopping."

"Fine by me. Let's check with Elizabeth."

Park knocked on the bedroom door. "Elizabeth? We're going shopping. You want to come?"

A muffled 'no' echoed through the door. Park returned to the front room. "She's staying."

"Let's go then. Maybe some alone time will mend her mood."

On their way out of the condo, the two girls ran into a young man that Park knew.

"Hi, Guy. Allow me to introduce you to my friend, Rose Hill."

Brendon Garrett broke into a wide smile. "Pleased to make your acquaintance."

"Charmed." Rose returned the smile.

"What are you doing in Fort Myers?" asked Park.

"Dorms closed; couldn't get home. How about you?"

"Same story. We're staying in a condo in this building that we rented for the week. Another friend is with us—Elizabeth."

"Three bachelorettes," enthused the pseudonymous Guy. "Every man's dream."

"Let me adjust your arithmetic," said Rose. "I'm engaged, and Elizabeth has a boyfriend."

"That leaves me," said Park. "Unless you want a shot at Elizabeth; she's had an awful fight with her boyfriend. They haven't talked in a week and a half."

"Break-up by mutual silent consent?" replied Guy. "That never works; one party reneges and they have another fight."

"Want to join us?" asked Park impulsively. "I'm about to die from boredom. The beach makes me think I'm lost in a kennel for Shar-Pei dogs. We're going to the mall."

"I'd love to. I'm at loose ends myself. No one here to hang with."

"Hang with us," invited Park.

The threesome climbed into Guy's car. He left the parking lot and headed north, then turned west onto a major thoroughfare. He steered the car and the conversation, and soon they were talking about Elizabeth again.

"She's being impossible," said Park. "She won't talk to him. Poor man couldn't apologize if he wanted to."

"What was the fight about?" prompted the impostor.

"He did something she told him not to do," said Park.

"Ah, I see," replied Guy. "She is justified in her anger, then."

"No, she is not," replied Rose. "She's the one out of line. If he wanted to do what he did, he was within his rights to do so. All he did was prompt my fiancé and me to talk about getting married."

"What's the big deal about that?" responded Guy.

"There is no big deal," complained Park. "Change the subject, I'm bored of this one."

The conversation turned on restaurants and places of entertainment.

"I can get you into a club if you want," offered Guy.

"Honey, you are a dreamboat and a life saver in one," responded Park. "How about it, Rose?"

"I'm not the clubbing sort," Rose demurred.

"You think Elizabeth will want to go?" asked Guy. "It will get her mind off of ... what's his name?"

"Montgomery," Park replied. "Montgomery Lee."

"The prescription for love sickness," opined Guy, "is good circulation."

He and Park laughed. "Ain't it the truth," she said.

Rose sat back. *Something's not right, but I'm not sure what it is. I'd better watch Guy. Maybe I should go to the club if Elizabeth doesn't.*

Mick let Cody tap the vein in his arm, and insert the hypodermic needle. He watched as Cody pressed the plunger pushing the heroin and cocaine solution into his bloodstream. After Cody withdrew the needle, he smiled, closed his eyes and leaned back.

"This is the life, isn't Mick," said Jack feigning an injection of his own.

"You said it, buddy," replied a cheerful Mick. "Y'all got me regulated, and showed me things I never knew would make me feel so good. This frat's the best thing that's ever happened to me."

"Gratitude," said Jack. "It's good to show gratitude. It makes a fellow want to know how he can repay his pals in the fraternity."

"You said it. Anything you want, I'm there. Tell me what to do, and consider it done."

"We can count on you, can't we, Mick," stated Cody. "You're one of us."

Mick smiled as the rush of the cocaine offset the drowsy effects of the narcotic and the waves of pleasure from the opium dreams took hold. "I'm one of you."

"Would you help us, Mick?" asked Cody.

"Absolutely."

"We need you to make friends with one of our pledges," said Jack. "He's a rough guy having trouble fitting in. He's prime S.O.B. material, but he needs someone to help him loosen up. That someone is you."

"I'd be happy to do it," said Mick. "Who is it?"

"Montgomery Lee," answered Jack.

"Monkey?" said Mick with surprise. "Monkey is a good guy. Sure, I'm already pals with him. I'll help you fit him in. Anything special you want me to do?"

"Be his friend," said Jack. "That's all we need."

Guy maneuvered the girls into the lingerie department of a major department store. "What do you girls like to wear?"

Rose was put off his charm by this move.

Park, however, was hoping to attract him for the week, so she flirted shamelessly. She picked up a black, lacy teddy. "Black lace is inviting, don't you think?"

"I'm going to the perfume counter," Rose announced. She moved across the store so she would be out of Guy's vicinity. Her disgust was rising.

"Black lace for black promises," Guy responded. "But red is what gets a man's heart going." He held up a red bodice.

"A woman doesn't wear that in her boudoir. It goes over her blouse, and ends at the waist. It would be a ridiculous garment to sleep in."

"Depends on whom she's sleeping with," leered Guy. He picked up another garment—blue and filmy. "Let's check the fit." He held the garment against Park's body. "No good," he announced. As he put the garment back on the rack, he let his other hand accidentally-on-purpose brush Park's chest.

"Watch it," she said playfully. She gave his hand a light swat.

"Have I offended you?"

"I hardly know you."

"I can take care of that."

Montgomery was enjoying his surfing lessons and learning how to grip the board with his feet to cement his weight in place, and then gripping the energy of the surging wave that bore him into the shore on those rare occasions when he interrupted his series of beginner's wipe-outs.

Travis was delighted to share his one life's passion now second to his new life's passion, his love for Jesus Christ. Both young men were enjoying the fellowship of the Surfers for Christ group with whom they had hooked up.

Midweek, the group had a bonfire on the beach. The wood on the fire crackled and snapped as the flames rose into the cool night air. Most of the young people were wearing sweaters or jackets but they stayed in their shorts and bare feet.

Travis and a couple others went up the beach for a walk. As they went along, Travis related his tale of his high school life and his first semester at college. He explained how he had dated Park, but drifted away. He'd started looking for a deeper part of life than he had before. He gave his testimony about the night he'd visited the Christian group, and was saved. He finished by describing his baptism.

"But there's so much I want to know," he said. "I've wasted my time till now. I've been reading the New Testament in my spare time. I've gotten to the letters, but I can't understand most of it. Maybe I don't belong in college."

"Silly," said an African-American woman of nineteen years and above-average height. "You do belong in college. You're doing what all college students should be doing: searching for the truth, and embracing it when you find it. Most kids treat college like an extension of high school: concentrate on the social life, do minimal work on academics—only enough so they can pass a test without ever thinking about the material, and grab a diploma they hope will bring them a job."

"She's right," confirmed a Cherokee boy. "Stick to your learning and master your subjects. Look at the New Testament as another course. You're barely into the second week on the syllabus. Understand what you can; ask questions about the rest. Pray for the Holy Spirit to light up your mind."

"What is the Holy Spirit?" asked Travis. "When I was baptized, the minister had me kneel at the shore after he put me under the water. Then he and some others put their hands on my head and said to receive the Holy Spirit. Then a big burst of wind came across the river."

The Cherokee looked at the African-American. "You first," he said.

"First off, I recommend you read C.S. Lewis: *Mere Christianity*. Many new Christians are not ready for it, but you have the intellectual gifts to understand his reasoning. The Father, that is God, whom Jesus knew and addressed as Father, begot the Son, who is Jesus. So we have Father God, and God the Son or Jesus. Then, somehow, between the two of them, the Holy Spirit streams out. He is another person. So there is God the Father, God the Son, and God the Spirit. Three persons, but only one God. Don't try to understand it; the human mind doesn't have the capacity to comprehend how three persons exist as only one being."

The Cherokee took up the instruction. "When Jesus left, he promised that Another would come to help his disciples, and by extension, all believers. What he promised was the Holy Spirit; God the Spirit would come upon them in power to enable them to understand what Jesus taught, among other things. Thus my advice: the Spirit rests on you, Travis. Ask Him to give you understanding of the Scriptures that you read."

"Scriptures?" asked Travis.

"Another name for the Bible," explained the woman.

"Tell me more about the Holy Spirit," begged Travis. "What else does he do for us?"

The Cherokee man smiled. "The Holy Spirit begins a work of remaking us so that we become like Jesus. He reforms our characters ..."

Back at the bonfire, Montgomery was still roasting sausages and eating them on buns with pickles and mustard. Montgomery had found the physical exertion of the sport taxing in a way that felt good. He was relaxed in the sense of having had a hard physical workout, which had produced an enormous appetite.

As he roasted a sausage, his thoughts drifted back to Elizabeth and the cold shoulder she had been giving him for almost two weeks. He was calling home every day to see if she had left a message. There had been no calls nor had she written any letters. Montgomery even had his mother check his e-mail: nothing.

Montgomery felt odd inside. *I know I did the right thing. Rick and Rose are grateful. I doubt I understand women in the slightest degree. Travis seems to have the female psyche figured out. He never lacks for female companions, and he never has arguments. His admirers adore him, and do whatever he asks. Why do I have so much trouble?*

It was a good night for watching stars. Montgomery finished eating, and lay back to look at the sky. He knew all the constellations; he spotted the visible planets easily. Montgomery kept looking as he grew introspective about his life and his freshman year on campus. Suddenly he sat up. Something new had appeared—a small dot, but a small dot where nothing was supposed to be.

Montgomery ran to his truck and pulled his telescope out of his cargo box. He brought it back to the fire, but set it up a little distance off. The group around the fire became curious about what he was doing. Montgomery explained that he was an amateur astronomer.

He looked in the scope, scanning the heavens where that anomalous dot had appeared. As he located the quadrant, he began a systematic search throughout the sector. Then he saw it. He extended the magnification power of the scope and focused. His mouth dropped open in wonder.

"What?" "What is it?" the others were asking.

"A comet," Montgomery replied. "A comet has appeared. If you look closely through the telescope, you can barely see the tail."

He let the others take a look. They were fascinated. "What's its name?" someone asked.

"We won't know until astronomers determine its cycle and period. Then they'll see if it is a known comet. If not, the first person to report it has the honor of naming it."

"Let's call it Montgomery's Comet," the group suggested.

"I'm not the first to see it; amateurs never are, protested Montgomery. "One of the great observatories has already seen it and reported it. The press has not publicized it, that's all."

Montgomery's Comet took its namesake's mind off his self-critique of his ability to relate to women, in particular Elizabeth. He began explaining to the group the theory of the Big Bang origin of the universe, and an energetic debate arose over whether the theory was compatible with the Bible's account of Creation.

In Fort Myers, Brendon had wormed his way into the girls' condo and was trying to put the moves on Elizabeth. He was not succeeding.

"Come to the club with us," he said. "That's where you'll find new people to meet."

"You don't need me. I'll be the third wheel on the bicycle."

"Do come," begged Park. "Meeting some new boys is what you need. It will take your mind off you-know-who."

As Park went to change clothes and get ready, Brendon was attempting to work his charm on Elizabeth. Rose had gone out to the balcony to read. She wanted nothing to do with Guy.

"You're very beautiful," said Brendon. "Does your boyfriend appreciate how beautiful you are?"

"I'm sure he does," snapped Elizabeth.

"When was the last time he told you?"

Elizabeth considered the question but did not respond.

"He takes you for granted. Most guys do. Now me—I appreciate feminine beauty. It comes from within: from their soul, from their strength, from their passion, from their independence. Facial features—hah! The same features look plain on a dreadfully dull girl, but lock into standards of classic beauty—like the statue of a goddess—on an exciting women of intellect and soul."

"Is that how you see Park?" Elizabeth stifled her laughter.

"A girl like Park is fun for a day on the beach or at the mall. But when a man goes home, he wants a woman—a woman like an Elizabeth who can hold a conversation and arouse his curiosity."

"Is that what you call it," Elizabeth said tartly.

"Well, that too," Brendon laughed. "But even that part of the relationship is enhanced by the fire of the passion in the woman's soul: her intellect, her will, her desire to dominate and to submit, and her strength. Most men would be intimidated. But I like the fire of the strong woman—a woman like you. Your deep, interior qualities are what gives a man his greatest pleasure."

"You talk a good game."

"What makes what's-his-name so special?"

"His name is Montgomery. He has a passion for astronomy. He's loyal and committed and dedicated; once he starts something, he'll finish it."

"Montgomery?"Brendon raised his eyebrows in mock comic skepticism. "Are you going out with a man or a city?" Elizabeth glared at him. Brendon realized he had asked if she was extremely promiscuous.

"He's selfish—only cares about his interests, not yours. Plus he's stubborn. He sounds like quite a guy," Brendon sneered.

"That's not what I meant," protested Elizabeth. "His family has a lot of history, and he's conscious of that tradition. He tries to uphold it all the time."

"He's a snob."

"You're twisting my words. He's great; he really is."

"Has he called you during the break?"

"No—" started Elizabeth. Brendon began peppering her with questions and comments to denigrate Montgomery and not give her time to think for the reasons why Montgomery had not called, such as Montgomery does not know where she is staying because she had been giving him the silent treatment for almost two weeks.

Brendon was beginning to make some headway when Park emerged from her bedroom in a stunning red dress hemmed at her ankles with a slit extending the length of her leg. Brendon stared. His mind went blank and he left Elizabeth alone.

"Are you coming?" asked Park to her roommate.

"No, you two have fun."

That we will, thought Brendon, *that we will.*

The roommates were not surprised that Guy appeared in the condo around ten the next morning. Elizabeth sighed.

"I know," Rose commiserated. "I'd like to get rid of the jerk."

"I was thinking how cheap Park has become," said Elizabeth. "She's one small step from charging money."

"Meow."

"Seriously, I'm concerned. Every date ends in bed. Park doesn't play hard to get anymore. She's become loose, a reputation which will ruin her. Do we dare talk to her?"

"Hypocrite."

"I beg your pardon?"

"Hypocrite," said Rose, slowly enunciating the word. "Montgomery suffers under your condemnation because he dared to say something to Rick and me, while you maintain he butted into personal business, but you're ready to butt into Park's business."

"That's different."

"No, it's not and you know it."

Elizabeth opened her mouth but Rose cut her off. "Don't argue with me."

Elizabeth closed her mouth, then opened it again, thought better of speaking, and closed her mouth again.

Rose wondered: *How has our friendship become so strained? Two weeks ago we'd have laughed at Elizabeth's demonstration of a fish.*

Guy stayed on for the remaining three days. Elizabeth and Rose were barely speaking to Park when he left. The door had barely closed when they let Park know how uncomfortable they had been with his presence, and that they felt she was inconsiderate for not discussing her invitation with them before allowing Guy to stay.

"Y'all are jealous," Park had said in an airy voice. "I had a beau and you lonely hearts had only each other for company."

"Beau? You mean trick!" snapped Elizabeth. She stopped short of speaking again. Tears came into her eyes. "What's wrong with me? I'm not like this." She ran into her bedroom sobbing.

Rose was tired. "Let's pack and leave. I hate this place."

Brendon was soaring in his mood as he sped off to return to Bacon. He had three fantastic days with one incredible woman. Three miles out of Fort Myers, however, he remembered he was supposed to get friendly with Elizabeth, not Park. He began to concoct a story to tell Cody.

The boys said farewell to their friends on the beach. They exchanged Internet addresses, and with the innocence of youth, promised to send messages to stay in touch, never realizing that they would not keep these promises because their lives would not cross again.

It had been a good Spring break for Montgomery and Travis. The only thing nagging at Montgomery's mind was the disruption of his relationship with Elizabeth. *It's the not knowing—if she wants to break up, we should break up. She should not keep me dangling and wondering if it is over.*

CHAPTER TWENTY

THE FOURTH TASK

IMMEDIATELY UPON RETURNING from Spring Break, Montgomery entered into the fourth task with diligence. He was determined to complete the assignments in time for induction with the Spring pledges. He moved into the house for the live-in portion of the pledge period. He became permanent kitchen help. He avoided confrontations with any brothers, especially the pledge committee, and they left him alone not wishing to incur more injuries.

Montgomery found a psychology graduate student for his counseling. Since the issues were bogus, his assignments were bogus, and the counseling ridiculous, he did not consider the competency of the counselor a concern.

Brad Dinkins sat in an overstuffed chair in his suite of rooms that attached to the rear of a faculty house. He motioned to Montgomery to sit anywhere he chose. Montgomery chose the sofa.

"My job," Brad began, "is to answer the concerns that your pledge committee stated in its last interview. I've received a communication from them that specifies the issues that are a concern to your effective functioning as a full fraternal member: one, difficulty relating to the opposite sex (Montgomery flinched, remembering his argument with Elizabeth); two, rebellious against authority; three, loner-type personality; four, bookish type, preferring inanimate objects over human contact—wait a minute, that's the same as three; five, cooperation with others; six, handling assigned responsibilities; seven, introversion—

that's not a psychological concern—it's only a personality trait; eight, ability to play; nine, subversive abnormality; ten, self-centeredness regardless of effect on others; eleven, authoritarian style of relating to others; twelve, contradiction between relating to self and relating to others.

"Whew! They piled it on, didn't they?"

"That's all they could think of?"

"The S.O.B.'s are aptly named. I'm being paid to do this, but that doesn't mean that I'm beholden to their agenda. When it comes to the S.O.B.'s, the only question I have personally is why a psychologically healthy person wants to join them."

"I want to help them recover their original purpose of being campus leaders and role models."

"Isn't it too far gone for that? There's no one left who doesn't have an alcohol and drug saturated brain that can think much more than obtaining another dose."

"A few brothers exist who want to turn the fraternity around. What they lack to revive the chapter and renew its life is effective leadership. There's a brain trust—the pledge committee—that rules the house. It's made up of five brothers, but even there, the real power is in the chairman. The others take their cue from him. Neutralize him, the other four go to pieces, and the membership can be persuaded to purge the drugs from the house. From there, we move on to scholarship and behavior."

"This is the subversive abnormality that the committee reports in its communication."

"The Clintonian technique of redefining words. I disagree with the actions of the pledge committee. I refuse to participate in illegal acts that place my health and life at risk. So they label me as subversive. Dissent means subverting in their view."

"Illegal acts?"

"They order their pledges to take hits of LSD. They call it a spiritual awakening or a journey of self-discovery; they say it opens the personality to welcome new experiences and new ways of viewing things. But the dangers are great; besides, I don't use recreational drugs. The fraternity is out-of-line for trying to force me.

"Then there's the courier business."

"Courier business?" repeated Brad.

"I asked questions to find out what was delivered, especially since most of the deliveries were C.O.D."

"You delivered packages for cash?"

"Check. No one would talk about it; the fraternity members are scared to hear it mentioned. 'Not in the house,' they'd say as if something terrible would happen if they were overheard."

"Why don't you drop it all? Are they worth it?"

"Them? As in Cody Spung and company? No, but the fraternity is. The ideals it used to represent are worth fighting for. The chapter has considerable assets to be used for good or for bad. Should we let the bad have the assets and the name without a struggle?"

"I see why they label you subversive. This is a whale of a fight you've entered. Are you going to win?"

"I don't know, but I believe the struggle itself is worthwhile even if I lose."

"What else have you refused to do?"

"I refused to allow them to throw food at me. They initiated three altercations and I fought back. This semester I refused to live in the house until I was ready. Because they loaded me down with assignments, work and participation in groups, I refused to be their servant."

"What kind of groups did they have you participate in?"

Montgomery laughed. "They put me in this feedback group where I met with three female grad students and a female professor. They would make these presentations about women and male oppression, and ask my opinion. Then they would give me feedback about how I was relating to the group. But they were so divided: all they saw was what they wanted to see. What a farce."

"That was you? You're the one who got the better of the shrew and the three witches of Macbeth?" Brad laughed hard for a long time. "Everyone in the psych department was talking about it."

Montgomery grinned. "One of them came on to me."

Brad roared. "What gave you that idea?"

"She would come out of the room after a session was through, speak to me alone, blow in my ear, and run off."

Brad laughed so hard tears ran down his cheeks. He gasped for breath. "Stop it. I'll lose control of my bladder.

"You're a very interesting person, Mr. Lee. I see why you're giving them fits. What they call subversive behavior is simply setting appropriate boundaries. Rebelling against authority is the same thing. Fascinating how they repeated concerns in different terms to make the list longer. We can check off numbers two, six, and nine, also five is in the same category. Not bad for one session; that leaves us eight to deal with."

"Too true," said Montgomery. "Too true."

As he emerged into the night, Montgomery took a look around him. The night was overcast threatening a steady rain. He started toward the frat house, but he reversed his direction to go to the north dormitories where Elizabeth was continuing her almost three week pout. Montgomery had tried every day to reach her by telephone, but the message was always the same: Not in to you.

Montgomery reached the door of the Alyssa Hawkins complex, and pushed the button for Elizabeth's room. A laughing Park answered the call, "Who's there?"

"Montgomery Lee, to see Elizabeth."

There was a pause. "She's out."

Montgomery heard a slightly familiar voice in the background saying, "Is the punk outside?" Then more laughter faintly transmitted through the intercom. "Go away. She won't see you."

Montgomery felt his heart break along with his temper. "Tell her I will see her now."

Another pause ensued. "She is through dating little boys. Little boys with little boys," Park giggled.

Montgomery was heating up. But in the back of his head he wondered why Park was saying these things. She was not acting like herself. "I'll wait as long as I have to. Sooner or later she'll have to leave the dorm."

Another pause, and then Park said, "You overstuffed moron, you don't understand anything about women. You'll never get another date. Go back to your stars."

Montgomery was seething. "I'm coming up."

Park laughed. "I think not. Goodbye, mongrel. If you knew how to satisfy a woman, you might have been a man. I suggest castration. She hates you, mongrel." The box fell silent.

Mongrel? What does that remind me of?

Montgomery was deliberately late for the next class in Western Civilization. He was angry and he was puzzled, and he was determined to have it out. As he entered the room from the rear, he looked over the heads of the students hunched over their desks writing notes about the Reformation in Europe, and the political and secular ramifications for the medieval society of Christendom.

He spotted Elizabeth in her now-usual spot. He walked over and sat in the row behind her. She had not noticed him coming in.

Montgomery took out his notebook, and opened to a fresh page. He dated the page, and began to copy the main outline the professor was displaying via an overhead projector. As he caught up, he moved ahead so he would not miss anything crucial to the class. Then he tossed his pen so it landed at Elizabeth's feet.

"Pardon me," he whispered. "I dropped my pen. Would you be so kind as to pick it up for me?"

Elizabeth started at the sound of his voice. "What are you doing here?" she hissed.

Montgomery ignored the hateful tone of her voice. "I take this class, remember?"

Elizabeth started to say something, then bent over and silently handed Montgomery his pen.

"Thanks."

Elizabeth turned her attention back to the professor's lecture. Her concentration was broken. She chewed the end of her pen. Tears dropped on the page of her notebook fouling her pen's attempt to make neat strokes of ink.

"Why did I have to love you," she whispered hoarsely. "Why?"

"As I recall, we had an argument. That was followed by three weeks of silence. Do you think love means we'll never disagree?"

"You don't understand."

"You're right about that. Help me understand."

"If you need me to tell you, then you will never understand."

"I'm supposed to read your mind?"

"Women are good at it."

"I'm not a woman if you haven't noticed."

"I've never had an opportunity to notice."

Montgomery, somewhat confused, recalled their conversation in December. *We didn't want to begin a sexual relationship. Is she saying the omission of sex is the cause of the impending break-up?*

"Are you breaking up with me?"

Elizabeth began to cry hard. She grabbed her notebook and fled the room. Montgomery stared at her with the rest of the class in amazement.

"That's a remarkable talent you have, young man," said the professor in an acid tone. "Would you like to upset another member of my class, or may I return to my lecture?"

"Sorry, sir," Montgomery replied.

"I may proceed?" inquired the scathing lecturer.

Montgomery nodded, his face flaming red and his temper redder.

"She ran out," repeated Brad the counselor.

"Yeah," confirmed a disconsolate Montgomery. "She grabbed her notebook and fled in tears."

"Do you know why?"

"No idea. We had this argument about—I don't remember what it was about. Ever since then, she won't speak to me."

"Nothing?"

"Nothing. I forced her to speak in class by taking a seat behind her and tossing my pen at her feet. She then asks why she had to love me. She tells me if I don't know what's wrong, she won't tell me. Her parting criticism was that we haven't been naked together."

"Whoa. Where did that come from?"

"I don't know. We talked about sex and agreed we weren't ready for a sexual relationship. That was fine until now. Now she seems to be saying that I've deprived her."

"Have you deprived her?"

"I'm not sure what your question is. If you're asking if we've had sexual contact, the answer is no. We were quite clear on our boundaries: kissing, okay; hugging, and holding hands, et cetera, okay; anything is okay as long as it didn't involve genital contact or putting hands inside clothing."

"Montgomery, that went out with the dark ages. Are you afraid to embrace your sexuality?"

Montgomery stared at the twenty-eight year old, bearded man who sat in his overstuffed chair asking personal questions like he might inquire about rain.

"Are you afraid to embrace your sexuality?"

"That's a loaded question full of assumptions about moral conduct. Does embracing human sexuality mean that we have to be sexually active? If a young man chooses to be celibate because of his religious beliefs, is he now a psycho?"

"Is it a choice or a fear?"

"A choice," Montgomery snapped.

"Are you sure?"

"Yes."

"You're almost nineteen years old. How many nineteen year old male virgins do you think there are?"

"Plenty."

"Few—less than five percent. Almost all of that five percent have repressions from neurotic fears or stifling religious beliefs. The statistics bear that out."

"Get new statistics. The ones you have are flat out wrong."

"The Kinsey report —"

" — was flawed from the beginning," Montgomery interrupted. "The sample of men was badly skewed because one-third of the men interviewed were in prison. The sample was overly biased toward non-normative sexual persons such as homosexuals. Kinsey hired child molesters to fondle children as young as two months old. Their screams and tears were interpreted as expressions of enjoyment. The Kinsey report is trash because it is based on bad data from a skewed sample that did not represent the general population. Therefore, all of its conclusions are in error. It's useless; in fact, it's worse than useless because researchers use its errors as truth and in turn, worse errors are made."

"Yes, but —"

"But what? But other studies? They're based on Kinsey's discredited work or suffer from statistical biases, intentional and accidental, of their own. Then there's the fact that there's no way to get objective information. All research is based on surveys and interviews. When it comes to sex, people lie."

"How can you make such an assertion?"

"Forgive me, but you're naive for a grad student in psychology if you don't know that people lie about sex. For example, after the 'sexual revolution' of the 1960's, people began to believe it was fashionable to be players and have multiple partners. By the 1980's, men were reporting an average partner number in the three to four hundred range; women in the sixties. Then the AIDS epidemic hit. Sexual conquest in high numbers became unpopular; committed relationships became the vogue. Suddenly, the number of men's lifetime partners plummeted into the teens; women about three or four. You cannot account for the change in responses to surveys except by saying that people lied on at least one of the surveys, most likely both."

Brad stared at Montgomery with his mouth agape.

"When the topic is sexual behavior, the best researchers can determine is what people are saying about themselves. How close that is to the actual truth can't be determined. For you to say that I'm afraid of sexual intimacy because you have some statistics is to make an erroneous application of an unsound conclusion based on uncorroborated data. Unknowingly to make such a mistake is ignorance. Knowingly to make such an error is irresponsible, at best. It severely indicts your integrity."

"You're not afraid of your sexuality," Brad said in an effort to salvage the conversation.

"I enjoy being grown up; I enjoy the company of women. I know who I am; I know Whose I am. I have made a healthy decision that I won't engage in sexual intimacy until I'm in the commitment of marriage. That protects my body and my spirit from dangerous risks. You ask me if I embrace my sexuality? That IS my sexuality. It's great, too."

"How do you deal with urges?"

"Like everyone else, I discipline my body with my will. If humans were slaves to their urges, then crimes like rape and child molestation would have to be made legal."

"What happens at night?"

"Same thing as what happens to every man at night."

"Do you —" Brad left off.

"Do you?" Montgomery let his eyes bore into Brad's.

Brad looked at his notepad. "Let's return to your girlfriend. If she wants intimacy, don't you owe it to her?"

"Owe? You mean like a mortgage or a car loan? We have no contract."

"But if it's good for her health—for her to feel like a woman—" Brad faltered.

"Maybe you need to visit the shrew and her coven."

Brad struggled unsuccessfully to form a response.

"You're so set in your assumption that sexuality must be acted out or there's something wrong with the person that you're blind to how healthy celibacy is for the single person," observed Montgomery. "Think about it."

Brad did not respond.

"I'll take it that we have now successfully dealt with issue one," Montgomery concluded, and he let himself out.

In the frat house, Cody was examining Brendon. "How goes the campaign of subversion?"

"Really good. I've been working on her mind non-stop since I made contact in Fort Myers."

"Is that all?"

"She's frigid," Brendon lied. "She rebuffed all my suggestions. She froze up. I backed off. I'm working her slow—letting her thaw out a few degrees at a time. But I'm making inroads to cut him out."

"How so?"

"I keep pointing out how inconsiderate he is and how he lacks appreciation for her femaleness."

"Femaleness? You don't use that term with her?"

"Why not? I keep harping how she's a strong, independent woman, which is fine by me but that he hates. She believes me."

"You're overconfident. Don't underestimate the foe."

"He hasn't seen her or talked to her for three weeks."

"Above all, he is resourceful. Don't be too sure that he isn't in some means of communication. Plant the ideas in her mind—the caustic statements that will tear at his heart. He must come to doubt himself."

"I'm working as we discussed. The seeds will come to fruition."

Travis was sitting in Park's room talking with her while Rose and Elizabeth were taking a break down the hall.

"Tell me again what happened between us," he said to Park.

"We went out; we had some laughs. It was fun for both of us. Then we moved on."

"Why did we move on?

"People like us don't form deep attachments." Park shifted her legs uncomfortably. "We connect, take it for what it's worth and move on."

"How did we disconnect?"

"You pulled out, we both got what we wanted and we're done." Park sighed, "Look, if it makes you feel any better, you're the best I've ever had."

"Tell me again what happened between us."

Park looked at her nails. She looked around her room. She smoothed her skirt. She played with a pillow. Travis maintained silence; he had learned this from Montgomery.

"I'm shallow," she said at last. "I move fast and never stay long. Be shallow, Travis."

"Activity masks the loneliness; sex numbs the need for love."

"Don't think! Take what life gives you; move down the buffet line."

"Is that what we did? We moved down the buffet line; then you went for dessert while I headed for the salad?"

"There's someone else. I have a new boyfriend."

"But we split up before him. Tell me again what happened."

Park was close to tears. "Why are you doing this to me? Why are you doing it to yourself? If you must know, you started to love me. I didn't want your love. You started to dip below the surface. I didn't want a deep relationship. I want a good time. That's it. I had to pull away; you wanted commitment and I can't form a commitment."

"The truth, at last. I did want a commitment; I did want more from our relationship. I was searching for love; I wanted someone to love me. I wanted someone to love. I was missing out on the greatest part of being human, and I wanted it. My only mistake was to think I could find meaningful love in a romantic relationship."

"Right. A mistake to want love—exactly."

"No, that's not right. The type of love for which I was hungry is not the love of a woman for a man. That was the mistake—hoping for that love from you when it comes from someone else."

"Whatever are you talking about?"

"The love of Jesus Christ—that's what I was missing in life—the difference that he's made for me. He loves me, Park. I'm his. It's not a mistake to want love; the mistake is to try to find it anywhere else before finding love from Jesus. He makes me important. I may be a slug on the planet, but Jesus loves me so being a slug carries great meaning. He gives purpose to my life. My purpose is to love him back."

"So you're a monk?"

Travis laughed a hearty, good-natured laugh. "No, but now I can really love a woman because I have his love to share. I want to share it with you."

"Rose said you went religious."

"Religious is not the right word. Neither is spiritual. I now have a friendship with Jesus; he's my best friend. Even Saint Montgomery is nothing next to him. I was shallow, but I was not made to be shallow. Jesus carved deep channels within me. You are shallow, but you were not made to be shallow. Don't you want to be loved, too?"

"Travis, what you have is right for you, but for me, —" Park was moving to a brush off.

"Don't patronize me! Jesus is right for all of us, but if he isn't, then he's right for none of us. Think of me as a kook; denounce me as a fanatic. But stop being nice with the 'I'm okay, you're okay, we are different kinds of okay' bit."

"I'm not interested. I want neon lights, admiration of the masses and a handsome man in bed at the end of the evening. There—I said it. I can't be any more blunt."

A light knock sounded at the door. Park answered; it was Brendon. "Come in, honey," Park said with obvious relief. Travis was surprised to see Brendon at the girls' room.

"Guy, meet Travis, a friend from long ago."

"Guy?" said an incredulous Travis.

"Right, Guy —er— Guy Travers," said Brendon in his nervousness to find a last name to complete his alias.

"Guy Travers, Jesus loves you, Guy Travers." Travis walked to Park, and gave her a hard, closed mouth kiss. "Goodbye, Park. Think about what I said and call me when the shallow stream goes over the waterfall and a deep pool looms in your future."

"What was that about?" asked Brendon.

"Kiss me," Park replied. "No, love me."

"What do we talk about today?" asked Brad cheerfully.

"Let's tackle loner, bookish, introvert and ability to play."

"Do that."

"Come with me." Montgomery led Brad out to his truck. In the back were the quadmates: Cat, Red, Shorts, Caveman, Travis and the Ghost. The boys started whooping and hollering when they saw Montgomery appear with the counselor.

"What's going on?" asked Brad.

"You'll see." Montgomery opened the passenger door for Brad and climbed in the driver's side. Brad got into the truck reservedly. Montgomery cranked the engine. It roared to life. He turned the radio up loud. In the back, the boys hollered and beat on the cab's roof. Montgomery threw the gear into drive and pealed rubber for half a block before zooming for the out-of-town spot where the boys loved to go muddin'.

Brad grabbed frantically for his seatbelt as Montgomery left town. When Montgomery hit the mud, churning the water in the muck with his tires, Brad clenched the handhold, his knuckles turned white. Montgomery swerved the truck right and left, and cut doughnuts.

"Can we take a break?" an ashen-faced Brad asked.

"Sure," said Montgomery, pulling up on a dry spot.

Brad opened his door and gingerly set his foot on the ground. As he shifted his weight to his foot, he found his leg muscles rubbery. Even so, he wanted to get out of the truck before Montgomery decided to take off again. He looked at the back of the truck and wondered where the boys had gone.

Whap! a mud bomb hit him squarely in the face. Whap! Whap! two more hit his chest and waist. Loud laughter erupted from the darkness. Whap! Whap! Brad ducked the mud and slipped, falling on his backside. More laughter roared across the churned-up ground.

Montgomery rolled down the windows and cranked the radio to full volume. In the mud, the boys danced and hollered, throwing mud at one another but making sure that Brad caught the worst of it. Montgomery joined his quadmates in the fun.

After fifteen minutes, the boys broke for the truck. Brad was covered head to toe. Montgomery pealed out of the patch and headed for the car wash. Once again, he cranked the radio loud and the boys played a rough game of tag as they washed the truck and then one another of mud.

When all was sparkling clean, they hopped into the truck, and Montgomery raced back to campus. He pulled up to Brad's rooms and stopped the truck, idling the engine.

Brad quickly jumped out. "You made your point, Montgomery. I'll write the frat and tell them what they're doing is unnecessary and stupid. Good luck with the rush."

Chapter Twenty-One

Hazing Huntsmen

CODY SPUNG WAS SPENDING much time out of the fraternity house. Most trips took him southeast to Miami and from there to points unknown. His purpose was known only to himself. The other four members of the pledge committee believed that Cody was arranging an occupation for himself as his time to depart the campus was not far off. Rip and Pete, the graduating seniors, had made no plans for their entrance into the working world. They were too bent on revenge to worry about something as trifling as that.

With Cody gone, the committee was free to operate as they wanted. They spent their days conceiving and executing ways to harass the pledges: the six recruits, the two holdovers, and the exceptional Montgomery Lee.

"I don't care who his old man is," Pete growled one day."No pledge is going to receive a free pass for beating fraternity brothers."

Rip scowled darkly. "Do you have any ideas? The assignments were no good. He's successfully completed each one. Now we have the problem that our experts pronounce him fit for membership. How do we get rid of him?"

Jack responded, "Carefully. Why don't we organize a scavenger hunt with the pledges as the scavenge? We can bring back the paddle boards and do some damage."

Pete said, "How would that work?"

"Simple. We have nine pledges. We station them around campus and in the Glades. We send out the brothers in groups of four to find pledges and bring them back to the

house. As punishment for being found, we let the brothers whack the pledges on the butt. Then we can administer punishment as we think fit, and where we think fit," explained Jack.

Rip smiled. "We'll break a few bones on the twerp."

"Just a few?" Pete upped the ante.

"Leave me out of that," said Brendon. "You know what Cody said."

"Cody isn't here, is he?" spoke Pete emphatically.

"As I said, leave me out," said Brendon. "But the hunt is a great idea. We're letting these pledges get off too easily, even if we did recruit them for membership."

"Leave it to me," said Jack. "Let's say Saturday night."

Excitement began running high in the Sigma Omicron Beta house as the news of the hunt spread. Brothers began forming teams of four, and discussing strategy for finding the most pledges. The minority faction met to discuss strategy for protecting the pledges from the surprises they suspected the pledge committee had dreamed up. Of particular concern was Montgomery Lee.

"Their purpose is to put him in the swamp," averred Black Jack. "If the gators don't get him, they will—no witnesses around."

"Without Cody's presence, no one is smart enough to leave the kid alone," said Gravy. "If they hurt him, Harrison Lee will put them in prison for life. The frat will be closed. Everyone associated with it, irrespective of good or bad or mixed up, will forever carry a bad reputation. There's a lot riding on keeping Montgomery alive and well."

"Alive?" asked Rusty.

"You're aware of the business conducted by this house," stated Gravy.

"Delivery, mostly C.O.D. We fill the niche left by the big players when they stopped C.O.D. deliveries."

Black Jack growled. "Don't be naive, Rusty. This house is the supplier of most of the illicit drugs on campus. That's what we deliver, and why we collect cash."

"I don't know when the house first went bad," said Gravy. "It lost sight of its original purpose. It no longer believed its ideology. It was carried away by current fashions in thought, especially by a pluralism that wiped out its historic doctrines, a tolerance that allows any aberration equal status with normalcy—it even redefines aberrations as normalcy, and pays lip service to the language of the original ideals by redefining the words but failing to tell anyone who would be offended."

"Indeed," confirmed Black Jack. "Who knows how or when the snake got into the garden of God? He was there when it mattered, and he corrupted the Earth. Now we have to deal with the aftermath. Here in the house, power was obtained and is wielded by the merchants of misery. Now we deal with the aftermath."

"The drug business is full of cutthroats," said Gravy. "Men who would kill their mothers for money. We have some of those types in the house."

"Rip Tilden," Rusty shuddered. The other two nodded.

"What should we do?" asked Black Jack.

"You two form a team. Recruit a couple others who are sympathetic. I have a friend in an electronics business. He can get us some radio gear and possibly a means of keeping a trace on Montgomery. We slip a tracer in his shoe or something. I'll stay here at the house to be Central. With the radios, the four of you can split up and cover a larger area. We have to get to Montgomery first," Gravy outlined.

Black Jack nodded his head. "We find him and hide him until the night is over."

"I'm scared," said Rusty. "But I'm in—all it takes for evil to succeed is for good men to do nothing. I forget who said that."

"Burke," said Black Jack. "It was never found in his writings, but the saying is attributed to him in a number of forms."

"If your courage runs out, you still have guts," said Gravy. "Remember that the Cody Spung gang is well entrenched and has the power. They're capable of anything, especially since Pete got his shiners and Rip had his nose flattened."

Montgomery sat with Shorts on Thursday and watched Elizabeth sail across the room.

"I don't get it," Shorts said. "She gives you the silent treatment: the deep freeze. She goes around crying, saying 'Why did I have to love you?' If she does, why won't she make up?"

"This makes five weeks. I've called every day, gone by her dorm, and tried to get her to talk. I can't figure it out. I'm not sure I want to figure it out. Whatever her problem is, she won't tell me. It was our first argument. One strike and I'm out. I'm not going to last much longer. Can a guy break up by e-mail?"

"Guys break up in many ways. I've never heard of it, but I'm sure it's done. Write your message and click send. If she replies, delete without reading. It's fairly neat and quick."

"How else to bring finality to the relationship? Maybe I should ignore her and date other girls. But things should be clear, and break-ups should be clean. I love her, but she doesn't love me. She may have an infatuation she can't rid herself of, but she does not love. Love doesn't remain silent for five weeks when the other party is making efforts to communicate."

"Did you try the false apology? Apologize despite the fact you were right."

"A man can't apologize when he can't say hello. Thanks, Shorts: I've only now realized that I must end the relationship. There's no hope."

"It happens to the best of us. At least you had a girl to break up with."

"Whatever happened to the names from the mixer?"

"I went through my short list, and moved on to my long list. Bottomed out a couple weeks ago. Nothing took."

"I'm sorry."

"When you're in the frat, and chat up the sorority girls, put in a good word for me," Shorts laughed.

"Check." Montgomery spent the period mechanically taking notes, but his mind took flight into the shadows of despair where the wreckage of relationships is junked. He sighed and thought about what was and what could be. Then he remembered what is, and strengthened his resolve to make a clean break.

"The plan," said Jack as he handed out a map with nine locations marked on it. "The pledges are sent to the following locations: the stadium, the student center, The Ring, the library, block 3D of faculty housing, Natural Science's observation post, the theater, and Alyssa Hawkins dormitory—they're having an open dorm party."

"We need a ninth location," Pete noted.

"In a minute," Jack replied. "The pledges may circulate within the defined area of their location. For example, the pledge in the stadium may stand on the field, go up in the seats, or underneath to the locker rooms. They must try to avoid capture, and the huntsmen are authorized to use whatever force is necessary to subdue them. If, in the judgment of the huntsmen, the quarry fails to try to elude capture, they may punish the captive appropriately."

Pete grinned. "I like this game."

"When they take the pledge, they bring them back to the house. We'll lock them into the first floor lounge. Each team may go back out until all the pledges are captured, or the sun comes up. Undiscovered pledges are required to report to the house within one hour of sunrise. That's when we'll declare a winner: the team with the most bags. In the case of a tie, the earliest team that brought their first bag to the house wins. The prize is Janet for one week exclusive." Jack looked proud of his arrangements.

"One thing is left undone," said Rip. "What about the mongrel?"

"Mr. Lee will wait at a certain restaurant in town where we have an overextended customer who is willing to wipe the slate clean by closing earlier than normal. I have a special team to go looking for him who'll be tipped off regarding his location. This team is Rip, Pete, Cookie and Croc. Can the four of you handle him?"

"You'll not be seeing him again," said Rip.

"I want no part of it," responded Jack. "You must understand that I know nothing about how you found out where I situated him, and whatever may happen after that. I—know—nothing. Don't forget that you'll have Cody to deal with."

"Cody should worry about keeping me happy, or he should watch his back." Rip laughed nastily.

Montgomery's fingers banged on his computer's keyboard:

My beloved Elizabeth, my heart is broke as I write to you to state the obvious: we are uncoupled. How my action in helping Rick and Rose could offend you to the point you would cease acknowledging my existence, to say nothing of not speaking to me for these past several weeks, is something I will never comprehend. All that remains is to say how happy I was when we were together, and that I loved you beyond measure. You reproach yourself for loving me; yet you won't love me. What happened to love, what happened to grace, what happened to forgiveness?

We did not survive the first argument; that causes me sadness and leaves me in sorrow. I love you, Elizabeth; but I cannot suffer your silence any longer. Make that past tense—I loved you. General Stuart, your request for reassignment of orders is granted.

Gen. Lee

Montgomery read the message he had composed. His vision blurred, and he rubbed his eyes with his shoulders to blot the tears. *If I send this message, I'll die because I'll have killed any hope. Yet to linger in the certain uncertainty that I'll never enjoy her company again, or hear the sound of her voice, except by chance, is unbearable.*

Montgomery moved his mouse to position the screen's arrow over the send icon. He pushed the button, watched the icon mimic being depressed, and then the sending message appeared on the screen. It was done.

Beep! Elizabeth's computer lit up. The screen showed an animated clip of a fuzzy bunny hopping to a rural mailbox with a letter. The clip played over and over as Elizabeth ignored the signals that she had received an e-mail. She was feeling despondent. She and Park were sparring daily, and she had never patched up her quarrel with Rose from Spring Break.

Should I transfer? Should I leave school now and start over at a junior college? I wasn't ready for this; the pressures of college have ruined the best guy I ever knew and lost me my two best friends.

The door opened, and Park walked in with Guy, a/k/a Brendon. "Elizabeth? Can I have the room?"

"Again?" Elizabeth snapped. "Is this the trysting center of the universe?"

Park heaved a dramatic sigh. "Is it too much for a girl to ask for some privacy when entertaining a gentleman?"

"Stay with us," urged Guy. "Join in the excitement. It would help you to forget the mongrel who cares nothing for you."

Elizabeth regarded him with disgust. "The only thing worse than rooming with a cheap whore is becoming one." She left the room, heading for the lounge in the center of the complex. But when the night beckoned, she went out the door into the darkness.

Elizabeth wandered around the northern residential area for an hour. Then she decided to go to the Student Center and kill some time by finding something to do.

At the Student Center, nothing on the activity board caught Elizabeth's attention. She went into the game arcade to pass the time. She took the first available game she passed: Space Explorers. She put her i.d. card into the slot, and punched up a game.

"I got it!" Rusty announced in triumph. "It took some doing and some daring, but I have the plan for tomorrow night's hunt."

"Good show," said Gravy. "What's the plan?"

"They picked eight campus locations for the eight pledges who are of no concern. The ninth location is specially selected for the RMCP."

"Who?"

"Code name for our special concern. Simple precaution."

"We can't be too careful. Good thought."

"The RMCP will bivouac at a greasy spoon in town. A special detail will be sent for him. The RMCP will be ambushed. End of story."

"If we know where he is, we can watch over him."

"Short of standing guard, and betraying our espionage, watching him won't help. I have a suggestion."

"Go," said Gravy.

"Each pledge will be given a location, and instructed to stay at that location until found by a team or dawn. Either circumstance will result in the pledge being brought to the house. The pledge is allowed to move within his location, and further is enjoined to resist capture or face punishment. The huntsmen want a challenge. Here's the thing: we switch locations. We move the RMCP to one of the campus locations and move another pledge to the restaurant. The pledges will receive an envelope tomorrow night with their location in it. They won't know the other locations to keep the game fair so a capturing team can't make a captured pledge reveal where the others are. We switch the names on two envelopes. Then, Black Jack, Cooper, Dooger and I find the RMCP after allowing a decent interval so no one suspects a fix. We bring him back to the house, and stash him in an upstairs lounge. You stay with him, and we'll go back into the night. At dawn, we produce him, the game's over, and all's well. For the time being, anyway."

"Excellent plan," Gravy approved. "Do it."

"I already did. I couldn't count on getting into Jack's room again."

Gravy smiled a rare smile. "In a couple of years, I want to talk to you about a job."

Travis sang with the rest of his Christian friends on the second floor of the Student Center. He listened as a girl gave her testimony about finding Christ when pregnant, and choosing adoption over abortion. Travis marveled anew over God's forgiveness of human mistakes.

Singing a parting song of praise, the group broke up in hugs of friendship. Travis smiled, and left humming a song of praise to himself. On his way downstairs, he ran into Dunbar Edwards. "Dunbar! How's it going?"

"So-so."

"What's wrong?

"Oh, I'm at loose ends. That girlfriend of yours—"

"Ex-girlfriend," Travis corrected.

"Yeah, well, that ex-girlfriend came back from Spring Break with another guy. I thought I had something good started with her, but without so much as a farewell kiss, I became a nobody."

"Sorry, dude. But she delights in her shallowness; she actually brags about it. Come on, play Space Explorers with me. Don't wander in despair."

The two boys went into the arcade. Travis led the way over to the machine, but did not recognize Elizabeth. He laid his i.d. on the console. "Challenge for the next game."

"Take the machine; I'm through," said Elizabeth. She let the spaceship die. She collected her i.d. card from the slot.

Travis recognized her. "Fascinating."

"What is?" asked Elizabeth.

"You freeze Montgomery out for weeks, yet here you are playing his favorite game."

Elizabeth froze. Tears sprang to her eyes. "Oh, Travis," she sobbed.

Travis opened his arms wide. "Come here." Elizabeth fell into his embrace and buried her head into his shoulder. Over his shoulder, Travis said to Dunbar, "You start."

Dunbar slipped his i.d. into the game's slot, fired up a spaceship and blasted off into the far corners of the universe.

Travis took Elizabeth over to a concession area and purchased two cans of Coke. He opened a can and offered it to her. She took the can and a sip. Travis opened his Coke and took a long drink. "Whenever you're ready."

"I don't know what to say to him. He—he's too good for me."

"How so?" probed Travis gently.

"He never gets mad; he's always even-tempered. He's responsible and caring; he's mature. He makes these grown-up decisions. He always does the right thing. He can't be manipulated or seduced; he's strong. He's intelligent, too—his mind works in ways I can't understand."

"Don't talk about him; tell me why you're not good enough for him."

Tears began to flow as Elizabeth opened her mouth to speak but could not make her breath aspirate vowels into her consonants.

Dunbar caught Travis' eye. "Don't move," Travis said. "Collect your thoughts; I'll be back." Travis walked over to the game. "Do me a favor, Dunbar. Stay here but watch her. Tell me if she runs off."

"Gotcha."

Travis tore into the game. He negotiated the asteroid belts that lay between the ship's launch pad and lucrative point fields. He discovered new planets, new elements, fuel sources, and four lost colonies. He came around a yellow star and smashed into a comet. His ship died.

"Your turn," he announced before returning to Elizabeth. "Take it slow. Tell me about you. Why aren't you good enough?"

Elizabeth hung her head. She took a deep breath. "Park doesn't know that her brother raped me when I was thirteen. He was sixteen. It was during a sleepover. I was so flattered that this older boy was paying attention to me. He asked me to come to his room after the others fell asleep. I was so dumb. He made me pregnant; I gave birth to my baby on my fourteenth birthday and gave her to adopting parents."

"I'm sorry. That's a rotten thing to happen to a thirteen year old."

"I went through a lot of counseling and my parents put me in private school—actually a home for pregnant girls—until the child was born. I entered high school at the beginning of my sophomore year."

Travis waited for Elizabeth to keep talking. She, however, saw a glow in his eyes. Something was reaching out to her—drawing her out—encouraging her to open her closet of secrets.

"I thought he loved me but he betrayed me. I never allowed a boy to get that close again. Then I met Montgomery. I never knew a boy could be so wonderful. My heart felt so full—at last a man worthy of my love. Then came the awful argument. He started to do something and I told him to stop. He ignored me and kept at it. All the feelings of betrayal flashed back upon me." Again Elizabeth focused on Travis' eyes. The glow was stronger and a figure seemed to be emerging.

"I don't know what to do," she said in a low voice. "Why did I have to love that man? I've been avoiding him because I can't face him. My feelings say he defiled me—violated me—like Park's brother. My head knows that's wrong, but my feelings are controlling me. I blame Montgomery now for what Park's brother did. I can't separate the two, and that's why I'm powerless to do anything but pretend he doesn't exist." She began crying.

Travis wondered what he should do. He opened his mouth to say something, and was astonished to hear these words pouring forth, "My child, you are burdened with shame. I hate what happened to you because I love you. I made you good; I created you, and what I made you is good. I will always love you; I will never abandon you. Your sins are forgiven because I died on the cross. I took the penalty for you. I did it of my own free will because I love you. Love me too. Will you love me?"

Elizabeth shivered. On Travis' face, the glow was now shining—two bright stars anchored on a vertical beam and crossbar. She gasped. A face was emerging from the stars; the most remarkable brown eyes gazed at her with complete love. A warmth came over her. The face was bearded with strong cheekbones. The kind eyes smiled to communicate acceptance to her.

Travis' voice continued to speak, "Yes, you love me too. Believe in me for I defeated the evil powers of the world. Believe in me to share my victory. I will cleanse you and make you new. I created you, and I will recreate you whole and pure and in my image." Elizabeth's heavy burdens were being lifted from her soul; she was crying profusely. She felt innocent and complete for the first time in six years.

She whispered, "I love you and believe in you."

From Travis' mouth she heard, "Be thou clean." And she was.

"Because you love me, I am giving you someone to love you. You know of whom I speak. I want you to love him for he will be your earthly companion. This is my gift to you. I am the Lord. My name is Jesus, and I am the Christ."

The face and the glow vanished. Dunbar had come to the table to tell Travis it was his turn. His face was white and his jaw was agape as he stared. Elizabeth wiped her face with a napkin.

"That was weird," said Travis. "I heard these words in my head and I knew I was supposed to repeat them. What did I say?"

Elizabeth laughed weakly but genuinely. "You said, 'Jesus loves me.'"

"Amen to that," Travis said happily. "By the way, I'll be happy to beat the snot out of Park's brother anytime you want. That should never have happened to you, and if I had been there, it would not have."

Elizabeth smiled for the first time in weeks. "Thank you, Travis. You're a breed apart."

Dunbar spoke up. "Can someone please tell me what's going on?"

Elizabeth said, "I should go back."

Travis said, "When you get back, there will be an e-mail from Montgomery. Delete it without reading it. Trust me, delete it; don't read it. Send him an e-mail with the subject 'Let's talk.' The frat has a stupid game going on tomorrow; you'll have to wait for Sunday."

"Check," said Elizabeth. Travis grinned.

"Dunbar, let's get back to our game," said Travis. "I regret that I can't fix your girl problems, but you can take your anger out on the asteroids."

Travis took his turn on the machine. He whipped his spaceship through empty hyperspace to arrive at a distant galaxy. There he found an advanced civilization threatened by a pulsar. It was a new challenge; Travis was figuring out how to push metallic objects into planetary rings to shield the civilization when he dropped into a wormhole. He popped out in a different galaxy and before he could get his bearings something whizzed across the screen and collided with his ship. It was a comet.

"Dunbar, you're up."

Dunbar took the controls, and made his launch. He took it very slowly through wide rings of orbiting space junk. "Travis, you've dated many girls."

"That I have."

"Can you explain them?"

"Dunbar, that's not your question. Why did Park ditch me? That's your question."

"Yeah," grunted Dunbar working hard to shed a magnetic piece of junk, which was following his ship.

"According to Park, she's shallow. Take her at her word. She got what she considered a better offer."

"I might be a football star in another year or two. What's better than that?"

"Your anguish betrays you; you care for her, which to her is threatening. Don't look at me strangely—this is what she said: 'Attachment is a reason to move on. Don't say break-up because you can't break something that doesn't exist.' She's dating a big wheel at Sigma Omicron Beta."

"A frat boy? With the S.O.B.'s?"

"Right. She met him over Spring Break in Fort Myers, which is strange: What was he doing in Fort Myers? Even weirder: he's using an alias. He isn't Brendon Garrett, feared member of the powerful pledge committee; he's Guy Travers."

"It sounds shaky," said Dunbar zipping around the Sun in an effort to send the piece of junk careening into the star.

"Dunbar, my friend and study mate, true redshirt freshman, you had a few laughs, forget her. Believe you me, she's forgotten you. When she tires of Brendon-Guy, she'll find someone else. Good idea with the junk. Better blast out before it comes back."

"Yeah, you're right, Travis. Look for a new girl."

Dunbar's ship suddenly nose-dived and crashed on an alien planet. The top panel slid back and the astronaut jumped out. Before

Dunbar could react, a strange creature pounced and bit his man. His final score flashed on the screen.

"Let's go," said Travis. "Somebody else can play my last ship. Come back to my quad; we'll see who's back, and how the parties were."

"Who's this?" said Shorts in a loud voice as the two boys entered the quad. It was 12:30 a.m.

"Hey Shorts," greeted Travis. "Dunbar is a friend of mine."

"Any friend of Travish ish a friender of mine," slurred Shorts.

"Good party," said Travis.

"The besh. Fish it May Beer Barrel Blasht off. Shelebrate the splace shustle taking off."

"Get blasted for the blast-off," laughed Dunbar.

"Right," grinned Shorts. "Uh-oh. 'Scuse the leak." He went for the bathroom.

"I hope he hits the target," laughed Travis. "I wonder if anyone else is back."

It appeared not. Travis invited Dunbar to play video games, and the two boys disappeared into his room. In a moment Travis came out and got a cold beer and a sweet tea from the refrigerator.

"Have a brew," he said. "Is the roundball up?"

"Ready to go. Who do you want to play?"

"College, Kentucky, 1993."

"Thanks for the beer. I'll take Duke, 1992."

The game machine whirled and clicked. It threw up a collegiate court and the two teams on opposite sides. The screen referee tossed the ball, and the boys began to play a rapid session up and down the screen.

The score was 45-43 five minutes into the second half when the door banged open and Cat, Caveman and Red appeared in the frame.

"What's going on?" asked Travis.

The three boys giggled. Travis raised his eyebrows.

"Full moon out tonight," said Caveman.

"You've got the wrong roommate," replied Travis.

"Triple moon," added Cat.

"Avert your eyes, Dunbar," said Travis, catching on.

"Where's a wet towel when I need one?" asked Dunbar. The boys laughed.

"What did y'all do tonight?" Travis repeated.

Red said, "We paid our respects to the S.O.B.'s."

"No wonder the moons were shining," said Travis. "Dunbar, more quadmates. Cat, Red and Caveman."

Cat looked at Dunbar's open beer. "I'm thirsty."

"Coming up," said Red. "Two brews; Caveman?"

"Naw, I don't indulge; haven't you noticed?"

The three boys crowded into Travis' room. They began shouting advice to both boys as the game continued. The close contest continued into three overtime periods. At last Travis edged Dunbar with a three-pointer from the top of the key.

Travis was willing to give up his position, but the boys decided to play golf because all could play. "What course?" asked Dunbar.

"TPC at Sawgrass," said Travis. "Bring it on!"

The boys began to play as the first tee popped onto the screen. As they talked, Dunbar learned more about the group of men with whom Travis lived. They talked about their studies and majors, declared and undeclared; they described their backgrounds and hobbies. Dunbar talked about playing football; he was at school on a partial scholarship. He roomed with two other players in the players' dormitory, but he was hoping to get out next year because the other players were not compatible with his interests.

"Why don't you move in here?" asked Red.

"Housing won't process the paperwork unless there's a serious problem," said Cat.

"Yeah, with only five weeks left plus exams, I'll tough it out," Dunbar figured.

"Forget the paperwork; just move in," said Red. "The Ghost has had a room to himself all semester. Take the other bed; we'll talk to him when he comes in. Move your clothes, books and stuff over here and swing by your other place once a day for mail. You're cool; you fit in here."

"If he agrees, I'm favorable," said Travis. The other boys noted their assent.

“That would be a great blessing,” said Dunbar. “Thanks y’all.”

By Saturday morning the matter was settled. Dunbar moved in.

Saturday afternoon Montgomery sent Travis an e-mail detailing the upcoming hunt that night where the pledges were the prizes to bag: *The brothers have carte blanche to punish pledges who are too easily caught because the brothers will be the judges and the administrators.*

Travis immediately wrote back asking if Montgomery needed a guard: *I have no doubt that you can take any one of those guys. But they’re attacking in packs of four, which are more than enough to overcome any man.*

Montgomery wrote back that he believed he was safe: *They know Daddy’s investigating. Thanks for the offer.*

Travis was not convinced and discussed it with the quad. Everyone was agreed that they would keep watch, and they worked to form a plan.

In the frat, preparations were at a feverish pitch. The pledges ate a hurried supper of black beans and rice with cornbread. They dressed in dark clothing and smeared black grease on their faces and hands. Montgomery wore hunting clothes (camouflage wear) and spread green and black and brown patches on his exposed skin to break up the lines of his profile.

The teams were making preparations of their own. They had the advance knowledge of knowing that they would be operating across the campus and town. They procured ropes for trussing their captives, straps for “punishment” as they were anticipating that they would be unsatisfied with their captives’ efforts to escape, gags, blindfolds, hoods, binoculars, and flashlights.

The special ops team, as Rip and Pete had tagged themselves, were also wearing camouflage gear and had coated their exposed skin to avoid exposure to prying eyes. They carefully packed a hood, gag, rope, set of handcuffs, brass knuckles, rubber hoses, and hard rubber batons. Rip told no one but he packed a small semi-automatic pistol. Their plan was simple: head out of the frat to a local tavern at nine p.m., the starting time for the hunt. At midnight, they would go to the restaurant, subdue Montgomery and truss him with a gag, hood and handcuffs. Then they would beat him senseless.

Gravy's team decided to use all their ideas plus a few more. Unknown to Montgomery, Rusty doctored one of his sneakers with a radio beacon that Gravy would monitor at the frat house. The four men each put on a special radio transmitter with undetectable earpieces in case they were separated by circumstances. Gravy would monitor all transmissions and be in communication with the four.

Gravy told Montgomery he would not be part of the hunt and asked to borrow Montgomery's telescope to search for the comet. Montgomery assented without suspecting that Gravy would use the telescope to monitor the action from the top roof of the fraternity house.

The team knew, thanks to Rusty, that Montgomery would be hiding in the theater. There was a play that night. With luck, he would think to sit with the audience. They would wait until intermission, and whisk him away. The switch would not be known until after midnight. They planned to have Montgomery safely locked away with Gravy guarding the room well before then.

At seven o'clock, the nine pledges left the fraternity house and headed for their assigned hiding places. Not one was aware that a special fate for one of their number had been worked into the plan. They moved to their locations, and by eight o'clock were hiding in the darkness with their nerves on edge and hearts pounding. Not one entertained the idea of ditching the hunt, and going somewhere else. The threat of punishment had their attention; the stories of S.O.B. discipline were known—very well known.

Travis stayed in contact with Montgomery by e-mail, and knew that he was going to be in the theater. Montgomery had received his envelope at six p.m. as the pledges scarfed down dinner in the kitchen. Montgomery promised to contact Travis after he returned to the house.

Travis found out how Montgomery was dressing, and three of the boys had similar garb so they prepared as decoys. The other four came and took up stations around the theater watching the doors. The three decoys entered the theater. One took an empty seat in the house, one slipped into the balcony and one found a way into the backstage dressing area.

At nine o'clock p.m., Jack assembled the teams in the front room. He reviewed the rules of the hunt. He stressed that captives must be brought back to the house for the team to receive credit. Dawn, or the capture of all nine pledges was the end. Finally, he said to exact proper punishment if the pledges failed to perform well. He winked. Most of the brothers laughed.

Jack had one more surprise: clues. Each team received a different clue to the nine locations:

Team One: This is where I stand and cheer; I'm not allowed to drink my beer.

Team Two: In this place I like to gather; play a game and hear some blather.

Team Three: On my finger I do linger.

Team Four: In this nook find my book.

Team Five: What do we have in common: glasses, CAD engineering, xyz axes, space

Team Six: Look at grass as gators pass.

Team Seven: Culture and art never here part.

Team Eight: Her cousin was Sadie, I love this lady.

Team Nine: You know the drill.

The carillon sang out on the top of the nine o'clock hour. The teams hustled out the front door to begin the hunt. They fanned out to separate themselves from the pack; then they huddled to discuss their clues. Team Seven moved through the faculty housing, and went north to throw the others off their movements. Team Nine, the special ops team of Rip, Pete, Croc and Cookie went into town to their favorite tavern, and ordered drinks.

Gravy watched from the roof. He radioed Black Jack that the teams were in general confusion—more beating the bushes to see if they could flush a pledge than knowing where to look or conducting a detailed search. Rusty split off from the team and doubled back to the theater. He made a surveillance of the perimeter, and radioed that it was clear of RMCP and hunters.

Rusty entered the theater. The lobby was half lit (university energy-saving plan). Rusty looked around watching for signs of movement with his peripheral vision. It was 9:30 p.m. He looked in the men's bathroom: empty. He came out and went for the theater doors. He stepped inside and waited for his eyes to adjust to the darkness.

"Rusty to home: in theater, RMCP not spotted, out."

Gravy responded, "Roger."

Rusty walked to the side of the theater and made his way down front. He looked up at the rows of theater patrons, and spotted a young man in camouflage clothing in the mid-section.

"Rusty to home: found RMCP ..." He caught sight of the young man looking at him and pointed, then held a thumb up to signal he was a friend. The young man stared blankly and looked away.

That's odd. Rusty spotted a young man in camouflage clothing sitting in the balcony. "... negative that spot, second cam wearer in balcony, over."

"Home to Rusty: confirm two cam wearers in theater, over."

"Rusty to home: affirmative."

"Blackie to Rusty: how long to halftime, over."

"Rusty to Blackie: twenty minutes, over."

"Home to Rusty: maintain position, over."

"Rusty to home: roger, ov—I don't believe it."

"Home to Rusty: describe, over."

"Rusty to home: third cam wearer backstage, observing from wing."

"Home to Rusty: repeat order, maintain position, over."

"Rusty to home: wilco."

"Home to Blackie: move to theater pronto. Tail three cam wearers, locate real McCoy, over."

"Blackie to home: wilco."

"Home to Blackie: out."

Meanwhile, Travis had snuck inside the theater after seeing Rusty go in. He went to the balcony, and conferred. Both left the balcony for the main floor. The cam wearer slipped into the main seating and conferred with the young man there. The second one, who had spotted

Rusty, pointed him out. Travis followed the gesture from where he was and began creeping down the sidewall. The young man in the wing saw Travis' movement, and circled around to the appropriate side of the theater. The two cam wearers separated and made their way to the corner through the aisles.

"Rusty to home: Cam wearers and civilian coming at me, over."

"Home to Rusty: hold position, over."

"Rusty to home: wilco."

"Blackie to home: what gives, over."

"Home to Blackie: dunno, decoys p'raps, over."

"Blackie to home: arrive five minutes, over."

"Home to Blackie: roger, out."

"Blackie to home: out."

At the nod of Travis' head, the four boys rushed Rusty, grabbed him and melted through the aisle door into the backstage area. "Who are you?" demanded Travis in a fierce whisper.

"Rusty Mingon, Sigma Omicron Beta. I'm looking for Montgomery Lee." Rusty depressed the talk button on his radio without the other boys noticing.

"What for?" demanded Travis.

"The frat is conducting a scavenger hunt for its pledges. My team received information he was here."

"He's not here," said Travis.

"Where did he go?" asked Rusty.

"That we're not going to tell you," replied one of the cam boys.

"Then I'll maintain my position," said Rusty.

"That's not possible," said another boy.

"Why not? Why are you interfering with a harmless frat activity?" asked Rusty.

"There's nothing harmless about your frat," the first cam boy cursed.

"Who are you?" Rusty demanded.

"Travis, his roommate, and these are his friends."

"Home to Rusty: confirm Travis, over."

The boys were surprised when Rusty said out loud, "Rusty to home: Travis affirmative, over."

"Home to Rusty: let me talk to him, over."

Rusty reached up and pulled a flesh-colored dot out of his ear. He stepped next to Travis, and put the dot on his ear. He mashed the talk button and said, "Rusty to home: proceed, over."

"Travis, this is Gravy from the frat. Do you recognize my voice?"

Travis nodded. Rusty pointed to his mouth. Travis flushed, "Uh, yes sir."

"Travis, Rusty is part of a special team formed to find Montgomery first and take him out of the action so he is safe. Do you understand?"

"Yes sir."

"Travis, your boys can help. Brilliant idea—decoys. Take your positions. Do you know where Montgomery is?"

"Yes sir, he's in the —"

"Not now; show Rusty," Gravy interrupted. "Travis, you can help. When the team spirits Montgomery out of the theater, I want you to move ahead, on the sides and behind them in case another team interferes. Will you do that?"

"Yes sir," Travis answered.

"Great. We have at least one bad team out looking to hurt him bad. You are a true blue friend to look out for him; you and your friends."

"Yeah, well, Travis three, Montgomery a million. I have a long way to go to even the score."

"Thank you, Travis. Put Rusty back on."

Travis gave the earpiece back to Rusty.

"Rusty to home: on the air, over."

"Home to Rusty: everyone resume position. Wait further instructions, over."

"Rusty to home: wilco."

Rusty looked at the boys. "We're on the same side. Tomorrow we'll compare stories. For now, take your original positions. Trust me; trust Gravy and our team. Show me where the RMCP is."

Travis looked at him strangely.

Rusty cryptically explained, "The Mountie."

Travis nodded and led Rusty out the door. He pointed at the orchestra pit.

Rusty gave Travis a thumbs-up and retook his position in the front corner. He noted that the other boys had found their places as well. Rusty motioned to Travis to stay with him.

"Rusty to home: all in position, roomie with me, over."

"Home to Rusty: roger, out."

"Blackie to home: at theater, wait instruction, over."

"Home to Blackie: join forces with homeys, balcony, floor, wing, over."

"Blackie to home: wilco."

"Blackie to Rusty: identify, over."

"Rusty to Blackie: southeast corner of main floor, over."

"Blackie to Rusty: roger—whoa! Blackie to Home: 911. Two teams converging on theater, over."

"Home to Blackie: spotted teams; neither special ops. Tip-off suspected. New orders: hide in strategic locations. Tail the teams. Blackie, you get to RMCP and stay with him, over."

"Blackie to home: wilco." Blackie directed Cooper and Dooger into places where they could tail the teams away or into the theater. He quickly jumped up the steps and went into the building. Blackie moved stealthily but quickly. He reached Rusty and was shown Montgomery's location. He went backstage and went into the basement and entered the pit from below. He saw Montgomery sitting among the woodwinds in the back row. Blackie went up, tapped his shoulder and held his finger to his lips. "I'm with the good guys." Montgomery nodded.

Intermission arrived as the two teams were entering the theater. The decoys rose with the people and mingled through the crowd.

"Coop to home: third team in ambush outside the building, out."

"Home to coop: roger, out."

"Home to Rusty: over."

"Rusty to home: over."

"Rusty, get the decoys to lead the teams out and away from the theater, over."

"Rusty to home: wilco."

Rusty sent Travis to put the plan into operation. Travis reached the first boy, and engaged in an animated scene with him. His quadmate winked, and fled toward the lobby bathroom. One team closed in on him from the rear.

Travis sent the balcony decoy onto the main floor toward the northwest emergency exit. The decoy reached the door, breached the seal and fled into the night. The emergency alarm went off and the theater lights began flashing. The second team tore after the decoy through the breached door.

By this time, Rusty had attracted the attention of the stage decoy and motioned him to the lobby. Upon gaining the lobby, Travis joined up with him and went out the front door. Upon reaching the pavement, the decoy sprinted up the street. The third team sprang out of hiding in pursuit.

Travis called the other three boys from their perimeter observation posts. They went into the theater. Travis checked out the bathroom; an exterior window was open. He smiled and shut the window.

The boys entered the theater as overhead speakers began to squawk, "Do not use the emergency doors to exit the building. It was a false alarm. Do not use the emergency doors to exit the building. It was a false alarm. Please resume your seats for the second act."

The crowd re-entered the theater unaware of the second drama playing out in the theater. In the orchestra pit, the musicians resumed their seats and began tuning their instruments. Black Jack pulled Montgomery into the bowels of the building. "Be ready to move," he whispered. "When I get the signal."

The orchestra launched into the prelude. The people applauded. The actors began taking their places on stage. As the orchestra reached the end of the piece, the curtain began to rise. Act two began.

"Rusty to home: over."

"Home to Rusty: over."

"Rusty to home: are we clear for move? Over."

"Home to Rusty: negative. Too much activity, over."

"Rusty to home: what now?"

"Home to Rusty: sit tight. Estimate of forces requested, over."

"Rusty to home: enemy negative. Us two plus four allies, decoys gone, over."

"Home to Rusty: theater clear outside. House two teams with bags arriving. Stay there, over."

"Rusty to home: wilco."

"Home to Rusty: out."

The actors kept the play moving along. Thirty minutes went by. Suddenly the radio crackled to life.

"Home to team: move out, repeat move out. Now, over."

"Blackie to home: on the move with RCMP, out."

"Rusty to home: covering rear, out."

"Coop to home: converging with Blackie, out."

"Doog to home: covering left flank, out."

"Rusty to home: allies on front and right flank, out."

"Home to team: roger all. Home front clear. Direct route clear. Avoid student center and town, over."

"Rusty to home: roger that. Out."

"Home to Rusty: out."

Gravy now spent ten nervous minutes waiting for the team to carefully bring Montgomery to the house. He felt better when he could see them approaching the fraternity. Then he saw something moving.

"Home to Rusty: over."

"Rusty here, over."

"Home to Rusty: use back gate, back door, back stairs, over."

Rusty to home: wilco."

The team moved around to the rear of the Sigma Omicron Beta property via the backyards of other houses in Little Greece. Black Jack opened the gate and entered the yard. He motioned the others in. Rusty, Coop, Doog, Travis and the other three quadmates accompanied Montgomery into the compound. They moved inside and went up the back stairs to the lounge.

Gravy was already there. He held up a hand to keep them from talking. "We are not done yet. Rusty, Blackie, Coop and Doog, go back out and good hunting. It's almost 11:30 p.m. In approximately thirty-five minutes, the switch will be discovered. I want to keep surveillance on the roof. Stay in contact by radio. Travis, spare the introductions. Y'all stay here with Montgomery until this thing is over sometime tomorrow morning. I'm locking y'all in; here's a spare key if y'all have to get out. I changed the lock this afternoon; no one else has a key. Be alert, be quiet. Don't let anyone know y'all are here." Gravy went out the door and turned his key in the lock.

"Whoa," said Travis. "Welcome to the Devil's Lair, boys."

Cat sat down. "Anybody got a beer?"

The Ghost said, "You people take your hazing seriously."

Shorts said, "Only for you Monkey; only for you."

Montgomery looked confused. "I feel like I've been spirited out of communist China. What gives?"

"You, of all people, know the cutthroats who populate this house," said Travis. "Don't you think it possible that they staged this game for payback time?"

"They've been running around with their tails between their legs scared of my Daddy who is investigating them. They wouldn't have hurt me."

"Guys like Rip don't care about your Daddy," said Travis. "If he gets his revenge, he will gladly go to his death."

The thought sobered Montgomery. He let out a big breath, "What have I gotten myself into?"

Two pledges were in, Montgomery was hid, and the teams were out hunting more game. Some of the teams had deciphered their clues; team one was running through the stadium seeking their quarry. Team four was methodically combing the library. Team three was arguing over how to search The Ring without the pledge slipping behind them.

Midnight arrived. On the roof, Gravy watched as Rip, Pete, Croc and Cookie left the bar and walked down the street to a restaurant. They went inside.

Streetlight fell into the darkened room. Rip motioned Pete to the kitchen. Croc went behind the cashier stand. Cookie looked in the bathrooms. There was a clash of pans and dishes falling to the floor.

The kitchen door burst open and Pete came out holding the pledge by the back of his neck collar.

"Got him," Pete sang out.

"Good," said Rip. The four members of the special ops team gathered around the pledge.

"I tried to get away, honest I did," the pledge stammered. "Don't hurt me."

"Who is this?" screamed Rip. He flashed a light into the pledge's face. "This isn't the mongrel! Wait till I see Jack."

Pete cursed too. "Where's the mongrel?" he asked the pledge.

"I don't know; they didn't tell us where everyone was going. My envelope said to come here. I've been waiting for someone to show since eight o'clock. Please don't hurt me."

Pete grabbed the envelope and tore it open. Inside was the slip of paper that named the restaurant and gave the street address.

"Jack wouldn't sell us out," he said. "If he did, the cops would be here. The papers were switched before they were given out. One of the punk's friends anticipated us and located the punk someplace else. They have him safely stashed someplace. Let's get out of here."

Rip's face was murderous. "Now there's two for me to take out."

Croc spoke up. "Don't talk like that in front of us. Be smart."

Cookie said, "Grab the pledge and let's go. So we missed administering a beating tonight. He's not free; we'll make the punk pay another time. I want to get drunk. I have 101 proof whiskey in my room: a half gallon which should last us all night."

Pete asked, "What should we do with the pledge?"

Cookie replied, "Take him with us so we don't look like chumps coming back empty."

Rip was pacing back and forth in a fury.

Cookie opened the front door and stepped onto the sidewalk.

Pete was following as Croc turned to address Rip.

The pledge spoke. "Thank you for not hurting me."

It was the wrong thing to say. With a roar, Rip slammed the pledge against the wall. The pledge's head hit the painted concrete block with a loud crack. Blood splattered everywhere. The pledge crumpled onto the floor.

"What did you do?" Croc asked in horror.

Pete sprang back into the room. He pulled the pledge's body away from the wall. The boy's skull was cracked on the side. Pete profaned the name of the Lord. "You killed him."

Rip was calm. He turned to Croc. "Leave. Now. You saw nothing. You and Cookie left Pete and me with the pledge alive and well. Understand?" Rip glowered at Croc.

"Yeah, Rip, I got it," Croc said.

"Make sure Cookie knows," Rip said menacingly.

Croc left the place and let the door slam.

"Grab a tablecloth," Rip said. "We need to dump the body."

Pete's eyes widened in shock. "This is out of my league, Rip. We need to come up with a good story and call 911 before the time of death trips us up."

"Do exactly as I tell you and keep your mouth shut. No story, no 911, the pledge left the joint with us and ran off. Period. Now let's wrap up the gator bait and wash the wall and floor. Then we dump the body in the Glades. Got it? Boy disappears—it happens. Distraught comrades don't know why. Pledge committee says he was having trouble. Everyone figures he got spooked and ran off. File gathers dust in the Missing Persons Bureau. End of story; there is no story as long as the gators are hungry." Rip laughed viciously.

Pete felt freezing fear slicing through his body. *How can I be a part of this? I'm an accomplice to murder. Even a half-competent prosecutor could make me a co-conspirator subject to the same penalties as the killer himself. There I am: being strapped into a chair with wires being attached to my arms, legs, chest and head; an arm reaching up for a lever, the lever moving down ...*

"Snap out of it!" Rip snarled. "Help me."

Pete shook all over. *How can I not be a part of this? Rip would kill me as easily as he killed the pledge.* Pete pulled a tablecloth off a table and began to wrap it around the body. Rip had mopped up the blood, and was using cleaning chemicals to wash the stained surfaces.

Pete found some plastic wrap in the kitchen and wrapped the body like a mummy so it would not spill blood when they removed it.

About 3 a.m. the two men left the restaurant. They carried the body through alleys and shadows, crossed the drive and entered the Everglades. They waded through ankle deep water, pushing through the sawgrass until they were five miles out from town. They dropped the body and moved back to town.

"Not one word," said Rip.

Gravy had watched the two men leave the restaurant carrying something. He did not realize what had taken place. Croc and Cookie were in Cookie's room getting rip-roaring drunk hoping the alcoholic haze would blot out the memory forever, drunk or sober.

More pledges were brought in. The stadium quarry, The Ring pledge, and the library pledge were in the house by the time Rip and Pete dumped the body and started back to town. Five pledges in, two pledges out, Montgomery in hiding and one dead.

No one figured out the remaining two clues or came across the pledges. The Alyssa Hawkins pledge grew bored after the dance was over, and came back on his own at four a.m. Frustrated or tired teams began returning to the house. The ink of the night began to dilute to purple. Gravy called his team in, and released Montgomery into their care. They took him downstairs; no one was wiser.

Travis led his quadmates out of the house and off the property.

The sun rose—it was Sunday morning. A cold and stiff pledge limped his way through the streets and entered the house. Everyone was exhausted. Jack was still up. According to his tally, Team Six made two bags, the only team to catch more than one. Most of the members had crashed on available sofas. Most of the members were sound asleep.

"Team Six wins," Jack said. No one applauded. The hunt was over.

Chapter Twenty-Two

Exam Ringers

ELIZABETH CAME TO SEE MONTGOMERY Tuesday afternoon. They left the frat house and walked down the street of Little Greece away from prying eyes and listening ears. Elizabeth asked Montgomery to listen and not talk until she was done. She talked of her childhood and of her early experiences. She talked of her friends, and the fun times they shared. She talked of their girlishly innocent sleepovers.

"But one night it changed. I was only thirteen. Park's brother was older. At sixteen he was a man of the world to my naive mind. He was bold and strong; I was fascinated. He would break into our silly girlish doings, flex his muscles or take his shirt off and ask how to wash it. He started paying attention to me, saying things to make me laugh and making special gestures to me. I thought I was hot. On a trip to the kitchen, he asked me to come to his bedroom after the others fell asleep. I was so bowled over I agreed.

"That night in his room he was lying in his bed. As I came in, he got up and came over and kissed me. I had many confusing feelings inside. I thought I was grown up, I had these feelings of desire at the same time I was confused and scared. I thought I was only a baby and I shouldn't be in his room. He locked the door. He led me to his bed and began telling me wonderful things: I was grown up, I was ready to be a woman, don't I want initiation into womanly ways. I nodded yes. It was then that I noticed he was naked.

"He pulled my nightie off my shoulders. I said no. He only smiled and continued to pull. It ripped. I went to scream but his hand was over my mouth. I was scared. He pulled the garment away from my body and forced me to lie on the bed. I began crying. He pushed my legs apart. I cried harder as he shoved himself ... It was over in five minutes.

"When I opened my eyes, he was grinning. 'There's more where that came from, kiddo,' he said. I wanted to run but he put his arm over me holding me in place. He did it two more times before he let me go. 'Tell anyone,' he said, 'I'll deny it. They'll never believe you. Besides, I love you. This is our secret.' I was so dumb I believed him.

"Then my belly started to grow. I was pregnant with his child. My parents were angry but dealt with the situation. They put me in a 'girl's school' where I worked in my classes until I had my baby. The baby was adopted. I received counseling at the school where I came to terms with the rape, the confused feelings, being a mommy and not being a mommy at fourteen, and understanding my feminine sexuality.

"I re-entered normal life and my regular school for my sophomore year. I had successfully put it all behind me, or so I thought. I came to college and met the most wonderful boy I had ever known. He—you were everything that Park's brother was not. I fell in love with you from the moment I met you. It's no accident we were taking Western Civilization together; I changed my schedule.

"All was well until you pushed Rick and Rose into talking about marriage. I thought it was a mistake. I told you to stop. But you went ahead. The confusing feelings returned in greater strength. I felt violated again. I transferred my feelings toward Park's brother, who ignored me after that night, onto you. It wasn't your fault. But I couldn't help it. I was so upset I couldn't speak to you; I couldn't bear to see you."

Elizabeth stopped speaking. They walked in silence.

"What changed?" asked Montgomery.

"Jesus took away my shame. He cleansed me of my past, and made me new. He has forgiven me, and now I ask for your forgiveness. Will you forgive me?"

"Absolutely," said a tearful Montgomery. "I'm in love with you, also. I'm sorry that I didn't know. I love you, Elizabeth Stuart. Do you love me?"

"I love you with my whole heart and entire being."

The feelings of separation, confusion and anxiety dissolved between the two. Montgomery opened his arms and pulled his sweetheart to him. They hugged for a long time, and resumed their walk holding hands. An animated conversation ensued. They had two months to catch up.

Back at the frat house, Cookie and Croc were in no condition to take their exam in American Civics. They began checking to see who might sit in for them and take the exam. Pete called the pledges together in a Friday meeting.

"Part of the fraternal experience is brothers looking out for other brothers. Two of our brothers need help in a class. Who's willing to help?" asked Pete.

The pledges looked at one another. With the exception of Montgomery, they were mediocre scholars, at best; they looked to the fraternity to help them, not the other way.

"What's the class?" asked Montgomery.

"Ah, Montgomery, you study well, thanks for volunteering," said Pete.

Montgomery was instantly suspicious because Pete used his first name, and secondly because he didn't order him, but characterized him as a volunteer. "You didn't say what the class was. I cannot volunteer to help unless you tell me what the subject is."

"Civics: high school level; these two guys aren't mental giants. They're majoring in remedial education."

Montgomery's feelings of discomfort intensified as Pete showed disrespect for members in front of pledges. "I've been studying Western Civ, not American politics and government. But if I can help prep—who are they, anyway?—I will."

"Your assistance is appreciated. You'll earn points with us toward admission."

"Who are they?" repeated Montgomery.

"Cookie and Croc."

"That's a tall order. Why don't you hack the computer and fix their grades?"

"We remain in a never-ending race to be one step ahead of new security measures. The old-fashioned way is better except in cases of extreme emergency."

"Cookie and Croc are an extreme emergency. Their minds are less than nimble. You believe they can cram enough into their brains to make it through their exam?"

"I believe that you can cram enough into your brain to get them through their exam."

"What good would that do?" I'm not taking the test—" Montgomery broke off. *I am taking the test: going to the exam and pretending to be one of the deficient scholars.* "No—negative. I'll tutor them and work with them, but I won't take the exam for them."

Pete sighed. "Why do you never cooperate?"

"Why do you always cheat? Why are you even here? You care nothing for learning or a degree. Why the charade? Wouldn't it be easier to buy a house in town to run your couriers? Why take over the fraternity?"

"Why must you always confront us?" Pete asked sadly. "The other brothers who are like you don't give us any trouble; they lay low. Why can't you? Haven't you been hurt enough? Why are you calling down trouble upon your head, and upon us all?" He choked.

Montgomery stared at him. Pete was about to break down into sobs. *Something happened during the hunt; I'm sure of it. Pete's team has changed; they're in great fear of Rip, who hasn't been seen much since that night.*

"I will not take exams for others. I'll help tutor anyone in the house to prepare and study, but they have to take the test themselves."

Montgomery began to leave.

"Montgomery," Pete called, "I'm sorry about everything. Please understand: I'm sorry about everything."

Montgomery left without saying a word.

"Right," Pete said briskly. "I need two volunteers."

Montgomery walked down the stairs and went into the kitchen. Gravy was sitting in his usual chair at the table reading a book. Montgomery took a Coke out of the refrigerator and popped the lid. He moved to the table and sat down.

Gravy marked his place in the book and set it down."I didn't think it possible, but the house has exceeded its previous level of weirdness," Montgomery began. "I thought last Saturday night was a fun game; y'all and my whole quad react like the Communists are going to shoot me at dawn, and stage a commando raid to spirit me back to the house keeping me guarded and hidden until the night is over. Pete and Rip form a team; the two brothers on their team return from the hunt and haven't been sober since. Rip is keeping a low profile, not blustering and threatening as usual. We have a missing pledge. Pete has also dropped his aggressive posture, lives in great fear of Rip, and has apologized to me, in his words, 'for everything.' He's asking for volunteers; not giving orders. People have changed; why?"

Gravy's face was impassive.

"You know something; I know you do."

"I cook, I work on my graduate degree, and this year I watch over you. If you knew the true nature of the men you confront, you wouldn't go around asking questions. You persist in pledging when you know these men want you to go away. I admire your persistence but question your sense. You have done much simply in persisting, but the house is much more dangerous than it was last fall. Go back to your quad; you have great friends. You'll find a better place among them."

"Thank you for your advice. And for everything else you've done for me. But I'm sticking it out." Montgomery drank a swallow from his Coke.

Gravy was silently praying he would not see Montgomery's body wrapped in a shroud being taken into the Everglades by Pete and Rip to dump.

CHAPTER TWENTY-THREE

HURRICAN ALAN

BLACK JACK came down the stairs, entered the kitchen and snapped on the television set that sat on top of the refrigerator. The tube warmed up, and a nineteen-inch face filled the screen.

"Mallard Swanson, our certified meteorologist has our top story tonight: Hurricane Alan bears down on Florida." The logo for the station's newscast came on with music. The faces of the six o'clock news team assembled in a montage, and faded to the actual faces on the set.

"Mallard, what's on tap?"

"Tap is the right word. Rain, lots of it, will soak southern Florida as our first hurricane of the year moves across the peninsula. Fortunately, it will be a weak hurricane although that still means sustained wind speeds of 73 miles per hour or higher. The thinking at the National Hurricane Center in Coral Gables is that the storm will hit Fort Myers with sustained winds in the eighties—a minimal hurricane—with heavy rains in the next 36 to 48 hours. Precipitation is predicted around twelve to fifteen inches of rain as the storm drags across land."

"It's unusual to see a hurricane this soon, isn't it?"

"Yes, but not unknown. We've had hurricanes form in every month of the year, although the season of June 1 to November 30 is when most of them come. We watched this one form in the Caribbean off the South American coast, scoot around the west end of Cuba and linger on its path toward us. When it hits land, it will disintegrate to a tropical storm which is good to keep damage from wind at minimal levels, but tropical storms tend to drop more rain than hurricanes so flooding is a major concern."

"What should people do regarding preparations?""Our viewers should check on their hurricane supplies and make sure they have plenty of everything on hand: fresh batteries, fresh water stored in jugs: a gallon per day per person including pets, radio, canned food and such items. Bring in all outdoor furniture, and anything else that is not firmly attached to the ground. Evacuations will most likely be unnecessary unless you live in a low-lying area prone to flooding in heavy rains."

"The storm will begin to affect us when?"

"Tomorrow night the first rains should begin. The day after tomorrow will be the worst of it."

"Thanks, Mallard. Our top story: Hurricane Alan Knocking at our Door. More news after this commercial break."

Animated conversation broke out in the kitchen following this news report. It was picked up in the dining room and predictably, the fraternity began talking about a hurricane party.

Jack winked at Brendon, and mouthed the word, "Football."

Brendon grinned and caught Pete's eye and repeated Jack's action, "Football."

Pete stared at the table. He had not been himself since the hunt. In fact, he was badly rattled. He lived in fear that Rip might eliminate witnesses. *Why hadn't I insisted upon calling 911 so we could pass the death of Rho off as an accident? The last three weeks should have calmed my nerves as the house accepted the explanation that Rho had bugged out and quit the frat that night. I packed up the boy's belongings and personally tailed the collection truck to know that the things were now buried in the landfill.*

Pete had no reassurance from Rip. Rip kept a very low profile, taking most of his meals in his room or leaving the house altogether. Pete had tried to talk to him a few times, but Rip only glared and threatened him with bodily harm if he mentioned the incident to anyone. Every time Pete saw a policeman, campus security officer or police car, he started and trembled.

These changes in Pete and Rip, also Croc and Cookie who now were never sober, did not escape the sharp eyes of Gravy and Black Jack. They conferred once a day on what they were finding out. Black Jack was tracking Rho, whose real name was Michael Miller Gee, through his campus classes and residence. Gravy was working inside the house to find out more about what had happened that night, and what Pete and Rip had taken to the Glades.

To date, they had established the disappearance of Rho, but it seemed only Pete and Rip knew what happened. Gravy was working on Croc and Cookie to open up, but had not been successful. Gravy's strong suspicion was that Rho had died in the restaurant, and his body was the bundle Pete and Rip had taken to the Glades. But he couldn't ascertain the truth of his hunch because evidence and eyewitnesses were not forthcoming.

Montgomery watched these goings-on as well. He kept his ears open, and knew something was very wrong. But if Gravy could not crack the puzzle, Montgomery was less able. He concentrated on his classes, his cooking, and his girlfriend. Montgomery was happy about one thing: whatever had happened during the hunt, it had spooked the pledge committee. Their hazing was half-hearted at best; they left him alone.

Montgomery found this turn of events welcome. His experience on the hunt had rattled him: no less than twelve young men spent twelve hours dedicated to one thing—protecting him. He felt his vulnerability keenly: *was I the pledge who was supposed to disappear?* He kept his suspicions to himself, but as he thought back over his two fights with the pledge committee, he was filled with marvel and fear.

Cody was an infrequent visitor to the house. He was angry about the hunt, and dragged the full story out of Rip. Cody made the decision to be rid of Rip. He had larger ambitions now, and was establishing himself with Miami gangsters who moved a large chunk of the narcotics that entered the nation through Florida ports. He couldn't afford to have an unpredictable cutthroat attached to him. Cody did nothing at present; it would be easier to dispose of Rip after graduation, unless he proved a useful sacrifice should the body of Rho be discovered.

Cody's plan was to put the house into the hands of Jack. He was disappointed in Brendon who had misled him about the assignment to move on Montgomery's girlfriend. Brendon had started dating the roommate, not the girlfriend. He had been able to sow seeds of doubt and turmoil, but he should have been upfront about the change of plan.

The next day the pledges and brothers worked to secure the house and property against wind and rain damage. Excitement was running high; the promise of a hurricane party was enticing as classes were cancelled for the next day.

Rain began falling as night arrived. Montgomery was with Elizabeth. Their relationship had strengthened once they had resolved the quarrel and the circumstances of Elizabeth's behavior after the quarrel. They were more deeply in love than before.

Montgomery walked Elizabeth back to her room. At the door, they paused to exchange a passionate kiss. They left off when the door unexpectedly opened. Both stepped back as Brendon-Guy came out the door. "I'll see you tomorrow night, then," he said to Park as he left. He had not seen Montgomery.

Montgomery looked puzzled. "That's strange."

"Who—him? I hate that guy—Guy."

"Guy-guy? What's a guy-guy?"

"No, that guy named Guy. We met him on Spring Break. Ever since then, he's been Park's lover. Real trash which is what he's turned Park into."

"His name is Brendon, not Guy. He's one of the jerks on the pledge committee at Sigma Omicron Beta."

"Are you sure? Maybe they look alike."

"No way. Those faces are emblazoned on my memory. I would know them anywhere. That is Brendon Garrett, tormentor and scum-bucket."

"Since he attached himself to Park, he's also shown a great interest in my life, particularly you and I. He has never failed to tell me how rotten you are, and how good he is. I thought him immoral and unprincipled to hit on me while he was sleeping with my roommate, but maybe they sent him to cause trouble between you and me. That's funny; I did well on that score without his help."

"My only concern is that they don't do it now."

"They have no chance—no hope," murmured Elizabeth nuzzling Montgomery's neck.

"Do we tell Park?" he asked, stroking her hair.

"Park isn't receptive to negative news. She'll only deny it. We aren't the same girls who arrived in Florida last August with dreams of academic achievement. Park and I are distant now. I doubt we'll room together next year."

"I'm sorry. Y'all have been friends for a long time."

"It was bound to happen. Our morals aren't the same. Sooner or later one of us was bound to lash out at the other. I'm sorry it was me, but I'm tired of finding places to go because Park's having a tryst. It's almost nightly."

"Are you unhappy because we don't—?"

"I'm content to wait. We don't have to have sex in our relationship to love each other as well as we do. That's where we differ from Park."

"I'm still committed to the idea of marriage before sex as part of my Christian lifestyle. What's happened to Travis has convinced me even more that I'm right to hold out. He's so regretful over his history."

"I'd like to know more. I've been an indifferent Christian. I'm wondering whether I should seek more. Ever since that night before the hunt, ..." She told Montgomery about her experience with Travis.

"Definitely. Start coming to church with me."

"Maybe we can also check out this Friday night group that Travis hangs with."

Montgomery kissed his girlfriend yes. He kissed her goodbye. Reluctantly the two young people said goodnight.

Storms lashed the windows and roof of the fraternity house overnight. As the young men in the house rose to greet the day, a steady downpour was falling. The party went into full swing. Someone had brought in several half-kegs of beer, and the first was tapped with breakfast.

By noon, most of the people in the house were half-drunk. With a giggle, Jack announced to the pledges that they were going out to play football in the rain. The rain had slackened in midmorning, but picked up again in the afternoon.

"All you need is your jockstrap," said Brendon.

"You have uniforms for us to wear?" asked Montgomery.

"You wear a jockstrap, nothing else. That's the fun of it."

Montgomery flushed with embarrassment at being outside and being so exposed. The other pledges laughed and hollered. It sounded like great fun to them.

"We assemble in fifteen minutes," said Jack.

Montgomery thought about not playing. But he also considered the consequences of refusing. *I might win admission to the house if I go along, and that would enable me to begin a campaign of reform. I might lose the support I've been building if I refused. But it's wrong, plus I'll feel ashamed to be undressed outdoors. Still, there's safety in numbers, and in the hurricane, no one will be out to see us.*

The pledges assembled in the familiar lounge where their activities were conducted or begun. Montgomery was beginning to associate every mark, every stain, every burn and every hole in the floor, walls, ceiling and furniture with a nasty hazing action inflicted by the pledge committee. The Hall of Shame he dubbed it.

Jack met the pledges in nothing but his jockstrap. The anxiety of the pledges that this might prove another bad surprise evaporated. Jack led the eight boys across the fields to the stadium. As the boys came onto the turf, already drenched by the rain, they groaned at the sight of ten fraternity members dressed out in full pads and cleats.

Jack laughed nastily. "The game is tackle, gentlemen. Regular rules. We'll kick off."

Jack joined the other ten and donned the pads, cleats and uniform they had for him. With a low kick, they began the game.

Pledge Nu fielded the ball and immediately lateralled. The ball squirted erratically on the soaked grass. Howard Libbell, a/k/a Epsilon, jumped on the ball. The fraternity members piled on mercilessly.

Montgomery quarterbacked. He knew that eleven on eight meant a fierce rush was coming. He took the snap and handed off to pledge Xye who threw a halfback pass into the arms of Brendon. Brendon took off for the end zone and scored.

On the ensuing kickoff, the ball squirted across the ground to Mick's feet. He had received a new injection and was dreamily contemplating the ball as the brothers came pounding at him. Montgomery pushed him out of the way and took the full brunt of the hit. Mick was dazedly looking at Montgomery as if he was a ghost he could see through.

Montgomery tried to get the defense organized, but it was apparent that the pledges were drunk, disorderly and concerned with staying away from the ball. He found out that getting tangled up with a blocker meant doing a fast dance on the field to avoid being stomped on the feet by their cleats.

Montgomery also tried to work the offense, but the same problems hampered his efforts. The pledges were playing a game of "hot potato": immediately handing off the ball whenever they received it, or throwing a pass or tossing a lateral. This happened regardless of the direction of the ball movement, or where they were in regard to the line of scrimmage.

The opposition was laughing too hard at the pledges to call penalties whenever their frantic efforts made an infraction of the rules. Their own state of non-sobriety also led to many errors on their part so that the score built up slowly. An hour later, when a halftime was called, the score stood at 35 to 7, fraternity leading.

During halftime, the fraternity members huddled under a ramp drinking beer and smoking marijuana. Montgomery sat on the sideline in the rain wondering how much longer this game was going to last. The other pledges sidled over to the frat members, and by begging and abasing themselves, were able to keep their state of non-sobriety at its game-beginning level.

The game efforts became worse, if anything. Nobody was paying much attention to the ball or playing regulation football. The padded players launched themselves at the pledges, knocking them to the turf and smearing them in the mud. The football was tossed from player to player without concern for keeping possession for their side. The meaningless score was forgotten as players scored for opposite sides and committed general mayhem.

The downpour grew harder as the afternoon wore on. Montgomery wondered if the center of the storm had stalled off the Gulf coast and was pumping water into the clouds it was sending over the land. The grey light steadily deepened and visibility became less. After another hour had gone by, the players called it quits. They came over to the pledges and congratulated them on their play—complimenting them as worthy of Sigma Omicron Beta.

"Nobody saw us," said a thankful Montgomery.

To his horror, he heard giggling and laughing from a sheltered part of the sidelines. Hiding behind a barrier were several girls: one holding a video camera wrapped in plastic.

Jack grinned. "Hurricane days are recorded for the frat's permanent archives. Besides, the other brothers want to see how well you played."

The girls came running over. Montgomery was disgusted to see that Janet was leading them. "Hi, boys," she giggled. Montgomery looked at their eyes and from the dilation realized that they were high. "Thanks for the show." Janet laughed hard.

Montgomery instinctively covered himself with his hands. The other boys had backed away. He saw something flash, and heard the snap of scissors as Jack, Brendon and Pete cut the jockstraps off three of the pledges.

"Woo woo!" screamed the girls. One grabbed at a boy's crotch. He jumped back, then turned and fled. Snap! snap! snap! Three more pledges stood stark naked on the field. The last pledge decided not to wait. He tore his jockstrap off and threw it into the air. The six boys danced around the others several times, whooping and yelling, before trotting toward the fraternity house.

That left Montgomery who was standing frozen to his spot on the field. He hadn't the presence of mind to escape when that was still an option.

"No, don't," he said, but Jack paid him no mind. Snap, snap! and Jack pulled away his covering.

"Let's see what you got," growled an aggressive Brendon who pulled an arm away from his front. Pete grabbed the other arm, and they held him there for inspection.

Janet had a big grin on her face. "I like what I see." She moved forward as a couple of members helped Pete and Brendon wrestle Montgomery to the ground.

Montgomery fought his handlers, but their grip was strong and he could not budge their combined weight. Janet went down on her knees and straddled Montgomery's legs.

Montgomery closed his eyes and willed his body not to react. But an eighteen-year-old boy's body, primed with a high level of hormones, has a mind of its own when faced with such stimulation. Montgomery felt himself react, and Janet's violation of his body.

Montgomery clamped hard with his abdominal muscles to stop his body from cooperating. He fought desperately as he might on a long car trip with thirty minutes to go to the next bathroom. But his body took over. He began to shudder all over as Janet over stimulated his nerves. Janet lifted her head in triumph when Montgomery lost the battle. The boys cheered and slapped high fives. The girls giggled. Janet laughed with deep pleasure.

"I'm losing my buzz," she said. "Let's go."

They left Montgomery lying on the field as they walked back to the frat house to smoke more marijuana and indulge their own passions, which had been aroused by watching Janet's oral rape of Montgomery.

Montgomery lay on the field and cried. He felt horrible and disgusting. He had kept something pure and precious for the greatest love of his life as a present on their wedding night. Now some common tramp had stolen it from him, and he would never have it back. He vented his complaint to heaven: *Why? You asked to me to pledge—why this? Why me?*

He heard no answer. He raged against a Divine Power that would set him up for this and then withdraw from him because of it. He sobbed and wailed. The heavy downpour muffled his cries as it washed away his tears and the evidence of the crime.

It occurred to Montgomery after the passing of a quarter hour that he would do well to find clothes before someone else saw him in this condition. He rose to his knees and remained motionless for several minutes. The shock of the violating disrupted his sense of time and motion. Suddenly he burst to his feet as a sprinter leaving the chock blocks for a race. He ran as fast and hard as he was able off the field and up a ramp that led to the outside of the stadium.

Officer Patrick Downey was slowly patrolling the streets of Bacon looking for flooding, vehicles in distress, downed utility lines and the like. He looked at the stadium and was amazed to see what looked like a naked figure sprinting up a ramp and into the rain. Officer Downey pulled over to the curb.

Montgomery had decided to run for his truck and put on a pair of shorts or swimming trunks he kept in his locker. He never locked the chest and he was on a dead run so he would not be caught in his naked condition. He was too humiliated to return to either the frat house or his quad.

Officer Downey muttered to himself, "Who would believe this? Stupid college kids," and radioed that he was on a call. He slipped into his raincoat and stepped from his car. From his trunk he pulled out a woolen blanket and moved onto the sidewalk to intercept the rapidly approaching Montgomery.

Montgomery had not looked up since he left the stadium. He focused his eyes on the ground so he could carefully place his feet upon the surface avoiding holes, stones, broken glass, and slipping. "Oomph," he grunted as he ran into the policeman and the blanket.

Officer Downey wrapped the blanket around the boy. "Stop right there. You're under arrest for indecent exposure. Come with me."

Montgomery was stunned. He felt the earth give way beneath his feet. He had a sensation of falling as he stood on the sidewalk hearing the gruff words of the cop.

"Grab this blanket and get in the car."

Montgomery adjusted the blanket so he could hold it around him and shuffled to the car. Downey put him in the front seat as he felt there was no danger from a nude detainee—no weapons. Montgomery looked at the floor with a countenance of total despair.

Downey got into the car and radioed his status. "What are you doing? This is no weather to be out in. Why aren't you wearing clothes?"

Montgomery mumbled, "Fraternity prank."

"Which one?"

"Sigma Omicron Beta."

"Figures," grunted Officer Downey in disgust.

When they arrived at the police station, Downey led Montgomery through the back entrance to where they kept their holding cells. He found a spare prison suit of coveralls, "Put these on." Montgomery was so grateful for clothes he dropped the blanket and immediately pulled the coveralls over him. Downey retrieved his blanket and led Montgomery to his desk for booking.

"Name?"

"Montgomery Lee."

"Address?"

"3F3 Somerset Johns."

"Home Address?"

"Sparksburg, Florida."

"Age?"

"Eighteen."

"What were you doing in the rain?"

"Playing football, sir."

"Naked?"

"No sir, we were wearing athletic supporters."

"Anything else?"

"No sir, it was a fraternity stunt; none of the pledges wore anything except a supporter."

"Stupid. What fraternity was this?"

"Sigma Omicron Beta."

"You a pledge?"

"Yes sir."

Downey appraised Montgomery's face. He was a veteran cop and usually had a good feel for the type of boy he brought in for these types of charges. He estimated that Montgomery had a good background, got mixed up in something and was unlucky to be the one who got caught.

"You want to tell me who was involved? It might go easier for you—even drop the charge."

"No sir."

Downey looked again at Montgomery. Montgomery was tense and unhappy.

"You don't need to protect those jerks. The S.O.B.'s are just that: S.O.B.'s. Don't become one. Tell me who was involved. Find a better house to join."

Montgomery was silent.

"I'm charging you with a misdemeanor: being unclothed in a public area. Because it's a misdemeanor, I'm issuing you a ticket, which is a summons to appear in court. The next court date is a week from today at 10 a.m. Come two hours early to meet with a public defender unless you hire your own attorney. This charge carries a maximum of thirty days in jail and a $1000 fine."

Downey saw the tears flowing from Montgomery's eyes. "Is there anything else you want to say?"

"Please don't tell my father," said Montgomery as he wept harder.

"You're an adult at eighteen years of age. Therefore, this department does not notify anyone. However, arrests are public information. This arrest will be published in the Bacon weekly paper, and could be picked up by any media outlet although it's doubtful such a minor incident would be considered newsworthy."

"Thank you, sir."

The officer turned and completed the paperwork. He pushed some forms at Montgomery for him to sign. He took the forms and dropped them into the process pile.

A couple officers kidded about the arrest. The three cops laughed, which only increased Montgomery's agony.

"Who was it?" one officer asked Downey.

"Some college kid; his name is Lee."

"Not Montgomery Lee?"

"Yeah, why—does that name mean anything?"

"That's Harrison Lee's kid. You didn't know that?"

"Doggone it. Why me? I can't let him go; I caught him in the act."

"If that's Harrison Lee's kid," said the second officer, "there's more to this than he's telling you. He didn't do this on his own, he wasn't put up to it, he was forced—I'd bet any amount of money on it."

"He won't talk," said Downey. "My hands are tied."

A week later, Montgomery stood in the courtroom of Judge Harold Bothams. A man in his fifties, with a full head of graying hair and a strong physique, Judge Bothams looked the part of a wise and intimidating judge sitting on the bench. And he was.

The clerk of the court read the charge of indecent exposure. The judge asked for the plea. The public counsel announced that the defendant pleads no contest to the charge. The prosecutor announced that he had no objection to the plea.

Judge Bothams went to accept the plea and rap his gavel when he heard an interior voice say to halt. Judge Bothams was a born-again, tongue-speaking, Gospel breathing Christian of a Pentecostal faith. When the interior voice of the Spirit of God spoke to him, he listened. The Spirit had established his reputation among his peers and the legal profession because it had prompted him on many occasions to dig further into matters to uncover the truth. He was admired for doggedly getting to the truth of a case regardless of the legal maneuvering.

Judge Bothams laid his gavel down and appraised Montgomery. Montgomery stood with his head down looking at the floor.

"The court would like to hear evidence in this case," the judge announced.

The prosecutor's head snapped with surprise. Scrambling to get organized, he grabbed his file and asked Officer Downey to take the stand.

Officer Downey was sworn, and the prosecutor asked him the basic questions. Patrick Downey had testified on many occasions, and wore a good demeanor in court. He prepped on all cases, though he knew most of them would be settled with a plea and no testimony was necessary, in case one of them would unexpectedly go to a hearing and trial. Officer Downey gave the facts: the day and time of the arrest, and his personal observation of the defendant in the act of committing the offense. Officer Downey knew not to volunteer any information.

The prosecutor declined to ask any other questions for it was an open-and-shut case. He was surprised the judge was pursuing it although he knew to expect the unexpected from Judge Bothams. The public defender also declined to ask any questions for she had no defense. He did it and he was caught. It did not get more basic than that.

"The court would like to ask its own questions," announced the judge.

A murmur went through the courtroom filled with friends and family of other defendants. It was highly unusual for a judge to ask his own questions.

"Did the defendant offer an explanation for why he was in a public place with no clothes on?"

"Pursuant to my questions, he stated that he was involved in a fraternity prank," answered Officer Downey.

"How did he describe the prank?"

"The defendant answered they were playing football."

"Was it a hazing incident?"

"He did not say."

"What did he say was his status with the fraternity—what fraternity is the defendant associated with?"

"The defendant stated he was a pledge at Sigma Omicron Beta."

Judge Bothams whistled. "I know something of them," he said. "Sick-Bees are regular visitors to my courtroom."

Judge Bothams looked at Montgomery. He felt compassion for a young man who most likely was not involved in breaking the law but was most likely someone else's victim. "What else did the defendant say at the time of his arrest?"

"Only that they had been playing football in the rain, the pledges were wearing only athletic supporters, and he didn't want his father notified."

"You may step down." Judge Bothams addressed Montgomery. "Son, you have the legal right not to say a word. But I would like to ask you if there is anything you would like to say about why you were there, what took place and how you came to be naked as you left the stadium."

Montgomery shook his head. *Even if I wanted to tell, no one will believe me.*

The Judge picked up his gavel. "The court will take a short recess. Both counsels and the defendant will join me in my chambers, please."

In his chambers, the Judge sat behind his desk, and motioned the others to chairs in front. "There is much more to this case than meets the eye. My feeling is that Mr. Lee did not commit a crime, but that he is the victim of a crime. My hope is that in these quarters Mr. Lee will feel more comfortable about telling us what actually took place. Mr. Lee?"

"No sir, I have nothing to say."

"Son, why are you protecting people who deserve to be prosecuted? They would not return the favor to you. The S.O.B.'s are aptly named. Anyone wishing to join should have his sanity examined. I've seen enough cases to know that their leadership and membership are malicious, vindictive and probably involved in organized racketeering committing numerous felonies daily. Get out of that place. Don't become mixed up in something that may make you guilty by association. What are people going to say if Harrison Lee's kid goes to prison?"

Montgomery looked up in shock.

"Yes, I know who you are. I infer from the presence of the public defender that you wish your father to remain uninformed of these proceedings. Both counsels are put on notice that the court wishes Mr.

Lee's desire to be complied with. The court would be most unhappy to learn otherwise. Montgomery, what was going on?"

"It was only a prank—playing football during the hurricane. Mild compared to their normal stunts."

"My sense is that more than a football game took place."

Montgomery's eyes widened in fear because the Judge was getting uncomfortably close to the truth.

"Montgomery, whatever you say within these walls will be exempt from legal proceedings. I'm asking you to tell me what really took place."

"Sir, we played the game as the officer said. Then the brothers made us take off our supporters. I was running to my truck to put some clothes on that I keep there when the officer got me." Montgomery began to sob.

"Is that all?" asked the Judge kindly.

Montgomery nodded his head. Shame prevented him from describing the manner in which he was assaulted and violated.

"Montgomery, there is yet more to be told. Your tears tell me that. But if you won't tell me, I may have to hold you guilty. You understand that? You may be sentenced to jail and to a fine which I doubt you can pay without having to tell your parents why."

Montgomery held his silence.

"Very well," said the Judge. "Counsels and defendant will please return to court. I will resume the proceedings in ten minutes."

As the door closed behind the three persons leaving the Judge's chambers, he turned toward his window and closed his eyes in prayer. Judge Bothams averred his belief in Montgomery's innocence and reticence to tell everything. His instinct said that something else had taken place. He asked for guidance. As he waited, he sang a hymn of praise.

Five minutes elapsed before an answer began forming in his mind. He began to see with his imagination the stadium field, the football game, the disorganized play and the end of the game. He saw Montgomery rooted in fear. Then he saw the group advance on Montgomery. The vision faded.

"Thank you, Lord, for revealing the answer to me. Thank you for withholding what I don't need to know: it's between you and Montgomery and the perpetrators. Amen." The Judge rose, straightened his robes, and walked into the corridor that led to his courtroom. Outside his door, he pressed the button that gave a discrete buzz to the bailiff that he was entering the court.

"All rise."

"Thank you, be seated. Mr. Lee, will you please stand. This is a most difficult case despite its 'open and shut' appearance. That Officer Downey apprehended you while you were nude is not open to question. What the court does not know are all the reasons you came to be in that state.

"You choose to remain silent; that is your constitutional right although the court believes that anything you would choose to say would help in establishing your innocence. I would like to ask you if there is anything you wish to tell the court."

"Only what I said in your chambers. We pledges were playing football wearing nothing but athletic supporters. The brothers made the pledges take their supporters off at the end of the game. I was running to my truck for clothes."

"Thank you. Will both counsels please approach the bench."

When the counsels had stepped forward, the Judge said, "This kid is not guilty of anything. The court will not entertain his current plea. Is there any objection to a plea of not guilty and dropping the charge?"

"No, your honor," said a surprised public defender.

"No, your honor," said a cagey prosecutor who knew a conviction on this case was nothing to fight for.

"Step back," said the Judge. "The court rejects Mr. Lee's plea of no contest. How does the defendant amend his plea?"

"The defendant amends his plea to not guilty," the public defender said quickly.

"The court enters a plea of not guilty. The court wishes to state that it is unimpressed with the evidence that has been presented. Would the prosecution make a motion?"

"The people move that the charge be dropped."

"The court grants the people's motion and instructs the clerk to enter in the record that the charge has been dismissed with prejudice." The public defender whispered to Montgomery that meant he could not be recharged at a later date.

"The court wishes to admonish the defendant, off the record, to leave his fraternity. And Montgomery, know that a Higher Court has assumed jurisdiction over what took place when you were pulled to the ground."

Montgomery could only blink in surprise as Judge Bothams left the court.

Chapter Twenty-Four

Attack of the Sick-Bees

IT WAS MAY, it was hot, it was humid as Hurricane Alan had brought the onset of the rainy season. The rain gave rise to an exploding population of mosquitoes. No one walked through the swamp now. They rode the bus to main campus but still swatted bugs throughout their rides as each opening of the door admitted new insects to bite and suck.

"Our decision," announced Jack to Montgomery, "is that you must continue as a pledge."

Montgomery was sitting in a room with Jack, Brendon, Pete and Cody. Rip was absent, but Montgomery was used to the fact that Rip was now always absent. Montgomery looked at Jack and saw the scorn that played across his face.

"I never had an interview. How can y'all make a decision if the house has not interviewed me?"

"We changed our rules," said Jack. "Now we review your case and decide whether your preparation is adequate to merit an interview. You're woefully unprepared. We're doing you a great favor allowing you to continue. If I had my way, we'd drop you. In fact, I proposed it. But the others think you can do better."

"I performed well on all my assignments. Y'all received good reports from everyone. What do I lack?"

Jack spit as he spewed his words, "You have an attitude problem. You always have had an attitude problem. You don't think you should have to do this work. You think you're better than us. We don't think you're ready. We might be wrong but that's your hard luck."

Brendon said with a smile, "We aren't disputing that you're meant to be a fraternal brother. It may be that you belong in another chapter of a different frat. Do you believe in God?"

"Yes."

"There you go," Brendon answered. "Your call to fraternal life may be directed to a different place, and we're helping you to find that out."

"That's stupid, dumb and ridiculous," Montgomery shot back. "First, either I'm qualified to be a member or I'm not qualified to be a member. To say I'm qualified in one place but not another is inconsistent and illogical. It's like saying I deliver a stirring oration in the House of Representatives but the same oration made in the Senate is boring blather. Either I can speak, or I can't speak. Second, y'all say y'all detect God directing me to another fraternity. But y'all don't determine that by prayer. Y'all make that determination based upon y'all's assessment of human evaluations. Y'all turn to psychological tests, psychotherapists, therapy groups, videotapes, and papers to determine God's direction. Ludicrous! Outrageous! Are *you* God that y'all make his decisions for him? When it comes to accomplishing God's will, y'all must go to prayer to find out what his will is."

"What you say may be true," replied a smug Brendon, "but we make the decision, and our decision is that you continue as a pledge."

"I can't believe I covered for you jerks. If I hadn't kept my mouth shut, y'all would be in jail!"

Pete was thunderstruck. Jack and Brendon had smiling sneers on their faces.

"What?" hollered Cody. He stood up and grabbed Montgomery by the shirt. "What have you done? Who did you talked to?"

"You don't know, do you?" said Montgomery coolly. "Your boys did something stupid during one of their stunts. I ended up in front of a judge. If I had told what they did, they would have been prosecuted. I still have that option to sing—statute of limitations and all that."

"What else do you know?" roared Cody.

"Nothing, except that we have a missing pledge who never came back from his hiding place during the Hunt. He's been missing for four weeks. Nobody knows anything about it—the story is he ran off. But the four dudes who went after him have been acting strangely ever since. What happened to Rho, Pete?"

"N-n-nothing," stammered Pete. "He ran off just as you said."

Cody gave a hard stare to Pete. Pete gulped and looked at his feet.

"Then there is this courier business," continued Montgomery. "Highly unusual for a fraternal activity. We take packages to people, which, oddly enough, are always Cash On Delivery. Not for odd amounts either, but always in multiples of five dollars: five, ten or twenty. The couriers return from their rounds with huge wads of bills. No one will talk about it. The packages are sealed to prevent inspection. It's enough to raise suspicions of drug trafficking."

Cody let go of Montgomery's shirt. "That's absurd. We fill a niche in the market place—no one will make C.O.D. deliveries anymore. We collect in round dollars so the couriers do not have to carry a large supply of change."

"This is exactly what I'm talking about," averred Jack loudly, "you have an attitude problem. Who are you to challenge us and our decisions?"

"Who—are—y'all," retorted Montgomery, "to sit in secret and make decisions unaccountable to anyone? Who—are—y'all to violate y'all's published procedures whenever y'all feel like it and the applicant has no recourse?"

"I've succeeded to Cody's place as chairman of the pledge committee," said Jack. Brendon looked sharply at Jack and then at Cody. Cody's face was obtuse.

"Therefore, understand the authority I wield as I tell you to get your things and leave the house. Your in-house privileges as a pledge are over." Jack's voice was firm and unyielding.

"With pleasure." Montgomery left the room. Outside the door, he found Rusty and Black Jack listening to the discussion. They gave Montgomery big smiles and silent high-fives. Montgomery went with them to Rusty's room where Montgomery had been staying.

In the room, Brendon was demanding loudly when Jack had been given the chairmanship for the committee.

"You fouled up," Cody cursed. "You seduced the wrong girl. You're so tied up in her you forgot your assignment. He and his girlfriend resolved their dispute and are closer than ever. Now you morons have made more mistakes. What was he talking about?"

"It's nothing," said Jack. "We had a little game of football in the rain. Then Janet gave him a licking he'll remember all his life. Probably his first time. He should be grateful to us." Jack grinned.

Cody cursed as he figured out what Jack meant. "Idiots! On whose authority have y'all stopped listening to me? Y'all disobey orders, and have nothing to say? I said, 'Don't hurt him; don't touch him.' I saw this coming. Now he has a hold over y'all. That's why I said to lay off—we were going to hit him through his relationships, not directly."

"I said to stop listening to you," said Rip coldly from the doorway. "The great Montgomery Lee would be gator food by now if you had listened to me. Now he's a greater threat to the operation than before."

"So nice of you to drop by," Cody sarcastically remarked. "Who held an election and made you king?"

Rip sneered. "I answer to no one now."

Cody reached out, grabbed Rip and threw him against the wall. Rip hit the wall hard and crumpled to the floor. Pete cowered; Jack and Brendon jumped up.

"Leave him," growled Cody. "I'm smart enough not to throw a body so hard his skull cracks open." He stared directly into Pete's eyes.

"He was alive, really," whined Pete. "We left the joint and he took off—no warning."

"Can it," said Cody. "I know the truth."

Jack and Brendon exchanged curious stares.

"Let's get a few things straight," said Cody. "First, I am still in charge. I will receive my master's degree in marketing from the business college. Little do they know that this operation served as the subject of my thesis." Cody laughed hard. Jack and Brendon chuckled along; Pete tittered in nervousness.

"Second, I'm leaving the campus. But I'll still direct the operation through Jack. I'm graduating to bigger prospects. But my word is what you'll obey. Do not cross me again; not in the slightest way or I'll remove you.

"Third, Pete and Rip also graduate. Neither one will remain on campus."

Pete interrupted, "I'm heading for the Southwest once I receive my degree. Y'all don't know me; I don't know y'all."

"Intelligent thinking," approved Cody. "Because your timidity is disgusting and disqualifies you from further opportunities with the organization. The mongrel spoke of singing. Know this: a Canary Pete is a dead Pete. Count on it."

Pete's voice trembled. "I'm out. We don't know each other; I'll be so lost you'll never find me. Supplying a need and making a profit is one thing; it was a protest against the government stepping on the rights of American citizens. I didn't mind knocking a few heads for discipline, but I never signed on for killing. Goodbye strangers." Pete left the room.

"Jack's in charge," said Cody. "Y'all need to recruit new men for the committee. We're in danger of losing the house. Most of the membership stays on our side because they fear us. Plus we give them what they want—stinking party boys. But they could turn if they see someone opposing us and getting away with it. So find three new men and discipline the house. Hit the first infraction hard; then the others will fear you and stay in line. There are about a half dozen men in the house that are not loyal to us. Root them out. Y'all know what to do. We need 100% backing. If we lose it now, our secrets come out. It's y'all's responsibility to see that doesn't happen. Mess up, and I will personally see that you two swing for it. Understand?"

Jack and Brendon nodded.

"Good. We get past this difficulty, and everything will be fine. We had it good until the punk showed up. But it's our fault. We were sloppy and arrogant—took things for granted. No more. Pinpoint execution from now on.

"Put Rip in his room. He'll wake up soon enough."

Brendon and Jack picked up Rip's body and disappeared. Cody lit a cigarette. He sat smoking until Brendon and Jack returned.

"Task One," Cody announced, "is to clean up your mess. I'll take care of Rip. I'm keeping him around to take the blame if that pledge's body turns up. Boys, learn to wear poker faces; I swear, you two, even a meter maid asking y'all when y'all put y'all's last quarter in the parking meter would put y'all on death row. The less y'all know, the better. Keep it that way. React to nothing anyone says, good or bad. The worst they can put on y'all is depression.

"Rip will take the fall, if necessary. Appropriate since he created the problem. We'd actually be helping the law." Cody laughed at this amusing thought. "If nothing happens, well and good. I'll take Rip out another way. Pete is going far away. That leaves the other two. Find a way to get rid of them that doesn't involve violence. Make sure you silence them. No violence." Cody was reacting to Jack's look of protest. "It's a wonder this place isn't crawling with cops now.

"Task Two: fill out the committee. I want three good men who'll answer to y'all and obey y'all without question. Tell them nothing. I'll decide how much and when they'll know anything.

"Task Three: root out the non-loyal members. Y'all know some of them; give the rest a loyalty test. I don't care what it is. Be sure that everyone in the house is loyal to us. We have let some opponents slip into the house. Bad news, opponents. Out they go.

"Task Four: get rid of that whore Janet. She's a liability. If she turns up, the house will be closed. No protest; do it. She's an excuse for the cops to comb the house. I'm sure everyone can find a more satisfactory replacement.

"Task Five is to rid ourselves of Lee permanently. Develop a plan but do nothing until I approve. Remember, no violence. The next man to touch that kid will receive ten times worse from me. Be suspicious of anyone new. His old man is continuing to look into our pasts and our activities. We have big trouble brewing there. I assured my new partners we could handle it. Don't make me a liar.

"Don't move on him until fall. We're too close to exams and summer recess. While he's home, we have to lie low. Don't do anything stupid!

"You have much work to do. Do it well, and you'll be rewarded. Foul up and I'll clean your clock." Cody stubbed his cigarette on the floor.

"Task Six: shred all the courier records. Everything. Then burn it. The only thing I want left by graduation is the customer list." Delivering a final threat, Cody left the house.

"How do we handle the rest of the pledges?" asked Jack. "With only the two of us."

"Let's post a list and take them in," said Brendon. "All of them. Let's not monkey around. Anyone we should have passed on can be run out with the rest after we find out who's disloyal. Even the two losers we kept to do our chores."

"Are things that bad?"

"We must remember that no one else is in the know. What appears disastrous to us is unknown to most of the house. We act cool like all is normal. We don't panic, and it will be normal."

"And I'm in charge," said Jack.

"Gee, Jack, if you have to say it, it must not be true," observed Brendon with a forced innocence.

Across the campus, Montgomery's homecoming was greeted with cheers by his quadmates. "We're all rooming together," said Travis. "As we are now. Hopefully we'll get this quad back so we won't have to disassemble everything we have done to the place."

"Great," enthused Montgomery. "How has Dunbar and the Ghost worked out?"

"You mean Football," said Travis. "He had to have a nickname—everyone else does."

"You don't. How did you miss out?"

"They tagged me, too. Disc, short for disciple. They had quite a discussion, some holding out for apostle, others for Paul or Stephen, but ultimately they decided that real names couldn't be used, and they couldn't figure out how to shorten apostle. Now I'm Disc."

"Football doesn't seem right for Dunbar. Why not Jock?"

"Too mundane."

"What position does he play?"

"Tight end or receiver. He doesn't know; he's practiced both. He plays linebacker on the other side."

"Why not Rush? It would fit his positions. If we called him that, everyone else will go along."

"Done deal. Glad to have you back, buddy."

"It's good to be back. I've survived and I'm free."

That was the occasion for a good party. The boys set aside their studies, cranked up the stereo and had a blast. Several hours and beers later, they went to bed.

But Montgomery and Travis found no sleep that night as they caught one another up on everything that had happened since the infamous hunt of early April. Travis was aghast to hear of the football game, and its brutish ending. As Montgomery detailed his arrest and appearance before Judge Bothams, Travis shook his head to keep sympathetic tears from filling his eyes.

"Everyone speaks in awe of your Daddy, the great Harrison Lee. But you have him beat. When the history of the Lees for this century is written, you'll outshine all your Daddy has accomplished."

"I'll never measure up to my Daddy. It's useless to try."

"Oh, yeah? Did you see that letter on your desk?"

"What letter—this one?"

"Right, the one from the International Astronomical Union. Open it and read it—I did."

"You opened my mail?"

"So sue me. I had to know whether to call you, didn't I?"

Montgomery slid his hand under the flap. “You resealed it well,” he said grinning.

Travis laughed. “Too bad I was saved; I had a budding criminal career.”

Then Montgomery let out an ear-splitting yell that brought their quadmates into their room. “What is it?”

Montgomery waved the letter. “But how?”

“Some of those Tarheels we met over Spring break were impressed with your find,” explained Travis, “so when they returned to Chapel Hill, they went to Morehead Planetarium on their campus and the profs had a look. The surfers told the profs that you discovered it on the beach. It stands to reason with the Outer Banks sticking so far out into the ocean away from heavy light pollution that impedes observation. Anyhow, the head dog of the department—”

“The dean,” Red corrected.

“Yeah, the dean,” Travis said.

“I like head dog better,” said the Ghost.

“Figures,” laughed Shorts.

“May I finish?” demanded Travis. “So the dean sends the discovery in with the affidavits of the surfers with the date and time of your discovery. It turns out you were the first to discover it. So the bigwig astro people ask UNC for a name. They said call it after you. So we now have the official Montgomery’s Comet heading toward Earth and appearing to the unaided eye sometime in July. Congratulations, Comet.”

“Comet?” wondered Montgomery.

“Of course,” said Shorts. “This is huge so we changed your name to reflect your newly-acquired status. Comet you are, and Comet you’ll be.”

“What do I say if people ask me where Rudolph is?”

“Tell them to be quiet,” suggested Caveman, “or you’ll leave something on their shoe.”

The room exploded with laughter. After this, there was nothing left to do but resume the party. Thus it was that quad 3F in Somerset Johns welcomed the dawning day with their internationally celebrated Comet.

Montgomery telephoned his home and received the hearty congratulations of his parents and sisters. They were very proud of his accomplishment. "People ask me all the time when I'm going to stop the star nonsense and bring you into law. Phooey on them," his Daddy told him. "Pursue your dreams and be the best. I'm proud of you, Montgomery, so very proud I call you my son."

Later that day, Montgomery and Elizabeth took a walk after Western Civilization. He filled her in on his news good and bad. She was delighted about the comet. His tale about the football game and his court appearance made her sober.

"I hate those evil men," she said vehemently. "They must be stopped, but not by you. I worry so much when you're living in the frat house. They're capable of anything."

"Too true." Montgomery told her about being continued again.

"They do pile on, don't they? When do they let up? When have you had enough and quit?"

"I'm waiting for the chance to have my say. When I've had the chance to make a difference, and I've had my say, then I'll quit: in the frat or out.

"Plus, a guy from my quad was taken into the frat. He fell into heavy drugs. I might be able to help him regain control of his life. I want to take a shot at that."

"Sir Montgomery, ever ready to ride his white horse."

"The better to rescue you, damsel-in-distress."

"Given what they did to you on the football field after the game, which was horrible, it makes me love you even more. We both have been through the same experience; I know you know how it was for me. You and no one else can have full sympathy for what I went through. I'll never freeze you out again. I love you, Sir Comet Monkey General Montgomery Lee."

"I love you, Miss Stuart. We have an understanding, then." His heart beat faster.

"Yes. No ring—not yet. But we're intended for one another."

Montgomery burst into an ear-splitting grin, and kissed the passionate love that consumed his heart and made it stronger.

That night the blissful couple went to dinner with Rick and Rose at the Brasserie.

"Here's to the enfianced couple," Montgomery toasted Rick and Rose with Sprite^{TM}. The four young people clinked their glasses together.

"Here's to the couple with an understanding," replied Rose. To Montgomery's questioning look, she said, "A woman knows these things." They clinked their glasses and drank.

"Have you set a date?" asked Elizabeth.

"August 9," said Rose. "So close."

"Are your parents unhappy?" asked Montgomery.

"They wish I was further along in my studies," said Rose. "They're afraid I won't receive a diploma because of changed circumstances. But they support it."

"What kind of changed circumstances do they foresee?" asked Elizabeth.

"Children," replied Rick. "But the earliest we'd have a child would be after I graduate. Even though we plan to wait until Rose graduates, if we did have a child, we could arrange our schedules so Rose can continue her studies. We are committed to the two of us finishing college."

"I reckon you won't be our floor advisor next year," mused Montgomery.

"No, we're moving into married housing," said Rick. "They don't believe there's enough space for a couple to occupy the floor advisor's room—to say nothing of sharing a bathroom with other men."

Rose laughed. "Even if they thought it could work, I veto the idea. No insult intended, but men are pigs. I don't want to live in their sty."

"Which means I'm flying solo," said Elizabeth. "I've talked to some other girls, but I have no firm arrangements for the fall term."

"I feel lucky," said Montgomery, "the quad is staying together for next year. We even filled the hole in room four."

"Have you registered?" asked Rick.

"I meet my advisor tomorrow," said Montgomery. "But it should be easy to register: math, physics, intro to astronomy, Asian civilizations of antiquity, astronomical history."

"The brain," said Elizabeth. "I'll continue exploring civilization with Montgomery, but must go my way with the classics: music, art, and literature plus reading skills—it's an education department class."

"What will you do about the fraternity?" Rick asked Montgomery.

"I don't know. Maybe I'll continue with my efforts to join, maybe I won't. I have the summer to think about it. The difference from a year ago is that if I make it in, that's okay, but if I don't, I'm happy going on without it. Maybe people can't understand, but membership in the fraternity is not a great prize that will leave me greatly disappointed and depressed over a failure to win their approval. I'll be a campus leader and role model as God determines, and the men at the frat have nothing to say about it.

"All they can do is prevent me from fulfilling my God-given call in their fraternity. They can't stop me otherwise. Therefore, it's about them, not me. Their failure to recognize my gifts is their failing, not mine. If they frustrate God in his will to put me into membership, they're the ones who have a problem with God, not me.

"All things considered, the turkeys must worry about their gobble, not me. I'm at peace."

Rick responded, "There's many more boards, committees and organizations who should learn from what you are saying in addition to the S.O.B.'s, even churches and ordination boards."

"I can't imagine a church's ordination board would put their applicants for ministry through the nonsense I've been through."

Rick countered, "Trust me: it happens."

Elizabeth burst out, "That's terrible."

"The 'Ins' of a religious hierarchy have always been jealous of their power and position," chimed in Rose. "I'm not at all surprised that they would be extremely difficult with newcomers. The more promise, the larger the threat to their position; thus they are more strict and harsh on the best candidates. They're afraid they'll lose their churches to the newcomers. This is probably more acute if the applicant is 'second career'. Such a person brings their experience of the business world and such and probably is better suited to handle the more complex situations. Jealousy is a much too common human reaction."

"I guess I'm naive," said Montgomery. "I would have thought the ministers—clergy—who serve on ordination boards would be mature in Christ and would have left those childish feelings behind years ago. I would have thought they would identify who God called and work to put them through the process with as little hassle as possible. I would have thought they would approach their work as a sacred trust. I would have thought that they would display the compassion of Christ and the gentleness of Stephen when they interact with applicants. I would have thought they would assess actual performance in determining potential."

Rose smiled gently and laid a hand on Montgomery's arm. "That is naive. There are those who will give applicants a hard time merely because they received a hard time, and it's their turn to harass powerless applicants."

"It's very sad," chimed in Rick, "but often the things you would have thought—maturity, sacred trust, and the like—are lacking in the people and the board as a whole. My cousin applied six years ago to an ordination board in this state, and not one of your 'would have thoughts' characterizes that ordination board."

"That doesn't give one much optimism for the future of the church," remarked Montgomery.

"It's horrible," said Elizabeth. "What this means is that the good ones quit, the dumb ones are turned down, and all the rest—the mediocre—make elder."

"That's right," said Rose.

"Bingo," said Rick.

"Check," added Montgomery.

Coming Next

Frat House: The Sequel

As Montgomery continues his efforts to join Sigma Omicron Beta, the murder continues to haunt Gravy and complicate Cody's plans to expand his network of distributing illegal narcotics.

Gravy works from the inside to gather evidence while Montgomery's Daddy and others work from the outside to pierce the inner workings of Cody's operation.

Is Park becoming the new "Janet" of SOB?

Will Rip exact revenge upon Montgomery Lee?

Is Mick utterly ruined as a drug addict?

In the middle of everything is the hellish pledge committee, whose members have changed but not its attitude. Does Montgomery gain admission in his second year at Florida Sawgrass University?

Watch for the release of ***Frat House,*** the exciting continuation of the ***Rush Week*** saga.

About the Author

ALARIC JAXARTES is the pen name of a former United Methodist minister residing in Jacksonville, Florida. A long-time pursuer of literary art, his work began to take shape through his experiences as a pastor of small, rural and small town churches. "Rush Week" is the first of several novels that "A.Jax" is writing. Pageturners Publishing Company is looking forward to bringing to market additional tales of his prolific pen.

Before coming to Florida, A.Jax worked in business, the resort industry and manufacturing. He earned his C.P.A. in 1979, and worked as an auditor before entering business. At one time he owned his own business providing management services.

A graduate of the University of Delaware, and Asbury Theological Seminary, A.Jax draws upon all facets of his widely varied background in constructing his tales. He lives alone with two dogs.

Pageturners Publishing Titles

PLANNED RELEASES

Rush Week: College freshman Montgomery Lee pledges a fraternity, which turns out to be a struggle over the future direction of an organization that has abandoned its purpose for existing.

Power In The Blood: A small, southern town debates homosexuality in the church as a spree of killings erupts. Is there a vampire on the loose? Why won't he obey the rules about vampires?

A Hunger For Intimacy: As a 13 year old boy comes of age, he struggles with questions about intimacy, sex and relationships with his friends and girlfriends.

Tattered Flags: The Boy Scouts are sent into a state forest to clean up a site polluted by industrial dumping, amid great controversy by environmental peers and the media. Are they helping the environment, or are they part of the problem?

Frat House: the sequel continuing the Rush Week saga.